The Disappe

Johnny Joh

Copyright © John Johnson
London: August 2021

The Disappearance

This is a work of fiction. Names, characters, businesses, places, events, locales, and incidents are either the products of the author's imagination or used in a fictitious manner. Any resemblance to actual persons, living or dead, or actual events is purely coincidental.

John Johnson has asserted his rights under the Copyrights Designs and Patents Act 1988 to be identified as the sole author of this work.

Original work completed in the UK June 2021
First published worldwide in August 2021

Table Of Contents

Chapter 1 – Empty

Chapter 2 – Moscow

Chapter 3 – Jumbo

Chapter 4 – The money supply

Chapter 5 – Beacon Hill

Chapter 6 – The vacuum

Chapter 7 – Blondy

Chapter 8 – A bit of coding

Chapter 9 – La La Land

Chapter 10 – The investigation

Chapter 11 – The Blockchain

Chapter 12 – Logan

Chapter 13 – The real boss

Chapter 14 – Resource allocation

Chapter 15 – Crypto One

Chapter 16 – St Basil

Chapter 17 – Breakfast in Chelsea

Chapter 18 – An Irishman in Moscow

Chapter 19 – Twin Peaks

Chapter 20 – Day two

Chapter 21 – The tennis club

Chapter 22 – Raspo's

Chapter 23 – Geneva

Chapter 24 – The savant

Chapter 25 – The message of hope

Chapter 26 – The golf connection

Chapter 27 – The replacement currency

Chapter 28 – Hank's new buddy

Chapter 29 – Monique
Chapter 30 – The Energy King
Chapter 31 – The trick
Chapter 32 – Meshchansky
Chapter 33 – Daylight robbery
Chapter 34 – Le trou noir
Chapter 35 – Crosstown traffic
Chapter 36 – Corroboration
Chapter 37 – Cat Mouse Fish
Chapter 38 – The escape route
Chapter 39 – Dinner in The West Wing
Chapter 40 – A digital gold rush
Chapter 41 – The Ides of March
Chapter 42 – Departure
Chapter 43 – The FIB
Chapter 44 – Millstatt

Abbreviations and translations

HMG - Her Majesty's Government. The UK Government

PM - Prime Minister: Head of the UK Government

Cabinet - The collective name for the UK's top Ministers

MI6/SIS - Former / current UK secret service units

CIA - Central Intelligence Agency. Their US counterparts

RRT - Rapid Response Team. A fictitious unit within MI6/ SIS

TECH - Technology

BTC - Bit Coin. A digital currency

COBRA - The UK Government's official emergency response team

Crypto - Crypto currencies. A new form of digital money

FSB - Russia's secret service, formerly known as the KGB

FIB - International cadre of bakers

IP - Internet Protocol. A technical standard used in digital networks

VPN - A Virtual private network

USAF - The United States Air Force

BA - British Airways

ARPANET - Advanced Research Agency Projects Network. The original internet

ICJ - The International Court of Justice in Den Haag

Python - A coding language

Linux - An alternative computer operating system

Ischeznoveniye - The Russian word for disappearance

Izhets - The Russian word for liar

Skrytyy - The Russian word for hidden

Quant - A financial modelling and analysis specialist

Dramatis Personae - Key characters

Harry Shepperton - Commander of The Nines. Aka Ten

Jojo Everett 9-1 - Radio and internet engineer

Mark Wright 9-2 - Weapons and ballistics

Paul Lambert 9-3 - Lawyer and negotiator

Jake Rivera 9-4 - Professor of physics and chemistry

Caitlin Yang 9-5 - Software designer and coder

Liam Dempsey 9-6 - Geologist and materials

Hazel Ingliss - Harry's boss

Johnny Marriott - English inventor

Brigadier general Zhang T'ang aka The Brig - Retired Chinese security service

Major Valeria Tietnoch - Senior FSB officer

Idris Smith aka 'Turbs' Turbanski - English journalist of Afghan descent

Andrei Umnymozgi - Software genius

Georgi Podlyavitch - Andrei's best friend

Anastasia Yurilenko - Their flatmate

Colonel Hank Wyatt - Retired USAF and CIA officer

Ivan Tertroothski - Russian journalist

Viktor Alliskaya - Russian fixer

Sylvie Danton - Swiss banker and FIB spokesperson

With huge thanks to Eileen and Sunny

For Lydia and Mark

With love

You are my inspiration for everything

THE DISAPPEARANCE

Chapter 1 – Empty

Sorry, service temporarily unavailable.

The message glared back up at him from the screen, unforgiving and final, the word 'temporarily' mere packaging to soften the blow and reduce the shock.

Harry reached down and withdrew his card from beneath the flashing green light.

It was exactly the same message that had appeared on the other machine in the first bank, the one he had just tried ten minutes earlier.

He thought briefly and then reinserted his card, being extra careful with the PIN.

ONE NINE SEVEN THREE.

He was going to be fifty next year and, although you were not supposed to do it, he liked to keep his passwords and PINs memorable despite the increasing number of automated promptings to use an asterisk, a hyphen or a semi colon. *Bloody idiots*, he thought, *how's anyone supposed to remember anything like that? Words and numbers are already hard enough on their own.*

Tap. Tap. Tap. Tap.

ONE NINE SEVEN THREE.

The screen flickered briefly and changed to a welcome menu.

He selected "view balance".

A number appeared, a healthy number.

Harry Shepperton was well rewarded for being TEN, the commanding officer of The Nines, the UK Government's latest RRT, the drop everything, go anywhere, fix the problem quietly, Rapid Response Team.

He didn't keep all his money in the bank these days; hardly anybody did any more with interest rates well under one percent and heading for zero.

Every month he would check his budget, leave a grand in there to cover eventualities and then transfer the rest out to Guillaume in Geneva to work his creative magic. His fund was smallish by Swiss investment standards but still somehow managed to deliver between fifteen and twenty per cent every year. *Need to pop over and see him soon for a review,* Harry had been daydreaming just half an hour earlier as he stepped out of his London townhouse on his way to the bank, quickly rehearsing in his head that journey from his home out to City airport, the one

that he had done so many times before.

But he wasn't daydreaming now.

He focused hard.

So the network part of the system was working properly because £16,575 was pretty much exactly what he'd been expecting to see, the same net amount after taxes as last month, give or take a few quid.

"Do you want another service?"

Harry thought for a moment and pressed yes.

"Deposit. Cash or Cheque?"

He selected "Cash"

Another flashing green light on the opposite side of the machine told him where to put his tenner.

The machine swallowed it, then spat it out again.

Sorry, service temporarily unavailable.

Two different machines.

Two different banks, just ten minutes apart.

Both high street majors. Same thing both times.

He glanced at his watch. 5:10 am.

Liam and Jojo would still be asleep and probably wrapped around each other, despite the team protocols. As their boss he was perfectly entitled to wake them up. As members of a crack intelligence unit he would expect them to respond and he knew they would. But if the world's financial system was going into cyber meltdown the two of them, plus the rest of the Nines, were going to face days and days of almost zero sleep.

So he settled for Code Blue, which always meant the same thing.

Top priority – get to the office for 7am.

Across town six mobiles pinged and six very bright young sleepyheads stirred and muttered to themselves as the words on the screen jarred them out of their warm slumbers.

Code blue. Fuck.

Harry took his tenner and his card, tucked them away into his wallet, and sent one more text to his old mate Billy Poppitt. *Special delivery required by 7am.*

Billy was always up at 4, his old army days long behind him, although the discipline of early starts still very much a big part of his daily routine.

Code blue. Blimey wasn't that…?

They didn't happen very often.

In Ealing, Chelsea, Greenwich, Stanmore, Highgate and Blackheath six rather stealthy white transits glided out into the soft dawn light and headed into the thin but growing London traffic to pick up their young charges.

No swish saloons for this team where inconspicuous was much more sensible and might keep you alive longer.

The fact that all of the vehicles had been heavily modified at considerable expense to Her Majesty's Government of the United Kingdom meant they were more comfortable in the back than most saloons. Had they wanted, the individual team members could all have clambered in and gone straight back to sleep. But they were all top professionals, were now in mission mode, fully on message, and headed in. The driver of the Stanmore van barely got as far as Harrow before turning round and heading back, allowing Mark the welcome luxury of returning to the warmth of his bed, Harry having quickly realized he wouldn't be needing his weapons guy for this particular mission and standing him down quickly.

Caitlin, Jake and Paul were now all wide awake and pondering the upcoming early morning briefing to which they were headed as a rather watery looking sun started to appear in the brightening sky.

Liam had already responded, quickly alerting Harry that JoJo was with him and they'd be coming in together, seperate pick ups not required.

Harry smiled a wry smile. He didn't want to discipline them for sharing a bed, he was too good a boss for that, but sharing a ride in was another matter. He'd have to find a way to make sure that didn't happen again. Way too risky when you never know who's watching.

And, in his world, and with his team, somebody was always watching.

But for now, he had something much bigger to worry about.

Two machines.

Two different banks.

Same behaviour.

They had said it would happen overnight.

And it had.

It had started.

Chapter 2 – Moscow

It's always cold there.

But then, what do you expect? It's Russia.

But it's survivable cold in Moscow. Freezing, or a few degrees below. Not great, but not Siberia where it's often twenty, thirty or even forty below. Your blood turns to permafrost and every waking moment is a battle for survival, a struggle for warmth. You can't concentrate because all your energy is being used just trying to heat yourself up and then staying warm. There's not much time for anything else. Your brain gets mushy and your thinking focuses more on basic survival than anything else. That's why dissidents get sent there. They can't think straight any more.

Which equals no more dissension, pretty quickly.

Andrei was only 19 but wise in the ways of the world. The cyber world that is, where hackers were king. The other world, the real non-digital one, was of less interest to him. He didn't visit it very much. Apart from the fact that it was where he needed to go to have wild sex with Anastasia, his beautiful and lusty 16-year-old girlfriend, it really didn't interest him a lot.

So he was quite a complicated character, intelligent way beyond his years in tech matters, otherwise more like a very young and naive teenager.

He needed his buddy Georgi to keep him grounded, to keep him sane, to keep him out of trouble, out of jail, out of the morgue.

'The Press will just spin it like mad, like they always do.' his friend had confided. 'People are so used to lies they barely notice any more, they just kinda' screen them out. Which is more than a bit weird when you think that we are all born with an inbuilt bullshit detector, a vital part of man's primeval survival kit, and then we just switch it off when those guys start speaking. It's understandable of course, there's just so much crap to screen out these days so we end up eliminating nearly all of it. Sad but true '

The two young conspirators were in planning mode. They needed to gauge the world's likely reaction to their latest robbery, not – in common with most cyber-terrorists – a word they really liked to use but, nonetheless, the correct one under the circumstances. For they were about to pull of a heist of global proportions and were – to their credit in some respects – spending most of their waking moments planning the

get-away rather than the actual theft itself.

After all there was no point in walking off with most of the money from the world's banks if you were going to get caught.

In their grandfathers' day, it had mostly been political crime that got you sent to the Gulags, where hard labour and dodgy clothing combined with the sub-zero temperatures to kill thousands. These days the crimes tended to be more of a financial nature, with embezzlement of state assets being an especially flexible favourite when it came to the larger schemes.

And *ischeznoveniye* was set to be one of the largest of them all. Although fraught with complexity and one of the most audacious bank jobs ever, the two boys were increasingly convinced that they could pull it off.

But the getaway remained a problem, remained the ultimate key to success, and remained a big headache. Especially when they couldn't confide in any one else, only had each other to share their secret ideas with.

But Andrei and Georgi were very bright and knew intuitively that their biggest problem, their main problem, would be the awful silence they would have to keep when amongst friends.

No one could know.

Not a soul.

Way too risky.

That would be one of the hardest things to pull off. Possibly the hardest of all.

'Remember Covid-19?' Georgi continued. 'The lies were off the scale. All of them. Death numbers, hospital bed capacities, effectiveness of vaccines, transmission characteristics of the virus. All bollocks. All made up.'

Andrei thought about asking why, but realized he didn't care. Covid-19 was old hat, something from two years ago, almost ancient history to someone his age.

What he did care about was *Ischeznoveniye* , the code name for their latest plan. *Ischeznoveniye. The disappearance.*

'So what does that tell us, then?' he replied. 'How can we learn anything from that episode that we can use here?'

'That the media lie. A lot. About most things. And they will almost certainly lie about this too?'

'So?'

'And much of it is state controlled and will always do the bidding of its masters.'

'So?'

'Do you think the world's Governments will want to make this story public?'

'Well, I can't see how they can keep a lid on it with everybody's money disappearing overnight. It's hardly like no one will notice, is it?'

'Yes, of course that's true. They'll have to say something. But it will be a series of half-truths, for that – in reality – is how they work. And how they get away with it. Big blatant lies are a bit obvious but if you boil them down to something else and then add in some stuff which is obviously true and finally tell people a few facts that they really want to hear then you're a long way towards a credible cover up. Sorry, cover story. For that's what it will be in this case. They won't be covering anything up because you have to be complicit to do that'

'I think I follow, but can you give me an example. I mean in our case. What kind of things do you think they're likely to print?'

'I reckon we'll see some PR guy who specializes in disaster management issuing a statement. I think it might even be a good idea for us to use that eventuality to get ahead, and keep ahead, of the whole situation.'

'Meaning?'

Georgi grinned.

'Meaning that we save them the bother and write the statement for them.' He continued. " After all, who better to know what really happened than the people who actually did it.'

Andrei looked puzzled.

Real world stuff.

Not his thing.

His friend handed him a sheet of paper.

'I thought you might ask ' he said. ' So I drafted something earlier.'

Andrei read slowly, attempting to place this piece of fiction into the overall context of their plan

This morning's technical confusion in the banking world seems to have been caused by a perfect storm of conditions that have led to a temporary period of disruption for customers worldwide. After being assured for years that online banking was increasingly safe, today's incident will have set their plans for even more automation back, possibly by as much as several years. What started as a series of platform upgrades and systems integrations, both intended to improve the basic

functionalities of global banking systems, appear to have caused the worst crash in living memory.

At present the exact amount of money which has gone missing is still being assessed. Customers are expected to be covered for most losses using the existing contingencies. Financial systems worldwide will be unavailable until further notice but are expected to be back online within a few days according to senior management sources. World Governments are expected to announce a raft of credit facilities shortly as part of a series of emergency packages.

He grinned at his friend.

'You really wrote that?'

'Yup. What do you think?'

'I think you're a bloody genius. Apart from one thing.'

'And what's that?'

'How do we get it to them? Without betraying ourselves?'

Georgi looked a bit downcast for a moment.

'Well, I cant think of bloody everything, can I? One step at a time.'

But then he quickly cheered up.

'I know,' he said brightly.

'I know how to confuse them.'

Andrei waited expectantly.

'We'll send them another note as well. At the same time. But in a different style and with a different type of message.'

'And what would that be then?'

Now it was Georgi's turn to grin.

'Do you remember Robin Hood?'

Chapter 3 – Jumbo

The team had spent all morning wrestling with their new task. The problem was easy enough to understand. The world's money had gone missing.

Not some of it.

All of it.

'Not really possible, is it?' Liam suggested, echoing all their thoughts. ' Just like that.' He threw his hands up in front of him, like someone shooing pigeons away. 'Poof. Inta' thin air. Loike some fekkin' magic trick.'

'Well, I know what you mean, its very hard to take in, but its definitely happened,' Harry reassured them.' Apart from all the obvious sources of confirmation available to this department, just switch on the telly and there's nothing else going on. It's the only story from here to Timbuktu. Big Ben could have fallen over and nobody would know.'

Multiple screens around their briefing room high above the Thames insisted he was right. All had the volumes muted but the subtitles told the story. The global media was in overdrive. All sorts of experts were being wheeled out to pontificate on the night's events, all well intentioned but all struggling to insert the relevance of their own individual expertise into the story.

The much-overused word *unprecedented* was, for once, justifiable and appropriate. And when the numerous correspondents started struggling with their various explanations, that one single word quickly became their best friend as a whole host of individual theories quickly ran out of gas.

'So none of the usual suspects are claiming responsibility then?' asked Caitlin, keen to eliminate as many of the world's better-known rogue groups as possible before they got started.

Harry's boss Hazel Ingliss chose that moment to enter the room, fresh from the Cabinet office briefing that was just starting to tackle the same problem.

'I can't really call this much of an update Cait', she said, grabbing the chair next to the Californian Internet guru ' because we still have next to nothing to go on. But I can answer that particular question pretty directly and it's a no. We haven't heard a peep from anybody at this stage, although it wouldn't surprise me if we do within the

next few hours.'

'Are we calling it a terrorist incident then?' Paul enquired.

'No, not yet, not officially anyway. Although that question is a bit of a teaser. Nothing has been blown up or destroyed, not in the traditional manner anyway. Yet the disruption will be the same, even worse in reality because it's going to have a worldwide impact on nearly everybody almost immediately. That's not something you can get by blowing up a bridge or carrying out an assassination. So I can imagine that most of that mob will want to claim it anyway. It will be like a badge of honour thing, making them princes amongst thieves. Won't make our jobs any easier though, that's for sure.'

'Can the banks fix it?' Jake wanted to know. 'Cos I sure as hell would like to know what they have to say about all this. I can see a big flashing red light shining on the latest damage to their reputation. Given the bad press they've received over the past fourteen years since the credit crunch, this could sound their death knell.'

'Hard to believe they're actually involved though,' Harry responded, 'their stated position at the moment is that they're just victims like everybody else. Although I think they're going to find that a pretty hard sell going forward.'

His team all nodded and concurred. The banks had a poor image, largely a result of their own actions and mainly something of their own making.

Too many excesses.

Too much greed.

Not much trust left any more.

If any.

'But I take your point, Jake. It's hard to see how they're going to come out of this well, if at all.'

'What does the Cabinet say then?' JoJo asked Hazel.

'They're still in session. Oddly enough they're partly waiting on us to see what options we come up with.'

'I know we're Rapid Response,' JoJo replied, searching around for a foothold to position the team appropriately, 'but please remember we need something to respond to. The world's money going missing isn't exactly election shenanigans like Iceberg, is it?' she added, referring back to the team's first ever mission.

'Or Wuhan?' she continued, referring to the second. 'In both of those we were able to identify the problem quickly. A threat to democracy in one. A threat to world

health in the other. Both a whole lot easier to understand than what's happened here.'

'Don't forget there was a major threat to the global economies in both of those cases as well.' added Paul. 'I think it's fair to assume the same thing will happen here. What with everybody's money disappearing from their accounts overnight. If that doesn't pull the rug a bit, I don't know what will.'

'Where do we think it's gone, anyway?' Caitlin asked reasonably. 'Banks have audit trails don't they? Normally it's impossible to just disappear assets or funds completely, as I understand it. Not if you put specialist resource onto it. You know, those forensic accountant guys. They're like bloodhounds, aren't they? Least from what I've heard.'

All eyes turned to Hazel.

The team didn't have secrets.

They knew about her non-departmental past.

'Yes, you're quite right, of course. There's no way it can just disappear. You can't really even lose a fiver these days with digital banking. If you know what you're doing and where to look and you have the time, you'll always find it.'

Liam stopped rocking on his chair and leant forward, tapping all his fingers together on the desk, a kind of mini drum roll. Not attention seeking, more a kind of nervous energy spilling over.

'Who's heard of David Copperfield?' he asked in his soft Dublin brogue.

Jojo shivered slightly, hoped no one would notice. But this was not Iceberg, their initial project a few years earlier, when she had first encountered the boy of her dreams. They always say love will turn up when you least expect it and then suddenly one day CRASH, there it was, slap bang in the middle of her life, just like that. Only in poor Jojo's case it happened in her first professional team meeting with her new colleagues. She remembered his twinkle across the table as Harry had introduced them and she'd had to steel herself from the onrushing train. Now, years later, her discomfort at that moment still came back and shook her sometimes, even though they had now been an item for a long time. The team all knew and, even better, both her bosses were cool with it. That accent though, she shivered and tingled slightly, as she always did when he spoke.

Irish boys.

Damn!

And her a convent girl....

'Dickens or that American bloke?' Paul snapped her out of her reverie.

'Da Vegas guy,' Liam continued.' by his own admission, just another magician. Only he did his tricks on an epic scale. Made a Jumbo disappear once in front of a live audience, as I recall. Only it hadn't really gone anywhere, had it? He did some smoke and mirrors ting, sleight of hand, whatever. Kazamm, now you see it, abracadabra, now you don't, kazamm, now you see it again. I remember watching it on da' telly. Hell of a trick. I mean, to all intents and purposes he had made this thing disappear. But he couldn't disappear it forever. Ten minutes later, or whatever, it was there again.'

'Your point, Liam?' Harry enquired.

'Well, it just occurred to me that he didn't actually have to do anything with it, did he? 'Cos it hadn't actually gone anywhere. If it had, then he might have really had a problem. I mean where can you put a Jumbo jet that nobody would notice. Not sa easy, huh? '

The team pondered this latest piece of whimsy from the Emerald Isle. Would have been complete bollocks of course except that their favourite Paddy had a knack of being right about the strangest of things.

'Well, whatever happened to the money, the current status' confirmed Harry, turning to scan the TV monitors which quickly confirmed that there were no new developments 'is unchanged. The world's money, as measured by all of the liquid assets of the banks, has effectively gone missing overnight, making it, as of this precise moment, the largest theft of anything in one single incident ever.'

He scanned the faces of his young team, all nodding along now in gentle agreement.

'Which means, ladies and gentlemen, that this incident has landed in our laps and we now have a new project. Effective immediately.'

He checked with his boss. Hazel was nodding too.

'Which only leaves us needing to come up with a…'

'I think he used a Lear-Jet actually, 'said Paul, 'although I must admit Jumbo would seem way more appropriate for us, given the size of the task.'

And so the team's third project was born and baptized by 9am, barely four hours after Harry had left his bank.

Her Majesty's Rapid Response Team was living up to its name.

Chapter 4 – The money supply

Money. One of life's great mysteries.

Where it comes from and where it goes, the former being almost impossible to answer, the latter only too easy.

We spend it.

So it disappears, although that is normally an entirely different and more comprehensible phenomena, fuelled by mankind's seemingly never ending desire for *more stuff* of various kinds, whatever it may be.

Those particular types of financial movements do, however, in and of themselves, raise lots of other questions. How much *stuff* does one need? Is there such a thing as enough? Can I be rich and spiritual, camels, eyes of needles and all that? Who do I give it to for looking after and safekeeping and can I trust them? All timeless and barely answerable questions, though many wise men have tried.

But that other one, that first one. Now, that really is a tricky question because the answer that we all really crave doesn't exist for the simple reason that there is no one single answer. Money may well come to many people as a result of their work, where they are making something perhaps, or doing something for someone else, rendering a service, as they used to call it in the old days.

Under those circumstances, still very familiar to most people, one person got paid and somebody else, often a company, would do the paying. But that doesn't answer the whole question, there is still a part of it that remains fathomless. Where did it really begin and what did it start with? What actually came first? Is it a bit like the start of the universe, which, even if it was billions of years ago in the oft quoted primordial soup, must still have had its own start somewhere else, its own origins in something that even preceded all of that.

In the beginning there was God, says the bible, and, in the absence of any better ideas, huge parts of the world's population continue to settle for that. It might not be very scientific or even culturally credible, especially given that there now seem to be so many Gods, a surplus really, almost one per region if looking at the global picture. Although that very idea is obviously absurd, can it be any worse than the raging headache caused by trying to understand the concept of infinity, that awful prerequisite for adequately coming to grips with most pre big-bang theories about the

origin of life?

Things must start somewhere, must come from somewhere.

Our human brains demand it.

No other alternative explanations seem credible.

Economists, those modern day practitioners of financial juju and mumbo jumbo, will happily explain it all away in a wave of theories.

Well, surely that should help. After all, wasn't it hard maths and physics formulae that got us to the moon, helped develop jet powered flight, built cities, bridges, tunnels and pretty much most of the modern world.

Maybe, but that stuff is all based on hard science, immutable, like the laws of gravity, and agreed upon by legions of peer groups worldwide, something that tends to happen rather less so with economists. Stick ten in a room and ten different opinions will appear on most subjects. They have a tendency to baffle to deceive, rather like university professors and dons who are so well read in and around their subjects and so steeped in their individual expertise that it is nigh on impossible for an outsider to deconstruct their arguments.

And so it is with money.

And so it also is with the money supply which is, at heart, an economics theory.

None of this mattered too much to Andrei and his friend Georgi, his co-conspirator in a get-rich-quick plan which had one significant and very major difference from all other such schemes which had come before.

This one robbed everybody.

Andrei and Georgi would win, but all the others would lose.

And lose a lot.

But for the sake of planning and being thorough they reluctantly concluded that they really did need to understand about money, its idiosyncrasies and nuances, its power and its weaknesses. How it worked in practice, moved around the world, caring and ensnaring, joking and provoking, doubling then halving then trebling again. The more they considered it with their keen young minds, the less possible it seemed to be able to move forward without understanding its multi-faceted behaviours properly, including the one big question to which they would always return, time and time again.

Where does it really come from?

If you are planning to make something disappear then you first have to

understand it properly. If you don't, how do you know it won't just come back?

So began a period of immersion into all things monetary and time spent away from the tech evolutions which usually drove their everyday lives.

The source of money.

More obscure than the source of the Nile and just as tricky to find.

Where was it?

Or should that be, 'what was it?'

'Looks like we'll have to put everything else on hold for a while then,' Georgi announced sleepily one morning after a particularly heavy night's research and reading had wiped them out, ' because this is sure gonna' take some time.'

Although they were generation Z kids, children of the Internet, the floor of their comfortable apartment on Staraya Square was strewn with pamphlets and heavy looking textbooks.

Although they were new world bandits, they were also old fashioned students, both with voracious appetites for learning, for understanding, for the absorption of knowledge, the gold seam from which everything else flows.

This attention to detail made the two teenagers stand out. Not in a conspicuous way of course, for that would be a disaster in the world of cyber theft, where anonymity ruled and the shadows were your friend. But in the sense that their approach to their task was so detailed that they planned for each and every possible eventuality that they could think of.

In their minds it made perfect sense to consider everything, without exception. Most robbers give scant thought to the origins of the things they plan to steal. They tend not to look back too much being, as a breed, not especially given to reflection.

Andrei and Georgi were different.

Very different.

And with a maturity way beyond their tender teenage years they now set out to try and understand the arcane theory of money supply. When he asked the rather obvious question for the second or third time, Georgi finally got a proper answer.

'In case we want to put it all back.' Andrei told him.

'What do you mean?'

'It's one possibility, isn't it?'

'What is? Putting it all back. Well, no, not really. Why would we ever want to do that? It's going to take all our skill and energy to steal it in the first place.'

'But we agreed that we need diversions, didn't we? And more than one. Several'

'How is putting it back a diversion? And, may I remind you, we still haven't entirely figured out all of the things that are essential for the main task, the actual things on the list that really need doing. So, apart from anything else, I can't see how that can be any kind of priority when we still have so many major gaps in our overall thinking. More like an unnecessary distraction than an essential diversion.'

'What did we predict would happen, day one?'

'Err, the world would go nuts?'

'Well, obviously, yes. But as a response from the authorities?'

'They would deploy an expert task force, among many other things,'

'To do what?'

'To find out what happened.'

'And....?'

'To try to find out where the money had gone. To find out what happened to it.'

'Correct. And where will they look?'

'No idea.'

'Don't you think it would be a good idea if we knew?'

'Well, I don't know. Maybe. But what possible use would that information be to us?'

'You remember when we came up with our code name for this?'

'*Ischeznoveniye.* Yes, of course.'

'What did we say to each other?'

'Andrei, that was weeks ago. I can't really remember. We were saying lots of things back then. Most of it connected to the basic idea and our chances of actually doing it and then getting away with it.'

'We said, we need to find some experts. Experts in disappearing things. So that we could learn from them.'

'You mean the magicians?'

'Exactly. And what is it those guys always say? It's not really magic, there's no such thing. It's all distraction, all sleight of hand, all smoke and mirrors.'

'True enough, that's what they say, alright. But I still don't see …'

'If we put it back it will cause confusion, always a major part of any distraction. How many bank robbers in history have put the money back?'

'Apart from Isaac Davis, none, as far as I know.'

'Correct, and we can make allowances for him because in 1798 banks were still a bit new and he didn't know you couldn't pay the money you'd just robbed straight back in. Poor guy. But he's the only one.'

'Hardly surprising.'

'Exactly. And there's our second good reason. The invaluable element of surprise. The money disappears but just as the police investigators turn up, or whoever it is they decide to send, it reappears. As if by magic. A classic trick. Now you see it, now you don't. Or, rather, in this case, now you don't see it....'

'And now you do.'

'And now you don't again."

'What?'

'Well, if we can disappear it, then reappear it, then disappear it again, that will cause even more confusion. The public will be clamouring for an explanation, and that always makes investigations more difficult. They're hard enough without the media pressure and something like this will be off the scale.'

'Hmm.'

Georgi was coming round slowly.

'And what if we just put some of it back?' he ventured, as he thought this latest idea through, 'and only in selected locations. As well as confusion, that might spark some greed and envy, some anger and conflict, because there will be winners and losers. Horrible emotions, but useful if deployed tactically.'

And so it was that the boys agreed on the importance of understanding the money supply, the creation machine. Only then could one reasonably expect to put the thing into reverse and restore the missing loot in a digital manner.

No walking back into the local branch of Sberbank for them, no shoving an old satchel full of roubles across the counter.

No, this was high crime.

The highest.

Fraught with problems.

Awash with risk.

But, oh, the fun of it, the sheer scale of the challenges. What else could two teenage Muscovites get so much pleasure from?

Just at that moment, a tall slinky teenage blonde in ankle boots and a skirt that looked like a pelmet wandered in, shaking the morning snow off her Cossack hat.

The boys stopped talking immediately.

Anastasia had that effect on most conversations.

'Hi guys.' She glanced at the network maps and open notebooks, replete with sketches and drawings.

'Anything interesting going on?'

Andrei had his back to her as she came in so had to turn around to address her. In doing so he failed to notice that his best friend winked at Anastasia.

She just smiled. Not sure who at.

Andrei and Georgi had been friends forever, well for eleven years actually. But time has a strange way of moving. In later life it seems to have a normal, almost leisurely rhythm, but, to the young, nothing can happen fast enough and everything seems to take forever. So the fact that they had met as eight year olds sooo long ago meant that their relationship was one of the very oldest things in their very young lives. As a result it was an exceptionally strong bond, forged in playground scraps and the usual teenage wonderings about the world, with all its beauty and mystery.

They were, literally, as thick as thieves and immune to much of the turbulence that so often troubles the young. Most things that would affect other boys their age didn't.

With one tall, very willowy, blond exception.

She turned her back on them as she took off her knee-length purple mink and reached to hang it on the old stand behind the door, her shapely young curves straining at her tight top as she stretched upward.

She was very self-aware and knew intuitively what effect she was having on the two boys. Although it can also be said that a woman can never truly understand the erotic nature of male chemistry, something that remains a societal issue of massive proportions to this very day.

But Anastasia knew enough, sensed what every young woman craves as she emerges into the bloom of womanhood. The boys had an eye on her and an eye for her. She liked that; it made her feel good in a way that she never sought to question. And why should she? It was her right to feel that way.

And if it was more than one boy, even several, well, so what? She was a pretty girl and so how the world went around. Little could she know that the boys' immunity to most things when it came to challenges to their friendship would be sorely tested by her very innocence.

She turned back round and sat on the high bar stool, all thigh and curve.

'It's just another tech project Ans,' Georgi assured her. 'Just a networky thing. Pretty boring really, but we like to keep up with all this stuff, you know, it's just too tempting.'

'Will you get any money for it?'

'Should do, yes.'

'How much?' Anastasia was a thoroughly modern Moscow girl, long of leg, and not short on ambitions.

The boys had known that question would come, so were prepared.

'Can't really say. Depends on a whole lot of variables.'

'I though you hated variables, said it made your projects too unpredictable.'

'That's right. They do. So we try to eliminate them. Which is where we are with this right now.'

'Do you think we'll ever have a million?' she enquired, her eyes moist, possibly still streaming from the icy weather outside, although probably not. It was her favourite question, one they'd both heard many times before. It was always a relief when she asked it because they knew that once they'd answered she would back off and turn her thoughts to other more important matters, like her next shopping trip

'We might. It's always possible.'

It wasn't a deliberate lie. Their audacious, somewhat mad plan was still in its infancy so, although they had an outline, much, if not most of the detail was still missing.

Oddly enough for two robbers, the one aspect that was normally the most important thing of all in such scenarios, the value of the loot, had not been properly calculated. The schematics which lay open and spread out across the table had plenty of numbers attached to them, but the figures did not represent pounds, dollars or roubles. They were engineering documents revealing the interconnectivity of several local and global VPN's, the Virtual Private Networks which guaranteed a modicum of privacy and security to individual internet users.

They work by providing an immediate reassignment of traffic routing options meaning that a user in Moscow could, at the press of a button, draw a curtain across his browsing habits by suddenly using a node in a faraway server to support his activity. Thus a local user, anywhere in the world, was not really active in his or her own real location any more, but was effectively initiating a set of computer

interactions somewhere else. Arguments were constantly made that this was a more efficient traffic distribution mechanism for the internet, spreading the available capacities around the globe at the touch of a keypad and thereby distributing heavy traffic loads more evenly worldwide.

Although this was undoubtedly true, invisibility, the happy by-product of this arrangement, also provided one of the anonymous cloaks which supported more nefarious activities. Accordingly the structure of these sub-networks was of huge importance to the boys as they crafted their master plan. Their compulsive planning ethic meant they had to master the detail of the available networking protocols before they could move on to step two.

Ischeznoveniye. The Disappearance.

In this regard Andrei and Georgi were not just ordinary teenagers, nor were they just another pair of random hackers born post millennium into a digital age that was already maturing fast.

More and more products and services were now running across the Internet, which was itself now an increasingly mature beast, fifty six years of age if you take the setting up of ARPANET by the U.S. Department of Defence in 1966 as its original birth year. Children born post 2000 never knew a world without it and accepted its reality in daily use unquestioningly.

Their fresh eyes, young blood and unfettered sense of adventure would soon take computer sciences and interlinked networks quite literally to the heavens and beyond.

The education of this new golden generation created precocious talent in new ways. The child prodigies of yesteryear had mostly graced the arts with their talents with the musicians remaining the most famous due to the continued ubiquity of their work all over the world hundreds of years later. Mozart, Chopin, Liszt, Handel, Prokofiev and many, many more. There were equally talented, although slightly less well known representatives from the worlds of science, physics and mathematics.

But computers are new, at least in their modern incarnations, as are the strands of copper, silicon chips, slabs of cobalt and streams of radio waves that support their inter-connectivity.

And the education is also new. So new in fact, that the educators – plus the fathers and mothers of these children – were often left behind when it came to the teaching. They delivered the basics, but using methodologies which struggled to provide much of the essential forward thinking. At a certain point, the children started

to do that for themselves. They had been handed laptops, smartphones and tablets for their second birthdays and accepted them into their cots like so many alien teddy bears, something to gaze at and interact with, although hardly a great cuddle. But these were the Gen Z kids, complete with proper human DNA and yet somehow wired differently, chipped by their environments.

How could mum and dad possibly keep up with this latest facet of human evolution?

Answer? They couldn't. These kids were off to the stars, dreaming impossible dreams, but then, isn't that what dreams tend to be anyway, isn't that what they are there for in the first place? Hazy manifestations of something that we struggle to realise or achieve in our everyday waking lives.

And so it was with the two boys, sharing their growing pains as they trudged to school in Moscow's regular two-foot snowdrifts, thinking, as all youngsters do at that age, about some version of an impossible future and then taking a first faltering step towards it.

They had the same insatiable curiosity as their own grandfathers had had in mechanical things. Cars were cool. So were planes. How did they work then? So they read, they observed, they tinkered, they acquired, they stripped down, they reassembled and they learned.

Two generations later, same process.

Only it was early i-Phones that aroused their curiosity, not the latest Volgas or Skodas. Andrei and Georgi jailbroke them for the local mobile phone dealers who sought to profit from the seemingly never ending propensity for the Russian economy to never have very much of anything.

Limited supply but plenty of demand was one of those few situations that economists usually could manage to broadly agree upon. They called it scarcity and said it drove prices up. They were right and, as the local shopkeepers finally found a decent sideline, the boys discovered money.

Far from being thought of as some evil form of third world child labour, this was not considered to be a problem in early twenty first century Russia.

The country was changing.

So much had happened, was still happening, that the political turmoil created massive ructions right through all the territories of the post Soviet Union.

Wealth became the new god, much of it stolen or mis-appropriated.

But then it usually is.

The economy lay wide open to rape as the changes washed across the upper layers of Russian society.

It had taken the best part of a decade after the fall and demise of Gorbachev, but by the end of the Yeltsin years – Gorbachev's ever-controversial successor – a new era had been ushered in, if not formally and publicly, nonetheless semi-officially.

It became – almost overnight, given the usual snail's pace of change in that vast country – ok to own stuff, to have materialistic impulses, to be envious of the west and the tendency of its people to want things, nice things, homes, cars, holidays, clothes, watches and so on.

It was a long list, especially for people who tended not to have too many of those things in the first place.

It wasn't the Wild West but it did become the Wild East.

Laws were broken, corruption became rife and the obvious happened.

The underworld grew stronger, inveigled itself into the financial mainstream through a series of manouevres and relationships, grew increasingly confident as it found new ways to escape and avoid detection, very often by coming up with a never ending series of new ways to improve one's lot in life.

As the general background conditions changed in support of these societal developments, the criminal fraternity became increasingly aware of several growing trends which they decided they would like to exploit.

But there was a problem.

Their traditional brutish methods would not be enough to leverage these new types of opportunities.

You don't get far kicking a computer or setting fire to a network hub. Technology cannot feel human pain and does not respond to intimidation, bribery or threats. As the penny dropped, it became clear that this particular change was especially momentous.

This was a changing of the guard moment and the young bucks inside these mafia type cells saw their chances and set about figuring out how to take advantage of them.

In order to have any kind of seniority or status inside a Bratva structure it had been traditionally required for the aspiring Vor – the Russian equivalent of the Camorra "*made man*" – to deliver something of exception to the group. In the old days this would usually involve something especially unsavoury, usually violent,

often murderous.

But as the guard changed, so did the requirements.

To stay alive you have to adapt, else you die, as true in the first half of the new millennium as it ever was. And this particular adaptation spelt good news for those youngsters who were proficient in the dark arts of computer magic, who could find treasure in the labyrinthine abyss of cyberspace, who understood millennial alchemy, creating gold out of nothing.

The good ones were suddenly much in demand; the really good ones were fought over.

Two in particular stood out.

Two old schoolfriends who insisted on working together or not working at all.

In the rather topsy turvy world of Russia around 2012, this rather tantrum like behaviour, which would have led the perpetrators to a quick and sticky end a few years earlier, was suddenly tolerated. The word came down from the Pakhan, the boss man at the top, they're only stupid kids, they don't mean no harm behaving like that and, by the way, they're not that fucking stupid really are they? Not if they can do all this computer juju stuff.

So no smacks and plenty of lollipops.

Just smile and agree. If they want to work together, so what, long as they can produce and keep their mouths shut.

And so, from being a bit unsure about what they were getting involved in at the start, the two boys went from a bit of occasional moonlighting after *shkola* to a situation where the *'additional homework tasks'*, provided by their new friends with the fancy cars, were becoming ever more frequent and eventually started leading to late nights, lack of sleep and declining marks in their exams.

Parental intervention quickly ensued, followed by some old school reasoning and persuasion – which was fading out but not entirely gone – and a few stuffed envelopes, the lubricants of the ages.

It was not entirely lost on Andrei and Georgi's parents that their sons' employment prospects were not too good. There was a depressed jobs market, but they also quickly realized that there was a burgeoning secondary shadow-economy where the pay was just as good, if not significantly better.

They worried about the risks of course, but the rewards started to outweigh them and, convinced of the overarching protection of the *vor y zakone,* they acquiesced,

their complicity made stronger by a stream of relentlessly repeated assertions about the 'special' training they were receiving in the world of computers and networks, which was quite obviously becoming the new lifeblood of the modern world.

Like drug users or alcoholics who start off with the mild stuff, the two friends, aged around twelve, started off with low-level crime, almost so innocuous that they might have been forgiven for not knowing that what they were doing was wrong. The fact that mum and dad, the ultimate sheriffs at most pre-teen rodeos, did nothing to inhibit matters, almost guaranteed the paths of their future lives.

After all, if not the parents, then who?

They didn't have to chase the work. It came to them, because the impossibly long tentacles of the underworld had their spotters everywhere, even in the schools.

In fact, especially in the schools.

Those that showed special aptitude were noticed, tested a bit harder than the other kids without being aware of it, given a bit more homework occasionally and generally watched from the sidelines, in much the same way as the future sports stars are observed by anonymous strangers sitting high up in the stands.

A star striker will always stand out, his goal tally irrefutable proof of an inherent ability, the creative midfielder won't have a string of numerical credits to his name but the talent will shine through brightly as opponents flounder in his wake, the top goalkeepers a mix of skill, daring and madness, all three ingredients essential.

Similarly the proving grounds of these young IT professionals were dotted with scouts from the outside world as well as the kindly teachers. They were lauded as the Corporate stars of tomorrow, for that was how they were coached, and they were encouraged to start thinking early about regular careers and becoming future captains of industry. In this way they would stay on track for a short while, their educations effectively providing a camouflage for the insidious preparation that would eventually lead them into the shadows.

By the time they were in their teens they were expert at programming and writing code, all platforms, all systems, no questions asked, because, by then, they had been officially recognized as stand out talents and were being given additional lessons late into the evenings.

Things at home were unaffected because the family monthly budgets continued to be topped up by alleged scholarship money and bursary payments designed to encourage and facilitate entry into university. This was the parting of the ways as well

as the parting of the waves, the moment where the parents either carried on with the whole charade or suddenly woke up and smelt the coffee.

In the case of Andrei and Georgi, a point of no return had actually been reached a couple of years earlier where their ability to assiduously dismantle some academic firewalls had set them on course for some extra tuition with some of those older 'operatives' who were already active and established on the dark side. Who better to rank and assess the upcoming youngsters than their peers, not really that much older in their late twenties, but actually light years apart in terms of skills development and sheer intuition. They reported back to their respective Bratoks – the go-betweens in the appropriate layers of the mafia hierarchies – one by one until the cumulative reports started to make people sit up and take notice.

At that point a job in industry for the two friends ceased to be an option any more and the defined arc and trajectory of their future lives seemed pretty much assured.

But life can have a funny way of turning out differently and confounding expectations.

Harry Shepperton and The Nines were certainly about to come up against a pair of extremely formidable opponents, given their near decade of over-achievement as black hats in a dark world.

But all of a sudden it seemed something rather peculiar had started to happen.

The boys were becoming self – employed.

Very weird for a Mafiosi.

Hardly ever happened.

Not this side of the cemetery anyway.

Chapter 5 – Beacon Hill

'I know its normal for us to hardly know where to start,' Harry admitted as he wrapped up the early morning briefing. ' But this time it does seem extra challenging. Anyway the Project is ours now, so let's just review where we are and hopefully, assuming you've all had your cornflakes, something will pop out to get us going'.

'Where was the initial hack? Have the banks said yet?' Liam enquired, rocking slowly back and forth on his chair, the soothing motion driving his best thinking. Or so he always said.

'They're staying pretty stumm right now ' Hazel told him, wrapping a long jazzy scarf around her topcoat and grabbing her trademark fedora.

She looked more like an eccentric artist than the head of UK counter- intelligence as she headed for the doorway. It wasn't an intentional disguise but it worked.

'I need to get back over to COBRA and see what they've come up with. I'll be in touch later. Take care children. Byeee.'

Her and Harry were both more than twenty years older than their precocious new charges and had a habit of revealing some rather unprofessional affectations now and then.

Quite endearing really.

And she was gone.

'We need to start from somewhere else then' Jake offered. ' We can't just sit around here waiting on those guys all day. Don't they know we're on their side? I mean, without their input, what exactly have we got to go on right now?'

'A world full of angry and frightened people' offered Jojo.' We could start by asking ourselves who that actually suits, who might benefit from it and why? Let's not forget the lessons of Covid, it was only last year after all.'

'You mean it's just about the money?' Paul stated, a quizzical look on his face.

'Oh, its always about the money, Paul. But what I mean is could there be something else going on, you know, behind it? A kind of alternative agenda?'

'Well, that's gotta' be the world's best ever camouflage then, if that's the case' Jake's Laredo drawl twanged softly in the small room. 'Heck, I hadn't even thought 'bout that. But what on earth could it be? What's bigger than this that it could need such a mind-blowing smokescreen? I mean, c'mon people, don't we have enough of a

problem right here with the main story without looking for a sub plot?'

But the table was suddenly quiet, the cogs were turning, and even as he uttered the words, Jake found that he wasn't even convincing himself. This was The Nines team, bright as buttons, sharp as tacks. They were not so much trained as naturally inclined to rule everything in until they could rule it out. No matter how preposterous.

'Ah, hell ' he said again, looking round at his silent colleagues. 'Really?'

'We have to consider everything Jake' Harry reminded him. That's how we work. Part of the fun but also part of the pain.'

'I know boss. Sorry, just a moment of frustration. Not helped by a wall of silence coming from the finance world. From what I seen a' those guys, they could ha stole it all themselves. Bunch of crooks. Where would they hide it all though?'

Again the table went quiet. They were all staring at Jake, grinning.

'Whad 'ah do now?'

'You're sure asking all the right questions this morning cowboy' Paul teased his colleague.

Jake rewound his thoughts as Caitlin helped him out.

'That's got to be a decent clue Jake. We're all using the same word here because it's all we've heard all morning from the media. Disappeared. That's what they keep saying, over and over, isn't it. *"All the money has disappeared."* Well it can't have, can it? That's just not possible. It's the wrong word.'

'And the right one would be?' Harry pushed his team along gently. They usually got there in the end with some mild prompting.

'How about *moved*? You know, like from A to B.'

More silence and cogs turning. Harry knew from experience that the longer it remained quiet, the more likely it was that they were on to something. Their individual thought processes were labyrinthine as they each wandered off down a series of dead ends and cul-de-sacs, eliminating, validating, prioritizing, and trying to fit the available pieces into a whole. Not too easy when you didn't really have any pieces to start with.

'You mean it's probably hidden?' Liam was rocking faster now, usually a sign that he was getting somewhere. ' And because much of it is in non-physical assets, then it follows that there's only two options. Either cyberspace or inside a server, one a dose big fekkers under da Arizona desert. And bein' as how they's really one and da same thing ...'

'What are?' enquired Harry.

'Cyberspace and servers, they just two fancy words for parts of da internet. The big parts, not the stuff in your home office, but the heart and soul of the beast, the hubs and the networks, those components that thread it all together. Loike da' glue.'

Harry Shepperton knew full well how most of that stuff worked. He was fifty, not eighty, but he still always believed in letting his team charge around wildly with their ideas for a while before settling on a course of action. It had always worked in the past so he left them to their thoughts for a few moments while his own mind wandered off.

He had a team of specialists, now commonly known as The Nines because of their high IQ's. He had expertise in physics, law, materials, geology, traditional engineering, computing and the internet, all at his immediate disposal but now, as he focused in and thought about it properly, he realised that he didn't have a money guy, a finance expert.

He reflected on their last mission, The Wuhan Mystery, which had benefited enormously from the inclusion of The Brig, a retired Chinese national who Hazel had seconded to the team to help unravel the source of Covid.

Now Harry found himself a man short again. This was going to be tough enough without somebody who possessed the latest detailed knowledge of how the banks worked and knew their latest trends, probably something that only an insider could provide.

He racked his brains. Who did he know in that world?

Somebody trustworthy, but maybe also a bit off centre.

A maverick.

Somebody who could do the left field, out of the box stuff, the kind of thinking that might pay dividends, trying to reconstruct what was beginning to look like the biggest robbery of all time.

Three thousand miles away in his Beacon Hill townhouse Colonel Hank Wyatt, formerly of the USAF, gazed down at the Charles river where the joggers on the Esplanade formed a constant and seemingly never ending stream of motion.

He had always been one of those people who was generally content with life, irrespective of whatever it threw at him. Like many of his colleagues who had joined the military while they were still young, teenagers in many cases, the first set of early

retirement options, with all their attendant benefits, had arrived after thirty years of service. The money was good, pretty generous in fact, as befitted those who had served. So was the rest of the package. Health care, comms allowances, travel and hotel discounts, even protection where necessary. So that should have made life nice and rosy and yet...

And yet...

He was still barely fifty, an age which seems like it might just be about half way to those of an optimistic persuasion.

He stared down at the new business cards which had just been delivered that morning and now lay staring up at him from his desk.

Colonel Hank Wyatt
USAF (Ret'd)
General Contracting

hnkwycolo@usaf.mil

Nice of them to let me hang on to my old e-mail address, he thought, although, in truth of course, it was hardly ever going to be of much use to anybody else.

He still agonized over the term 'General Contracting' which sounded both oddly suspicious and completely innocuous at the same time, and yet it summed up his capabilities and his intentions pretty well.

So he stuck with it.

But it was the word in brackets that bothered him most.

Ret'd. Retired.

It was a true description so it was accurate. That wasn't the problem. It was more the connotations of the word, which shouldn't really have been that negative, but nonetheless were.

Washed up.

Finished.

Put out to pasture.

Over the hill.

Of course the very fact that he was setting himself up as an independent investigator meant the complete opposite. At the rather appropriate age of 49 Hank was doing what everybody should do around that stage of their lives.

He was trying something new.

Connected as it was to the first part of his life, it was still a departure, a new beginning in some respects, a jump into the unknown. He hadn't really thought the whole thing through to the n'th degree, but just knew instinctively that he needed to do something fresh, both for himself as well as for the world around him.

Contribution, the Americans liked to call it. Giving back. That set of activities, which, if carried out anonymously, could provide so much nourishment and development for a man's soul.

Plus he'd be getting paid, of course, the draw of the Yankee dollar never being that far away. With the modern world so interconnected and so turbulent he felt sure that opportunities would present themselves. One only had to look at the media to be reminded of that, as that morning's TV news bulletins were all proving.

It had crossed Hank's mind, of course, that this latest blow up in the world's banking system could provide some work for him, although, like most everybody else on the planet on that particular day, he was completely flummoxed by what was going on and had absolutely no idea what to make of it.

Having absorbed several hours of television 'experts' trying to make sense of it, he'd finally had enough around lunchtime and decided to head over to The Hill Tavern for a few beers with the locals to see what the consensus was.

In this small but elegant enclave of Boston there were a lot of smart residents who were probably planning to do exactly the same thing. Somebody would be able to cast some light on it for sure and then, better informed, he could return home in the late afternoon and get stuck into some serious planning.

As he crossed the landing to head downstairs and grab his jacket his mobile pinged. It wasn't the usual alert though. Like many people he'd made use of his i-phone's multiple ring-tone choices by allocating separate melodies to different people.

This was one that he hadn't heard in a while.

He looked at the screen, just to check, as he answered the call.

'Harry Shepperton ! As I live and breathe.'

He could hardly believe his luck. On a day that was turning out to be as momentous in world history as 9/11, this was unlikely to be a social call.

'Hello, Hank. How's life treating you?'

'Exceptionally well, thanks. Although a bit short on fun recently, truth be told.

37

Wuhan and Covid seem an awful long way off now, especially considering that it was only last year.'

'Yes, I know what you mean.'

And the two men reminisced for a few minutes about The Wuhan Mystery, as they had come to call it, and the rather strange adventure they had shared in Holland at the International Court of Justice.

'So, she did do it then, Harry, did she? The girl? Married him in the morning, betrayed him in the afternoon!'

'Well, that was the thing with Covid and the whole story. Turned out to be the ultimate whodunit?'

As he brought Hank up to speed on The Nines' last mission, Harry sought some clarifications.

'Did I see somewhere that you've retired recently Hank?' he asked.

Hank had wandered back upstairs and was now sitting at his desk.

The joggers hadn't stopped jogging and his new business cards hadn't stopped staring.

'Officially, that's correct. I am now in receipt of a rather generous pension from Uncle Sam, although I gotta' tell you, at my age, it feels mighty strange.'

'So, what does it say on your new business cards then?'

Hank felt a shiver.

Fuck. How could he know about them?

'Have you got my house bugged, Harry?' he enquired, only half in jest.

The guy was running England's top elite response unit. He would know stuff, lots of stuff, and what he didn't know, he could probably find out in an hour or so.

He heard a chuckle come back down the phone.

'Hardly. I just figured the Hank Wyatt I know, former CIA and USAF officer, spare time geologist and space scientist amongst other things, was unlikely to spend the rest of his life sitting on his arse. I kinda' guessed you find other things to do.'

Hank breathed easier.

Just for a split second there…,well, you never knew with spooks.

And Harry Shepperton was Ten, no ordinary spook.

He was one of the few people in life who also knew about the small gap at the start of Hank's career when he had dabbled with a career in financial services and spent a lot of time, wildly successfully, in casinos, something which had brought him

to the attention of the CIA recruiters who had wanted to know what his *system* was. He didn't have one, as he repeatedly told them, he was just *"pretty good with numbers"* because of a rare emotional gift, something which turned out to be a bit of an understatement for one of the world's top quants.

There was a list of "other things" with Hank Wyatt.

It was a very long list.

'I am considering my options, Harry. That's true. But as I've been watching TV all morning I'm afraid the only thing I'm focused on right now is my personal bank account and trying to find out whether I've actually still got any money left in it. That floated quite naturally to the top of today's to do list, I'm afraid to say.'

'What are they telling you?'

'Who?'

'Your bank?'

'They're not telling me shit. I can't get through to them. Just a recorded message telling me how important my call is to them and referring me to their website which, apparently, can answer most questions. Only it can't, can it? It can't tell me what the fuck's going on? And that's today's one and only question.'

'Are you contracted to do anything for the next couple of weeks?'

Ah, there it was. The real reason for the call was emerging.

How available should he make himself?

Was this a time to play hard to get?

To negotiate?

He quickly reflected on what he knew about his friend in London, who he was, what he did for a living, who he knew, the fact that he had a Rolodex and a contact network second to none.

Midday in Boston was 5 in the evening across the Pond in old London town. The fact that Harry had probably been calling people all day and that he might just as well have been the fiftieth as the fifth suddenly paled into insignificance alongside the rather pleasing fact that he had thought to call him at all.

All the old training kicked in, the service ethic, the duty to fellow citizens. Whatever the hell was going on, this was hardly the time to be discussing expenses. Especially with one of the few people on the planet who stood any chance of making sense of it and had a team at his disposal who had been hand picked to fix global problems fast.

Hank made a quick decision.

'Not really Harry, no. Why do you ask? Is there something I can help you with?'

Hank suddenly realised he had access to a much better source of information than his Cambridge Street neighbours down at The Hill Street Tavern.

He'd had an inkling that using the phrase 'General Contracting' would provide him with plenty of latitude for his future projects, might even stretch him a bit, take him off in some new directions, keep him from getting stale, get him involved in some newer stuff.

Little did he know …..

'There might be.' came the reply from across the Atlantic.

'Do you know anything about Bitcoin?'

Chapter 6 – The vacuum.

Harry was still working long into the evening on that fateful day when the world's money had suddenly vanished. Even though he'd been up at 4am in the morning, there was no tiredness, as is often the case with people who are genuinely busy. The subject matter can be pretty much anything as long as it engages the brain and stimulates the mind, the body then utilizes one of its numerous sub-mechanisms to ward off sleep, not indefinitely of course, but for a few hours at least, or maybe several if the stimulus is sufficient and there's enough adrenaline.

The very nature of his job as Ten, Commanding Officer of the UK Government's recently appointed Rapid Response Team, ensured that most days were like that. When he finally hit the hay he never had any difficulty in dropping off, never needed pills, never needed a sleep therapist. What the hell were they anyway other than symptoms of a rather unbalanced society? His regular day nearly always depleted him and drained his energies completely. And this, by any standard, had not been anything like a regular day.

So he was still feeling relatively fresh at 7pm in the evening when he responded to Hazel Ingliss's summons and strolled the fifteen minutes across Blackfriars to her office for the long awaited two-way update, him to her on the assembled thoughts of his team, her to him on the output from COBRA.

His boss swung open the door of the walnut drinks cabinet and cleared a small space on her desk for the Glenmorangie Signet, her tipple of choice. She placed it next to two cut glass tumblers and fetched an ice bucket from the fridge.

She didn't ask. It was early evening and they'd both had a rough few hours. It was time to review both the day's occurrences and the events that had led up to them.

'So they weren't bluffing then?' she started.

'Seems not.'

'Are we any closer to identifying the source?'

'No, not yet. We should have something by tomorrow morning though. I've got Jojo and Cait pulling an all-nighter. Our guess is Russia, based on a few of the cipher signatures.'

'What are they?'

'A bit like vanity watermarks, things criminals tend to leave behind when they

yearn for recognition but cannot readily admit it to themselves.'

'You mean they want to be identified? Deep down they actually want to be caught?'

'Yes, exactly. It's an increasingly well-recognized pattern of behaviour, almost like a syndrome. And it probably will be one day as soon as some boffin somewhere dreams up a name for it.'

'Why would anyone do that? Don't the bad guys always want to get away with it?'

'Yeah, you'd think, wouldn't you. But don't forget there's a significant age aspect to factor in with a lot of these cyber crimes. They're often youngsters and sometimes they can even be a whole two generations away from us. It can be a bit like children playing. And part of the game, and it's often a really big part, is toying with the opposition. That's us, by the way. They like to taunt and to tease. The sig-ciphers are part of that. They're leaving us clues and saying " catch us if you can."

'Which makes the whole thing much more infuriating, And I suppose they will know that and it forms part of their fun. And so the whole thing builds.'

'Yup, that's very much the psychology of it. And that's why we suspect Russia. That's very much their kind of thing. From the top down. Knowing that we know but can't or won't do anything about it. Double fun for them. They absolutely love that.'

Hazel Ingliss poured out two more shots of the hard stuff and pushed the ice bucket towards Harry. Each to his own with the diluting.

She kept hers neat.

So did he.

That's the kind of day it had been.

'Any consensus from COBRA?'

'Only that it didn't appear on any radar. You know how we normally end up kicking ourselves because all the signs were there, loads of clues but we missed most of them. Well, not this time. Absolutely diddley squat. Nada. Nichts. A total blank. Not so much as half a whisper.'

Harry furrowed his brow.

'Really. Well that is, in itself, a clue of sorts. I mean there's usually some chatter somewhere isn't there, however indistinct? So that's actually very unusual'

'Which, without blowing our own trumpet too much, means that all of the usual suspects are pretty much immediately eliminated. Plus for the last twelve hours The

Five Eyes have concentrated on pretty much nothing else and they haven't got a Scooby either. Because of the very nature of the incident there's also a rather unprecedented top level of co-operation starting to emerge amongst the non-aligned nations, as we once used to call them. Bit patronizing that, when you come to think of it, but anyway, they seem to all be drawing a blank as well, at least that's what they're telling us. So what do you conclude from all of that?'

'That it's a very small group of people, working alone, and with no overt political agenda.'

'Very small? How small is very small?'

'Two kids in a bedroom.'

'Have hacked into all of the control servers for the world's banks and have accessed everybody's accounts, including the banks' own reserve deposits? That is seriously not possible, Harry. Please tell me that can't be true.'

'Well, it's not actually me saying it.'

'What do you mean?'

'After you left this morning, we kicked a lot of ideas around. Most of them were pretty whacky, but then if this whole thing isn't really whacky, then I don't know what is.'

'Ok. And..?

'Whenever we're a bit confounded, we tend to revert to the old Sherlock principle. After you've eliminated the impossible, whatever else is left, no matter how improbable, must be the truth. He used it to solve murders and eliminate suspects; last man standing is the guilty party, that kind of thing. Or last woman. But as a theorem it does have a general applicability that's kind of stood the test of time. So we started to compile a long list of possible suspects but then, about fifteen minutes in, we realised we had set ourselves a rather ridiculous task, well an impossible task really, for the simple reason that pretty much everybody could be a suspect when it comes to motivation. Almost everybody who wanted to gain a large sum of money could be on that list.'

'So where's the elimination in that?'

'Exactly. There isn't any. So we needed to add a few more layers to the simple question of *"why would anybody want to do it?"* the main two obviously being *"who has the knowledge to do it?"* closely followed up with *"how are they planning on getting away with it when everything in the digital world leaves a trace?"* They're not

always that visible of course, the clues, but they are always there, assuming you know where to look.'

'And that's what Jojo and Cait are working on right now?'

'Literally, as we speak, yes. The first being a needle in a haystack, the second more like a teardrop in an ocean.'

Hazel Ingliss sat back in her large comfy swivel chair and slowly absorbed what her trusted lieutenant was telling her.

She took a long swig of the Scotch and stared out through the bulletproof glass of her top floor office in Spook central. The lights along the ever-busy South bank, just over the Thames on the other side, were starting to glow across the river's surface.

'Why not the other way round?" she asked.' Surely the latter will be easier if they've left the digital version of fingerprints behind.'

"Well, because you have to try and get your head round the enormity of this thing. The scale of it is stupendous. Not only has all the money disappeared, but because all the usual mainstream repositories for it have also all been affected, it means that there's effectively nowhere left to put the money. There is, in effect, no hiding place, because the whole system has been compromised in one fell swoop. And yet, there obviously needs to be one somewhere, because all the loot is digital. This is not a raid by guys in balaclavas carrying stripey bags with Swag written on them. That's our first puzzle, the first task to solve. It's not actually a *why* or a *how*, now that I come to think about it a bit more. It's a *where*. It's all gone, all right. The banks have finally confirmed it. But where to? Where the fuck is it?'

He reached across for the ice bucket. If he was going to have a third shot, he'd best dilute it. Gonna' be a long night.

'Because there is, on the face of it, absolutely nowhere for it to go.'

Chapter 7 – Blondy

The plain fact of the matter was they were both in love with her. And a pretty intense love it was too, the kind that can have seismic implications for people and situations the world over, for such is the power of that beautiful, powerful emotion.

When it hits, it's like a freight train, when it departs it leaves a hollow gap, the kind that won't ever have been felt before, a bewildering emptiness tinged by the dawning of a sudden realisation that there is now a hole where another person used to be, the one who was there just yesterday, warm and full of fun and laughter, now gone, don't know where, don't know when, definitely don't know why.

The cruelest of all cruel things in an often cruel world.

And yet the price is worth paying, always worth paying for that sense of elation, of floating on air that comes as part of the unspoken bargain. The occasional brutal lopsidedness just one more unfair penance inflicted on the unwary, the unwitting, the uncertain, the unready and the unprepared. Because it may happen repeatedly, over and over again in its relentless quest to dishearten and despair, but it will only ever happen a first time just the once, probably because that level of pain might otherwise kill through overexposure.

Better to have loved and lost, they say.

Definitely.

Better to be safe than sorry.

Hmm. Not so sure.

And so the world's young lovers wander around in the fog of their teen emotions, not seeing everything too clearly perhaps, but nonetheless feeling it very intently and, emboldened by youth, unconcerned about haphazards or pitfalls.

And so it had been with Andrei and Georgi, thrown together in the playground, battle forged in the scrapes and scraps of their schooldays and their younger years, sharing the spoils of life, even at such a tender age, destined to be friends forever, or at least until they were about seventeen, which amounts to the same thing for a fourteen year old.

Those are important years, the awkward years, as some older people like to call them, not because the kids feel awkward but because they do. Sexual feelings emerge

like something coming out of hibernation, unsteady and stumbly. It all feels perfectly right, whatever it is, and yet there seem to be walls of resistance, all erected by old people, apparently for the benefit of the young, although they never appear to have been consulted on the matter, youth apparently being too inexperienced to know its own mind, a rather questionable and partial truth at best. Throw in a beautiful fourteen-year-old girl and the flammability of the mix immediately becomes highly combustible, barely needing any kind of spark to set off a series of psychological and physical explosions.

And so it had been with Anastasia.

Already tall, even by Russian standards, where long slender legs were quite common among young girls, she was a natural looker, possessed of a pretty face and the kind of curvy body that would distract boys and give them instant brain fog.

Although an undoubted beauty to behold, the girl inside Anastasia was complex, more aware of her own striking looks than would ever be good for her, she could be flighty, envious and spiteful, three characteristics to be avoided at all costs in a young woman if at all possible.

Regrettably the poor girl had never had any real choice in the matter, brought up as she was by a mother and a father who had created her biologically but had then forgotten to love her, the ultimate human crime, the sin to end all sins, he all consumed with the vodka that had remained the scourge of that immensely sad country for centuries as it was let down again and again by its political leaders throughout the ages, she equally addicted to a skewered outlook on life brought on by the drudgery of the local bathhouse where she was leered at constantly by fat men with bad breath, bald heads and broken teeth. The one shining light in their lives, right under their noses every day, a small bundle of curiosity, was ignored and abused, too much trouble, needing too much energy, too much attention, too much money and then one day suddenly a teenager without a soul, destined to a life of excess negativity that would reflect their own.

Such an outcome was not guaranteed of course, being more a probability than a completed destiny, and yet her treatment of the boys that had started to pass her way did not bode well. In much the same way as the child who tortures animals often turns into an adult monster, Anastasia was now a nasty tease, taunting the poor lambs with her feminine loveliness, but not offering any kind of love or genuine affection in return, for the very simple but very upsetting reason that she just couldn't, for she did

not know what that was, or how to do it.

Although her looks made her a genuine magnet, it would have been better for all concerned if, in her particular case, the polarity had been switched and she had repulsed rather than attracted, at least that way she would have learned to appreciate the true value of warmth and genuine friendship and not been so fickle with the ready feelings of others. But life is what it is and that was the hand that had been dealt to all those in her circle – and there were many – as she blossomed and grew, ever aware of her changing body and increasingly haughty with her manner.

She quickly discovered that she had the pick of the boys and chose Andrei because she liked his floppy fringe and cool clothes, although she also liked Georgi who could play guitar, Mikhail who knew about science and stuff, Sergei whose dad worked on the council, Boris with the funny hair who lived next door, Piotr who wanted to join the ballet and. …well, quite a few more as well.

At fourteen this is quite normal for a teenage girl so she left a trail of emotional debris and destruction behind her as she flitted from boy to boy, like a butterfly hopping from flower to flower, free and easy with her charms as she went, which only made matters worse as her young conquests all imagined themselves to be in love with her.

The reason all this mattered so much was that she was actually destined, although she did not know it, to play a leading role in solving one of the world's most memorable crimes, initially just a bit part player but then hugely instrumental towards the end and the final unraveling and denouement.

The two boys who could not be parted by anything, despite the wiliest attempts of their *vor y zakone* handlers during their formative years, would see their deep friendship founder on the rocks of infidelity as Anastasia took her pleasure with both of them in that one way which is always guaranteed to destroy genuine affection.

One knows. One doesn't.

One knew. One didn't.

And then the delights of sexual embrace quickly become toxic, almost overnight. Just at that particular time when they needed to be completely sure of their tight bond, of their rock solid friendship, there would be an explosion of mistrust, an outbreak of disillusionment. They had been a solid team, had kept each other going through all the doubts at the beginning of their extraordinary adventure. Would they, could they, dare they? Nobody knew, because what they were planning had never been done before.

But they felt secure enough since it would be safe to try because only the two of them were involved.

Sworn to secrecy, no one must know. Not even Ans, especially Ans, because she could be a bit, well, you know, a bit gossipy, the one thing they really couldn't afford.

So they didn't tell her.

But she found out.

Found they had a secret from her. Had hidden something from her.

Even though she had let them both fuck her.

Bastards. How dare they do that.

To her.

To the queen bee.

She felt, well, what was that feeling exactly? Something very weird. Difficult to put into words. Didn't feel good though, no, not at all, like they'd let her down or something. Was it betrayal maybe, a word that she'd heard of but couldn't really understand properly at her tender age, and it didn't really fit the situation accurately anyway. So she struggled for days to try and identify the feeling, the way only a girl or woman will do, agonizing over it, yet all the time quite sure, in herself, that she'd been wronged, even insulted maybe, such a horrible feeling.

And yet, all that had happened was that the boys had had a secret, one that they had kept from her, and that had been enough. Even though it wasn't really anything to do with her, somehow she felt… let down …disappointed …rejected …what on earth was that feeling.

Not nice, anyway.

And she'd been good enough to let them both fuck her.

And then they had done this.

Turned on her

Bastards…

Chapter 8 – A bit of coding

Well, more than a bit actually. In reality quite a lot was required for even the simplest of tasks in the year 2022, as the penetration of the internet as the most advanced computer network the world had ever seen continued apace into all corners of everyday life.

The first clues about the full extent of its software capabilities were already there to see way back in the eighties when the earliest developments of Fly-By-Wire were slowly introduced into aircraft development. It led to planes effectively being capable of flying themselves with only limited intervention by the pilot. Fast-forward about forty years and self-driving cars is now a reality, as is the automation of nearly all large-scale systems which drive and support modern life.

And it is the internet which supports the worldwide connectivity that joins all those systems together, its magic being made possible by use of a specialist language although, oddly enough, it is not one that people speak, for it is the language of machines, which they alone can understand and respond to and yet, even more oddly, that language has been created by man.

And so the youngsters of the sixties and seventies, who were among the earliest practitioners of coding, found themselves true pioneers as the whole world started to slowly gravitate towards total computer dependency.

They wrote books and manuals and became teachers to future generations of computer science students, destined to affect profound change on the world. Their names should be known to all of us. Some are, in the case of the founders of the huge modern American corporations, and yet many are not.

Brian Kernighan, Denis Ritchie and Ken Thompson for example, all language developers extraordinaire. Yet even they, early though they were, had their own predecessors like Alan Turing and Ada Lovelace, from as much as fifty and one hundred years earlier respectively.

So in some regards it could be argued that all this stuff isn't really so new after all. Until, that is, one factored in the internet and the awesome power of interconnectivity. That really did change everything, as plenty of people had kept saying back in the late nineteen nineties although, regrettably, many were charlatans

hyping the latest IPO's in businesses they didn't fully understand but were fully invested in.

That period was characterised by a whole host of fly-by-night, get-rich-quick companies who managed to achieve astronomical stock market valuations without ever earning any real money or making any profit. Apart from for their investors of course, who laughed all the way to the bank chanting the mantra of the time *"The internet changes everything."*

Huge numbers of those businesses failed but a very small number survived, grew, and prospered hugely, becoming titans of the modern world. So the mantra was proved correct, although the dramatic nature of that change took many more years to materialise fully.

And so it came to pass that one particularly ice cold morning in January 2022 Georgi had uttered those immortal words to his friend and partner in crime. They had been up all night – again – poring over the blueprints which were destined to become the source of so much future trouble with Anastasia.

'It's gonna' take a bit of coding' he concluded softly, uttering one of the great understatements of the twenty first century.

Andrei was perched on his barstool in the open plan kitchen of the flat they both now shared, having concluded several months earlier that co-habitation would be a boon to their rapidly advancing planning.

'We're going to need to calculate the man-hours numbers now,' he responded cheerily, undaunted by the sheer scale of the task they had set themselves. 'Then we can start to form a proper timetable.'

They had now reached a kind of mid-way point in their *project,* for that was still how they thought of it. It had always been inevitable that they would need to write their own instructions, the orders and sets of commands that would corrupt the workings of the world's financial systems and allow them to take control to carry out their *Ischeznoveniye,* their pet code name for what was set to become the world's greatest robbery.

'I'm still less worried about getting in, than what we actually do once we're in there.' Georgi said, still tracing a finger across one of the routing protocols laid out on the coffee table. 'We need a whole plan to pull this off. It doesn't help if the first part's brilliant and the second part is rubbish. We want to get away with this as well as just do it. No salt mines, remember.'

'Agreed, I think we need to switch focus now and start concentrating on the BitCoin architecture. How refined do you think it really is? It's got all this fabulous press down the years but c'mon, is anything really that unhackable?'

'Especially hard to believe that nobody's ever tried. I reckon plenty have but they've just managed to suppress the story in the media.'

'Why, though? Isn't that something that people would be interested in and would want to know about?'

'Absolutely, no doubt about it'

'There's plenty stuff about mining hacks out there. Some of those vids look legit, but just as many are really flaky. But the core programme itself? That's something else. Bombproof, allegedly, or so they say.'

'I can understand all the interest in the mining stuff. That's where the money is for the main player set. And those characters are light years ahead of the big corporations and they have the right attitude. High risk but high reward. Very high in fact, as long as you can get your money out.'

'Which should not be a structural problem with Crypto because the liquidity should always be there. You don't have to make markets like you do with traditional equity investing, the stocks and shares stuff.'

'No, its not a structural issue. It's confidence in the people. It's about who you have to depend on to get paid out. If you have no control or leverage over that then your position is so much the weaker.'

And so they went on, sounding, for all the world, like a couple of fifty year olds who'd been working in banking their whole lives. In reality, this was just the release of years of absorbed knowledge accrued from multiple sources and a myriad of conversations in their formative years spent working on a raft of quite sophisticated illicit intrusions into the world of finance at the behest of their underground masters.

But with Andrei and Georgi, it was a whole lot more than just knowing the lingo, just talking the talk. They understood this stuff in all of its extreme technical detail.

'And that's very a systemic weakness as well as a positive strength. The hardware is incredibly robust but the trading conditions in the marketplace that surround it are highly volatile.'

'You mean corrupt.'

'Well, lets settle for unpredictable. The algorithm is rock solid – at least up to now – but the people are not. So that's a worry if you're buying Bitcoin as a hold,

even a short term hold, because you'll only ever find a buyer who's another speculator.'

'But isn't that true of most investments these days? They're all a bit of a gamble, all a bit scammy. I remember when I first heard about the markets I mistakenly thought they couldn't be manipulated. I mean, how naïve can you get? Anywhere there's money, things can get manipulated. And they do. And the larger the pot, the greater the potential manipulation.'

'I think that's right. But it's not our problem, is it? Not if we're going to put it all back.'

He paused for a second, thinking through this, the trickiest part of their whole operation for the umpteenth time.

'That's not something we'll need to worry about though, is it? Our problem is the same one small children have when they play hide and seek. There's only so many places to hide and eventually somebody who's looking will look into all of them.'

'Apart from somewhere they're really not supposed to be' suggested Georgi with a grin.

'How do you mean?

'Well if they're playing in the house, they shouldn't be in the garden. If they're playing in the garden, they shouldn't be in the park. And so on.'

'Which means what, in our case?'

'That we need a wealth store where nobody will look'

'But they'll look everywhere. We already know that'

'Apart from somewhere unhackable. They won't look there because nobody can ever get into it. Or, more accurately, they haven't until now.'

And so the boys had their plan. Not the detail but at least a good outline. The world's greatest ever robbery would not be a theft.

It would be a transfer.

Smoke and mirrors.

A trick.

But on an epic scale.

And nobody would know about it, about how they were going to do it, about the exact detail, about the small percentage that might not make its way back, might disappear permanently, you know, just to cover their expenses.

That would be their strength.

Their invisibility.

Because only they would know.

Only them.

Perfect….

Chapter 9 – La La land

Cyberspace. What is it?

Does it exist as some other final frontier for the USS Enterprise to investigate?

Or is it all in our heads, like all the spiritual stuff ?

Or is it just a repository of data, some trove of digits, of ones and zeros, of binary code, parked in the Nevada desert or the backwaters of The Ukraine or wherever it is these days that the global concentrations of server farms happens to be?

Irrespective of location it remains, for most, a place of mystery. Things happen there which we cannot see, hear, smell, taste or touch and yet they affect us in all sorts of ways.

Very important ways.

For this is the dark domain where all of those strange languages get spoken, where the software engines talk to each other, where the codes are decoded, then recoded, then decoded again, all without any human intervention. Where data packets are disassembled, fragmented for security purposes, and then reassembled, often far away on the other side of the planet, into something meaningful, not to us as humans, but to a chip, to a programme, to an algorithm. Discs are reformatted and complex security signals allow the firewalls to open, those guardians of the night who immediately yield up the secrets of whatever lies beyond to those with the right key.

This is a world within a world. Something which just fifty years ago was pure science fiction, believed in by the very few, but ridiculed by the very many, is now a part of everybody's everyday lives.

Indispensable.

Unavoidable.

Inescapable.

Yet so few understand it.

Or its laws.

Or how it works.

Or its frailties.

Does this matter?

Very few understand how electricity works.

Or how cars work.

And yet they are both exceptionally dangerous, killing in large number every year, although their deadly nature does not seem to unduly concern people who continue to use both all over the world on a regular basis.

At least cyberspace doesn't kill people.

Well not directly anyway.

It does not appear on death certificates as a cause of death like electrocution or a car accident.

So in that sense it could be deemed harmless. You can touch it and use it without ill effect.

Yet when one considers that's where all the world's assembled, saved and stored data is kept, then things begin to look a little different.

For data is the modern – day knowledge and knowledge is power.

"Data is the new oil," they like to say. And normally a repository of anything required to attain and keep power, like the armoury inside the castle walls in olden days, is a thing of value, in constant need of protection by some, whilst sought after with avarice by others.

And so cyberspace has – almost inevitably – become a kind of battleground where, without being too dramatic about it, the current and future forces of good and evil confront each other on a daily basis.

The innovators continue to come up with incredible new ideas that make lives better, easier, more comfortable for the masses. The bad guys plot robberies and dream up a never-ending stream of scams to upset and destabilize.

It is the modern day equivalent of Agincourt and Stalingrad, of Waterloo and Gettysburg, of Hastings and The Somme, where the fate of millions will ultimately be decided, not by axe, cannon, bomb, bullet or sword, but by technology, not by something loud, visible and noisy, but by something silent and unseen, not speaking French, Russian, German or English, but by speaking in those other tongues, the ones that only the machines can understand, C+ and Python, SQL and Apache, Java and COBOL, Limbo and Delphi, Pascal and Fantom.

There is something almost biblical about this strange place, unholy though it would seem at first glance, where a digital version of the tower of Babel exists through this multiplicity of languages, not created to confound or confuse, but to enlighten and facilitate, to make things happen, either right in front of your eyes or all

the way over there, on the other side of the world.

It is regularly referred to as a domain. Dictionary definition: A realm of administrative autonomy, authority and control within the internet.

And there you have it.

An unwitting description of what it really is.

A fiefdom, albeit one without a Laird who owns it.

At least for now.

A strange place of dark secrets only known to and understood by the very few, by those who are intelligent enough to enrich themselves through the acquisition of wondrous knowledge. But to the many who use it on a daily basis, without truly understanding it, it has a certain mystery, like electricity and the motor car.

It is a place of magic.

It is La La Land.

And, although no one controls it in its entirety, there are some increasingly high profile examples of partial control. Fortunately these are mostly benign at present, although their inevitably destructive effects on old style business models has led to many a painful transition.

It was into this heady mix of global change, digital evolution and electronic networks that two young Russian hackers rode pretty much unchallenged in the early spring of 2022.

They did not control but they did understand.

They were not magicians but they were about to do a disappearing trick.

They looked like thieves but then again, appearances can be deceptive.

Very deceptive.

La La land would never be the same again.

Chapter 10 – The investigation

Caitlin Yang and Jojo Everett were no strangers to the bewildering world of interconnected computers and worldwide networks. Although one was more the theoretical physicist and the other more the engineer, they knew enough about each other's disciplines to form a good team, a sub-team in reality, a team within a team.

Harry often deployed his troops like that, being a great believer in the power of synergy, two minds complementing one another by sharing and focusing knowledge.

Or three minds, as it would soon be in this particular case, as Colonel Hank Wyatt (Ret'd) of the CIA and the USAF headed out to Logan that same evening, bound for the late BA flight to Heathrow. He would be joining them the following day to add his understanding of the latest iterations in fintech to their own deliberations. In the meantime they just focused on summarising what they knew so far in order to be able to brief him thoroughly in the morning.

Cait had dropped anchor about six thousand miles from home in the ever fashionable district of Chelsea, where she had grown increasingly fond of London life and the idiosyncrasies of the English with their strange accents and constant ability to laugh at themselves. Jake had told her a lot about Hank Wyatt with whom he'd worked on their last mission and she was looking forward, as all ex-Pats do everywhere, to hanging out with someone from back home, even if, as it was in this case, he was a generation older and came from the opposite coast.

But that was for tomorrow. For now she had a long night ahead of her with Jojo who duly arrived at her Ifield Rd flat around the same time as Harry's COBRA debrief with Hazel Ingliss was winding up. She'd be crashing in Cait's second bedroom that night and was delighted to learn from her cabbie that the converted house was not on the side of the road overlooking West Brompton cemetery, one of the Capital's largest graveyards.

Jojo was a tough girl who could handle herself well in all situations but everybody has their own particular sensitivity and hers was with death in general, a subject she avoided as best she could at all times.

They ordered a take away Chinese and some beers and got stuck in.

The earlier briefing session had already started to focus on the option of using

geography to kick-start their thinking. There were competing, and very good, reasons for choosing any one of the various other events along the story line as a start point, location itself being so fluid these days. People could move so quickly from place to place, taking their assets and families with them, that it almost seemed counter intuitive. And yet there was always something grounding about an address, even if it was an Internet Protocol one that identified a computer source rather than a building on a street. You had to start somewhere and, as all good policemen will tell you, just one tiny clue is like a small tree that will grow, develop and spread its many branches in lots of different directions.

'I kind of understand why they do it, I suppose' Jojo offered, starting their deliberations off in a rather unexpected place.

'Why who do what?'

'The hackers. Because that's what this is, isn't it? It's a very sophisticated one but nonetheless it's a hack. Whatever the media are calling it.'

A bundle of newspapers and printouts on Cait's kitchen table confirmed her point with a sparkling array of nifty eye-catching descriptions of the overnight events. Even on day one of a global crisis it seemed the headline writers were determined to have their fun.

Cyber bandits carry out global stick'em up.

Your money is safe, Governments advise penniless citizens.

Banks can't count, "we don't know how much" they admit.

No witnesses to the world's largest robbery because nobody did it.

Facemasks seemingly not required in Covid – secure theft.

"Invisible robbers arrived and left undetected," say clueless cops.

'That last ones a bit rich' Cait observed, a bit miffed because The Nines team were now essentially the leading detectives on the case.

'Number one we're not clueless, number two it's only just happened last night, number three, how do they know that. They don't really, do they?'

'Same old, same old' Jojo comforted her.' A basic smattering of facts, very basic in this case, and the rest of it, they're just busking. Making it up as they go along.'

'Yeah, I know. Still smarts though. Bloody William Randolph fucking Hearst has still got a lot to answer for, over a hundred years later. And him a countryman of mine. Arrogant bastard. Now what did you mean again?'

'About what?'

'Hackers.'

'Well, when you look at the way people make money by just pushing paper around, it can make you sick, can't it? And not just a bit of money, we're talking billions, many billions in the case of the Corporations and the Institutions. Meanwhile normal people are working their socks off for the meagre salaries that just about keep them and their families afloat.'

'You mean the world's not fair. Is that what you're saying?'

'Well no, course it's not, we learn that as we grow up. Still doesn't feel right though, does it? When you see people earning so much without really making anything or doing something for somebody else, or for the advancement and benefit of society.'

'Sorry, is this little bit of homespun philosophy helping us with Jumbo in any way?' Cait attempted to bring her friend back on track. ' Or are you just venting?'

'Sorry, you're right. But there is a serious point. This could actually be one of those Robin Hood groups, so pissed off at the excesses of the last decade that they just couldn't stand it any more'

'In which case, what? They're going to hand all the loot out to the world's needy and dispossessed? Can't see it, Jojo. Very unlikely.And how would they do that anyway?'

'Well, they've got this far, haven't they. They've managed to nick it. All of it, it seems, so they're not bloody daft, are they?'

Cait pondered this piece of blunt wisdom for a moment as she finished brewing up some coffee. She wandered back in from her snug kitchen with a tray and two steaming mugs. The beers would come later once they had some traction, but they needed their brains for now

'I'm not discounting that' she said, pouring out some caffeine, 'But didn't we agree in the meeting to start with territory, with a *where* rather than with a *who*? On the understanding that we would then at least have a start point for our ground ops teams, you know, give them a kind of target zero location to home in on and start asking those difficult questions they're so good at. Even if it's still like a hundred square mile zone with The Kremlin in the middle. Just somewhere to start, because, as of right now, we got nothing.'

'I agree it might shut the media up for a few hours, that's always a blessing. But it could also go the other way and start a frenzy. You know how they can be when

they get their teeth into something. Not a pretty sight. If we so much as hint at anything like that, they'll be all over it within a few hours. But anyway, annoying though they are, they shouldn't be our main focus, should they?'

'No. And, in the absence of any clues about the involvement of any known groups, I suppose there is some merit in Harry's lone gunman theory. Although the logic that suggests at least two, maybe more, seems pretty strong to me. It just doesn't seem feasible that any one single person acting alone could have done this.'

'And are we any the wiser about how they did it? What was in the Cobra update from Hazel?' Jojo enquired.

'Well, it seems that the banks are trying to work together by joining their disparate tech teams into one single response unit. Their version of us, basically, but with all the benefits of a whole raft of insights into their own sector. Nothing formal from them so far, only one rather rambling telephone call with Harry promising us that we'd be the first to know soon as they come up with anything. Bloody good of them, considering we're on their side. I don't think their tech guys are being stuffy, as a breed they tend not to be, but the upper reaches of banking management certainly can.'

Their work and years of training had given both girls plenty of regard for the I.T professionals who made the modern world go round. They would be just as eager to find out what had happened as anybody else, perhaps even more so. To them, something like this was a bit personal, compromising, as it had, their own strenuous efforts over several years to provide a secure and safe system for global banking, specifically designed to prevent the unthinkable from happening. That particular unthinkable that had just happened!

'Was that where the first info about the Sig ciphers came from?'

'Must have been. Who else could have provided that if not them?'

'So what do we know?'

'That all of the coders and programmers are aware of them and it is barely conceivable that they would not take steps to at least disguise the kind of markers they leave behind. As they pass through the various layers of the networks they will always leave a trace, something like the striations on bullets, peculiar and exclusive to the journey taken by each and every data bit. They will conform to a particular pattern for each and every individual byte in any one given transaction. The capacity and the transfer rate doesn't matter because it's not about content, complexity or speed

because they're designed as identifiers that serve to effectively watermark all throughputs. It's not possible to modify or eliminate them, at least not for the average Joe. But we're not talking about him, are we, but about a much higher level of expertise. These guys are the absolute best in terms of raw knowledge. They know exactly what they're doing. That's why the clues are enigmas. Are they deliberate, set to throw us off? Or, is it just possible that they are the first mistakes, maybe even the only mistakes? In which case we're obliged to follow them, are we not?'

'Yup, guess we're obliged either way really aren't we?' Jojo summarised. 'Correct me if I'm wrong here, but you absolutely cannot switch those things off, can you?'

Cait had her physics hat on now and was in immutable law mode. The raw maths that underpinned the functionality of modern IP networks had certain behaviours which always followed the same sets of rules.

'No, you can't. They're like the protocols, essential parts of the whole infrastructure. You can't mess with them at all.'

'So the banks have got the raw data, the instructions and commands that implemented the traffic re-directions?'

'Must have. Inconceivable that they haven't '

'So where is it?' Jojo asked, flicking from screen to screen on her tablet, 'cos they've sent us loads of stuff but not that, not that I can see anyway.'

'Then they must be still working on it, their own tech teams I mean. And they're trying to pool their efforts aren't they, which always means a delay while the people and the systems start to interact and get used to each other.

Let's say the world's top twenty banks are fronting this up, that'll be a team of, what, three or four from each, that's sixty to eighty people trying to share data right across the world and a few disparate systems. Never going to happen overnight is it?'

Jojo took a large gulp of her coffee and leant back on the sofa.

'Why not?' she said softly. ' The robbery did.'

They both paused, as if realizing for the first time the enormity of the planning that had gone into this.

'We definitely eliminated an inside job at our briefing earlier, didn't we?'

'We did, yeah. Completely impossible. The instructions were buried inside a set of Trojans, almost certainly delivered by a cohort of Bots at a pre-arranged signal from one master control unit. You put those on a time switch to co-ordinate the kick

off and then wait. Minutes, hours, days or even weeks later it goes bang and you're off, the final action happening in just a couple of seconds.'

The arrival of malicious software into the world of computing continued to wreak havoc despite the constant evolution of patches, upgrades and fixes which were applied by Cisco and all the other global practitioners responsible for the build out and scale up of the World Wide Web.

One of the more nefarious examples of black hat thuggery was the now prevalent habit of hijacking random computers around the world to do their dirty work. This was achieved by slipping a small piece of rogue software into the main drives of large numbers of unsuspecting devices across multiple regions. Once installed and functional those machines would effectively become zombies, only obeying the instructions of their new masters, usually thousands of miles away, somewhere else on the planet. Phalanxes of these computers of varying sizes would then be effectively hooked up together to create a rogue base with the sufficiently large capacity necessary to create major mischief on behalf of large numbers of shadowy figures, intent on personal gain. Known as 'bots', their robotic behaviour cast shadows everywhere and sucked up huge resources as the good guys fought to stay ahead in a non-stop and seemingly never ending battle between what can only really be described as the forces of light and the powers of darkness.

'So that's why we're now in location mode. Not who, or why, but where?'

'It's a start, isn't it. And that's what we need right now. But Harry's throw away line about two kids in a bedroom. You don't think…?'

'Harry doesn't really do throw away lines, does he?'

They stopped and thought.

Two!

Just two!

Really!

Just as Sherlock said, when you've eliminated the impossible, whatever's left, however improbable, is where you have to start looking next.

Chapter 11 – The Blockchain

Andrei and Georgi continued to work on their *project* ceaselessly, only surfacing for air and temporary exposure to the analogue world when they had to. They lived a kind of inside out, back to front, wrong way round kind of existence compared to most.

All of their friends were pretty geeky – the rather cruel word used to describe those for whom the world of computers takes up an inordinate amount of time – but still had time for all the usual pastimes, had pretty much normal lives with jobs, bosses, relationships and pressures, just like everybody else.

But if you treat the digital domain like some kind of extreme sport, then you can end up giving yourself over to it, sacrificing way too much time and energy, leaving others behind outside in the *real world* although, to the converted, it was becoming an increasingly moot point as to exactly where the divide between the two actually lay.

Some, probably still the majority in 2022, still regarded the internet as somewhere to go and spend time, to hang out, to do work on an intermittent basis. Consequently, they would just log on now and then, spend some time, a few hours maybe, amusing themselves or completing some tasks, then log off and go back to their lives.

For the hardcore, it was completely the other way round. This had the happy side effect of not arousing any suspicions about the plans that were being hatched in Staraya Square. It was hard to avoid talking shop with their other friends but they found they could do that quite easily without being too specific about *ischeznoveniye,* the rather tough discipline of staying stumm about money and work related matters having been something they had already mastered in their mid teens as their local handlers had guided them through the labyrinth of behaviours needed to stay alive on the fringes of the underworld.

The great advantage of this was a total lack of distractions – apart from the welcome appearances of Ans a few times every week to show off her latest outfit complete with matching boots and fur hat – by the outside world. They could touch it whenever they wanted, but were essentially now locked away in a temporary prison of their own making. Their favourite café, just across the park, and their local

McDonalds, sustained them and a short break once or twice a day was enough to help recharge their batteries. They would often work on through the night surviving on just a couple of hours of rather light sleep, not good, not particularly healthy, and definitely not recommended. But at that age there is a tendency to think one is indestructible, a feeling that is prevalent amongst all the youth of the world, probably because, for them, at that stage of their young lives, it's largely true.

The net effect of all this was the creation of a true haven of peace where concentration came easy, which was just as well because the plotting of an escape plan had continued to take centre stage in their thinking and was now consuming all their waking moments.

The central conundrum remained. If they compromised all of the existing storage and repository locations with their initial raid, where could they go with the loot?

Its very non-physical nature was both a plus and a minus. The good news was that it was digital and had no bulk, There were no giant swag bags. The bad news was that their own initial actions had destroyed the only known habitats of those types of invisible assets. There would be no home for them.

None of a conventional nature anyway.

As they considered this not inconsiderable roadblock to their plans, it also became apparent that this particular inconvenience might also compromise their second vital imperative.

Their own getaway.

Obviously that was never going to be the screeching tyres and false number plates variety so splendidly redolent of twentieth century bank jobs. Truth was, of course, they had never really finished off planning properly for that either. And so now, as they focused in on Phase two and those two issues started to come into sharper focus, they began to wonder if, instead of having two very large headaches, the solution to the first might also be the solution to the second as well.

'I kind of understand it in principle' Andrei said, wiping away the crumbs of an early evening sandwich and swigging some water.

No alcohol at work till this was over! They needed all their faculties, full concentration required.

'But the actual core architecture is not something we've ever really got too close to before, is it?'

Georgi, as usual, was poring over several documents that looked like blueprints

for some complicated network, a council building scheme, a set of architect's drawings, a large scale wiring diagram.

His head was still in Phase One, which was coming along nicely, but hardly finished. He stopped tracing his fingers across the documents, one on the screen of his i-Pad, one on a couple of hard copy print outs, and looked up, the expression on his face confirming that he'd been miles away, lost in his own thoughts.

'Sorry, too close to… ? What were you saying?'

'The Blockchain. None of our activities have involved it yet, have they?'

'And you think this might be the right time?'

Georgi tuned in extremely quickly. They had kicked the idea around once or twice of doing some BTC work, their parlance for hacking into some of the world's burgeoning BitCoin accounts.

Or at least trying to.

Possible, but really not easy. They were notoriously difficult to crack, much of the protection around them having been designed and implemented by other black hats, many of whom continued to switch sides at the sight of a healthy pay check. In other words, they would have been going up against their peers, which was not really a problem, just a tad unnecessary when there were so many easy pickings to be had elsewhere.

They had learnt growing up – had been taught by the older and the wiser – to pick their battles.

So they did.

As a result the whole BitCoin and Blockchain landscape was still largely unfamiliar to them, at least in terms of first hand experience. How much did that matter? They now started to consider, and quite seriously for the first time, whether that might present a possible solution to their problems or whether it could just lead them into a trap.

Was it the way out of jail?

Or the way in?

Pretty big difference.

Digital money is already here in many respects, as anybody who uses online banking will know. And there are millions who do that each day all over the world. So it is, in most readily accepted senses, already established.

However a digital currency is something else.

In much the same way as the pound is the currency of England, the dollar of America, the Yen of Japan, the Franc of Switzerland and so on, it is the currency of that other increasingly well know global territory, the internet, that realm of administrative autonomy which wasn't really there fifty years ago. It never had its own currency before, never needed one. Why would it? It was a domain without people back then.

That's hardly true today though when, in a sense, it has become a second home to everybody in the world, and yet a place without its own Government, or a police force, or a set of borders, or a single language that it could claim for itself.

Or a currency.

Until now.

Something fundamental was changing. Suddenly, in the first part of the twenty first century, all those things had started to evolve, somewhat inevitably.

And, although it will take a while yet, along the way the changes are likely to be momentous and, amongst the most seismic of all the likely eruptions and tidal waves, will be the arrival of crypto currencies, not initially to replace, but to work alongside all of the existing ones.

There may, in time, be several, as individual nation states try to develop and launch their own. But there is already a market leader and it is called Bit Coin, generally referred to as BTC.

It is the current darling of currency speculators and many investors the world over, having leapt in value considerably since it's emergence just over a decade ago. The fact that its origins are shrouded in a bit of mystery contributes no end to the intrigue, the suspicion and the confusion, pretty much in equal measure.

Written as an algorithm, its structure is highly futuristic, something which lends to its appeal. All other existing currencies are, and always have been, created traditionally by the world's central banks. Not to be confused with the retail ones on your local High Street, these are national banks, run and managed by individual Governments, regulated and overseen by various federal and independent agencies.

In contrast BTC was developed by a computer programmer and coder called Satoshi Nakamoto, who may, or may not, be a real person, may, or may not, be several real people. Although this name exists for attribution purposes, the identity of the source is, essentially, anonymous, something which worries many who suspect fraudulent intent, but excites just as many others who like the idea of distance from

Government controls.

Whoever he, or she, was or is, one of the key features of Nakamoto's BTC – and there are many – was the absence of any printing press, not required because worldwide circulation as required of necessity by the old paper stuff, would now be taken care of by the new fangled wizardry of technology, meaning you can no longer put one in your pocket or actually hold it.

Quite obviously this, all on its own, was more than enough for some people, the type who are naturally sceptical and suspicious by nature, to cry foul and damn the whole project as beyond dodgy. The wild speculation that followed the launch of BTC in 2009 only fuelled that particular fire, something which is extremely unfair given that all the international equity markets and stock exchanges are, in truth, driven by the same speculative fervor and fever on a daily basis.

One of the other main wonders of BTC, or commercial differentiators as the business community might prefer to call them, is what is generally referred to as its architecture, the tech engineering that supports its existence. In coming up with an appropriate structure Mr, Mrs. or Ms. Nakamoto devised something rather unique.

As well as being a store of value, the software that supports and creates the currency has its own inbuilt transmission protocol, meaning that anybody who wishes to use it as a payment method can do so without engagement with any third party.

It is, in effect, a currency and a bank, all rolled into one, in the sense that it provides the functionality and customer service that have hitherto always been provided, albeit at arms length, by two completely separate entities.

This concept is, quite literally, revolutionary. It offers the distinct possibility of introducing something completely new at the not inconsiderable expense of doing away with something very old. Quite how the established banks feel about this threat to their future prospects, possibly even their very survival, is not too difficult to determine. Despite their poker faces being very much to the fore, they are confused, fearful, horrified intimidated and outraged, pretty much in equal measure, at the mere thought of the type of changes which lay in wait.

Time will tell, but one thing they can no longer do is ignore it, or, more correctly, ignore them. For BTC, hugely important though it is as a landmark in monetary evolution, is no longer alone.

Others, like Ethereum and Stellar, are gaining traction and several major Governments are all busy announcing their own crypto currency plans.

This is no longer a future trend.

It is something that is happening right now, at the start of the twenty first century.

It is the Zeitgeist and Andrei and Georgi were about to do what they did best with advanced computer technologies.

They were about to take Bitcoin and The Blockchain on a wild ride.

Chapter 12 – Logan

The Big Dig had more than lived up to its name. The construction phase of the civil engineering project to link downtown Boston to the city's airport began in 1991 and eventually took an astonishing sixteen years to conclude after running into all sorts of problems. Taking into account an earlier planning phase which had started in 1982, the whole exercise, much to the annoyance of just about everybody who lives in that fine city, ended up taking an incredible twenty five years to complete, thereby making it the lengthiest and single most expensive highways project ever undertaken anywhere in the US.

Which is why Colonel Hank Wyatt had a wry smile on his face as he sat in traffic in the tunnel under the Charles River, wondering whether those leaks which had plagued the project so often had started up again. The red light had kept his cab stationary for twenty minutes as the large emergency works equipment heaved to and fro just up ahead.

Normally a big headache for anyone chasing a plane, Hank wasn't too worried about the jam, having left home a full hour earlier then necessary to allow for exactly that kind of contingency. Even all these years later, The Big Dig still had a reputation for its propensity to suddenly cause big headaches en route to the airport. So one planned accordingly.

The expected delay also gave him time to read Harry's briefing documents which had been scanned across to him a few hours earlier. With luck he would finish them before taking off, leaving him free to have a couple of nightcaps and get some sleep on the way over to England before landing at Heathrow early the following morning. Harry had given him the name of a hotel in trendy Chelsea where he was due to meet up with Jojo and Caitlin for breakfast and to review progress. That didn't allow too much time for rest so he wanted to avoid spending the whole flight reading if he could help it. The Big Dig was actually, and as he'd expected, doing him a bit of a favour.

He flicked back and forth through the print outs trying to get a general feel for what had happened the night before. The details were mostly there, absent the input from the bank's own technical team which was still being compiled, along with a series of bullet point conclusions which had been arrived at by the Jumbo project team at their Code Blue meeting in London earlier that morning.

Like a lot of people in a hurry, he focused in on those first, the time pressures of the situation encouraging him to fit those conclusions backwards into the facts rather than checking whether they were the correct and most appropriate logical deductions to actually derive from those facts.

He knew Harry's team. The Nines were good, among the best. They wouldn't have missed anything, their logic would be impeccable, their own internal intelligence briefings and general awareness of world events would be bang up to date, their assessments likely the most clear sighted of any. No doubt in his mind that was the best place to start. The conclusions were in the Exec summary at the back, on page four.

Good briefings were always short.

He looked at them.

* Unlikely to have been carried out by any previously known external actors, although many will claim responsibility for what they perceive to be invaluable P.R.

* Suspicions about an inside job by bank executives persist due to their inability to shake off the whole industry's poor image following the '08 credit crisis.

* However our preferred option at this early stage is neither of the above, but rather a black hat group, currently of unknown origin.

* No communications have been received for ransoms yet and there are no other demands at this stage, which means the motive is currently unknown.

* Demands for money seem unlikely because, in the short term at least, it would be a bit incongruous because there isn't any.

* Other reasons could be societal, demanding some form of political change, blackmail, demanding payment for data restorations, or criminal, requiring some form of prisoner release.

* Global issues cannot be ruled out requiring actions that affect the whole world. These range from introducing universal benefit schemes to the adoption of green eco-agenda items to immediate disclosure on UFO and extra terrestrial matters.

* First steps should focus on the geographic, not an obvious place to start for a cyber crime, but one that can yield quick local feedback if we get the zone right.

* The tech knowhow required to pull this off is extreme, not only the gaining of initial access, but also the subsequent ability to shelter and hide.

* Grapevine chatter is red-hot across all platforms and we continue to monitor.

He continued scanning down the last few lines to the bottom of the report where the date and the signature were written.

Jake Rivera
Project Jumbo
Nines Special Ops
London: March 2022

Hmm, the Brits finally got to him then, he thought, noticing that his old friend and acquaintance from the Wuhan adventure, Professor Jake, had omitted his professional credentials from his sign off.

It could hardly be said to be common practice across the world for those with academic qualifications to willfully choose not to use them in matters of formal communication, but it was certainly true of an increasingly large cadre of such people in England.

The UK could sometimes be a very confusing sort of place, very elitist at one end with hairdressers and time servers getting all sorts of gongs, but also extremely modest at the other, where many people who had achieved much for their country and society only displayed their talents and contributions very modestly.

It was certainly not Nines' official policy to demonstrate such humility in this manner and yet all six of them did it that way just the same. They all had the highest possible qualifications in their specialist fields but they seldom spoke of them.

At recruitment for the team several years earlier, seasoned examiner Colonel Blinky Duff and his co-interviewer Archie Webster had both remarked upon the final "optional" question in the notes and comments section.

Please use this space for any additional comments about the candidate. Especial attention should be drawn to their overall bearing and mannerisms in the context of suitability for a position as one of the highest-ranking intelligence officers in Her Majesty's Government.

They had quickly realized that this adjunct to the usual questionnaire was an attempt at informal character assessment to round off the interviews, although they had largely been based on intelligence, top IQs being very much the order of the day for recruiting the six Nines officers.

"*Obviously not looking for any toffee nosed Old Etonians, I suppose*" Archie had ventured, "*which is just as well because we certainly haven't found any today.*"

The final six were qualified to the hilt but it was not something any of them ever volunteered, all preferring to let their abilities speak for themselves.

Now, a couple of years later, as Hank's taxi dropped him kerbside at Logan departures, he took the opportunity to catch up with his fellow countryman. He didn't know the whole team, having spent more time with their negotiator Paul Lambert than anyone else, but he had met the Texan in Holland where they had both given evidence at the ICJ as the team investigated China's role in Covid-19.

He glanced at his watch. Just coming up seven, so midnight in London. The 214 wasn't due out till half nine so plenty time for a beer and a pizza at Monica's, then he could skip the B.A. hospitality and go straight to sleep.

Best ping him first though, just out of courtesy.

He'd barely had time to order his snack when his mobile rang.

The Laredo drawl at the other end was unmistakable.

'How ya' doin' buddy? Been a while since ol' Den Haag.'

'Hello Professor. Still shy about using the Academics, I see.'

'Ah, you must 'a been readin' this morning's briefing docs. I though Harry might call you in, what, with you bein' a financial wizz an'all. You comin' over?'

'I'm sat at Logan right now actually. Just busy digesting your thoughts alongside one of Monica's finest pizzas. Bit weird all this, to say the least. Anything new since you wrote the report?'

'Jojo and Cait are doing a tech review as we speak down in Chelsea. Cait's got a flat there now, just up a bit from the football ground. You should probably head straight over there when you get in. I can ping you the address. You remember our two lovely girls of course?'

'One's going out with the Paddy, isn't she?'

'Liam. Correct. What a good memory you have'

'And the other one's the Californian girl, right. Quite tall, curves in all the right places. Not exactly inconspicuous.'

'Yup, that's her. Caitlin, Frisco gal. Nice as pie but deadlier than Nightshade. As a few have discovered to their cost.'

'So they're Harry's tech team?'

"Exactly.'

'And who else is doing what?'

'Paul Lambert is liaison with the banks. Liam is on his way to Russia and I'm deputising as Harry's number two. Because of the need to go at this right around the clock we've decided to do a kind of rota system. Even the great Harry Shepperton can't go without sleep indefinitely so I am effectively the night shift. Which is why you got me straight away at midnight. I've just clocked on, so to speak.'

'What's the Russia angle? I didn't see that in your briefing.'

'Just in the past few hours Paul has started to get the first feedback from the banks. They're having to cooperate but their individual privacies and securities have hamstrung things a bit so, until they get going properly, it's a bit of a stuttering start.'

'Well with all the world's money suddenly gone missing from everybody's accounts, I struggle to see exactly what else they have to do apart from solve this. So an inability to liaise properly is hardly what people will be wanting to hear from them right now, is it?'

'Agreed. But I think by the time you land in the morning, things will look a lot different. Everybody's just been in shock all day today and it's only really now that I get the sense that a proper response is kicking in.'

'And Russia?'

'It's a long shot but we have nothing else at this stage so we're running with it. The world is awash with hacking tools, most of which are very easy to get hold of and very simple to use if you have any basic programming or coding proficiency. What's less common is seeing developmental work around a whole bunch of these tools in any one location in a very short period of time. In other words taking them in their basic format and trying to refine them to do additional levels of layering.'

'But surely it's in the nature of the hacking community to try and improve their capabilities all the time. Just like the legit software and hardware manufacturers do. It's just that they're on the other side of the fence, right?'

Hank wasn't the tech guy but he was going to need to understand as much of this as possible if he was going to be of any assistance to The Nines and be able to contribute to Harry's team's efforts.

He cut another slice of pizza, took Jake off the hands-free and clamped the cellphone to his ear. Probably not a great idea to be broadcasting this type of stuff out to an airport lounge crowd.

'Of course' Jake agreed. 'And it's a never ending and ongoing process which

makes it hard to identify anything anywhere that could provide clues.'

'Clues, like a spike of anomalous behaviour somewhere. That kind of thing you mean?'

'Well yes, something like that would really help give us at least a starting point. The difficulty is that visibility only really occurs once you break cover and start doing your experimentation out on a network. If you're just at home working on your PC or your Mac then everything is self-contained, it all just sits there on your own hard drive. You just blaze away in private; nobody has any idea what you're up to or what you're really doing. Invisibility is your friend. And our enemy.'

'And yet somehow the bank guys have spotted something in Russia which has made them sit up. What was it?'

'It was a break out of sorts. A sudden rush of network activity using Aircrack, Bully, BetterCap and HashCat, all established Wi-Fi hacking tools, much loved and widely used by that community. You go to a Hacker's convention – and yes, such conferences actually do exist – and you'll meet a hundred experts on all of those.'

'Wow, really. That's pretty scary.' Hank washed down a slice of meatball pizza with a draft of Sam Adams as he took in this piece of unexpected information.' I had no idea.'

'Even worse, they hold competitions to see who can crack the access to all sorts of networks with points awarded and top prizes given out. I mean there is something more than a bit bizarre about it. But then the upside is, they like fixing the bugs as well, those flaws that are so often the weaknesses in many installed systems. So they can claim, with some legitimacy, to be a force for good as well as scaring the pants of everybody. I'll grant you that though, it is very odd.'

'Harry should recruit some of those guys.'

'Don't worry, Jojo and Cait are pretty well known in that world. They attend all the seminars, workshops, conferences and know most of the players. That's actually been one of our main secondary sources for backing up the bank's own initial suspicions. Obviously they don't go as themselves, if you see what I mean, but it's like on the job training for them. I've seen them when they come back from those things and they're really stoked, ah mean, like you wouldn't believe.'

Jake's Laredo twang had been slowly diluting since he'd relocated to the UK, but it only ever took a few minutes conversation with one of his own countrymen for it to come back. Once a cowboy …

Hank checked his watch. Still plenty time to get to the gate. He probed a bit deeper to try and flesh out the rest of the story. After all, the media would only ever tell you so much, only ever knew so much, especially with a global news story like this one. He wanted to understand all the angles and he was talking to one of The Nines, one of Harry's guys. If anybody was up to date and had all the pieces it would be that team.

'What about the civic fallout, Jake? What's the official response gonna' be to all this? People will want their money back. And pretty damn quick too.'

He finished off his beer, reflecting for the third or fourth time that day on the several hundred thousand dollars of lifetime savings that he was missing personally.

'Including me.' he added, as a rather unnecessary afterthought.

'Well, including all of us, actually.'

Two rather unnecessary afterthoughts.

Jake didn't have too much to give him.

'I wish 'ah could tell you right now not to worry but ah'd jus' be lyin' if I said that. Truth is, nobody right now got a damn clue what to do. There's no blueprint for this, no training manual, no contingency plan. All 'ah can tell you is that the world Governments are tryin' real hard to come together to present a united front. Ah'm sure they'll get there eventually but it won't be quick. Holding statements will be issued everywhere tomorrow in an attempt to calm things down.'

'Are they planning to underwrite all the losses?'

'Well, that's one of the many tricky and unanswered questions. The present status of the money is *"missing."* So these are not, strictly speaking *"losses"*, at all, at least not yet. Not until we know much more about exactly what's happened.'

'Well, I can't see that satisfying anybody'. Hank asserted.

He hadn't been planning a second beer but the nature of this conversation made him suddenly feel rather thirsty. Besides, filling in as much as possible now on the phone with Professor Jake meant he could get straight to sleep on the plane. No more reading required. Easy decision.

'That will just sound like a total cop out when the people really need support. Or at least the promise of it.'

'Ah agree completely. But you have to factor in one more thing.'

'What's that?'

'That media headline about the banks not being able to answer the *"how much"*

question.'

'What about it?'

'It's true. They don't know how much is missing?'

'But its all gone, right? All of it? Every last cent.'

'Yup, that's what they're sayin', right enough.'

'So the question is not dependant upon individual account totals then, is it? It's all of them. All of them added together. The sum total of all the accounts in all of the banks, all added together."

'That's the retail loss, yes. The losses ascribed to all of their customers.'

'What else is there?'

'The banks' own money. All of their own assets. Where do you think all of that is kept?'

'What, and that's the part they can't count?'

'Plus all of the Governments funds.'

Hank was momentarily stunned. At this rate he was going to need a third beer.

'You mean all that quantitative easing. All the credit that was ever issued. All of those trillion dollar estimates of our nation's GDP. Of the individual country GDP's around the world. All of the savings, the institutional as well as the private. All of the positive cash balances held by the individual exchequers. All of the outstanding loans and the other debts. None of the bookkeeping for any of that has been done sufficiently well to provide an accurate enough figure for a restitution programme, or whatever they want to call it?'

Jake knew the difference between a question and a statement and so realised that he didn't actually have to answer, and he probably wouldn't have done were it not for the fact that he was talking to an ad hoc team member, somebody who was now very much on their side, part of the solution. For Hank was, unofficially, 9-9.

'They will probably come up with an estimate of the total, if you want my guess' he suggested, placidly.' Something not legally binding but sufficiently adequate to form a basis of some sorts for thinking about how to set up and implement a support programme. So it might not be too accurate to start with, but it will act as a construct to put something in place and calm the mood, or at least dilute the outright panic and chaos, which is what we will have without it.'

'And this will be led by the World Bank and the IMF presumably.'

Another statement.

Hank's USAF training may have been extensive but he was going to need some coaching on asking open-ended questions.

No matter, Jake played along again.

'They will be part of it but people will be much more likely to trust their own Governments more than faceless institutions, that is if they manage to trust anybody at all. The predominant feeling right now is one of anger. Having a bunch of unknown bureaucrats turning up out of the blue right now is unlikely to help anyone.'

Hank factored all of this into the dawning realization that this was actually an appalling problem. If the combined brainpower of the banking community failed to come up with at least some way of getting the various credit mechanisms up and running again, then everything, everywhere would just grind to a halt, at a Government level, at a business level, and at a personal level. This was actually, the more he thought about it, an outright attack on society, on the way everybody lived their lives, on modern civilization in general.

As such, he suddenly found himself thinking more terrorist than thief, more revolutionary than robber.

This could switch the lights off.

As of right now life looked normal. There he was, sitting in Departures at a major North American airport and everything was open, everything was working, his taxi had got him there ok, albeit with a slight delay, his beer and pizza were great, his flight was on time, his mobile phone had a signal and was supporting an international voice call. On the face of it, nothing had changed, people everywhere were busy going about their business, although, now as he watched and took things in, he noticed for the first time that people did look a bit more anxious than usual, were behaving a bit jumpy, seemed to be having slightly more stressed phone calls.

His old CIA training kicked in and, in his head, he fast-forwarded a few days.

He didn't much like what he saw.

'I don't think we're going to get too much time with this one Jake,' he offered. This is gonna' be a solar eclipse type mission, will get dark and cold real quick. People are going to get scared, real scared, even more so if the politicians don't handle things properly. What time does Liam get to Moscow?'

'Should be there early morning, will try to set up some quick local liaisons, due to report back in the afternoon, so we should have his initial assessment sometime tomorrow, although remember he's got hardly nothing to go on, so I'd say he'll need

at least twenty four hours.'

'Remind me of his specialism again?'

'Well he's not short on I.T skills and what he doesn't know he picks up from his beloved.'

'Right. But that's not his main area, is it. Not his background by training?'

'No, it's not.' Jake confirmed

'He's a geologist.'

Hank ordered his third beer.

Chapter 13 – The real boss

When Sir Walter Tweedy first suggested that the UK set up a new kind of task force he had met with some seriously stiff opposition. That is, of course, quite normal for anyone proposing change, for there will always be many who are quite comfortable with keeping things the way they are. That is not to say that they are right, because such resistance is very often born out of protectionism of one kind or another. Looking after one's job, one's career, one's finances, one's friends, one's colleagues, all play a role. Usually, the more portentous the change, the louder the voices shouting it down.

So it came as no surprise to the crusty old mandarin in the elevated ranks of the UK's civil service structure that he was making new enemies. It was something he was used to, something that, in effect, he had made a career out of. For Sir Walter was not a man who was typical of the breed, where cushy lifestyles and inflation proof pensions were often the dominant thoughts of those occupants of the numerous Government offices straddled along the Thames in central London. He was a visionary, a man blessed with good insight and the courage of the convictions which it brought him, attributes that one needs in abundance to take on the collective might of the military, that group of people who have always seemed so essential down the years, not just in England, but everywhere across the world.

One takes them on at one's peril for they are always so well connected, the ability to be both the first and the last line of defence against either a foreign enemy or an internal insurrection always being invaluable to political leaders around the world. Proof of this, if any were needed, could always be found in their ability to secure the most ridiculous budgets and develop the most preposterous weapons, two capabilities which many felt were generally much more of a threat than the oft imagined enemies without and within.

It was not that Sir Walter's latest bright idea directly threatened the generals, the air vice marshals and the first sea lords. On the contrary, he was actually a huge fan of their contribution to global democracies. The key issue, and the thing that worried them the most, was his latest plan, his idea to set up a new type of RRT, a rapid response task force, who would be completely unarmed. They saw this initiative – and especially that particularly unusual feature of it – as a threat. Sir Walter saw only

opportunity.

'Too many bombs.Too many bullets.Too many dead bodies. If anything, we really need less, not more of all that' he explained to Blinky Duff, the seasoned head of special ops recruitment, on the night before the final interviews for The Nines, the name he had chosen for Harry Shepperton's new team of special agents.

'Strange name sir?'

'They've all got exceptionally high IQs, averaging out at 150 each across the group.'

'I see.'

He didn't really.

Sir Water smiled at his old chum.

'We only need six, Blinky. It needs to be a small unit'

'Ah, yes, of course.'

He still wasn't too clear.

'Six officers with IQs of one fifty each. Total combined IQ nine hundred. I didn't really want to call then The Nine Hundreds. Sounds a bit, you know, Sparta or something. So I thought we'd call them The Nines. Bit snappier, don't you think?'

'Why only six? The world's not exactly short of problems is it. We could probably do with nine hundred.'

Sir Walter smiled, the knowing smile that often came with high rank, his lofty position providing him with an overview of global situations often denied others.

'These are in addition to,' he explained, 'not instead of. The usual resources are unaffected, they'll all still be there to do the usual firefighting.'

'What will they actually do then? And who selects their missions?'

'They will. They choose their own.'

Blinky was somewhat taken aback at this.

'Bit of a departure from the usual drill then.' he commented, keen to find out as much as possible about the backdrop to this, Sir Walter's latest piece of radical thinking. He would be interviewing the final candidates in the morning so it would be good to know as much as possible for his own purposes, even though he wouldn't necessarily be sharing it with the six hopefuls.

He flicked again through the summary sheet outlining the brief bios of the final six.

'So there's six posts in total then?'

'Correct.'

'Just the six, no more, no less?'

'Correct.'

Blinky turned the file over and lifted the back cover up, as if he was looking for something.

'But there's only six candidates.'

'Correct.'

'What happens if one fails at interview?'

'They won't.'

'How do you know?'

'Because they've been carefully selected. Hand picked, you might say.'

'By whom?'

Sir Walter had a proper steely stare which he brought to bear on situations now and then. It wasn't particularly hostile, but it wasn't over friendly, not patronizing, but not too encouraging either. It was an experienced and very senior manadarin way of closing down any series of questions that ever started to snowball out of control.

Colonel Blinky Duff was a civil servant too by that time, his own military days now behind him.

He knew the code and moved on.

'And no weapons? An unarmed unit. Are they all Ninjas then?'

'No. Not all.'

'How will they get out of the inevitable scrapes?'

'They won't get into them.'

'How do you know?'

'Because they're bright.'

'That's hardly a guarantee, is it?'

'I agree. But we want to try to break the mould a bit with this unit. If they're as smart and well briefed as I want them to be, they'll be more than capable of doing their jobs without blowing things up every other day.'

'But the kind of tasks an RRT normally engage with are fraught with danger.'

'Agreed.'

'So their ops are going to be different somehow?'

'I doubt it.'

Blinky scratched his head.

'I'm sorry sir. I don't wish to appear unsupportive, but aren't you putting them in harms way a bit. What are they supposed to do if somebody shoots at them?'

'They should try to avoid such situations, usually doable with proper planning.'

'With all due respect, the military might disagree.'

'The military, Colonel, will be there to back them up if necessary. We're not planning on disbanding them anytime soon, far as I'm aware.'

Blinky shuffled his papers again and had another quick look at the summaries.

'Bit of a mixed bag, aren't they. A lawyer, I notice. What the heck will he be doing in the heat of battle?'

'He's the best blagger we could find. More negotiator than anything else. His job will largely be making sure there are no battles.'

'An internet guru?'

'The internet rules the world these days, Blinky. Have you been asleep for a decade? Plus she's from The Valley, so she'll know some serious computer nerds. Always handy.'

'The Valley?'

'Goodness, you have been asleep for a decade.'

'A physicist? Presumably not to make nuclear weapons but to defuse them?'

'Well, hardly. I'm hoping Lambert will be able to do that and negotiate them away if we ever come across some. With the help of some decent politicians if we can find any.'

'Lambert?'

'Paul Lambert, Blinky. The negotiator. Have you not read the notes yet old chap? You're on at 9.30 in the morning.'

'A geologist?'

'Anybody who really understands how the world is formed is invaluable.'

'At a dinner party, maybe. But what's his likely role in this team?'

'I don't know yet. Bit of a wild card. But he's a Paddy, can talk the hind legs of a donkey and charm the girls till they faint. You'll like him.'

'I tend not to pass people just because I like them, sir. Doesn't really work that way.'

But Blinky was making a mental note. He already had an inkling that the six interviews scheduled for the following day were all effectively just rubber stamps on some decisions that had already been made.

He decided to ask. No harm.

'You know him then?'

'I wouldn't say I really know him but, yes, I have met him.'

'And the others?'

'What about them?'

'You've met them as well?'

'I have, yes.'

'May I ask in what capacity?'

'Socially. At an informal occasion.'

Blinky was being nosey now. But he still had an inkling.

'Just the six?'

'Just the six, what?'

'At this informal occasion. Was it just these six?'

Blinky had a bit of a steely stare of his own, not quite as persuasive as Sir Walter's because, as his nickname suggested, he couldn't really stare at anybody or anything for very long. Nonetheless, he had his own way of making his point.

'The six who will be The Nines.'

He was hinting, as forcefully as he dare, at his rubber stamp theory.

That would be something very unusual.

Unprecedented even.

Sir Walter, being a knight of the realm, was blindingly quick on the uptake.

'It's not a *fait accompli*, Blinky. We need them stretched a bit more first, just to be sure. But yes, they've been pre-selected up to a point. Hardly any sense in seeing twelve people for half a dozen posts when the top six favourites all turn out to be ready, willing and able.'

'And available.' Blinky was rifling through his files again.

He furrowed his brow briefly.

'Seems like they could all start tomorrow as well. Not too much baggage and really not too much about their previous work or experience.'

'Ah, yes. All checked out. You needn't concern yourself too much with any of that. One less thing to worry about.'

Blinky's suspicions about that *"social occasion"* were quickly confirmed.

Classic headhunting.

Find a credible excuse, throw a drinks reception, and make sure the targets attend

without making them too aware of exactly what's going on. So no invites, as such. If they're worth their salt, they'll catch on pretty quick anyway. And then its just a two way Q and A disguised as general conversation. Lots of innocuous chitchat as a front for an unspoken selection process which would be quietly churning away in the background. Twenty or thirty short-listed. Most rejected. All done in a few hours. Highly efficient use of time. No buggering about with unnecessary interviews.

Blinky looked directly at his boss, nodding slowly.

Ah, ok. Understand now!

He checked his papers again.

'A chemist?'

It hardly mattered now because his normal routine asking questions that were specific and relevant to each individual was suddenly less important. Still, the professional in him wanted to do a good job. The more he understood, the easier that would be.

'Yes, who's also a trained biologist. Just in case we have to deal with a germ warfare attack or a virus or something. As I mentioned earlier, you can't defeat everything with guns.'

'Wouldn't you need an epidemiologist or a diseases guy for those things?'

'To treat the effects, yes, sure. But to prevent them in the first place. That's something else entirely.'

Blinky was slowly getting the picture. This was going to be a specialist unit like no other. Rapid Response was one thing. But the very nature of what they would likely be responding to was now making him begin to wonder.

'So they can all double up a bit, then. A Lawyer turned negotiator. A chemist slash biologist. Your Internet guru can code and do programming. The physics major is also a structural engineer. And a Paddy geologist who builds radios in his spare time.'

'Ah, good chap. You have read the brief then."

'Of course. But this last bloke. Mark.'

'Mark Wright.'

'Say's he's some kind of weapons expert.'

'Does it?'

Blinky stopped reading and looked up.

'What. That's wrong then?'

'I didn't say that, did I?'

'A weapons expert in an unarmed RRT. Isn't that a tad, err, incongruous?'

'I don't see why.'

'Let me guess. You have to know how to build one if you want to break one.'

Sir Walter smiled. It wasn't quite as menacing as his steely stare, a softer version of his shut down tactic, but nonetheless effective.

Blinky let it go.

But he wasn't quite finished with his own, less than subtle, debrief of his boss.

'What exactly am I looking for tomorrow? You know, when I stretch them? 'Cos they're as good as in post already aren't they? Just one final tripwire.'

'The only thing we couldn't really test at the dance,' he began, 'was their reactions. Not like Quick Draw McGraw reactions, more like decision making, especially under pressure.'

Blinky thought for a minute.

How to integrate that into his process.

'I'll give them some situationals. You know the kind of thing. You're in this particularly sticky spot. You've got three options, a, b or c. Which one do you choose and why?'

'With the best answer always being option d, the one of their own choosing, showing an ability to think for themselves and not be bullied into someone else's decision.'

The following morning JoJo Everett, Paul Lambert and Mark Wright all breezed through their face-to-face sessions with Colonel Blinky Duff and his gruff Scottish sidekick, Archie Webster.

Mark still had no idea he was joining an unarmed unit.

At around 3pm Professor Jake Rivera met the second American on Harry Shepperton's crack new team on his way out. Caitlin Yang's striking good looks were not lost on him but his heart was back in Laredo with his Texas sweetheart. The only breakout of romance destined for Harry's new team lay with the Dubliner with the laughing eyes who now waited nervously in the outside seating area while Caitlin nearly self sabotaged over her multiple choice question.

'I do apologise for keeping you waiting Mr.Dempsey,' the pretty young blond receptionist announced, smiling over at the tall fit-looking Irish lad who was now a full twenty minutes overdue. 'They're running slightly late, shouldn't be too long

now.'

Liam grinned back at her, his sparkling eyes lighting up an otherwise drab room.

'No problem darlin', tanks fer lettin' me know.'

A moment later her internal phone rang and she pointed over towards the door.

One of the two elderly men behind a large cherry desk rose to greet him while the other smiled

'Good afternoon, Liam. My name is Algernon Duff and this is my colleague Archie Webster. Thanks very much for coming in today.'

And so, by around six thirty, Her Majesty's Government of the United Kingdom had a new fully functional but highly secret operational unit.

Colonel Blinky Duff and Archie Webster popped into The Sanctuary for a meat pie, a couple of pints of Fuller's finest and a quick reminisce over the days rather strange proceedings.

JoJo Everett went back to her single bedsit wondering if there was the possibility of any Irish boys joining this new team. There was.

Paul Lambert wondered if he'd made the right choice after his rather odd meeting with Nick D'Allovite. He had.

Mark Wright started thinking that he might be joining some sort of weird space patrol. He wasn't.

Jake Rivera wondered if he'd lose his accent if he had to leave home and come to live in England. He wouldn't.

Caitlin Yang calmed down quickly at her early evening yoga class, still wondering if her emotional outburst had hurt her chances of landing her dream job.

It hadn't.

Liam Dempsey finally left the building around seven with a blond on his arm and another phone number in his pocket.

It had been quite a day.

Six candidates, two interviewers and one Knight of the Realm all slept well that night.

And The Nines were born.

Chapter 14 – Resource allocation

And so it came to pass that the redoubtable Harry Shepperton became Ten, Commanding Officer of The Nines special ops RRT, and with a considerable amount of talent and resource at his disposal. And yet, as Colonel Blinky Duff, he of the not inconsiderable military experience had remarked, six is a pretty small unit.

Compact. Yes.

Tightly knit. Undoubtedly.

Very skilled. Indisputably.

But still only six, whichever way you looked at it. A stretched resource, even with that built in capacity to double up on skill sets.

Harry already had a plan for managing this partial restriction using his impressive personal contacts network, his GPR plan he called it, referring to his Gold Plated Rolodex, which was actually silver by make, just gold by nature, possessing, as it did, all the contact details of the many and varied people with whom he'd had the pleasure of working over the past twenty five years since passing out of Officer training at Sandhurst, back in the late nineties.

From day one he had complemented his team as required with a selection of those people.

With Michaelangelo Volante in California, who had become Caitlin's instant lover within hours of that Pony ride back from LAX to his Wonderview penthouse. With Idris "Turbs" Turbanski, who had helped him nail Hassan Al Shalawi in the Muslim White House takeover plot. With The Brig, Brigadier Zhang T'ang, formerly of the Red Army and the Chinese Communist Party, during their unravelling in Wuhan of the truth about the source of the Corona virus. With USAF Colonel Hank Wyatt, now retired, the guy with the unbelievable past, ex CIA, ex USAF, multi millionaire, banned from casinos everywhere, the person who shared with Caitlin Yang, that greatest of all the great honours, that of saving a life. That same Hank who was due into Heathrow the following morning and with whom he was looking forward to catching up and running through his own plan for managing Jumbo, including the many gaps in it.

As he considered his team and how to best fit Hank into it again, he continued flicking through his GPR. He had, in the past, often just stumbled across somebody, a

name from the dim and distant sometimes, other times more recent. He would let his mind go blank and drift across the cards and images. The faces would usually come back to him quickly and then he would just spend a few minutes thinking about the various individuals, wondering how they were, where they were, and whether they would ever be a good fit for any of his rather unusual new projects as they came on stream.

At the back of his mind on this first day of a world suddenly devoid of money he was thinking banks, high finance and, of course, money.

Who knows a lot about all that stuff, he thought?

Apart from Hank. What kind of person?

He continued to let his mind freewheel.

There were a lot of people in that GPR from assignments old and new. Hank was one but he would need to know by tomorrow if he had enough resource to solve The Nines' latest challenge just using the core team. He had the right people, never any doubt about that, but did he have enough?

'Six, boss?' he'd remembered saying to Hazel Ingliss. 'Not many is it?'

She'd only smiled.

'Still got that Rolodex, Harry?'

Well, you can't lie to your boss, can you?

Colonel Hank Wyatt met his driver landside at Terminal 5, British Airways dedicated hub at Heathrow, the largest and oldest of London's five major airports, three of which were barely in London at all but nestled miles away in the leafy Sussex, Bedfordshire and Essex countrysides. Siting one anywhere closer to a city centre would be planning madness in the twenty first century as the trend grew to locate major transport hubs away from built up population areas for health and safety reasons, notwithstanding the fact that air travel was statistically still the safest way to do any long journey. Being shuttled into town from twenty miles out had pretty much become an accepted extension to most international journeys.

They headed down the Great West road past Osterley, Isleworth, Chiswick and Hammersmith before turning South and heading down towards the river in Chelsea. Hank didn't need the radio or a newspaper that morning to catch up on the overnight news; He had that ever ready and always on source of non-stop information called a driver. Sitting behind the wheel all day was not the worst of jobs, especially if you

actually liked driving, as a lot of people do, but it could be a bit of a solitary profession and some company in the back seat was always welcome.

'Of course, it's got bloody worse since yesterday' Billy told him.

Harry had sent his own personal security detail along to make sure Hank was looked after properly.

'All day long, a never-ending procession of people on the telly supposedly telling us what's going on. I mean I do appreciate the circumstances are unprecedented but even so, nobody was making very much sense. I suppose they were all in as much shock as the rest of us, assuming they'd all lost everything overnight as well.'

'Did it sound like there was going to be a short term plan?' Hank asked him.

'They said credit facilities would be restored as quickly as possible so that some semblance of normality could resume.'

'The banks said that?'

'No. The Government spokesman.'

'Did he say when?'

'She didn't. No.'

'Or how?'

'Not in any detail. No. In fact she said a lot more about what had happened and finding the perpetrators than she did about getting the money back into peoples' pockets.'

As the seventh – yet unofficial – member of The Nines, Billy Poppitt knew full well that the '"*Government spokesman*" had been Hazel Ingliss, drafted in at extremely short notice from Thames House to front up the immediate public response, not because she knew that much, but because she at least knew marginally more than anybody else.

Her true credentials as Head of UK counter intelligence at MI6 were not disclosed during the broadcast. After which she had disappeared back into the shadows and headed for her seven p.m. meeting with Harry.

'Any word at all from the banks?'

'They're due to issue a statement at lunchtime today. I think the girls have an advance copy of it.'

'And the international reaction?'

'A lot more subdued than you might expect. I think everybody is a bit stunned, understandably of course. Under most circumstances there's an immediate blame

game whenever a high profile incident like this occurs.'

'What, and that hasn't happened?'

'Hardly at all, no. The finger pointing will no doubt start at some stage but for now nobody has any idea who's behind this, much as we'd all like to know. I guess they've got no obvious suspects, no one to accuse'

'Any signs of panic?'

'Not yesterday, no. It was just eerily quiet everywhere, not too many people out and about on the streets. Reminded me a lot of two years ago when the virus hit. Lots of frightened people, lots of staying at home, glued to the news, trying to figure out what the hell just happened.'

'Did they close the schools today?'

Billy glanced up into his rear view mirror. He wasn't in one of the Nine's specially adapted transits today, Harry was spoiling him with the department's long wheelbase Jag XJL which Hazel Ingliss wouldn't be needing for a few days while she was holed up at Chequers, the Prime Minister's country retreat.

It was a roomy saloon, very comfortable and spacious, allowing passengers to recline and stretch out a bit in the back, so Billy had a good view of him. It wasn't so much that it was an odd question, more the way he'd asked it.

"Ex CIA", Harry had told him on the phone before he'd set off for the airport, confiding in one of his oldest friends, so this would be a guy who knew stuff.

'Sorry, sir. The schools? Not with you. What do you mean?'

Hank glanced down at the tablet on his lap. It had just pinged an alert and was demanding his attention.

'Seems there's been an incident at a school just outside Paris earlier this morning. And there are two other breaking news stories about a couple more that are happening right now, one in Germany and one in Spain.'

'What sort of incident?'

'The reports are a bit blurry so it's too early to be sure but they look like kidnappings of some sort.'

'What, and that could be connected to the money thing somehow?'

'Well only in a roundabout sort of way.'

'Something to do with getting this fixed quickly?'

'I'm guessing yes, that could be possible. If people don't feel they're getting the response they want from the authorities they'll often resort to extreme behaviour. You

know, that direct action stuff.'

'Like kidnapping kids? That doesn't make any sense at all. How does that help anybody get this fixed?'

'Well the first reports, sketchy though they are, seem to be suggesting that these are focused activities. Rather than just being randomly targeted, it seems the children are all those of local mayors and civic functionaries. So something designed maybe to ramp up the pressure on the politicians to sort the mess out quickly. Nothing will get your attention quicker than having your child kidnapped.'

'Well, apart from all the money in your bank account disappearing overnight.'

'I agree, but the timing seems weird so it's difficult to avoid making that connection. Three in one morning, and on this particular day as well. I'm surprised the stories even made the news actually, what with all the clamour going on around the financial meltdown but, if I'm right, we'll find out soon enough. The people responsible will make some sort of announcements and then we'll know.'

He switched the tablet off and gazed out at the sprawling Westfield shopping complex as they navigated the Shepherd's Bush traffic and then the mansions of Holland Park.

'But it is concerning that we might already be in Phase two. Phase two on day two. That's never happened before.'

'Phase Two, sir?'

'Hank recalled his sign off with Harry Shepperton on the phone the previous afternoon. *I'll send Billy to pick you up. He's not a Nine but he might as well be. Been keeping us all safe for years.*"

'Have you heard of the seven stages of acceptance?'

'Is that that alcoholics anonymous thing?'

'That's one version of it, yes. It's a kind of psychological profile of how we process incidents which shock our system. There's a bereavement variant as well. Plus several more.'

'What, and the perpetrators of those school incidents are in more shock than the rest of us? That's a bit of a stretch.'

'Not so much that, as they've just gone straight to step three. That's what's so unusual. If, indeed, that is what's going on here. I am guessing a bit.'

'Bypassing step two.' Billy was racking his brains but couldn't quite remember.

'Sorry sir. Remind me.'

'The first stage is denial. The shock being so strong that the body's protective systems cannot process it. So they reject it. Pretend it didn't happen. Or, to be more accurate, trick themselves into believing that. The human body and the human mind are both wonderful preservation mechanisms, remember. Their survival instincts all powerful.'

'And that's where we are now.'

'Exactly. This is a seismic shock. Something that should never happen. Indeed, has never happened before. So it's very profound. And then it's compounded even further by the fact that it's actually happening to everybody else at the same time.'

'Like the Corona virus shock, for instance.'

'Yes, there will be similarities. No doubt about that.'

'What exactly is step two?'

'Anger. The search for someone to blame. Who did this? Or more specifically. Who did this to me? And then that starts to bring in some layers of guilt. Maybe it's my own fault. Why did I do this to myself? How could I have let myself down like that? Let everybody down. It's very destructive. A proper death spiral of negative emotions.'

Billy quickly understood.

'So avoiding step two then, if you can manage to do it, would appear to be not such a bad idea, on the face of it.'

'Exactly. It's almost impossible to avoid. But it's certainly possible to minimise. Although seldom this quickly'

'So what might be going on here then, do you think?'

'Well, it becomes interesting when you remember that step three is generally referred to as bargaining, which is kind of where you start to wrestle with it, whatever it is. In one sense it's where the affected party is already starting to begin making peace with the event, coming to terms with it, so to say. But what's really significant is the manner in which that happens, because the mechanism is participatory.'

Billy didn't understand. So he said so. 'Sorry, sir. You lost me again.'

'Well, it takes two to tango, as they say. You can't really bargain with yourself, although actually you can but that's something a bit different, but phase three is where you confront the wrongdoer, the person who had brought the bad news, the inflicter of the pain, and you start to challenge them, you start to say *"hey, this ain't right, I don't deserve this, why are you doing this to me?"* And that's quite a big turnaround from

92

step two where you are still being submissive. Step three is about regaining control, or at least attempting to. Much less passive'

'So, if your theory about these kidnappings is right, what does all that mean exactly? How does it fit into the robbery, into the disappearance. Into Jumbo?'

Hank remembered Harry's words again. "*Not really a Nine but he might as well be.*"

No problem opening up a bit with Billy Poppitt then, who was slowly getting back on track as the Colonel continued his explanation.

'Well, regrettably, I think it's actually bad news. Although on the face of it sounding like a positive thing, the reality looks like an acceleration towards step four much quicker than anybody would have ever thought possible. This level of assertion, although generally welcome as an indication of potential recovery, is normally a slower part of the overall process, taking weeks rather than days.'

'And step four?'

'Normally, in an individual, we call it depression.'

'But this isn't that, is it?' observed Billy. ' I mean its got lots of individual's in it, if you see what I mean, but it's more like a group thing, isn't it. A society thing. Because its affecting everybody.'

'Correct. In which case, we would call it something else.'

'And what would that be?'

'I think the most appropriate word is panic.'

Chapter 15 – Crypto One

Andrei came back with the burgers at around midnight. The twenty-four hour McDonalds next to the park was proving a godsend and the dietary implications of too much fast food were completely lost on anybody under twenty anyway. They did at least vary their choices from the menu, which was a lot better than just choosing a quarter-pounder with chips every day. The boys had seen enough American movies about Wall Street and all those high-pressure trading floors to know that eating at your desk while you ploughed through hour after hour of screen based concentration was actually the right way to do things, the proper path to riches. And that's where they were headed, where they wanted to go. So, at least in that respect anyway, they were emulating their heroes.

But in reality he and Georgi were playing for an altogether different level of wealth. Their stakes could not be higher. It was, in gambler's parlance, the whole pot. There would be nothing left on the table afterwards. The cupboard would be bare. And that was a concern. One of many in fact, but, as the spring days rolled past, and they started to zero in on their final plan, they realized it was probably the main one. They would not just be making enemies of a few people, they would be making enemies of *everybody*, of *everybody everywhere*.

This dawning realization troubled them more and more. In truth it had always been there of course, been there from day one, but it was only as they got stuck increasingly into the detail that this rather unhappy byproduct of their rather extreme plan became clear.

It was suddenly a truly awful and very frightening prospect. They would have nowhere to turn, nowhere to go, no lawyers to get them out of jail, no cops to protect them from whoever came after them, no island in the sun to escape to. The more they thought about it, the more the whole thing suddenly started to seem like a truly bad idea.

'Probably because we were focused too much on the tech.' Georgi suggested, as he finished off the ice cream.

'Bit late now.'

'Well it's not is it. Not really. Not until we actually do it. We can actually stop anytime we want.'

'But stopping is pretty irreversible. We'll simply never get started again if we stop now. And there's no real way to scale back either. We can't half do it. It's all or nothing.'

'Which we always knew in terms of the financials. Just didn't think about the other aspects of it enough, maybe.'

'Well, we had enough on our plate with all of that stuff on its own. Still have really.'

And so began the reflective period, the period of doubt that often precedes great ventures.

This was either negative thinking or just being brutally realistic, and, as usual, it proved very hard to draw a line between the two. The full flush of youth can often bring with it feelings of omnipotence, of indestructability which can mask dangers which would be noticed and acted upon by older people, who would then reach quickly to engage either neutral or reverse gear.

But the young are wired differently and tend to display that natural sense of abandon which is such an essential part of growing up. Their appetite for sheer adventure is undaunted by risk, their inherent sense of natural caution diminished by the irresistible triple prospects of fun, excitement and stepping into the unknown, the vital ingredients of youth.

It is entirely possible that had they both been just a few years older that this particular moment – the moment when they temporarily hit the pause button – might never have even happened. But there is a big difference between late teens and early twenties in that regard and so, what could have been a gloomy period of introspection lasting days, turned out to be nothing much more than a minor wobble during one rather long and miserable night where they didn't actually get much done while they brooded over this sudden and unexpected downside, the one that, in reality, had been there all along.

After a couple of days they were right back on track, with, if anything, a renewed sense of determination to succeed. If they ended up in trouble, well, so be it. Their lives since around the age of twelve had always been on the edge and this was now just the next iteration of that.

And so they plunged back into the online tutorials about cybercurrencies, for those digital conundrums were now central to their plans.

They knew a lot about them, their recent history being something which both

boys had grown up with, not so much as background in their case, much more foreground. The early variants and the dominant brand, Bitcoin itself, had all started to emerge from the shadows when they were about nine years old. Like all kids born in the early part of the twentieth century they inhabited the digital world effortlessly, never really having known any alternative. Unlike their parents they didn't have to get used to the internet or the alternative and seemingly parallel universe which it created. Its existence and its very use in all sorts of daily applications was second nature to them, no different to breathing, something they did automatically and without thinking.

So anything new that came along in that domain was not a shock to the system. They would readily accept it and integrate it into their lives effortlessly. The reality was that they had just as much trouble, maybe even more, with the basic concept of old style money and how that worked. A new form of digital currency seemed to them, if anything, inevitable and long overdue.

So they studied them with interest, but, because of their young age, more with a kind of juvenile academic curiosity than the greed and intrigue which the sheer vastness of the attendant opportunities created in other, older people.

They had already started, around the age of twelve or thirteen, to play around with these cryptos – as they had begun to be known – in much the same way that a cat plays with a mouse. It was a DNA thing. They were drawn to them on an increasingly regular basis, couldn't help it, a little dabble here, a bit of experimental coding there, some conversations with their local minders now and then about the alleged impossibility of any creative hacks until gradually, over a period of two or three years, they found themselves increasingly in demand for their knowledge of the subject and their capabilities with it.

The bad guys had started to smell easy money and, at that stage of their lives, Andrei and Georgi were still a few years away from the luxury status of self-employment. They were not in any position to refuse.

They couldn't.

So they didn't.

And Crypto One was born.

Chapter 16 – St Basil

Paul read his Russian guidebook on the plane. It's a modern day pastime enjoyed by millions of travellers all over the world whilst en-route to their latest holiday destination, cramming in advance for all those local sightseeing trips that await them in their temporary homes.

'I've never been before,' he had exclaimed toward the end of the first Jumbo meeting that morning. 'Anybody got any tips?'

'Avoid vodka with breakfast. They will offer it to you.'

'Go to the cathedral. It's amazing.'

'Don't mention Rasputin. They're still a bit touchy.'

'Don't let any leggy blondes get you pissed.'

'Lovely' he'd replied.' Like I'm off for a jolly weekend as a tourist or something and I'm going to have loads of spare time.'

'Ok, then. Well, just go to the cathedral. It's amazing.'

So he did.

And it was.

As he crossed Red square, the central point of Moscow and replete with history, St Basil's cathedral loomed up out of the early morning mist in a stunning display of magnificence and glory. A truly astonishing sight just as a piece of architecture, the overall beauty of its form and flow further enhanced by the rainbow of colours which cover the domes and spires.

Just as much a work of art as it is a functioning cathedral, St Basil's rivals, maybe even outrivals, most of the other splendid old world churches that boast strong design pedigrees across Europe.

La Sagrada in Barcelona, the Duomo in Florence, St Paul's in London, St Stefan's in Vienna, the list is almost endless as befits man's paltry attempts at tributes to the almighty. They need not be splendid to look at, and yet they mostly are, with some just being off the scale beautiful to behold.

But they also serve who hide away, waiting gently and patiently in the dark backwaters of small villages and threatened communities around the world, offering quiet shelter, succor and sanctuary to the frightened, the poor and the dispossessed.

And it is on that truly divine list that the Russian Orthodox cathedral of Vasily the blessed in the heart of Moscow, usually referred to by its more common name of St Basil's, features, right up at the very top.

Like most people abroad on business, of whatever kind, Paul really did not have too much time for the attractions. And yet, this is no ordinary sight.

It stopped him in his tracks for a few minutes as he took in the grand splendour before heading on down past The Kremlin to The Metropol, the city's oldest and most distinctive hotel, just up at the top end of Red Square.

For a guy with a fine mind and a clear head he found himself arriving slightly befuddled at check in. Trying to make sense of Jumbo was bad enough. Trying to make sense of the historical enigma that is Russia was something else.

Just behind him outside was the seat of political power, where numerous senile representatives of Communist and semi- democratic Governments had symbolically threatened the rest of the free world as battalions of tanks, men and improbably large rocket launchers had paraded past their robotic clapping on elevated balconies. And now here he was in an actual building where Bolshevism itself had flourished, in The Second House of All Soviets, as it had been known in 1918, when the fires of revolution had raged. It was a stately and elegant edifice, like so many others in Moscow that had seen so much and yet kept their secrets close.

In that country, and in that city, that's never a bad idea.

Sure enough the receptionist was a six-foot blond. All arse and tit, as his own mother had rather unkindly labeled all shapely and well-bestowed young women for reasons that Paul never quite managed to discover. The description always seemed to fit a certain type perfectly though, although this one had a smile warm enough to unfreeze the Moskva.

Which was just as well, because he was now a stranger in a strange town, a situation where one needs friends, of whatever persuasion, as quickly as possible.

Being bright and feisty, like most modern young Russian women, she was straight out with both her greeting and her question.

'Welcome to Moscow, Mr. Lambert. Are you going to share the joke?'

Paul quickly realised his mum's old prejudices had made him grin and were now in danger of betraying his temporarily sexist innermost thoughts.

'Ha, yes, thank you. I'm really very pleased to be here. No, I was just thinking how lucky we all are these days, you know, compared to 1918,' he fibbed, only half

convincingly.

Like all women, Valeria's feminine instincts told her he had been thinking about things other than century old politics, but she was well enough trained and seasoned enough in her job to quickly move the conversation along.

'But maybe not feeling so lucky today, though' she replied quickly, 'with everything that's happened yesterday. What do you make of it all?'

'I'm not sure. Don't think anybody is, really. Have to wait and see what the banks have to say later on.'

'Yes, of course. The lifts are down that way. You're on the third floor. I hope you have a nice stay. Do let me know if you need anything.'

It was only slightly loaded, the way she'd said it, but loaded nonetheless.

Not *" let the concierge know "* or *" Just dial 0 for reception "* but *" do let me know."* Paul knew that she would obviously be aware of his last minute booking, sorted out anonymously by one of Billy Poppit's boys around six the previous evening. That, in and of itself, would not betray his reason for travelling, but in a world turned upside down overnight, the very fact that a rather sharply dressed and well spoken young Englishman would turn up in Moscow at very short notice the following morning was more than a bit striking.

For a top lawyer, turned ace negotiator, Paul had a rather mischievous mind.

He thought back to the ad-hoc advice from his team. Ah, what the hell.

'Do you happen to know The Rasputin Bar?' he ventured.

Gosh, that was quick. No messing about with him. Valeria liked that.

What she liked slightly less was the detail of his question.

'It's a bit early for a strip club but yes, I know it.' she replied.' I'll write down the address for you.'

Now Paul really did grin, then he dropped his head and laughed lightly.

Well that had gone completely wrong. Could he explain without digging a larger hole?

'I'm sorry' he started ' That won't be necessary. I should confess.'

'You're hardly in church Mr. Lambert but I'm all ears.'

'You see, I've never been to Russia before' he decided to try, 'so I asked some friends for a few tips and one of them said *"Don't mention Rasputin"* so I ...'

'You guessed there'd be a bar with that name and you wanted to see my reaction. But you didn't know it was a clip joint.'

Now he felt really lousy, like he'd taken advantage of her friendliness, although it was of course just a professional friendliness, her being a hotel receptionist and all that. And yet, in that imperceptible undercurrent that swirls away in those gaps between men and women, between boys and girls, both were actually having other thoughts on a completely different wavelength.

Valeria: Who is this guy, turning up here at short notice, today of all days?

Paul: She's obviously local. She'll know people and places.

Valeria: One day, someone from somewhere else will walk through those doors and whisk me off, transport me to a magical life somewhere else.

Paul: I need an ally.

Valeria: He's pretty cute.

Paul: She's pretty fit.

Valeria: Stay professional; let him go first, boys should always go first.

Paul: I kind of need to apologise here, to make up for that a bit.

So he did.

'Look, err, Valeria' he said, clocking her name badge,' can we start again. I mean, sorry, what I mean is, can I start again. I'm really sorry'.

Goodness, he was making a mess of this.

He put his small overnight bag down.

'I guess I'm just a bit over-tired after the flight and all the turbulence of yesterday. Plus absorbing all your local culture and history. It's a lot to take in and I wasn't too sure how the whole trip would work out, what with so many systems being down everywhere.'

She wasn't cross, more amused than anything else, but she was still weighing him up.

'Come' she said, making up her mind in an instant, and walking around to his side of her desk. ' We're very quiet this morning. I'll walk you down.'

The Moskva unfroze again.

She clicked her fingers and a porter followed them towards the old fashioned lift which looked like it could have been there since 1918.

She pressed the call button and said something in Russian to the porter before sauntering back to her desk.

'Bye' said Paul, a bit flustered.' Thanks.'

Porters are either young and dead keen or older and less so. This one looked like

he came with the lift. The good news though was that he obviously wasn't going to get lost in The Metropole's labyrinthine corridors, down which they now wandered, one by one, one after the other.

It was a very large building.

Finally, he opened a door and shepherded Paul inside, showed him the TV remote, the minibar, the heating controls and the view back across onto Theatre Square. Paul thanked him and slipped him a few dollars, US currency still being the preferred medium of choice for tips just about everywhere.

He was surprised when the porter gave him something in return.

'She said seven, gives you all day to rest. Looks like you need it.'

Paul scrutinized the scrap of paper.

Rasputin bar. Tverskaya 41.

'It's walkable, but I'd cab it if I were you. First day in town. Always the best idea.'

He might have been getting on a bit but his English was perfect.

Not for the first time in his life Paul felt Britguilt.

Everybody else spoke English but the English….

Aww, never mind.

Have to think quickly though.

Seven was far too late. He needed her earlier.

For work not pleasure.

He pulled a twenty out of his top jacket pocket where he always kept a hundred in loose readies. Just in case. The emergency fund.

'Thanks Leo, appreciate that. Can you do me a favour?' Good old name badges.

'That seems to be my main function in life these days.'

'What time does she get off shift? Do you happen to know?'

"She does five till one today.'

'Perfect.'

He pressed the note into Leo's hand.

'I'll be in there at one. Tell her I'll wait half an hour. No longer.'

'No problem.'

The World Bank announcement was due 12 noon local time. He'd be up for that. Then about 3 he would see the teenager girl, the first of several cranks no doubt, chasing the reward money, although her story, at least, was sufficiently detailed to

warrant some investigation. In between he would attempt some temporary recruitment.

There is a reason why people say some things are timeless. Even in the midst of a twenty first century crisis brought on by a whole host of negative reasons – greed, envy, anger, betrayal, revenge – calm words of peace, forgiveness and wisdom from the past can be invaluable for soothing the troubled mind.

Paul had been transfixed by the beauty of St. Basil's earlier for several reasons, but one of the main ones was the words that now rang through his head again as he thought back to his very touristy reading on the plane and some of the local inscriptions.Words from the Orthodoxy came back to him from the Moscow Patriarchate. Old words about emerging from darkness. Always symbolic, always full of hope, words that were timeless and always relevant. Especially right now as Day two dawned and one of the world's darker chapters started to unfold.

For those who do wicked things will always hate the light and will shun it lest their works should be exposed. But whoever does what is true comes towards the light and welcomes it, so that it may be clearly seen by everybody that their works have been carried out in God's name.

His shock at learning that he'd been booked into a former Bolshevik hotel right next to the Cathedral of the Intercession had begun to subside and he dozed fitfully in his comfortable room, the restlessness of the previous day still causing uncertainty and turmoil even to him, one of the small band of professionals who were charged with resolving and fixing the problem. It is hard to rest properly when the mind is troubled by something. Nonetheless, the short sleep did him some good and he awoke in time to get himself a strong coffee before switching the television on.

One normally needs a massive sporting event to get a TV audience of billions. The football world cup will do it, so will the Olympics and a few other random events. The much-loved American boxer Muhammad Ali actually broke the world TV viewership record five times all on his own between 1975 and 1980.

Now that's an individual world record that will never be broken.

Those types of events are largely enjoyable so people tune in. News events tend not to be enjoyable so people don't. The Apollo 9 moon landings were an exception. So was Live Aid. The current record going into 2022 was 3.6 billion when about half the world's population watched first the London, and then the Rio Olympics in 2012 and 2016 respectively. No doubt the Tokyo event will outstrip even those remarkable

figures if they ever get round to holding it after the Covid postponement.

Yet all of those records and numbers would pale into insignificance as an approximate two thirds of the world's 8 billion people now got ready to tune in to a special announcement from a specially appointed panel representing the world's largest banks and, by proxy, the world's smallest banks too. It seemed they had all somehow found a way to speak with one voice in addressing the crisis and would now, in turn, address the world. If anybody had been expecting a political speech, they were going to be surprised. This was not a time to be coy about anything. And they weren't.

He looked fit, tanned and healthy, whoever he was, and spoke English with just that slightest and mildest touch of an accent, imperceptible to everybody apart from, well, apart from an English person. He had a calm reassuring manner as he read his prepared statement off the autocue. It wasn't very long because he wanted to focus in on the numerous questions from the world's press so he just covered the basics before getting to his more detailed responses to the broadcast journalists.

"Yesterday was a day in world history that we never expected to see. It has affected all of us and, I'm afraid to say, in an absolutely terrible way. Not in the sense that there has been loss of life or a planetary disaster but we all woke up yesterday morning as victims of a global mugging. The world's money, of which we, the people who are represented around this table, are the legal and moral custodians, has disappeared. Not some of it, but all of it. It has, quite simply, gone. We don't know how. We don't why. We don't know where it has gone. We don't know who has taken it. We have, at this very early stage just one day and a half later, still got no idea about any of that. They are the four key questions and, it is very much my regret, that we still have no answers to any of them.

What I can say is that the banks' own investigation teams are working flat out in an attempt to address that situation. There will be another global broadcast at the same time tomorrow when I will speak to you all again about what we have found out.

I can also confirm that we are working with a host of official and unofficial agencies who are providing worldwide assistance. Their input will prove invaluable and I hope to be able to incorporate that into our own findings as we strive to find out exactly what happened."

"And I hope to be able to help you," Paul mumbled to himself as he finished off his coffee and some of the Metropole's biscuits. "But by tomorrow? That's pushing it

a bit."

The banks' spokesman shifted camera angles to indicate the start of the second part of the proceedings. Behind him, through a large plate glass window, the sun played gently on the surface of a lake where a waterspout plumed its way skywards.

" Hmm, Geneva," though Paul. The almost inevitable location to be chosen for making any significant financial pronouncements on behalf of the world's global banking community.

And Switzerland.

Where so much of that money was kept, some openly, much of it much less so. That beautiful country in the very heart of Europe that always manages to weather all of the worst storms that politics can ever create and sail serenely through them, sticking two fingers up at everybody else as they go.

Well, if other countries are stupid enough to quarrel incessantly until they have wars, why should we get dragged into that?

Not daft, the Swiss.

"So I will take questions in no particular order and do my best to answer them as openly and honestly as I can. Please identify yourself and state your affiliation."

The camera panned across the room.

"Lucy Diggs. BBC London. What immediate support measures are you taking to restore credit and how quickly can that happen?"

"We are in the process of getting the data that supports all credit histories back from the Cloud. Emergency provisions of a yet to be determined sum will be made as quickly as possible, we hope by midnight tonight. I estimate an allowance of three thousand dollars per person for everybody, right across the planet. It's a completely arbitrary figure. There's no personal profiling or fancy calculations. Everybody gets the same amount. Full stop."

"Robert Watchinit, New York Times. There are already signs of panic as many people across the world start to line up outside banks demanding their money. What's your message to them?"

"Very simply, this is not 2008 and this is not a bank run. No one institution is responsible for what happened yesterday. All are affected equally and there is no one single solution that will suddenly restore individual banks to a position of health. The fix for this, when we have one, will be universal and, in so far as it is possible, will be rolled out to all banks at the same time. Please don't ask me for timings though, that's

not a question I can answer this morning."

"Hannah Freiheit, Bild. How did this actually happen when all banks have been telling us for years that their systems are completely safe?"

"This is the most difficult question because we simply don't know. It is quite obviously a type of computer theft based on extremely advanced hacking techniques. The whole financial community has steadily migrated across to the types of platforms you mention over recent years and always with the toughest security protocols in place. I can only surmise that the people who did this are the best hackers in the world at the moment which is quite strange because we usually attempt to employ those people ourselves for a whole raft of reasons."

"Charlie Oyeah – Wright, Straits Times. Is it true that all the government money has also vanished?"

"Yes, at least all of it that was lodged with any of the banks has. Which is, as far as I am aware, most of it, so probably, yes."

"Jacqueline Trouvére, Le Monde. Is there any way that this could have been an inside job? Will not all explanations citing external forces be met with some skepticism given the banks rather low trust ratings these days?"

"Well, I agree we have a trust issue which we have been wrestling with for over a decade now and, I think, making very good progress. But no, this could not have been an inside job. Strange as it may sound, I don't think we would have the necessary skills to pull it off. This has been done by a team of people working right on the cutting edge of digital technology. We have many such people, of course, and they will, I hope be part of the eventual solution. I know of many who are working on that right now, literally, as we speak."

"Bruce Well-Buggameeblue, Sydney Morning Herald. We are constantly told that it's gone. The money's all gone, was the phrase that was used during the initial announcement. Well if it's all gone, where the bloody hell has it gone to? Where do you think it is?"

"I wish I could give you a better answer but we simply don't know. All I can tell you is that all accounts, right across the world, were zeroed overnight on the night before yesterday. It appears to have happened simultaneously which is, well I want to use the word impossible, but clearly I can't because it has just actually happened. As for where it is, the current location remains unknown pending the outcome of our investigations which remain ongoing and will continue apace until we can resolve the

situation."

"Ivan Terrtroothski, Izvestia. Can you say anything about some reports which broke earlier this morning suggesting that you have already identified some geographic locations where you are planning to start your investigations?'

"I can neither confirm or deny any such reports. What I will say is that the international hotline telephone number, which we have set up, has been ringing off the hook night and day. It is unsurprising, yet still very gratifying, that so many people want to help. Each and every call is, and will continue to be, taken seriously. We will follow them all up but the volume is daunting and, as I'm sure you can imagine, will include a lot of crank calls, hoaxes and, qu'est ce que c'est le mot en anglais, ah, yes, nutters."

Ah, French then, thought Paul, but then a banker from Geneva, what do you expect, but still that was the first time he'd missed a beat in search of the correct English word. Impressive.

The grilling continued for another twenty minutes or so as correspondents from the world's top media outlets continued trying to shine a light into the darkness of world banking practices as they looked for clues. Finally the spokesman started to draw the proceedings to a close.

"Well that's it for today. I will be back here again tomorrow morning at the same time to update you all with whatever we have found out. Any final questions?"

The camera panned the room one last time and found Ivan with his hand raised again.

He was looking quite serious.

"Are any of those nutters in Moscow?"

Chapter 17 – Breakfast in Chelsea

Billy cruised past the football stadium and a succession of upmarket furniture and rug shops before swinging the stylish long wheelbase Jag into the row of smart Edwardian terraced townhouses in Ifield Rd.

He pinged Jojo as he pulled up.

Special delivery, Boston Mass.

The large heavy looking front door opened a fraction. Hank bade a cheery goodbye to his driver, went inside and greeted the two Nine's operatives who were both still sat around the large oak kitchen table where they had spent most of the night, wrestling with the technical absurdities of their latest mission.

The laptops and tablets had been removed to one side so that that they had room for their other special delivery, the luxury of a home delivered breakfast from Cait's local deli.

Hank had skipped his free in-flight meal after Monica's pizza had filled him up at Logan, but now the smell of the freshly baked fluffy bread and the coffee brewing on the Aga in the corner made him suddenly feel inexplicably ravenous.

As he tucked into a hot crusty bacon roll dripping with brown sauce, the girls brought him up to speed.

'The banks' joint tech teams will announce some more detail later,' Cait started,'at which point we should start to get something more substantial to go on. In the meantime we concentrated on the likely scenarios based on what we know.'

She took a large drink of coffee from her CFC mug and summed up.

'The night before last all of the bank accounts linked to ATM networks were hacked and the accounts emptied. Although there is a perception amongst the general public that these cash machines are local, popping up as they do at garages, shops, bars, stations and all sorts of other places where people go about their daily business, the reality could not be further from the truth. One only need stop and think that a similar looking machine on the other side of the globe will not only recognize you but also spit out your holiday money in that country's local currency before you realize that the underlying networks are international. Not only that but they are also extremely sophisticated. You may be in Tibet or Timbuktu, in Mongolia or Madrid, it

won't matter. As long as you comply with the protocol the cash machine will recognize you and will pay out. Pretty astonishing when you think about it, especially those security aspects which keep everybody safe.'

'Agreed' said Hank, wiping a brown splodge off his chin with a napkin. ' They're a great example of tech supporting everyday life and making people's lives easier. We know that. What's your point?'

'That the backbone network that supports all those transactions, the thing that makes it all so easy, is, in reality, quite a complex beast. For a start, its not really just the one network, its hundreds of micro networks, VPN's mostly, all of them interconnected and plugged into each other. Seamlessly, of course, so the many millions of daily transactions can happen fluidly and effortlessly. People get their money and barely bat an eye. They hardly even notice any more how wondrous the whole operation is, until, of course, it ceases to work.'

'Which is essentially what happened on Monday night.' Jojo chipped in. 'At least that's what everybody thought at first. But of course it wasn't a fault this time. By around 4am the banks knew they had a problem as they noticed the accumulated balances of an increasingly large number of accounts reducing steadily. We were actually a bit slow here in London when it started to happen, but across the States and Asia Pac, where it was still daytime or evening, the penny was dropping much quicker as the banks ops screens slowly went dark and their colour-coded methodologies for highlighting emergency alerts kicked in.'

'Who noticed it first?' Hank enquired.

'Oddly enough, the Tokyo trading floors. With global finance so interconnected all their investment indicators suddenly started to show bank liquidity problems, something that will normally only happen when a key institution has a major crisis. So it doesn't happen very often and they certainly don't all come along at once, as was the case on Monday night, or Tuesday morning rather, as it was in Japan. Their guys rang the bell. Within minutes, dozens of tecchies all over the world were in fault finding mode, trying to fathom what was going on. After they started talking to each other about an hour or so later, they began to realize that there was something else going on. They escalated and the senior management teams got involved, dragged from their beds at some unearthly hour across Europe, and it was at that point that they alerted the authorities and we knew we had a much bigger problem.'

'How did you guys find out?'

Jojo and Cait grinned at each other.

'What?'

'Harry likes to pound the streets before dawn. Says it helps him think as well as keep his weight down. He's coming up fifty next year, you know, not so keen on the gym and the weights any more.'

'I see.'

'Plus he likes the City at night, well, just before dawn to be more specific. He says 2 o'clock is too early because its all people going home, the night revellers, but 5 o'clock is completely different because it's people who just got up and are starting their day, are off to do something.'

'You mean the guy running one of the UK's top intelligence units just walks around London in the dark on his own. That sounds a bit high risk. But then he'll be armed won't he, so maybe not quite so concerning.'

'We're not armed, Hank. It's part of our ethos.' Jojo explained.' If we're doing our jobs properly, we don't need to shoot anybody.'

'Ah, yes, apologies, skipped my mind,' said Hank, to whom, as an American, this was a wholly alien concept. His country had more guns than people, a disastrous situation which American politicians and law makers seemed unwilling to resolve because the US constitution had guaranteed the rights of all citizens to bear arms. The fact that the second amendment, ratified over two hundred and thirty years earlier in 1788, had been drafted and implemented to prevent an occupying colonialist power from seizing and confiscating householder weaponry, did not seem to unduly concern them, despite the country's wretched record of gun crimes and a worrying numbness to school shootings.

Cait shrugged her shoulders. As one of the two Americans on Harry's team she was slowly getting used to life in England.

'Same thing with the cops here. It seems very weird but the country seem to be able to make it work. Personally, I have to say I admire them for it. It's all very civilized and a very British thing. You go anywhere else in Europe and they're armed, just like our guys are at home.'

The ex-military Colonel Hank Wyatt (Ret'd) of the United States Air Force just decided to let that one go.

'So Harry's out beating the streets and what happens? He gets a call?'

'No. He goes to a bank and finds out the hard way.'

'Oh. Ok.'

'You have to remember that there had already been a couple of warnings about an attack of some sorts. They were a bit ambiguous, as those things often are, but they differed from the usual run-of-the-mill stuff by specifying one thing that was very different.'

'Namely?'

'That the hits would be of a financial nature.'

'Ah. Ok, and what else did they say?'

'That was the most surprising thing. They didn't.'

Hank furrowed his brow.

'Well that is unusual. No threats. No demands. No ultimatums?'

'Correct. Just some advance information. Almost like a tip off.'

'And your assessment of that?'

'Got tidied away in the round file.'

'What. You binned it?'

'Well no, not exactly. But it was deemed not to be worthy of any immediate follow up at the time'

'Nobody bothered to try to investigate the source?'

'Not as far as we can tell, no. It wasn't any of us, of course, things like that will always get dealt with centrally. As a tight resource The Nines don't tend to get that kind of stuff. It's all filtered out before it gets anywhere near us.'

'But presumably you've now gone back and had a look?'

'Yup, did that last night.'

'And?'

'Well, we were expecting high tech, obviously, given what's just happened. But it wasn't. It was a note. About as old school as you can get.'

'A written note? On paper?'

'Yup. Here, take a look.'

Cait handed him a sheet of A4 lined paper.

When the world goes dark

It will be us.

We'll make our mark

It ending thus

No more cash
It all be gone
That greedy rash
We will move on
In the night
We will arrive
At first you'll think
We can't survive
But time will show
Such trite remarks
To be the child
Of media sparks
We must be lighter
Must become
So much brighter
More as one
Less divided
Is the way
And more united
'til the day
It all comes back
It won't be long
Was just a hack
There's nothing wrong
But learn we must
To share it Jack
The golden dust
Or we'll be back

Hank scanned it, looking bemused.

'No wonder nobody took much notice. At first sight its almost meaningless as any kind of genuine threat. Just a bit of schoolboy we-must-have-a-better-world type of poetry.'

He read it again.

'Not bad though. Could be any one of a hundred of the anti-poverty, anti capitalist groups out there. There's loads of them. More than ever since the US stock market had a record decade and so many people got minted.'

'And so many got left behind' Cait added.

Hank handed the note back to JoJo.

'Who's Jack?'

'Probably an indirect reference to *Do it Again*, Steely Dan's masterpiece, about man's propensity for making the same mistakes over and over again and constantly repeating them without ever breaking the cycle. That's all we got on that.'

'So this was written by people angered by injustice?'

'And by the lack of financial equilibrium in the world.'

'And now they've essentially switched off the money supply overnight. Well that's hardly a course of action that could ever have been deduced from this note. And why would it have been? They – whoever they are – have pretty much pulled off the impossible. '

'Well, that's the current thinking, yes. The other references in that note all fit quite snugly into what actually happened. So we've eliminated all the other stuff, the cranky, the weird, the plain certifiable and the end of the world warnings and we quite like this one now. It's ticking boxes.'

'That's what you've been up all night doing?'

''fraid so. Harry said *" we've got nothing, we need a start point. Get me one."*

'And you think this is it'

'It is. Well, at the moment, yes, it's all we've got.'

'I can get it to some of my old buddies from the profiling team in the firm if it'll help.' Hank offered, referring to his old CIA days.' It's amazing what those guys can come up with.'

'Thanks. Already got their input overnight' Jojo confirmed, showing Hank an e-mail on her i-pad.' Just scroll down to the summary.'

He flicked the screen and read.

At first glance a somewhat anarchic message with especial references to cash as money and division as disunity. The implied threat – although no longer implied because of what just happened last night – is one of disruption, albeit on a temporary basis pending some kind of societal response aimed at a rebalancing of sorts, although, again, quite what that should or could be, is not made expressly clear.

The use of a pop culture reference would normally suggest youth although the fact that this is from 1972 – if we've got the reference right – is initially baffling until you factor in the land of milk and honey reference in that particular song. Then, in the context of the tone of the rest of the message and what it is trying to achieve, it looks like the right call.

The veiled threat can be construed two ways. Either the protagonists don't know exactly what they want and therefore cannot stipulate it. Or, alternatively, they are demonstrating a small measure of patience and tolerance by suggesting the authorities come up with some kind of response of their own first.

Although initially seeming to be somewhat immature in nature, there is actually a note of quiet determination in the text as suggested by some kind of inherent ability to do it again if required, no pun intended.

The recipients – i.e. us – are being told to right these perceived wrongs. We are being given a chance to do so within an unspecified timeframe which we can only guess at. Days or weeks, we would surmise, probably not months. In the absence of any such initiative it seems abundantly clear that there will be some kind of follow – on action, the nature of which is not made clear.

This was not remotely considered a cause for concern when the message was first seen. But in view of what has just happened, it is now extremely worrying as the capabilities of the people who carried this out must now be seen in a completely different light. This is no idle threat any more.

The use of a plural may be inadvertent but nonetheless the tone is consistent with a group, albeit a small one. From a behavioural standpoint it would probably be desirable for the people behind this to be compelled to silence. We know from history that the more people involved in a group crime, the less likely it is that it can be kept quiet. It only takes one person to become unhappy about something for the best laid plans to start to unravel. Secrets work best when they are kept between just two. Three is a very dangerous number.

The slightly utopian sense of a world that can find a fairer way to look after its peoples is, of course, never far from the heart of world politics, both recent and historic. It has to be concluded, regrettably, that although some general improvements have been made in that regard, much of the required work is left undone. This communiqué is a call to arms to get that process finalized. The impatient tone suggests that just starting something will not be enough, will just be seen as

further procrastination, as more jaw jaw. Action and a result are required here, not the launching of an inquiry.

Hank handed Jojo her i-pad back, his bottom lip scrunched up over the top one. He wasn't scowling, he was … what was that look?

Something like mild amusement, almost a wry satisfaction.

Not the look that Cait and Jojo were expecting anyway.

'Communiqué? '

'That's how it came. In an envelope marked *communiqué*. Just that one single word. Gets your attention a bit, doesn't it?'

'Well, yeah, it's obviously designed to. Then your guys threw it in a bin!'

'Not just our guys, Hank. Everybody's guys.'

'Explain'

'The same note. Five times. London. Washington. Paris. Beijing. Moscow.'

'The P5.'

'Exactly. Although we're not thinking at this stage that there might be a nuclear dimension to this, it has to be an additional concern. They might not necessarily still be the world's most powerful nations but they are who they are, with all that that implies.'

The United Kingdom, the United States, France, Russia and China were, and still are the only five permanent members of the UN Security council which was established as part of the post second world war global restructuring.

Set up in 1946 the English, the Americans and the Soviets, largely seen as the victors, shaped the post war political order. To the winner the spoils, so those three nations called the shots. With incredible foresight US President Roosevelt invited China to join as well so that *"the far east"*, as it was then known, did not feel left out on the global stage and could be included – and be seen to be included – in world politics. UK Prime Minister Winston Churchill agreed on condition that France also join, thereby providing Europe with some semblance of negotiating bulk in the face of three global giants.

To solidify their power the Permanent 5 were each given an individual veto on the weighty matters which come before the security council, these ranging from local spats to large scale wars. All five need to agree on any suggested course of action. If any one of them does not agree then in theory – and usually in practice – whatever is being proposed won't happen. Interestingly the Europeans have used this considerable

power less and less over the last thirty years, the larger nations much more so.

Geo-politics tends to have a certain scale all its own.

'And, what, all hand delivered to preserve some anonymity?'

'Only the Russian one.'

'Ah, so that's why Liam's out there.'

'Plus he's keeping Paul Company.'

Hank froze.

'Harry's got two of his Nine's out in Moscow. How did I manage to miss that?'

'We have to keep some things a bit quiet, Hank. You know. Secrets. Two people. Three people. All that stuff.' JoJo smiled.

Hank quickly realized that a lot had happened behind the scenes overnight while he'd been a guest of British Airways. The redoubtable Harry Shepperton had obviously been making quiet progress. Based on, well, on what exactly?

'I remember meeting Liam in Den Haag after the Wuhan thing. We had a few post mission beers after he got back from China. Isn't he a geologist?' he ventured, seeking confirmation of what Jake had told him on the phone at Logan, but, in reality, also some kind of clarification.

'By training,yes. But he's also got other talents.'

Hank raised his eyebrows. That's always a discrete question.

The girls were skilled enough to know that.

But they also knew that Hank was like an unofficial team member, that he'd been on Sir Walter's short list for interview for the original Nines team, that he was completely trustworthy and that they could tell him anything.

But he didn't have to know.

Not yet, anyway.

And he hadn't actually asked.

Not yet, anyway.

Always default to " need to know " whenever possible. It's just safer.

Suddenly, there was Jojo's grin again.

This time Cait joined her.

Two very attractive, very disarming smiles.

'More coffee, Colonel?'

Chapter 18 – An Irishman in Moscow

'You'd best go join him, Liam.'

Harry put down his mug of tea. It was now late afternoon and the Jumbo briefing had been finished about an hour. As was always the case with Intel it kept unsocial hours and had a habit of turning up in reverse order. The stuff you didn't need to know first. The stuff you really did need to know last. It could be infuriating but that was its nature. And if you had made an operational decision based on something that came in at midday, you would quite often be faced with changing it, or adapting it, by the middle of the afternoon.

While he had been in session with the team, a small army of backroom staff had been going through everything that had been assembled by another small army of backroom staff charged with digging out recent suspicious activity.

'What exactly we looking for?', came the usual question.

'We're not really too sure.' came the usual answer.

'Then how the hell we supposed to find it?'

And yet find it they usually did, although, in keeping with most of the weirdness in that particular world, they mostly didn't know that they'd found it at the time, that dawning realization only coming much later.

The communiqué was one such item, filed away as a low priority, non-response message which had been received weeks earlier. It had only been kept at all because some junior staff member had decided it had a certain novelty value after spotting that the note that had appeared in London was the same one that had turned up in Washington.

'Bit strange, but too cranky looking' had been the verdict, so nobody really took much notice, nobody really did anything, and nobody actually noticed that there were actually not just two of them but five of them. Not until three o'clock the afternoon of day one.

Harry had called Liam back to the office as soon as he found out.

'What, all foive a'dem?'

'Yup. And nobody spotted it till just now. A bit disappointing but it happens.'

'Well it reads so funny, I don't know that anybody would a done anyting

anyways', Liam suggested, scanning the note for the second time. 'And what would we a done wid' it anyways, even if we'd decided it actually meant something?'

He looked at his boss, searching for clues.

'No, exactly, I agree. It was a bit too easy to miss and you could hardly call it a set of demands, could you? So, on that basis, you're right. Nobody's fault it got overlooked, or rather that they got overlooked, I should say. All five of them. The question is what we do now?'

Liam was reading again, slower this time.

'What do da profiling guys say?'

'The Yanks are reviewing it, we'll know in a couple of hours.'

'It's a call for a fairer society, isn't it? Can't really blame anybody for wantin' datt I suppose. Da language is odd do', half student, half rebel, but then they're quite often one and the same ting anyways. How were dey delivered? All by hand I suppose to avoid a trail and then that would suggest some kind of worldwide group.'

His boss suddenly had an unusual expression on his face.

'What?'

'Only the Russian one. The rest were faxed.'

Liam's surprise was evident as he sat back suddenly in his chair.

'Faxed. But aren't they all obsolete, woiped out by da scanners?'

'Apparently not. They're still in use in a lot of places, embassies and High commissions being amongst them. Something to do with totality of access, I think they're calling it these days. You know the kind of thing; it's essential to have all the options available so that all communications channels are open and usable. That way, nobody misses out any information.'

'Well that's great of course but then they still don't know what to do with sometin' like dis when it drops in they're laps. Honestly, you get a fax like this one out of 'da blue and it just gets ignored. Da mind boggles.'

'Agreed. But still, it's our first clue. Our only clue. Now we have to decide what to do with it.'

'But are we sure its linked, you know, linked to Jumbo? Could it just be another rabbit hole to go down? We're not exactly spoilt for time here, are we, with the PM and COBRA breathing down our necks?'

'If you read it, there is a kind of fit, albeit a rather loose one. So, no, we can't be sure because that kind of certainty never really exists in our world, but on the balance

of probabilities, it's a reasonable bet that the people – or person – who wrote this is responsible for – or is at least connected to – what's just happened.'

'Which makes it what? Still a robbery? Or a political ultimatum?'

'Both. Which means we now have a much wider net to cast.'

'And a whole world to cast it in judging by 'da faxes. Did the trace teams identify any source details from the original transmissions?'

'They looked, of course, but they were all sent using prefix blockers. Could have come from anywhere.'

'But the Moscow one?'

'Delivered by a teenager on a bike. Hardly apocalyptic.'

'Did they trace him?'

'Well, they have the CCTV of course but it was posted into their equivalent of a council office, the kind of place where locals go to pay all sorts of bills. So it's not like an embassy, it's a place with pretty minimum security. And it's a twenty four hour facility so the imagery is just a constant procession of people all pushing envelopes and packages into a type of outside post box where the staff collect everything the next day.'

Liam thought about this scenario.

'Then how do they know which person it was?'

'They went through every single drop over a ten day period prior to the date stamped on it by the mail room when it eventually reached its final destination.'

'And that gave them the time window?'

"Correct. And within that they magnified every single one until they found the only one that looked likely.'

'Based on what?'

'The fact that it had one very large word on the envelope followed by a couple of smaller ones.'

'Let me guess. The larger one said Communiqué and the smaller one the specific address.'

'Correct. They blew it up to its max enlargement to be sure.'

'And the boy on the bike?'

'Had a pigtail, so may have been a girl. Other than that, baseball cap and shades so the usual anonymity.'

'And after he zoomed away. Or she?'

'Few street cams, then disappeared into a McDonalds.'

'And then?' Liam was still visualizing.

'Bought a wrap and some chips. Munched away for half an hour. Went to the loo. Never came back.'

About sixteen hours later Liam was on the AeroExpress train that connected Domodedovo airport to the city centre. The forty five minute ride confirmed yet again the ongoing trend to keep major airports a safe distance away from increasingly crowded and built up metropolis hubs, about twenty five miles worth of safety in this particular case. As he changed at Belorusskaya and entered Moscow's beautiful underground system he was surprised, like so many before him, at the magnificent architecture of the local Metro.

Chiseled pillars and marble tiles appeared to be everywhere, with all of the lengthy walkways being illuminated by extremely bright chandeliers, all so ridiculously splendid that they can only have been liberated by the Bolsheviks from any of the large numbers of hidden secret palaces built for the Tsars.

He changed at Pushkinskaya and took the 7 line to Kitay-Gorod where he emerged out into the cool spring weather on Lubyanskyiy Proyezd leaving Staraya Square behind him before turning right at the first main intersection. He didn't know of course that he was walking away from the scene of the crime rather than towards it but detection is seldom an immediate business.

The sign was in Cyrillic but the first three letters gave it away, as did the world famous golden arches and the gaggle of teenagers hanging out by the entrance.

He decided to look for himself first before trying the manager. As suspected no windows in the toilets, as is often the case in many McDonalds branches all over the world, so no escape possible there. He blundered into the ladies just long enough to confirm the same arrangement whilst being rebuked by three leggy blonde teenagers.

'Sorry, sorry. Tourist', he shouted back. " Turist.Turist' before disappearing back into the gents for a second time, as if to try and prove his genuine mistake.

He and Harry had considered passes and various false Russian ID's but the language barrier had got in the way. No point in pretending to be from the local goon squad if you couldn't speak the lingo.

"Dermot McMahon, customer services Director, Europe and Asia. Sorry to drop in unannounced like this, we get a better feel for things that way."

The young and willing Russian manager was only too willing to oblige. Cleanliness protocols, yup, all observed to the letter, here's the duty sheets, new menu items, yup the chocolate cake slices are going down a storm, the salads much less so, this isn't California you know haha, takeaway probably only about ten per cent or so of overall business but the home deliveries were definitely rising, late night drunks, no not really a problem, our cops are pretty hardcore on stuff like that, security cams, yup, one over there, two down the side, one over the door, no, of course I don't mind , make yourself at home, I've got plenty to do out front, we're two down again, that's probably my single biggest problem, if you could mention that in your report please, that would help me out quite a lot, thanks very much , yes , was very nice to meet you too, Mr. McMahon.'

And with that Igor returned to the fray out front where the youth of Moscow were busy confounding a century of alarmist foreign propaganda by consuming American products in unbelievably large numbers and having a great time into the bargain. The old Politburo would have turned in their graves but then they were never bothered about anything but themselves. The kids will always find their own way, given time.

Liam's undoubted acting talents parked now for a while, he settled down in the small back office that doubled up as storeroom and general overflow area and whizzed back to the appropriate date and time on the video footage. Ah, yes, there, you are. Hmm, well maybe? But no pigtail. Try to zoom in. Seems possible but only a bit, leaves much clarity and definition of the images to be desired. But the time matched perfectly. The street cams had the deliverer of the communiqué tracked most of the way back across town, definitely went in to McDonalds at 15:03, marched up to the counter and ordered, paid cash, itself unusual and borderline suspicious, sat in the small booth in the corner for about twenty minutes, munch munch, tap tap, munch munch, tap tap, burger left hand, mobile right hand, then headed to the loo at 15:24, how long does that normally take, say five or ten minutes depending. Liam ran the tape back and forth, somebody must have come out who didn't go in, given no windows that was the only option, ah yes, here we go, wow, what a looker, tall, blonde, the false pigtail and sports beanie presumably now discarded and tucked away in the pocket of the reversible denim jacket, black going in, now blue coming out, different set of shades, long hair flopping down, but it barely took seconds to realize that this was not any of the people who had walked in.

So the quick-change merchant was definitely a girl. But who was she?

Liam left his small hidey-hole and became Dermot McMahon again for a few minutes, she's wanted for fraud, has she been in before, I'm sure I'd remember her, Igor told him with a grin, although we do have a lot of girls in this city who look like that, here, show me again, well I never, she went in like that and came out like...., well I'm blowed, of course when I look at the film it's totally obvious, but in here, well it's just so busy all the time, I really don't think anybody would be likely to notice , but you've got a time stamp for her order so I can get her card details if that will help , oh she paid cash , wait , what day was that again, well I can ask Dimitri, it was him who served her, *Assistant manager* it said on young Dimitri's name badge alongside *how can I help you*, so Dermot McMahon explained his theory, Dimitri reflected briefly then remembered, she came back later, 'yes I'm sure, no, not that one with the pigtail, the other one with those Superdry Yakimas, they're so cool, I love them, what do you mean it's the same girl ,really , wow, why would she do that, anyway I admired her sunglasses, you know how it is, with a beautiful girl you just grab at anything at all to say, right, just to connect, to get a reaction and she says , ha ha thanks, so I'd kind of broken the ice a little bit , so I said , you don't look like a two double quarter pounders and chips kind of girl, kind of flirting a bit , which all girls like, right, and I was right because she left with the food, yes I'm quite sure, I remember watching her walking towards the door, it was a lovely sight, no, Igor , I don't perv on all the customers, I know the company rules , I was just admiring her figure , she was quite something , be a lucky so 'n so who shared her chips.

How does that help, thought Liam as he left, apart from knowing she's got a hungry boyfriend somewhere, somewhere nearby obviously, two hungry boyfriends maybe.

He walked back the way he'd come, down the broad road that led to the park. Igor had allowed him to return briefly to the little storeroom. He'd found sunglasses girl on the CCTV leaving but she'd been walking, no bike. There were no reports of anything being abandoned outside so where was it? She must have returned later, he thought, or somebody else had picked it up for her. Or maybe it hadn't been her bike at all; it had been lent to her for her courier drop. But by whom? That would have meant there was at least one other party involved, maybe more.

Lost in his thoughts he traversed the western side of the park and crossed Staraya Square, not really focused on the long row of elegant apartment blocks that now faced him from across the other side of yet another impossibly wide road.

In common with hundreds of policemen, detectives and investigators of all sorts down the years he was unknowingly walking right past the scene of the crime, the flat where Andrei's body now lay cold and motionless on the sofa.

Chapter 19 – Twin peaks

A month earlier the preparations for this audacious and unprecedented attack on the world's financial systems had started to take their toll. Although teenagers have the boundless energy of youth and can stay up all night and survive on much less than the suggested six or seven hours sleep deemed necessary by the experts, there always comes a time when the accumulated effects start to catch up on you.

After going at it hard since the previous Christmas the two boys had both now reached that point where they needed a short break to escape the relentless intensity. A couple of days should do it, just enough time to think about other non-tech matters for a while, to escape the wonders of the digital world and spend time with the wonders of the real world. They decided that Andrei would have a complete change of scenery and go and stay with his sporty elder brother across town. That would give him the chance to play some football and some tennis, the cardio activity and the social aspects of both games being hugely beneficial as a relaxation and a release.

Meanwhile Georgi would stay in the flat and paint, not paint the flat, but paint some country scenery from the photographic images of nature that he loved so much. That had always been his other thing, ever since he had discovered his talent for drawing at an early age. It came to him naturally, became his second hobby, his therapy, his method of escape whenever he felt the IT world starting to close in.

He kept everything he'd ever done in a kind of loose scrapbook and would take much pleasure in looking back at his own work now and then, not in a vain way, but more aesthetically. It always did his human soul good to look at images of beauty from nature, pictures which he had created himself, always adding some small touches and flourishes here and there to personalise them, not in an arrogant way, for nature is perfect on its own, but using what many call artistic license, the right of everyone to see things their own way and create interpretations accordingly.

His method was very basic, he had no formal art training so was very intuitive and spontaneous in his approach. He would scour the internet or the glossy magazines for something that he liked and then pin it on the wall next to his small easel, mix his oils up, and begin, outlines first, then the general shape, then the detail.

Mountain meadows were a particular favourite, all a bloom with yellows and

greens and small white flowers and he would often lose himself for hours on end in the majestic beauty of the snowy Alps or even the slightly greyer rock strewn Himalayas while he busily fashioned his creations.

He had a particular quirk when painting and liked to wear a kind of loose fitting smock, the type beloved of the artists of yesteryear, over his regular everyday clothes. And it was like this that Anastasia had found him on the second day after Andrei had departed for his sporting interlude.

'Nice outfit.' she teased, slightly surprised to see him wearing what appeared to be a small sheet with holes cut out for the arms.' You going to a fancy dress tonight or something?'

'It's my art thing' he told her, taking the pins out of his mouth for a moment and standing back from the wall.

'Isn't it beautiful. It's called Millstatt. It's in Austria. I'm going to go there one day after this latest project is all over. I can't believe anywhere can be so beautiful. See how the lake reflects the image of mountain above it.'

Ans tilted her head slightly to one side, as if the loveliness of the picture could somehow be improved by rotating it through twenty or thirty degrees.

'We've got plenty of places like that in Russia' she chided him, putting the sandwiches, cakes and bread from the local baker on the table. 'You don't have to leave the country for that.'

Georgi thought for a moment about telling her his recent worries, about confiding in her a bit, just a little bit, letting her know that there might be a time in the coming months where he would be obliged to try and hide, maybe even to run and hide.

As *Ischeznoveniye* became more real and came ever closer, he had suddenly started to envisage the life of a fugitive and the rather unpleasant prospect of being pursued by people he did not know and could not see. He had spent a couple of extremely restless nights working himself up into a state about the whole thing, only slightly comforted by the notion of having so much money after the event that he would be able to do pretty much anything he wanted.

But he would have made enemies, not just powerful but ubiquitous, which in a sense made the whole prospect of flight a bit ridiculous. If they were everywhere how could you possibly get away from them? Clearly you couldn't. And yet taking flight was very much a natural reaction, a primeval response, a survival instinct and, as such, not something that could be easily rationalised away.

But he chose not to say anything, not just yet anyway. Keep it quiet. That was the agreement he and Andrei had with each other.

Nobody should know. Absolutely nobody.

'And what's the point of painting a photograph anyway? I don't get it. You've already got the picture haven't you. What's the point in doing it twice?'

'I suppose it's the idea of creating beauty. I did think about sitting over in the park for a while but the trees are still a bit bare looking. Plus it's February and I'd probably need five layers whereas in here its at least warm and I'm way comfier in my trendy smock.'

He waved both arms around like a windmill in a strong breeze.

'Look, see what I mean.'

She giggled one of her naughty laughs.

'You don't have to rely on scenery for beauty, you know' she added, looking back at the wall again and cocking her head to the other side for another alternative view of Millstatt.

'Did you ever consider doing still life?'

Georgi laughed out loud.

'What, like a bowl of fruit? Two apples and a banana.'

He laughed again.

'Or a bottle of vodka with two glasses. And some ice cubes. Not really Ans, no. Not really my thing.'

'What about people?'

'What about them?'

'Don't you think people are beautiful as well. Maybe even more than nature. And if you want to be a great artist you should be able to capture that as well.'

'Capture what?'

'Real beauty, both the inside and the outside, although one is probably a lot easier than the other.'

'Not sure I follow.'

Anastasia's naturally flirtatious nature was suddenly being confronted by a rare opportunity. She was hardly ever alone with him but now the flat was empty, apart from the two of them.

She knew this was her boyfriend's best pal and, as such, should be out of bounds. But she also knew that he fancied her quite strongly as well. If anything, he'd started

indicating something more than just friendship and warmth over the past few months. A few winks here and there, some ambiguous comments, the peck on the cheek which lingered and lasted just a little bit longer, that certain look which the female radar can lock on to with absolute unswerving accuracy, the look which is less than ambiguous in its intent and carries with it a latent fire to ensure the message arrives with the appropriate impact.

So, although her instincts were usually infallible, she had the curiosity of the woman about her as well.

She needed to know. To be sure.

'Well, for instance, if you thought I was beautiful, you could paint me instead of some stupid mountain.'

Georgi had, of course, half seen that coming, had kind of hoped for it in a way.

But now the game was on.

The dance had started.

Need to choose the right words carefully and get them in the right order. Not always easy, especially with the rampant hormones of the young in play.

'Ans, you are beautiful, everybody knows that and everybody says it too. There's not too much doubt about that really, is there?'

'Well, I'm not talking about everybody. I mean you.'

Hmm, bit forward. This could get interesting.

And she was a stunner so of course he was interested.

BUT, she was his best mate's girl …

AND he was hardly short of options himself …

PLUS she had a bit of a reputation.

As he pondered his next move, she chose the moment to discard her heavily distressed leather pilots jacket with the fur ruff. As she removed it she twisted her shoulders back and forth to slip it off. It was a slim fit jacket and underneath she was wearing a tight top. A very tight top. The lateral movement gave her cause to inadvertently stick her chest out. Her tits looked firm and pointy as she tugged down on the short jumper in a rather futile attempt to cover up the midriff it had been purposely designed to expose. She threw her hair back and shook it, like a swimmer emerging from the water and drying off.

'You know, one advantage of doing a mountain is that it doesn't move. I can take my time. Probably be the same with the bowl of fruit or the vodka now that I think

about it. But how long could you sit still for?'

'How long would you need me for?' she retorted, unfazed it seemed by the thought of maybe having to remain motionless for a few hours.

'Depends what I'm doing, I suppose.'

'What do you mean?'

'If it was your face, we could probably stop and have natural breaks. There's no position involved is there, no posture. But if I were doing your body, then that's completely different.'

'Doing my body?'

'All of you, rather than just face, or head and shoulders. After a couple of hours you might need a break, a drink, a pee, whatever, and then you have to recline again in exactly the same position. That's very hard to achieve.'

'Recline. What, like a nude, you mean. They recline, don't they?'

'They do, yeah, although that's not actually what I meant.'

'Why did you say it then? You said recline. Not sit down or stand. Recline.'

'I was just pointing something out, that if you…'

'I don't mind.'

'Sorry, you don't mind what.'

'Reclining in the nude. If that's what you want.'

Georgi's mind was slowly becoming a kind of gooey mess as the willowy blonde vision before him began to suggest that she wanted to take all her clothes off and pose nude for him, let him look at her naked loveliness.

'Well, I honestly hadn't considered it. But if you're serious then we should think about it.'

'What is there to think about?'

'Well, for a start, reclining is very old fashioned and probably quite difficult to pull off, especially the first time. It's a rather odd position when you think about it, I think it was only favoured so much in bygone days because it provided an opportunity for some modesty.'

'How?'

'Well, you can't see everything can you. The models always have their legs crossed.'

Anastasia pondered this minor roadblock for half a millisecond.

'I don't mind showing you my cunt' she continued. 'As long as you can paint it

properly. It's quite small, just a tiny little slit really. And quite tight. Do you think you can get something like that right?'

Georgi's cool was starting to evaporate. A kind of brain fog descended as he involuntarily envisioned the prospect of this delicious sight and he began to stir.

Not only a strip, but a full flash was on offer.

Well, no, you could hardly really call that a flash could you, not if she undressed willingly to pose in that kind of manner. Managing to capture that properly could take hours, days, weeks…

He snapped back to reality.

'I suppose I could try', he offered valiantly. 'There's probably harder things to draw than a little slit. I mean, it's not exactly a difficult shape, is it. Not like glass or water.'

'I don't mind if you need to get close to it. I mean, we do know each other pretty well now, don't we?' she cooed. 'And I would want you to get it exactly right if we did it. So you'd need to be able to see it all properly.'

As his excitement grew, he suddenly started to notice another emerging feeling to go alongside his arousal, a feeling of being trapped as she closed her net in around him.

She was gorgeous and still in that early bloom of the teen years when a young woman's body is bursting slowly into maturity. And here she was offering to disrobe for him so that he could paint her and, well, who knew what else.

He wanted to of course, wanted her in the way that men will always want women, but he was conflicted. Conflicted and more than a bit confused now as she piled on the pressure and continued her seduction, like a Venus fly trap, about to snap shut on it's prey.

'It might even be easier if I just lie down. That way I can open my legs right up and you can see everything properly.'

'Your tits won't look right.'

'Sorry?'

'If you're lying down, I mean. Tits become a different shape depending on your posture. Standing up is better for tits. That's a man's perspective anyway, you can just see the whole of the female shape much better, the roundness and the lift and all the cleavage. At least I would imagine it's the same for an artist, although I can't honestly say I've ever actually drawn a female nude so I am guessing a bit.'

'What about if I stand up but put one foot on a chair or something. Then you can see my tits the way you want to, but also my cunt as well. Something like this, maybe.'

She kicked her trainers off and lifted a very long shapely leg up so that her heel was atop the bar stool, a full metre above the floor. She looked like a ballerina doing her beam warm ups, tall, slim and graceful but with a much heavier chest which Georgi could now see in more detail as she started to pull her top up.

'Whoa' he started, 'Hang on; there's a preparation phase first. I need to get set up.'

But the top was suddenly off, revealing a lovely floral pattern bra complete with yellow and green leaves. Her perky breasts strained to escape the twin cups which were just about managing to resist the challenge.

'Need to get my brushes and mix a few oils.'

She was sliding her jeans down now. Her legs seemed to look ever longer as she discarded the garment onto the back of the sofa.

'Make some space, figure out the perspectives, the distances.'

She turned away from him so that he could watch the unclasping of the bra – that loveliest part of a female striptease – from behind. Her back was a lovely curvy shape, turning in at the waist where her hips broadened out into the classic hourglass figure, not something found in too many of today's teenagers, their dieting preoccupations often compromising nature's sweet curves.

'Decide on colours, I'll need lots of pinks and flesh tones. Haven't got too many of those. Don't normally need them for mountains.'

The pants matched the bra. She slid them slowly down her legs before turning round. Her pert breasts jutted out like twin cones with two perky red nipples pointing slightly upwards above the toned firmness of her tummy. Her erectile mechanism appeared to be functioning well without any external stimulation as they hardened and stiffened all on their own. A glistening moistness lower down suggested that Anastasia was now in the early stages of sexual excitement.

Georgi's resistance had been well intentioned but was ultimately just not strong enough in the face of such a skilled operator.

She put her foot back on the barstool, this time resplendent in her nakedness.

'Do I look better than an Alp then?' she giggled, shuffling her body slightly and very deliberately so that he had the best possible view of, well, of everything.

Throughout the history of mankind, various factions of most societies have always made proclamations about the sex act, forbidding it under so many circumstances that it would be hard to list them all.

The majority of these artificial restrictions seem to have been aimed at men who were told constantly that it was wrong to want to give way to their desires, that there was something base and animalistic about it, that self denial was somehow a route to spiritual improvement, that self gratification – a particularly nasty phrase that hinted at the total denial of the existence of any female pleasure – was indulgent and selfish, that repression of natural biological urges should be encouraged to build moral character, that abstinence was somehow clean next to the act of copulation which was somehow not clean, that the physical aches and pressures that accompanied lengthy periods of celibacy should be ignored.

Meanwhile those lawmakers, priests, government officials, and other assorted thugs who sought to impose such rules on others, generally failed to practice what they preached and roamed the planet as deviant predators, satisfying their own lusty desires regularly whilst simultaneously telling others it was wrong.

It would be hard to imagine a worse case of hypocrisy

Fortunately we now live in different times where much more openness prevails and education has overcome bad prejudices, as it often will. Women are much less subjected to poor sexual teaching and in many societies detailed discussions about the multiple ways females can enjoy sex without any associated feelings of guilt are actively encouraged. The internet age, with explicit porn on every cellphone, has started to remove many of the last taboos as access to multiple experiences has become available to all at the push of a button.

This accumulation of advancements, which probably began as mass movements with the free-loving hippies of the sixties, has now reached a point where guilt free sex is becoming the norm.

No more darkness.

No more confusions.

No more angst.

No more self-denial, unless as a matter of choice.

No more ignorance.

No more repressions.

And, of course, many more Anastasias.

As a fully liberated child of the new millennia she had enjoyed a full set of sexual experiences regularly and often since the age of thirteen, deriving even more pleasure at the time from the knowledge that she was knowingly breaking somebody else's stupid rules and intuitively suspecting that there was just something plain wrong about somebody else someplace else, somebody she didn't know and would never know, telling her what she could and couldn't do with her rapidly flowering woman's body.

She learnt as much as she could about the whole subject, the ups and the downs, so to speak, about contraception as well as the pox, about different positions as well as the strange power she seemed to be developing over the boys, about the pleasure of sharing her thoughts and experiences with her girlfriends in a way that would have been almost impossible just fifty years earlier.

So Georgi was actually in very safe hands, was being seduced by a girl who, despite her tender years, was very much an expert. He really needn't have been worried about anything at all, should have just sat back and enjoyed it, let it all happen.

And yet this current age of enlightenment has given rise to some different issues as the male of the species has to learn how to deal with – and overcome – the rather new set of challenging emotions generated by sexually assertive females. Dominance, it can be said, is usually a much more male trait and it can take a considerable mental shift to allow the testosterone to do its thing in the face of a strong exhibition of oestrogen.

But there are also other feelings that are even stronger than a natural and healthy sex drive, and Georgi was also now finding that his strong bond with Andrei was manifesting itself in a strange way and needed to be dealt with.

This, he thought to himself, as Anastasia jiggled her lovely bottom around again on the stool so that she could thrust her wetness closer to his face, was rather bizarre.

'How about something like this?' she enquired with all the natural innocence of a teenager choosing a new frock in a shop with her girlfriends.

He stared at the rather damp looking entrance to her body. It was, as she had explained earlier, very small and didn't really look like it would be capable of having anything inserted into it. The wonders of nature, of course, would always take care of that, even in the tightest of girls.

'Err, yes, that's very good, yes, that will probably work ok.'

'And do my tits look alright like this? What do you think of this position, Mr. Artist, sir?'

She stuck out her young chest.

'How do you like them Alps?'

He was still somewhat transfixed by the close up sight of a moist, bald female cunt, a sight which most men would be happy to look at forever and which was now just a foot or so away from his face. He was so tempted but, oh, the confusion.

His erection was strong now, very hard and probably very noticeable.

He forced his gaze back and upwards, over a soft taut tummy, slightly bronzed by some light sessions at the tanning salons that were now springing up all over Moscow.

'They look err, spectacular actually' he conceded, noticing as he gazed from below in an upward direction, just how solid and firm the underneath part of her breasts were, so soft yet so solid.

And all natural.

All thriller, no filler.

Anastasia in the nude was a truly magnificent specimen of womanhood.

'Do you want to finger me a bit?' she said suddenly and just as naturally as if she had asked him if he wanted to go for a walk in the park.

But before he could think of an answer – and he was no longer thinking properly anyway – she adjusted her bottom again with another little wiggle and his tongue was suddenly on her, first on the outside, just tasting a bit, the sweetness like a rather earthy kind of honey, a natural nectar, then as she lubricated more, around the distended lips and then, as she clamped both her hands firmly down onto the top of his head, fully inside.

She rocked slowly backwards on the stool for a few moments, thrusting her teenage tits up towards the ceiling as her tension grew, wobbling slightly as she felt herself starting to lose control.

He now felt her ruffling her fingers through his hair as if searching for an anchor point, something firmer to grip on to so that she could steady herself. He tried to pull away for a second so that he could glance up and look at the blood gorged nipples which were now rock hard and providing a kind of pleasurable aching sensation across her whole chest area.

But she resisted, kept his head glued firmly to her crotch with one strong hand while grabbing his fingers with the other and rubbing them slowly across her upper

stomach area before allowing them to naturally move even further upwards.

She was now pressing so hard on him that he had to move his other hand away from holding her smooth bottom to the leg of the coffee table for extra support.

As he did so Anastasia started to feel a growing sense of release and began to elicit small moaning sounds. They had a light rhythm that matched the now vigorous movements of his tongue and had the immediate effect of increasing his own arousal. He quickly swung his spare arm back from the coffee table and grabbed her bottom with it again, pulling her towards him, closer than ever, further down and further in.

He squeezed her bottom tighter, partly out of pleasure and partly to try and introduce some stability to an increasingly unstable structure. Squeezed it, squeezed it harder, then squeezed it again.

Anastasia suddenly let out a loud moan and shook violently. Georgi felt his mouth fill up as a spurt of fluid from deep inside her cunt ran down his throat, and, as he swallowed to try and cope with the volume, gagged slightly, allowing the rest of her ejaculate to spill out onto his lips and run down his chin.

There was a lot of it.

She was now shaking his head quite violently with clenched fists and making strange gasping noises.

Georgi tried to swallow again. Wow, he thought, although it could hardly be called a normal rational thought, that's a lot of cum, really a lot.

As he swallowed a second time, she spurted again, arching her back this time as the pleasure of the ages ran through her young body.

Then, as quickly as it had arrived, it subsided. She went quiet and sagged forward a bit, breathing deeply.

Suddenly she clumped him hard on the shoulder.

'Fucking bastard. Taking advantage of your apprentice model like that. I should call the cops. And me just turned fifteen.'

Georgi started. ' What, you always said you were a year older.'

The legal age of consent in modern Russia is sixteen so this was potentially a two-year problem which could easily become a twenty-two year problem if either party was found guilty of statutory rape.

This was all of a sudden beyond worrying but then, in just a split second or so, he noticed her mischievous grin.

'Haha, gotcha. I think you forgot my little Yamaha there for a moment, silly

boy.'

Of course, her little bike. That meant sixteen at least.

Sixteen. All that mattered.

She'd clearly got her breath back now although the expression on her face was still a bit weird, a kind of sexy determination.

'Anyway I'll let you off as long as you fuck me now. Come on, get your cock out. Let's have a look. I hope you haven't already come in your pants.'

He hadn't, but probably only because his boxers were quite tight and gripped him so snugly.

He did as he was told as she turned around and tipped her torso slightly forward so that she could slide onto him. The lucky boy was then treated to the sight of his young life as her beautiful back and bottom bounced on him as she started up again, quickly into a gentle rhythm and then, after a few minutes of vigorous thrusting, the moaning began again.

Her normally long and free flowing blonde hair was in pigtails for the day so it seemed the most natural and obvious thing for him to do was to hold on to them and use them as light leverage to pull her ever more forcefully down and towards him, taking his cock deeper inside her with each rise and fall.

Georgi hadn't already come, but it didn't take him long now and, as she pressed down on him slowly for about the tenth time and gasped ever louder, he shot a large teenage load into her incredible body which was now lubricating even more than usual around its entrance.

The colourless liquid that had been running down her leg was now mixed with a white creamy substance that started to seep out from inside her. She thrashed about for a few more seconds like a fish caught on a line, all involuntary spasm and shudder, until she suddenly went quiet again, jerking and twitching slightly as his flaccid penis slipped involuntarily out of her, job done.

It had all happened so quickly, as sex does in the bloom of youth, the excitement being all too much.

But just as Georgi started to recover and ponder the full implications of what had just happened, she hopped off him, wiped herself with a tissue, grabbed his hand again and led him into his bedroom.

'Lick it' she insisted.' Lick me out.'

Georgi had imagined his afternoon's work to be over. He was less than keen.

'The rolls will go cold' he tried, not over enthused by her latest demands.

That a young girl could be so forceful, have such an appetite. No wonder Andrei had seemed so tired some mornings.

And he'd thought it was just the heavy duty coding text books.

She ignored his hesitancy and flopped back onto his bed.

'There's no point in buying them warm and then not eating them quickly,' he tried again, aware that he was probably sounding a bit unconvincing.

She opened her legs wide. Her slit looked different to how it had been just fifteen minutes earlier. A huge chasm, now inflamed and a bit raw looking and a very vivid pinkish red in colour, had replaced the very small hole. It appeared to be still producing some fluid, as if she were leaking. Suddenly she quivered again and Georgi realized that she hadn't actually finished. She was having a delayed action orgasm.

'Call me a dirty bitch' she insisted.

Better play along now, he thought.

She was becoming like a wild animal, clearly in the throes of something.

'Dirty bitch.'

'Put your spunky cock in my mouth.'

'It's not hard any more.'

'I don't care. Do it.'

Georgi obliged, just managing to summon up a slight modicum of semi-stiffness.

She sucked hard and then shook again, grabbing his hand and stroking her tits with it.

Georgi got a bit harder.

She removed him for a moment.

'Call me spunky mouthed bitch. I am spunky faced bitch.' she commanded.

'That's an instruction and a statement,' he told her, quite accurately.' Which one do you want me to…..?

'Aaaaaaahhhhhhh' she suddenly shook again, quite violently.

From nowhere Georgi suddenly managed to summon up some more semen which he now fired into the back of Anastasia's mouth with a short hot spurt.

It obviously agreed with her

'Aaaaaaaaahhhhhh. Aaaaaaaaaaahhhhhhh. Oh my god,. Aaaaaaaahhhhhhhhhh. I am a dirty bitch cunt, dirty spunky biitch. Aaaaaaaaaaaaaaahhhhhhhhhhhh.'

And then she froze and went kind of rigid, but still gripping his hand tightly.

'Do you want me to say all that?' he enquired, chivalrously.

She shook one last time and gazed at him with a kind of faraway look on her face. She was wearing a strange expression, almost a sneer. Her lips were slightly parted and her head bobbed slightly as she nodded four, five, six, seven times in quick succession as if some one was tapping her on the back of the head.

Then it was over.

That was the last of it.

It was only mid afternoon but they dozed, the sheer intensity sending them both off.

Chapter 20 – Day two

Harry Shepperton was a cometh the hour, cometh the man, kind of guy. Unlike the many previous incumbents who had carried that particular mantle before him, people like Winston Churchill for example, Harry didn't just show up once. He made a habit of it by leading his team of talented and bright young operatives on a series of successive missions. They were all characterized by levels of complexity which required multiple skill sets to unravel and solve. While his team were a bunch of energetic twenty and thirty year olds, Harry was slowly approaching fifty. Still fit, strong and vital, he possessed all the necessary leadership skills required to manage The Nines effectively.

Good communicator, loads of integrity, totally supportive, good problem solver, uncanny intuition, results driven and on and on. But there was one other attribute he possessed which made him stand out most, even though it was totally invisible and never on show.

Harry Shepperton could sleep like a baby.

No matter how troubling or worrying the mission, he had the natural ability to switch off at night. No matter how late it was, or how tiring the day had been, Harry could shut it all out. He wouldn't even spare the day's proceedings a second thought. As soon as his head hit the pillow, he was gone.

And so, despite a lateish de-brief and a few shorts with Hazel in her office the night before, he awoke fresh as a daisy at his usual time around 5am on the second day of what was now officially project Jumbo, in effect the hunt to track down the world's largest ever missing elephant, one which had now been gone just over twenty four hours ever since his pre-dawn stroll to the bank the day before.

Despite his ability to demonstrate non-stop flexibility whenever required, Harry was also a creature of habit whenever that was permitted by the rigours of his job. If circumstances allowed, he would always take breakfast on his own, not too difficult for such an early riser, while his family continued sleeping peacefully upstairs in their sprawly double fronted three-story townhouse in Chiswick which backed on to the river. As he brewed his morning coffee his only companions were the crack–of–dawn rowing crews who powered up and down the Thames, just beyond the bottom edge of

his lawn.

Having a kitchen up on the second floor gave him something of a panoramic view as they appeared under Kew railway bridge off to the north, and sped past moments later. Despite the hugely strenuous exertions on display, he always found it soothing and calming, something that he was used to, something that anchored the start of his day.

Whether it was the relaxing nature of the water or the rhythm of the rowers, he could never say. What he did know was that it always helped him with his period of reflection, as it now did on this rather odd morning where the whole world was waking up strange and completely different. A world without money had a very peculiar feel to it and, although his team had a kind of rough plan, he knew that they would need to step up more and more with each passing day.

It would have been a daunting task for most men. But he wasn't most men. And The Nines no normal team. Rapid acceleration came easy enough to them. They were used to it, designed to do it, thrived on it. Nought to sixty, under a second. No problem

He reviewed.

JoJo and Cait had been working on the tech all night. Hank Wyatt was flying in from Boston and meeting them for breakfast. Between the three of them they should have some thoughts on how the whole thing had been done by lunchtime. The banks' own teams had also been flat out now for twenty four hours and were giving a press conference in Geneva at 9am. All the immediate red herring claims had been examined and discounted by various members of the security services all over the world. Only one semi-serious contender had survived their scrutiny although the communiqué had plenty of detractors because of the style of the message with its street punk poetic idealism. Nonetheless he had sent both Paul and then Liam off to Moscow to pursue it as the only lead of any significance they had.

Up the road in The Bunker, recently renamed in a flurry of woke politics, Professor Jake was point man and would have been up all night, tracking developments.

The toaster pinged a couple of times. Harry buttered his toast, covered it liberally with Golden Shred marmalade, then sat down in his window seat and called him.

'Morning boss, get your seven hours in ok?' Jake's warm Texan twang always sounded so cheery, the perfect guy to talk to first thing any morning.

'Yes, I did thanks. The world may be broken but at least my sleep isn't. Some small consolation, I suppose. Everybody ok?'

'So far, so good. Hank's early, picked up some Jetstream on the way across. He's due in to Heathrow round eight. Billy's just left to collect him and then they'll heading straight over to Ifield, ETA in Chelsea with the girls, around 9:30.'

'You speak to him?'

'Yup, he rang from Logan so he's up to speed.'

'Good. Paul get in ok?'

'Yup, in the early hours. Decided to get his sightseeing in before he started work. Started the day with a very long walk, just as it got light.'

'Not a bad idea. I always try and do that after a flight if I have time. Good way to kick start yourself in new surroundings.'

'Yeah, said he hadn't been before so a bit of orientation en route to his hotel'

'And Liam?'

'Still in the air, he's about four hours behind Paul. Had to work his way through a load of security footage. You know, bike girl?'

'Or bike boy with pigtail? How far did he get"

'As far as a local branch of McDonalds, would you believe.'

'And then?'

'Trail seemed to go mysteriously cold. So that's his first port of call, to follow up on that.'

'Ok. Any more whispers anywhere?'

'No, nothing. But then yesterday was a strange day all round, wasn't it and I think everybody was knocked off their feet a bit by what happened. Remember how we all were in the briefing. I know it was only 7 in the morning but you could sense the shock. Despite all the training, some things are so totally unexpected that you kind of seize up a bit. It'll pass quickly, I'm sure. I'll be surprised if we don't hear anything else today, the whole incident is just such an impossible thing to keep under wraps.'

'Well, lets hope you're right. We could use a break from somewhere.'

'Anything back from the banks?'

'They've accepted our offer of direct help. We can attach somebody from here to their own task force from anytime after lunch today.'

Harry took a long gulp of his Arabica and watched yet another double scull cruise

past through the early mist on the low morning tide. The four oars glanced across the surface of the water in perfect symmetry as a faint dawn light broke onto the trees and rooftops on the opposite bank.

'After lunch?'

'That's what they said.'

'Any particular reason?'

'All hands on deck for this morning's presentation.'

'Which is 9 London time.'

'Correct.'

'And then what?'

'They have a long Q and A with the world's press.'

'What. All of them?'

'Well, hopefully not. They're quite a large team. We reckon around a hundred.'

'And they can't spare anybody to de-brief one of ours till the afternoon? Don't seem right somehow.'

'Agreed. You want me to be a bit more insistent?'

Harry pondered the situation for a minute.

'Well, I had Hank penciled in for it, what with his financial background and all. Odd though it is'

'Understood, I agree completely. He's our best guy for that, definitely.'

'Nothing to stop you attending their press conference though. Might be a good use of your time. Get yourself over there.'

'Ok, I'd best grab a couple of hours first then, can I put on a divert to you as you're now up and running for the day?'

Harry watched yet another boat glide by, this one headed south where it would shortly hit the next kink in the river, a broad curve that would take it round a bend and then back up under Barnes bridge on the other side. In less than a minute it would disappear from sight. It would still be there of course, but Harry wouldn't be able to see it.

'Of course. No problem. Catch you later on.'

'So long, boss. Speak soon.'

Harry stood up and craned his neck.

The boat had vanished.

An image of David Copperfield suddenly popped into his head.

Chapter 21 – The tennis club

There are those who insist that the best way to deal with a crisis is to become completely immersed in it. Quite a few others believe that space and distance lend objectivity and perspective, essential ingredients for most solutions. Hazel Ingliss belonged firmly in the former camp. She was a highly social beast anyway so networking her way through life came naturally. Why stop when things get difficult?

Since her last debrief with Harry she had been flat out on Jumbo. That drop – everything – just - do- this kind of moment doesn't come along very often. Her job usually meant keeping lots of balls in the air simultaneously most of the time, a skill which she managed with consummate ease. Tackling six or seven major problems every day was very much part of her routine.

But so was downtime. The way she figured it, relaxing and exercising not only helped, they contributed positively, both to her wellbeing as a person and her effectiveness as boss of the top team.

Over the years she'd tried most sports until, like many people, she found the one that suited her best. Squash was great but too violent. Jogging was great but boring and the road shock was a killer for the knees. Swimming was also great but even more boring. Cycling made her bum hurt. Gym workouts were a bit too punishing.

But tennis, now that was different.

Tennis suited her down to the ground.

It was mostly outdoors so lots of fresh air.

It was part cardio, part co-ordination, part balance, so offered a degree of variety.

But mostly it was highly social so it offered lots of networking opportunities. Usually with a few G and T's thrown in for good measure.

She had a regular group of girlfriends with whom she usually played. They would often sit for hours on the terrace outside the club afterwards dissecting the post Covid world and all its strange changes. Some good, some less so.

Hazel was not the same early bird that Harry was so it was late morning by the time she parked up her new BMW i3 at the club.

Old Father Thames rolled slowly past the small wall at the bottom end of the car park, as it had been doing forever. She paused to look at it for a few seconds. No matter the tribulations of the world, watching the river flow always seemed to soothe

most situations, somehow the more troubling the problem, the more the balm of the rhythmically flowing water seemed to ease it.

The Putney club was barely a mile from her house and she could have easily walked it with her kit thrown over her shoulder. But she knew her friends had all heard about her new all-electric car so she didn't want to deprive them of a viewing. They would, of course, have plenty else to talk about that particular day. The lunchtime match was only for starters, the pally banter that came later being very much the main course.

Kelly and Smiffy teamed up against her and Mags and they sweated a couple of hours away playing doubles under a light midday sun before heading for the showers and the bar.

The four old school friends had known each other forever and always treasured their time together. It took a lot for them not to be able to meet up regularly and they aimed at once a month or so.

Even on a day like this, as a global crisis was unfolding around them, they managed to find the time for some sport. Truth be told, that was very much the secondary reason, since all the girls had a very good sense of Hazel's lofty position in MI6 and couldn't wait to get some inside track.

'How can something like that even happen?' Mags started them off.

She was the one real sports star of the group having taken up pro golf as a teenager and made a handsome living from it over the years. As a result she had probably lost more than all her three friends put together the previous day, notwithstanding the fact that they were all well off in their own right.

'It's bloody computers to blame' Kelly offered. 'It was inevitable that something like this would happen one day. Using them for money was just a disaster waiting to happen. Governments should have banned that years ago, shouldn't you Haze?'

Hazel was used to being the target for all and anything which had a Government component to it. People tend to conveniently forget that nations are run by very large groups of people with very little individual accountability.

Therein, of course, pretty much in a nutshell, lies much of the problem.

'I'm not the PM, Kells,' she responded softly ' and even if I was, things like that have their own momentum. Be a bit like trying to stop a runaway train. It's just evolution, you know, the world changing. Just part of life.'

'But it can hardly be called progress when we go backwards, can it' Mags

continued, understandably the most agitated member of the group after finding herself about twelve million down overnight. 'Remember that Greece thing back in '08 or whenever it was. All of a sudden people could only get 50 Euros max from the machines because the system had a partial collapse. Why weren't any lessons learnt from that?'

'I'm not a banker, girls,' Hazel reminded them. 'Those guys have their own rules and live in their own world. You only had to look at this mornings broadcast from Geneva. Did that guy look worried to you? Don't get me wrong. I'm pleased he was so calm and collected but I did think it kind of summed up that whole world. Sailing serenely on while everything else all around us starts to fall apart.'

Smiffy was poking her vegetable bake with the kind of professional curiosity her status as a celebrity chef demanded. She was going to thoroughly enjoy eating it but only after she had managed to crack the secret code of the mixed ingredients. She tried a mouthful with a dreamy look on her face.

'That is just so good' she told them, slightly disconnected.' Sorry if I drool a bit for a moment. Do carry on. I am listening.'

'I mean I use computers a lot, all the time really I suppose' Kelly started up again. 'In my line of work, they're unavoidable. If we don't keep on top of the latest trends, we're dead. '

Kelly's love of design and colours and styles and cultures had taken her from college into the global fashion industry where the pace of change from day to day was a genuine force to be reckoned with.

'No doubt about their value to us at all. We can track stuff, replicate changes overnight or tweak them into something new, and then deliver to anywhere in the world within days. No computers, no business. Simple as that.'

'This isn't going to be the end of digital technology,' Hazel reminded them, 'that's here to stay. It has its ups and downs and we just have to get used it'

Her three friends all looked at her.

Even Smiffy seemed to finally tune back in.

'Are you saying this was a normal setback, Haze. Something that was always going to happen? That's not what that smarmy banker bloke said, was it. Totally unprecedented and unexpected, I think were his exact words.'

They had been a bit taken aback that Hazel sounded almost as if she'd been expecting it, that dreadful thing that had just happened. The harsh reality was that in

Hazel Ingliss' world she was always expecting the unexpected, was in fact trained for it, a fact she now attempted to explain to them.

'No, I'm not saying that at all. My point is just the opposite. It feels like a setback but in reality it's really just brutal evolution. When man first split the atom, it was a scientific breakthrough. Nobody could draw a straight line from that to a nuclear bomb.'

'Exactly. Most innovation tends to be for the good. And then the bloody military get hold of it and 'eff it up.' Smiffy obviously felt strongly enough about that particular point to temporarily pause her enjoyment of today's artichoke special.

'You think the military are behind this then?' Kelly asked her.

'Why not? They're behind most things aren't they? After all, it's them that's always preventing disclosure, isn't it.'

Smiffy was the team hippy, her pacifist views and dreams of life on Mars all well known to her dearest friends.

'The CIA know everything, you know.' she continued to confide. 'They even keep stuff from the President so he doesn't have to lie when reporters ask him. You should call the CIA up Haze. They'll know what's going on. They always do.'

Hazel thought about the text update she'd received from Jojo in her car on the way over. Colonel Hank Wyatt of the United States Air Force (Retired) and formerly of the CIA was her 3pm, in just over an hour.

She just grinned back at Smiffy, who was now busy tucking in again.

Smiffy acknowledged the look by raising her right palm. *Ok, so obviously you've already done that, course you have love, silly me, sorry.*

'Have you got one of your teams on this yet.' Kelly wanted to know. Their knowledge of exactly what Hazel did was pretty good but necessarily imperfect. A general awareness was essential, otherwise how could she share anything with them at all, her nearest and dearest, but the detail was something else.

They'd heard about a special team within the UK security service that had been specially recruited to get involved in these types of situations. Whenever they teased her about them, she just teased right back.

'You know those brainboxes with the fancy IQ's. They'd be good at this as well Haze. And aren't they our guys mostly? So no need to call Uncle Sam.'

The girls had no way of knowing that five of that team were now directly involved and working flat out on their third project in an attempt to save the world's

money.

'I never know what all the different teams are doing at any one moment' Hazel said, quite truthfully.' There's always so much going on.'

'But this is a priority, surely. A global emergency.'

'Yes, course it is, I agree.'

'So, come on Haze, spill the beans. Tell us who did it. I bet it's the Russians, those devious Cossack bastards.'

Well, that's a bit uncanny, she thought to herself, immediately wondering what Paul and Liam were up to in Moscow and whether they had made any progress yet on their rather slender leads.

They were her 5pm.

'I can't tell you what I don't know Kells,' she offered, again, quite truthfully. 'It's a tech jigsaw as much as anything else at the moment. We've got some of the pieces and we're putting them together, but there's still quite a few bits missing.'

'How can it have happened in the first place' Mags asked her that same question again. 'All them bank safeguards and security measures and passwords and whatnot. Aren't they supposed to have their own firewalls and things? I mean hacking one bank is allegedly impossible, but all of them?'

She took a large swig of Chardonnay.

'And all at the same time. I mean, come on. Please.'

Another swig.

'A coordinated hit on every single bank network. It's just so unlikely, so improbable. You cannot possibly believe that this is just a rogue hit by a couple of expert hackers. It's organized crime, isn't it? Must be.'

One of the things Hazel got from these meetings with her friends was the chance to see the problem of the moment – whatever it was – through the eyes of others. They would normally just have most of the same thoughts that her own people had but even that – repetitive though it was – was helpful in its own way by way of corroboration.

The genuine majority view was always that of real people rather than the driven agenda of the mass media. Mags was only just emphasizing the predominant thoughts of most people around the world as they woke up that morning to day two of the crisis.

Hazel had her finger on the pulse.

Day one: shell-shocked.

Day two: recovered a bit and started to think normally again.

A common theme was starting to emerge. Most people had now formed the opinion that this was a heist that had been organized on a grand scale. Nothing else made any sense.

Hazel sensed the drift in opinion. Not away from anything in particular and not towards anything in particular, because the authorities had never given any serious indication about their own suspicions. For the very good reason that they were still largely clueless about what had happened.

Mags, in inadvertently confirming the mood of the moment, had worried Hazel, worried her a lot.

As head of the UK's internal security, it was never her job to have a preferred position on any of the numerous work packages which dropped on her desk. Her role was to analyse them, to understand them and then to allocate resource appropriately – to Harry's team and The Nines in this case – in order that others may solve the problem, whatever it was.

To be effective she had to be an ace delegator. And for that to happen, she had to be able to let things go. Not completely of course, but just enough to allow her troops enough breathing space to do their own jobs.

By necessity, that implied a certain distance between her and the operational moment. And what worried her now was that gap. What her team were working on very much had the feel of something that had been carried out by individuals. And clearly nobody else in the world was thinking that.

She was used to being in a minority of one. But this, given the stakes involved, suddenly somehow felt different.

'We don't have any reason to suspect The Mafia, Mags.' she offered.' Although it would be very much their kind of thing. I'll give you that, right enough'

'How come they wheeled you out to do the telly briefing yesterday anyway?' Smiffy asked, polishing off the rest of her bake and a spinach and soya side dish. 'I nearly peed myself when I saw you come in. I was in the bloody studio next door you know, doing some rehearsals.'

'Sorry Babes. I didn't know you'd be in there or I'd have pinged you. Not that I really knew where I was going. God, I barely knew what I was doing. They gave me an hour's notice.'

'Hmm. The mighty Hazel Ingliss didn't know what she was doing. Well that's a first' Kelly offered.

'True in this case. They just needed a holding statement and somebody put my name up. Didn't like to refuse. It was a bit like a King and Country kind of thing. Needed doing. And sharpish.'

'Are your guys working with the banks now then? Kelly asked.' They're all well dodgy if you ask me. Wouldn't trust them as far as I could throw them.'

Hazel thought about Jake's morning flight to Geneva.

Harry had told her he'd sent him on a whim, a hunch, a feeling, something.

Undefined though it was, that was always good enough for her

Jake was her 7pm.

'I can neither confirm nor deny,' Hazel said, raising her G and T. ' Cheers.'

Kelly, Smiffy and Mags always knew intuitively when they had got as much as they could from Hazel. They loved her to bits and, their rampant female curiosities notwithstanding, fully respected her professional boundaries.

They ordered another round of drinks and spent the rest of the afternoon talking about the idiocy of bike lanes, the mysteries of electric cars and the cool young Italian waiter who was on duty that day.

But not necessarily in that order.

Chapter 22 – Raspo's

It is a commonly held belief that Italian Catholics are amongst the most devout believers anywhere in the world. But the same can easily be said for followers of the Russian Orthodox Church who have sought refuge in religion for much of the twentieth century as the scourge of communism ravaged their country.

As an ideology it had no place for any competition. Anything which was thought to distract the citizenry from their duties to the state was initially frowned upon, and then banned. Such circumstances quickly lead – as they inevitably will – to persecution on a grand scale and, in order to deprive believers of their right to worship, large numbers of churches were destroyed on a massive scale all over Russia.

In their madness the Soviets even obliterated their own history as they went along. Places like the Old Trinity Cathedral in St Petersburg, a building revered by the locals and where Peter the Great had been crowned emperor in 1721, and the Cathedral of Christ the Saviour in Moscow, were both torn down in a rage of political righteousness. The logic was brutal. If they could get rid of all thoughts of God and Emperor in one fell swoop then so much the better.

But the good people of Russia took scant notice of the demands of the monster Stalin and his brutal henchmen and took their chances in the large numbers of secret chapels which had sprung up all over the country. Many of them paid for their disobedience with their lives as they refused to betray their consciences. To this day the country has not forgotten those dark periods in its history and the magnificent churches of modern Russia once again soar to the heavens in colourful splendour and with a renewed vigour.

So in much the same way that the Vatican is touchy about unfrocking misbehaving priests, so the presence of a controversial religious figure bang in the middle of the country's predominant revolution is still a sensitive subject in Russia today.

The fact that Rasputin was not actually an ordained priest but more likely what we would call today an alternative therapist is part of the confusion. His behaviour confounds historians to this day but, as a court outsider who suddenly developed

much favour with the Empress Alexandra by providing unexplained medical assistance for her haemophiliac son Alexei, he quickly fell foul of the inner circle.

In December 1916 he was poisoned, stabbed, shot and then thrown in the Little Nevka.

Whoever it was who had him murdered weren't taking any chances.

At 47, he had been almost the same age as Tsar Nicholas and his alleged lover, the Empress herself, who barely outlived him by eighteen months before being murdered by the Bolsheviks in a cellar in Yekaterinaburg on the collective instructions of the unlikely sounding Ural Soviet of Workers' and Soldiers' Deputies.

Rumours of the involvement of the British SIS in his death have never been confirmed or denied, there having been much speculation that he was trying to persuade the German born Empress to promote a separate Russian peace with Germany, something which would have dramatically affected the balance of power on the western front in World War One.

"Blimey," thought Paul, as he finished off this piece of local history reading in his taxi on the way over to Tverskay41, *"no wonder they're still a bit touchy about him. I wonder if Harry knew about that last bit."*

He probably didn't.

Not many people do.

You have to be careful with the word *bar*. In most places it's just a drinking joint, a watering hole. But in other countries it will be a loosely disguised brothel, a bordello, occasionally a laufhaus.

Quite what this one would be didn't really bother Paul too much. It was 1 in the afternoon, that's a very different 1 to its post-midnight sister.

What he was primarily bothered about was that Valeria would show.

The Bankers' press conference had overrun slightly after the reporter from Izvestia had prompted a bit of a furore with his final question, so Paul was running more than a bit late. He'd needed to hear the responses though, the answer to the question about nutters in Moscow. If the bank spokesman knew what the Izvestia correspondent was referring to, then he did a very good acting job as he dismissed it out of hand.

But then, that is, of course, what professional spokespeople do the world over. They are nothing if not great actors.

He needn't have worried.

She was there.

And somehow, for somebody who, as Leo had told him, was not due off shift till 1 pm, she had managed to change.

One should never underestimate the propensity of women to manage to look their best under the most demanding of circumstances and at extremely short notice.

It wasn't so much a short skirt as a pair of very long legs that made her posture on the high barstool so striking. Everything else though was very understated, not in the least flirty. Because she hardly needs that, Paul thought, noticing straight away on this second meeting, quite a lot that he hadn't really taken in before. Her face on the small side but with beautiful almond coloured eyes, her hair long and lustrous now she'd let it down properly, her skin lightly tanned but the right side of orange, so probably genuine, her smile a proper Russian icebreaker.

She broke off from her conversation with the barman who wandered off as Paul came over, all ready to do that one thing men should never have to do when meeting a lady.

Apologise for being late.

She beat him to the punch.

'Mr. Lambert. I hope you are well rested. I got your message from Leo. I hope your room is to your satisfaction. Can I offer you one of our local specialities?'

Paul was about to object.

It was his invite.

He should be doing that. Not her.

Too late again. The barman was back.

'Martini Moscow' she ordered.

Paul looked at her quizzically.

'Shaken not stirred.'

The barman smiled.

Paul rode the wave well.

'Interesting choice. That what 007 drinks when he pops in?'

'I wouldn't know. I've never met him. Have you?'

She held his stare.

Ok, this was suddenly beyond interesting. Had she rumbled him or was this just a joke.

'Not recently, no. I don't get out much these days.'

'You got to Moscow pretty easily at short notice.' she observed drily. 'In the middle of a crisis.'

'Well yes, but I'm sure going back will be harder. The next few days are likely to see a lot of changes.'

'I agree. How long are you staying?'

'Till I get my work done.'

He was going to have to tell her some of it so he'd need to open up a fraction. He decided to take his chance.

She was ahead of him again.

'You're part of it aren't you.' she cocked her head slightly to one side in inquisitive mode.

Do all young Russian women do that!

'Whatever it is.' she continued.

All of a sudden she wasn't looking like just your average hotel receptionist any more.

'Well not really, no. Not in the kind of way you're thinking.'

'How many ways are there?'

Goodness, she was sharp.

'Well there's two. There's only ever two.'

'Explain.'

'There's the right side. There's the wrong side.'

'And in between.'

'Is just a chasm of confusion. Not somewhere you really want to be. Although, regrettably, it is where most people end up.'

'I think you talk in riddles now. You could be Russian.' she teased.

'Well I'm not. You've seen my passport. Did it look fake?'

'It looked convincing.' she answered, intriguingly.

Now that's not an answer you get very often, not put like that.

'So which side are you on then Mr. Lambert. You good guy or bad guy?'

'I tell you what. I'm going to let you be the best judge of that' he offered.

'Ok. Well I'd supposed you'd asked me to come here for more than just a drink and a chat about the bar owner.'

'Sorry.'

'A chat about Raspo.'

'The owner is really called Rasputin?'

'My,my, Mr. Lambert. You really wouldn't be any good as 007, would you? Don't you know you have to do your homework to be a good agent.'

She was teasing him again. Who was this girl?

'And if you'd done it you would know that my friend here,' the barman waved cheerily over at them both 'is called Ryszard Rasputin, or Rik for short because that's Richard in Russian. And that when he bought the bar a couple of years ago he had the dilemma of calling it either Rick's or Rasputin's, choosing between either the world's most famous American bar or the world's most famous Russian person. Or one of them anyway.' she smiled knowingly. 'Personally I think he made a good choice.'

And with that she raised her glass.

'Cheers, Mr. Englishman. Nostrovia'

Paul made his decision.

'I need to do a few local things while I'm here' he started. 'And I'm going to need some help.'

He paused for the reaction.

'Ok. I'm intrigued, but I do have a day job as well you know.'

'And what is that exactly? The real job behind the job?'

'Ah, Mr.Lambert. Russia can be complicated. A riddle within a mystery wrapped up in a puzzle. Isn't that what your nice Mr. Churchill said?'

'An Enigma.'

'What?'

'He said enigma, not puzzle.'

'Sounds like some sort of coding machine. Same thing though.'

'You'd know about coding machines then, would you?'

He grinned at her, the laugh lines around his eyes breaking out.

'In your day job as a hotel receptionist?'

'What is it you want, Mr. Lambert. I need to know that before I can figure out if I can help you at all. What exactly brought you to Moscow?'

Now it was Paul's turn to cock his head slightly to one side. He was just weighing up how much to tell her when his mobile rang.

It was only day two. Most things were still working. Airlines. Hotels. Phones. Bars. But how long would it be until the deterioration started. A civilization based

largely on the ability of everybody to perform financial interactions would soon start to struggle and disintegrate without them.

He looked down at the screen.

Dempsey 9-6.

'Sorry, the office. Just give me a tick', he waved his cell at Valeria as he backed away a short distance.

'Liam. You get in ok?'

'Yup, no problems. Well, not until now that is.'

'I'm listening.'

'I tracked pigtail person to a McDonalds. She went in, grabbed some lunch, went to the loo, did a quick change, went back to the counter and then vanished.'

'Well we hardly expected the author of the note to be an innocent bystander in all this, did we?'

'No, that's true. She did leave a clue though. Well, kind of left one, but didn't.'

'What do you mean?'

'She arrived on her bike. Left on foot.'

'With burgers or without?'

'That's what I thought. You'd want to keep the food warm wouldn't you? If you were taking it home, that is. So clearly she wasn't.'

'What did she order?'

'A couple of quarter pounders with chips.'

'Food for two. At least two.'

'And there's a park almost directly opposite.'

'What's it called?'

He looked back at Valeria, who had re-engaged Rik/ Raspo in conversation while he'd wandered off.

'Hang on. I'll check.'

She looked up and smiled as he came back over to the bar area.

'Left your briefcase in the office Mr. Lambert? You'll have to nip back for it then. What a bummer.'

'Have your guys got any surveillance in Staraya Park?'

She stared at him.

Well that hadn't taken long.

Rik / Raspo heard the exchange and reached down behind the bar, his hands out

of sight. There were a load of glasses down there that needed sparkling and polishing.

It wasn't them that Paul was worried about.

'It wasn't us.' he said quickly. 'And now I'm starting to believe it wasn't you either, otherwise you wouldn't be quite so interested in me, would you?' he concluded.

'Unless it's personal of course.'

He smiled at Valeria and the laugh lines lit his face up again.

Hmm. Pretty cool guy, Rik /Raspo thought, considering I could kill him right now and nobody would ever know.

'But they would know.'

Valeria and RR looked at each other quizzically.

'Know what'

'If you picked up that gun and shot me.'

RR's hands froze.

'Because I'm filming you. Here, look. Say hello to Liam'

He turned his phone round.

Liam waved a cheery wave.

'Top of 'da mornin' to yous.'

'Your office is in Staraya Square?' Valeria asked, quickly spotting a rather familiar looking statue in the background.

'We have a lot of offices. They tend to be wherever we tend to be. If you see what I mean.'

'Always make the most of whatever you find around you.' RR chimed in. 'We obviously share the same training manuals.'

As Paul had suspected, she'd led him into a Lion's den. That's what happens when you let somebody else have choice of venue. Although that wasn't quite the case here.

He looked at both of them, searching for the next clue.

'So who do I deal with?'

RR had his hands back on top of the bar now and had started sparkling up his glasses.

He nodded in Valeria's direction.

'Well, she's the boss.'

Chapter 23 – Geneva

The Swiss are good with money. Everybody knows that. The country is a magnet for savers the world over looking to squeeze that extra one or two percent more interest out of their investments. And the numerous banks and funds which reside there are remarkably good at delivering on those perennial customer requirements.

That is nothing new. It is a strikingly beautiful country but one with secrets, one with possibly even more enigmas than the ever – increasing number of Russians who had started flocking to their shores since the late nineties. They were suddenly the world's *nouveau riche* – the new rich in English – although somehow the original French phrase seems to summon up the spirit of such changes in circumstance much better.

Perhaps unsurprisingly many of these new arrivals still liked the old ways when it came to trusting their money to somebody else to look after.

And the Swiss have been doing that for centuries.

Legends abound of the gold and art of the ages being secreted away there, stashed in clandestine vaults and being discretely managed by professionals of various persuasions. Some of it booty from the church, some from the crusades, some from the newer wars. Once it ended up there a certain quietness would usually descend on any issues of provenance and legacy ownership.

They sure love their money but they don't always talk about it too much

So modern day Switzerland has a reputation to protect, something it thinks about on a daily basis. The country needs to keep its guard up against the gangsters and charlatans of the world of whom there will always be a large number and who come in all shapes and sizes, the villains and ruffians of yesteryear now the digital bandits of today.

These are difficult enemies to fight, tricky opponents to combat. A bit like the modern day terrorist, they tend to use the cloak of invisibility to carry out their attacks. The French have a word for them too – *les brigands du nouvel age.* These are not armies who appear on the horizon through the morning fog marching towards their fight. Their key weapons are not the roar of the cannon, nor the cries of terror from mother earth as her soil is ripped and shredded by explosive artillery.

It is, in fact, the complete opposite.

Stealth and silence.

Swiss banking is, therefore, perhaps best considered as a global brand, with a set of values that are the foundation of the promise it makes to those who will use it.

It is discrete and will not tell.

It is fathomless in its ability to create new wealth.

It is honest in its application of international law.

And, finally, it is hugely experienced and has seen it all before.

Well, most things anyway.

In his seventh floor office overlooking the lake, Guillaume Sagné was busy finishing off the email to his old friend Harry Shepperton.

Yes, Harry, of course we can fix a time to review your accounts.

I will get Sandrine to call you with some dates.

Might have to wait a few weeks though till this latest nightmare is over.

Quelle catastrophe

All the best

Ton Ami

Guillaume

He was surprised when his PC pinged again almost straight away.

Thanks Guillaume

Probably best I come a bit earlier.

Soon as, in fact.

See you in the morning

Hope that's not too intrusive, you know, duty calls and all that

Cheers for now

Harry

As an essential part of modern banking practice Guillaume had had to ask Harry a few questions several years earlier when he had first wanted to open his account. Governments everywhere, in their rush to tax anything that moved, had introduced so called money-laundering regulations so that they could snoop even more on their citizens, allegedly to spot the bad ones, in reality to exert even more control on the good ones. The banks had a new code of practice to follow to enforce this tyranny and there was a bit of a script.

He looked away from his screen for a moment and smiled as he thought back.

Outside it was a beautiful spring day and now, at lunchtime, the sun dappled the waters of Lac Leman with the occasional choppy wave washing across from the small tourist boats which were adding to the light almost imperceptible movements of the water.

He was over six hundred miles from Putney but Guillaume felt that same sense of calm that Hazel Ingliss was experiencing around the same time. The soothing power of the waters, rhythmic and eternal. He remembered that Harry had commented on the beauty of that view from his sixth floor terrace where they had chosen to sit outside.

It had been an identical type of day.

'How much do you wish to deposit, Monsieur Shepperton?'

'Two fifty.'

'Pounds presumably? Although the denomination doesn't matter to us.'

'Yes, pounds.'

'And the source of the funds?'

'Her Majesty's Government of the United Kingdom.'

'Ah, some kind of contract.'

'Err, no. Not quite.'

'I see. Explain please.'

'I work for them.'

'Ah.'

Guillaume switched gears faster than Lewis Hamilton in the back straight. As the youthful Director of a Swiss boutique bank he had already mastered the art of asking people about their money.

The direct approach was always doomed to failure.

Can you tell me how you came by this money?

No. Fuck off. What's it got to do with you?

That was twenty years ago. After the new changes had been introduced all new clients had become obliged to answer that question.

But there was still a way to ask it.

'Ok, just indulge me for a moment here. If I asked to see your tax records would you anticipate any problems in providing them?'

'No, of course not. But I would need a good reason why you need to see them.'

'It's the law.'

'Then there's no better reason, so no problem.'

Harry spent his life protecting life and liberty under the law so he not only respected it, but knew a whole lot about it too.

'Just out of curiosity, is that Swiss law?'

'No, it's international. You Brits, the Yanks, the Japs, everybody. It's a new way of catching the bad guys.'

'Funny that I haven't heard of it then because that's pretty much what I do for a living.'

Guillaume's tried and tested softly softly approach was working.

Slowly, slowly.

'You're a government lawyer?'

'No, not even close I'm afraid.'

Harry had his own rather direct way of disarming people who got too nosey about his work.

'I run a team of spies.'

Guillaume, like most people, laughed at first, and then pondered the correct follow-on response.

It was nearly always Fleming related.

'Oh, like double o double o's. Licensed to kill for Queen and Country.'

'Quite the opposite, actually. My guys wouldn't know one end of a gun from the other. Well, one would, but he hates guns.'

'Unarmed spies. That's novel.'

'I was joking Monsieur Sagné. Do you think people who really do that for a living own up to it.'

'Then what exactly do they do then? Your guys.'

'They solve problems.'

'The type that involve clean up crews turning up later?'

'I'm afraid you've been watching too many movies, Monsieur. We don't do dead bodies in hotels anymore. Hell, people have to sleep in those places.'

But Guillaume's slow dance was working.

Slowly, slowly.

'Well, yes, that's true, I do. It's my favourite form of escapism. But then I did always think the general image of that profession was a bit off. It just can't be that glamorous, can it? I mean not knowing who you can trust all the time. Absolutely

unthinkable in my line of business.'

'It's not quite that bad.' Harry said, slipping into the trap a bit. 'I'd trust my guys with my life, for example.'

'Must be all hand picked then? I presume you chose them all yourself?'

'Didn't quite work out like that actually. Not this time.'

The recruitment of The Nines had always jarred a bit with Harry.

Not that he had any problems with any of his team as individuals. Far from it, their calibre was beyond question. It was just that they had been served up to him like some fine dinner on a silver plate. Selected somewhere else by somebody else. The legendary Sir Walter Tweedy, no doubt.

HIs analytical mind didn't like gaps and this was one that he'd had to learn to live with. Still didn't like it though, especially when it just cropped up innocently in conversation.

Like now, for instance.

Harry continued to tip toe around this sensitive subject, aware that he would probably have to divulge more than he really wanted about his profession in order to pass these latest onerous tests as currently imposed by the global banking community.

Guillaume soldiered on.

'And can we expect additional deposits on a regular basis. Perhaps in line with your salary payments?'

'Yes, that's rather the plan.'

'And, if you'll just humour me a bit longer, Monsieur Shepperton, how much are they likely to be?'

Harry felt himself being backed into a corner, not a feeling he enjoyed.

'About ten to twelve.'

'Weekly?'

Harry glared, feeling slightly miffed now.

'Do I look like a Premiership footballer?' he retorted.

'Ah ok, ok. So every month. Shall we call it about 100k annually then?' he asked, scribbling free form on his desk pad with the rather expensive looking fountain pen he kept specially for these initial sessions.

He had several Montblanc special editions, all different colours, each of which he only used for specific types of meetings.

Opening new accounts – like today – the blue one, assessing riskier investments,

the red one, working with a client who he thought was going places, the multi coloured green one, dealing with loss situations or closing accounts – always sadder occasions - the black one. It somehow kept him on track as he navigated his way through the different sets of rules and requirements presented by each situation. The fact that he could see the real Mont Blanc from the terrace of his elegant chalet home high up in the hills behind Geneva made his pen of choice an even more obvious selection for those regular daily facets of his work.

Harry was currently vacillating between blue and multi-coloured en route to becoming a client although he still didn't know that.

Just a few more questions and then Guillaume would decide on the appropriate account and welcome yet another new customer to the ancient tradition of Swiss banking. But, ever cautious, like the good Swiss he was, he still needed a bit more clarity.

So, when in doubt, or even just struggling a bit, always try resorting to a tried and tested old chestnut.

'That's enough about work. Now, why don't you just tell me a little bit about yourself.'

It's generally surprising how most people struggle with five minutes talking about themselves without betraying some details of their work life. Guillaume normally managed to flesh out enough of whatever else he needed to know in that short additional piece of time.

But Harry Shepperton wasn't most people.

Fifteen minutes later he was none the wiser about Harry's job, but he was a lot clearer about Harry the man.

Some people just have a lot about them. As a banker Guillaume knew how to count. He could add up two and two and he was getting the right answer. This guy was the real deal. The body language was right, the back story made sense, his education and experiences all added up. He had the bearing of the British army officer who had passed out at Sandhurst twenty five years earlier and who had subsequently moved across to the other ranks where intelligence was even more key.

He'd given his home address as Chiswick which Guillaume knew well from attending that annual English curiosity known as the boat race, where teams of rowers from Oxford and Cambridge competed to beat each other in a mad dash along the river from Hazel Ingliss's house to Harry's, or from Putney bridge to Mortlake, as the

organisers preferred to describe it. As a fervent rower himself he tried to visit London every spring, to lean on a wall somewhere and watch the two university crews speed by in a blur of athleticism. The obligatory trip to the pub afterwards had taken him into several of the Capital's most scenic hostelries along the Thames towpaths and he knew the area well enough to guess that his prospective new client's townhouse would have a two million plus valuation. Bankers liked to get the fuller picture wherever possible, today's saver quite possibly being tomorrow's borrower, so best to ask now, find out as much as possible up front.

The full picture of Commander Harry Shepperton was ticking lots of boxes.

Just one final question now.

Not really essential but he asked it anyway.

Partly the professional banker, partly the curious human being.

'Thank you for sharing and being so open, Monsieur Shepperton' he started, using the same phrase he always used at this stage of his screening interviews, irrespective of whether the applicants had been successful or not.

'You won't be surprised to know we use social media a lot these days for client evaluation. We do it with everybody. Company policy, I'm afraid, I don't personally like it very much. Feels like snooping.'

'That's because it is,' Harry told him, in no uncertain terms.

Guillaume persisted.

'So obviously we profiled you as best we could before agreeing to this meeting. No point in you having a wasted journey, obviously.'

Harry glared at him. A fact of modern life.

Still didn't like it though.

'And I discovered that you have a military rank.'

He put his pen down and pushed his chair back and away from his desk creating a kind of natural pause.

'And I was just curious why you left that off your application form?'

He waited for the natural pause to do its natural thing and fill up the awkward silence with a response.

'Because I am applying for an account in my capacity as a private citizen. You no doubt have a large detailed file on my financials already, which should support my case. Now I think I have told you enough about myself Monsieur Sagné. So do you want my business or not?'

A robust response indicating a conclusion, at least for one party.

Guillaume Sagné was not about to become the first Swiss banker to turn down a quarter of a million pounds in new client account deposit money. He also knew when the civic interrogation was over, something which happened at different stages for different people, and he took the hint.

Sandrine duly processed the paperwork and the two men shook hands, destined from that moment on to become good friends over the years that followed.

As a highly skilled assessor of people and situations Harry had actually quite enjoyed being on the other end of a grilling for a change. He knew exactly what Guillaume was doing with his questioning techniques. They were something which he himself had studied and practiced much over the years, and consequently he respected anybody who could deploy them well.

To make it feel less like bullying and more like a natural conversation was really quite a fine art.

And now, on this sharp spring morning with the world in a spin, he had flown in to Cointrin at alarmingly short notice to meet up with the one – and only – man he knew and trusted implicitly in the world of high finance.

He cabbed it the short distance over to the Crowne Plaza, checked in, showered quickly and then went back downstairs to the lobby.

The large black S class, which Guillaume had sent, was parked directly outside.

Harry glanced at the reply e-mail on his mobile to check the details -

Mais, oui, d'accord.

Tous compris

Can you be at the usual hotel by midday?

I will send Leo. Black Merc – GE 6767

Come up to the house.

Monique will cook for us.

Always a pleasure

Ton ami

Guillaume

Harry was about to get some invaluable insights into the rather secretive world of global money.

And Guillaume, still curious after all these years, would try and fill in a few more blanks.

'I still don't really know, ma cherie' he confided to Monique. 'when we first met, he told me he was a spy.'

Monique looked up from the Raclette recipe book she'd been studying and raised an eyebrow.

'I have never met anybody who ever said that,' she told him, with the good strong common sense of womanhood. ' Even in jest.'

'That is also exactly what he said' her husband replied. 'That nobody who really was one would even joke about it like that.'

'Does he confuse you?'

'Only that part.'

'Then I'll ask him.' she volunteered cheerily.

'He won't say. He's way too polished.'

'Willi,' she chided him with an alluring smile. ' have you no faith in me?'

Half an hour later Leo turned into the steep driveway.

It was Day two.

Midday.

Chapter 24 – The savant

Jake was looking forward to catching up with Hank Wyatt. They'd last met a year earlier when the ICJ court case had managed to involve The Nines in the dubious internationally convoluted scam called Covid -19. Being two Americans, away from home and working in Europe, the two men had found lots to talk about and had enjoyed plenty of Dutch beer together while they were in Den Haag.

Billy Poppitt had managed a short kip after a quick fry up in Gino's café before getting back behind the wheel again. As Harry landed in Switzerland he was back on the road again in Hazel's stretch Jag heading for Fulham with the redoubtable Professor Rivera in the back seat for company.

Normally the Brompton road at lunchtime would be absolutely teeming with shoppers but today it looked positively bizarre. There was hardly anyone about as the full implications of *Ischeznoveniye* finally started to begin impacting life everywhere.

'Just so strange.' Jake commented as they cruised past Harrods, normally an epi-centre of commercial activity, the retail hub around which so much of London's swanky and swell Knightsbridge district revolved.

'I guess yesterday everybody was in shock and it still kind'a looked and felt normal. But today! Boy what a difference.'

'Only ever seen it like this once.' Billy told him, glancing up in his mirror. 'Two years ago in Covid. Just apocalyptic, streets deserted, stations closed, nobody around. And now this. Twice in two years now, something I never thought I'd ever see even once in my lifetime.'

'And it'll get worse before it gets better. No chance of this ending quickly from what I can see.'

Billy's heart sank.

He knew that Harry had left Jake in overall control of ops as The Nines' point man, the one to whom all the others reported while they whizzed around on Jumbo. If Jake didn't like what he was seeing then that was seriously bad news.

'What did you make of that banker guy?' he enquired.

'Don't really think he could have said anything much else.'

Billy observed his passenger placidly. The life he'd had had taught him not to

panic too much. Things always had a way of working out. But he was also naturally suspicious, especially when it came to people and money.

'Well, no, suppose not,' he agreed, 'but then he didn't really say a lot, did he?'

Jake thought for a bit.

He'd taken the Geneva statement very much at face value.

'Whatcha' gettin' at Billy?'

'Well, like it reminded me of one of them types of statements you get from the professional PR firms when there's been some sort of huge cock up and they get brought in to smooth things over.'

'Really.'

'Yeah, you know, a reassurance thing. There's a name for it.'

'You mean damage limitation.'

'That's the one. Exactly.'

'They only do that when they're covering something up though.'

'I know. Yeah'

Billy's good natured optimism was well known by the whole team. Always so cheerful, nothing ever seemed to get him down.

But he also had a bit of a reputation for reading situations very well. He may have just been their driver and security guy, but when Billy spoke they all listened.

Jake had decided to hook up with Hank and the girls and get their latest thoughts first before flying out to Geneva.

Was that still the best thing to do?

He pondered the situation in the light of Billy's comment.

Harry had seemed keen for him to be out there quickly, as if sensing that something might have been brewing.

'Can you turn round and head for Northolt, Billy?'

'No problem. Do I need to tell them?'

'No. It'll be ok. They were expecting me for one. I'll just be an hour early. Stand-by will cover it.'

Northolt is a small RAF base in West London used by both the military and the Government. A small fleet of Bae 146 STOL (Short Take Off and Lift) four engined jets are stationed there for rapid VIP transport. Hazel Ingliss had commandeered them for Nines duty twenty four hours earlier.

Being on stand-by meant RTR60 – ready to roll in 60 minutes. The guys who

looked after that small but select band of aircraft were all highly trained RAF personnel. Whenever they were put on special alert they always took much pride in ignoring the official RTR requirements. Usually that gets you into lots of trouble in the military. However the 32 Squadron special ops crews deployed their own version of *" we need to leave quickly"*

It was known as RTR 10.

Parking your car would usually take longer than getting off the ground.

The face to face debrief now abandoned, Jake called JoJo.

'Morning Professor.' She picked up straight away.'Hope you're hungry, got a nice little Bistro booked just round the corner.'

'Sorry Jo. Change of plan, regrettably.'

'Anything to do with the TV briefing.'

'Well, yes and no and don't really know to be truthful.'

'What did you make of it?'

'Classic holding statement. Not good. Not bad.'

He spied Billy, watching him in the mirror.

'Didn't really say a lot though, did he?'

Billy grinned. Always nice to have your input recognized.

'Hank and Cait are here, wait, I'll just put you on speaker.'

Jake expressed his regrets again and explained his sudden change of course.

'Harry wants somebody to join up with the bankers team asap so we can see what they're up to first hand.'

'Are we worried about them for some reason then?' Hank spoke for all of them.

'I think it's more about being thorough than anything else.' Jake told him.

'I'm surprised they haven't come up with anything more by now though' Hank continued. 'They were notified in the early hours of Monday morning and were already involved when Harry was trying to use that cash machine. It's now coming up Wednesday lunchtime.'

'And they've got a small army of people working on it' Billy piped up, from the front seat, determined to let his general view of banks and bankers be known.

'Morning Billy' the two girls responded.

Hank looked surprised.

Caitlin explained about 9-7.

'Anyway, what have you all been up to since yesterday' Jake continued.' Any

166

progress?'

'We've been through everything in detail now to try and build up some kind of picture with a timeline' Cait continued. 'Seems everything went dark at 3am London time and everything else around the world shut down at the same time.'

'So that's all the ATM's then. All the cash machines?'

'Correct'

'So the cash was still in the machines presumably?'

'But the network crash meant it was inaccessible to customers. The whole distribution system became instantly inoperable.'

'What happened to all that cash then?'

'Still sat there, awaiting the fix."

'Well, they certainly didn't make that too clear in their press conference, did they?'

'Because nobody can do anything with it right now and they've got all their energies focused on examining the infrastructure to try and understand exactly what happened and how they can resolve it.'

'And what about the banks internal systems.'

'Dead as a dodo apparently. Completely unusable'

Hank chipped in now.

'Which is what we've been mainly focusing on because, if there are any clues anywhere, that's where they'll be'

'Explain' Jake pressed him.

'The deep level infrastructure is where all the magic juju happens. You can think of it like a subterranean labyrinth. Completely invisible to almost everybody apart from those who boldly go. Either because they need to – i.e. it's their job and they work there – or they want to, in which case one has reason to question their motives.'

'Essentially hacker central, then?' Jake enquired.

'Yes and no', Cait answered him. 'Remember Jo and I are part of that community, albeit incognito. To them we're just a couple of nerdy academics who turn up at the conventions in loud jumpers because we're bored.'

'Or just looking for a shag' Jojo intervened.' Not remotely true of course, but that's how they see us sometimes. Couple of girls on their own, you know, the old stereotypes die hard. But the point is you would need some very specific skills and knowledge to get inside a bank network. They are, in general, about as secure as

anything can be. Obviously, otherwise they wouldn't be fit for purpose, be totally useless.'

'Which is where you come in Hank, I assume?' Jake wanted to know, still slightly foggy about the exact reasons why Harry had brought in a retired USAF colonel with a background in chemistry, space physics, and casinos.

Not quite your average guy, but then The Nines were not quite your average team.

Jake also remembered something else about Hank, something Paul had told him after they'd first met up in Boston on their previous mission, something about dyscalculia, which generally meant problems with understanding and rationalizing numbers, making him an even stranger choice to be seconded onto Jumbo.

Still, no matter, Harry always knew what he was doing.

'I'm here to dissect the Blockchain and see if it might fit into this actually,' Hank replied, rather matter of factly, as if he was discussing the weather. 'In fact, that's what we've been doing most of the night.'

Jake suddenly remembered the other thing that Paul had mentioned about him.

"He's a bloody savant, your countryman, a borderline genius."

'Wow, ok. Well I suppose we need all the expertise we can get on anything that might be in play.' Jake replied, struggling a bit with this latest nugget of information.

'We thought the same thing, Jakey,' JoJo reassured him, noticing his mild skepticism, 'but, now we've had a chance to think it all through, it does make a kind of sense.'

Flexibility and a ready acceptance of new ideas were common traits of all The Nines.

Jake moved from slight bewilderment to instant approval in a heartbeat.

'Great. So what do we know now then?'

He settled back in to listen, stretching his long legs out in the back as Billy passed by the imposing looking Scrubs prison, soon to become home to some very senior members of one of the world's oldest professions.

He nosed the Jag around one last corner and pulled up onto the ramp for the Westway.

They'd be at Northolt in about half an hour by which time Professor Jake Rivera was going to be a much wiser man as Colonel Hank Wyatt (Ret'd) of the US Air Force revealed an uncanny ability to theorize with great clarity about his preferred

version of recent events.

The rather strange dyscalculia which had manifested itself so strongly in Hank's earlier years as an ability to read emotions and colours had recently morphed into something else.

Something called hypercaculia.

Which was actually the complete opposite of dyscalculia, being the ability to process and perform an alarmingly high number of mathematical calculations at lightning speed.

The doctors struggled to explain it.

Brain functionality can change, they would say, we still know so little about it, but, yes, the scans and tests were pretty conclusive and they were all in agreement.

Hank was a walking computer.

Chapter 25 – The message of hope

It was now late February and *Ischeznoveniye* was in its final planning stages. Crypto One was its hatchery and the learning from it proved invaluable as the boys worked through the final stages of their scheme to disappear the world's money.

They knew the phenomenon could only ever be temporary because, unlike BitCoin and most of its successors, old style money could just be created out of thin air. The printing presses had always existed of course but their deployment in the first part of the twenty first century went from a practical emergency measure to a mad out of control spiral.

The dangers of inflation may become complex and confusing when explained as part of economic theory but the basics remain pretty simple. If you produce too much of anything the surplus creates a depressing effect on price and value. If you produce too little then the scarcity does the opposite.

And so it is with money. Failure to maintain some kind of link between paper money – or fiat money as it is commonly called in economic circles – and a stable value store like gold will create a distortion where the net effects can be pretty nasty. If everybody suddenly has millions of pounds, dollars, francs, yen, euros or whatever, then what will happen to the price of a loaf of bread? Will it still cost one unit of that currency as it did before?

Answer?

No. It will cost more.

Much more.

Much, much, more.

The examples throughout history are legion. The famous and high profile cases range from the Weimar republic and Germany between 1920 and 1923 to the much more recent, Zimbabwe from 2008 and Venezuela from 2019 onwards. There are many, many more examples from before and many, many more in between. Much simpler and softer versions also occur, being generally just referred to as rising prices caused by completely normal everyday effects like wage increases or demand surges for specific products.

The good news is that such episodes are much more rare in modern westernized

democracies, mainly because they are usually the product of extreme political mismanagement.

The bad news is that there's a lot more of that about.

The net result is that any new or replacement monetary system that claims to be able to reduce inflationary tendencies should be welcomed with open arms as long as they are easy to deploy, easy to use and easy to understand.

It is exactly those three hills that all existing Cryptos die on.

Not too many people understood this.

But Andrei and Georgi did.

And they also knew that they were going to be working in a kind of time vacuum, where everything which they had caused to stop would exist in a kind of limbo for a short while until, inevitably, the printing presses would burst into life and the clock of normality would start ticking again.

How long would they have and what should they do in that time?

About a week, they thought, was the answer to the first question.

The second one was much trickier. Escape detection was the obvious number one priority. But assuming they could do that, what else?

And that's when the communiqué was born.

It was another late night, fish and chips were on the menu this time from the Golden Arches, not a patch on the English version but still very tasty and enjoyable. The company that continues to feed the world extremely well for not very much money was being as reliable as ever.

The boys were all tecched out and drifted into one of their other realms of conversation, almost without intending to.

'Should we give some of it away?' Andrei asked on a bit of a whim, 'you know, assuming we pull it off.'

'I thought we were just going to park it for a week or so and then reverse everything.' Georgi seemed clear enough on the original plan. 'Probably not a good idea to bugger about too much with it at this late stage.'

'But is it wise to not make any kind of statement. They'll be expecting something won't they?

'Let them.'

'But it will just be a deafening silence.'

'Well, exactly. Isn't that good for us?'

'Maybe, I don't really know. It's not like we've done this before, is it?'

'No, but making an announcement is…'

'That's not what I was suggesting.'

'Well, let's call it breaking cover then. However you dress it up, we're suddenly visible.'

'I don't see it like that. Not if we're careful.'

'You can be as careful as you want. That's still leaving a clue where previously there wasn't one. I can't see the point. What's the upside for us?'

'We use it to create a distraction. You know, like a sleight of hand, maybe.'

Georgi stopped playing with his phone and looked up.

His friend had suddenly got his attention.

'Go on.'

'If it's an interesting enough message then a lot of the media will start to pursue it.'

'And a lot of them won't.'

'But it would provide us with a kind of divide and conquer tactic. Some of them running one way, some the other.'

'I don't think I'm overly concerned about the media, Andi. They're not the guys that are gonna' lock us up.'

'But they'll all read it, won't they? And they'll all react to it. Everybody will. They'll have to, in the absence of anything else.'

Georgi put his phone down.

Now he was really focused.

'What do you mean *"interesting message?"*'

'Well, look. No message equals no distraction. But then, just one message from us changes that.'

'Yeh, ok, I get that bit. But saying what? It would have to be something pretty profound, pretty earth shattering. Remember we're going to be Public Enemy Number One. In most countries that means wanted dead or alive. Not so funny then if we start advertising our presence and providing a trail.'

'But that's my whole point. If it's a well laid trail it can lead them in another direction, lead them away from us.'

'It would have to be something extremely well crafted to do that.'

'Like a Robin Hood letter.'

'I *thought* that's where you were going with this.'

'Well, don't you think it might work. It would make for a pretty sensational news story.'

'What, like they won't have got one of those already? The world's money has just disappeared. All of it. *Ischeznoveniye,* remember. I think that might just make the front pages.'

'But think of the frenzy. Even if the source and veracity remain unproven, it's the kind of thing that would capture the public mood. And I mean everywhere.'

'The Socialist dream finally comes true, comrade. Redistribution of wealth on a hitherto unimagined scale. They might even like that here, although I rather think that the scourge of Capitalism has got to most Russians these days.'

Georgi was coming round.

Slowly, but he was coming.

'Definitely has a divide and conquer feel to it, no doubt about that. I can see that now.'

'But we would have to be careful not to be too specific.'

'We'll just need to get a politician to draft it then. Load of hot air dressed up as promises. Isn't that their speciality?'

Andrei smiled.

'Absolutely, it is. The problem is I don't think we know any, do we? And even if we did....'

'Yeah, agreed, that's just too much break out. Way too risky. If we do it, we have to do it ourselves. Can't be that hard, surely? Just need some thinly disguised hints about greed and global imbalance. It's pure and classic socialist fayre, the kind of gobbledygook the reds have been trotting out since 1917. It always has an audience, that stuff. Always will, like any message based on hope.'

'Well, let's get scribbling then and see if we can come up with something.'

So they did.

And they did.

And then Ans turned up.

'What's going on boys?' she eyed the temporarily discarded laptops, tablets and mobile phones scattered across the tables and sofas.

'Anything I can help with?'

Chapter 26 – The golf connection

Paul Lambert always felt more secure when he had plenty of background before he embarked on any aspect of a mission. If there were places involved he would scout them out, if there were documents in play, he would read them, gadgets, he would play with them, people, he would try to meet them. Regrettably it wasn't always possible, especially when it came down to his fellow human beings, quite often the most unpredictable of all of those various categories.

And this was the situation he now found himself in as he started to navigate a rather tricky situation in Rasputin's bar on Tverskaya. Earlier that morning he'd decided to try and second the attractive hotel receptionist to help him navigate Moscow, not just geographically but in a few other ways as well.

Regrettably, although in some respects rather predictably, Valeria was turning out to be someone who had a similar day job to his own, a situation with beautiful women that was all too common in Russia. His immediate dilemma was not life threatening so it could have been worse. But it was time critical, so he was feeling some pressure.

Harry Shepperton, like most people, was very sensitive about his own boss, and specifically about keeping her happy. That was usually pretty easy because Hazel generally left him to it, totally confident in his abilities. But occasionally she liked to help. And the previous evening she had told Harry that her golf pro buddy Mags had struck up a good friendship with an up and coming young Russian golfer whose father was an oligarch, a rather strange word that had its own meaning but had come to portray something else in England thanks largely to The Sun and other similar newspapers where, according to them anyway, it just meant 'rich bastard'.

Could that relationship be useful while Paul and Liam are out there, she had pondered?

So Paul now had a 3pm meeting set up with either one of them or both of them – still not sure which – at a location that had still to be confirmed – security implications always paramount – without knowing the people involved – happened a lot but still bad for the nerves – and, it now seemed, without the innocent local girlfriend who he had been trying to recruit all morning to give him a cover story – who was now turning out to be FSB.

Or similar.

Plus he had a real life Raspo with an itchy trigger finger, now wandering up and down behind the bar, to worry about as well.

Sometimes the truth was your friend.

Sometimes it could get you killed.

Fine lines.

Half truths would work sometimes. Depended a lot who you were sharing them with.

Paul's mind raced as he computed.

She'd be highly trained.

She'd be well briefed.

She'd know who he was.

She was almost certainly on the same mission.

Maybe not the ally he'd been hoping for, but maybe she might turn out to be an even better alternative.

Russia could be very tribal. Much depended on Mag's dad and where his political allegiances lay. That guy that he didn't know. The father of that girl he didn't know either.

He made his decision and took his chance.

'I'm guessing your superiors are just as worried about the current situation as everybody else,' he started. 'Maybe even more so given their individual stakes in the matter.'

It was an oblique statement but she would get the meaning. The modern day leader of that vast country was oft rumoured to be the richest man in the world. Nobody knew for sure of course, most people in the political sphere who manage to amass such enormous fortunes seldom allow them to be counted accurately.

Or publicly.

Valeria cocked her head slightly to one side, that strange thing again, and peered at him.

Raspo stopped pacing.

Paul had their attention now.

'Everybody is concerned Mr. Lambert, right across the world. But, before we go any further, perhaps you could explain one thing.'

Paul cocked his head slightly and peered right back at her.

Two could play at that game.

'And what would that be?'

'Why have MI6 chosen to send one of their top agents to Russia? And at very short notice.'

The plain truth was that it was very much harder to be clandestine in person these days.

The digital world had many advantages.

Protecting secrets was not one of them.

'I don't work for MI6' he told her, partly in truth.

The Nines actually worked directly for the P.M. who, being a rather busy person, inserted a couple of managers into the situation for practical reasons.

'Maybe not, but Hazel Ingliss does and she's your ultimate boss, isn't she?' Valeria remarked curtly. ' The lady who likes playing tennis.'

Paul let that one go.

'Playing tennis with golf professionals.'

Her awareness and her inside information suddenly made it easier for him.

Like the Swiss, the Russians aren't daft.

'I've heard she's friends with Mags Mollitsky. What of it?' he replied.

To the untrained eye it would have appeared at that stage that Paul Lambert was suddenly on the back foot, had been pushed into defensive mode. However, as a skilled negotiator, that was not something that he ever allowed to happen.

He had allowed her to turn the conversation that way for a reason.

Now she had to elaborate.

'Mags is allegedly great friends with Yelena Alliskiya. No doubt you've heard of her too?'

'No, not really.'

This was good. His 3pm meeting was starting to come to him.

'She's one of our top golf Pro's.'

'Really. Didn't know you had any.'

'It's a growing sport here. Neglected for a long time but now increasingly popular as our Country continues to be much more open.'

'And much more tourist friendly, as I saw this morning when you greeted me so warmly at The Metropole.' he grinned, continuing to defuse the situation.

Valeria smiled at this truism. The fact that so many people from all over the

world had started to show interest in visiting her motherland made her proud and happy. It was one of the main reasons why she'd suggested to her own boss that it would be a good idea for her to do occasional hotel shifts, an initiative that ticked several boxes. Some professional, to do with surveillance and awareness. Some personal, to do with meeting men like Paul Lambert, who might be able to offer her alternative options for the future.

'So I'm guessing the reason you told Leo you wanted to see me at short notice might have been connected with Viktor Alliskiya?' she asked.

Paul was winging it now.

He didn't know who that was.

So he said so.

Valeria and Raspo exchanged glances.

This was interesting. Could their information be wrong?

Seemed unlikely, given the source inside a rather large building a mile or so further South along Red Square.

One rather intriguing notion about money – and there are many – is that it truly affects everybody on the planet. In its inimical fashion it can cause problems if one has too little and it can cause problems if one has too much. Plus a whole host of other almost unimaginable issues which can arise in between.

Ischeznoveniye was rather unique in that it affected people all over the world at the same time in the same way. Nobody liked losing money in normal circumstances. And these were anything but normal.

For those who had nothing it was little short of disaster.

Rather oddly, for those that had everything, it was exactly the same.

And, despite its thin veneer of backward poverty, modern Russia had arrived in the twenty first century with blinding speed and was now home to a growing number of billionaires.

Some were in business.

Some were in politics,

They all had one thing in common.

Power.

And lots of it.

And crossing people with power is never a good idea, a concept which Andrei and Georgi had debated vigorously deep into many a long night before deciding to go

ahead with their improbable adventure anyway.

And so it was that word had gone out very quickly from centres of power the world over – and there are many of them – to quickly investigate and solve the puzzle posed by this act of grand larceny, this exercise in cyber theft, this dramatic international robbery.

And one of the first things that powerful people usually do under such circumstances is enlist the help of other powerful people, their friends and acquaintances, to get things done.

Viktor Alliskiya was one such friend of one of the most powerful of them all. And Mags Mollitsky had mentioned him to Hazel, exactly as Valeria had surmised.

'He's one of the country's richest men,' Valeria assured him.' They call him the Energy King. He supplies gas, coal, oil, and nuclear.'

'Not all in the same truck, I hope' Paul joked, hoping some levity would help.

Valeria and Raspo were stony faced.

Obviously it didn't.

'His daughter Yelena is a close friend of Mags, and Mags is a friend of your boss. Am I getting close?'

'She's not actually my boss.' Paul offered, seeing a glimmering light at the end of this particular tunnel.

He thought back to the message he'd received from Jake who was acting liaison for Jumbo back in London at the moment when The Nines started to deploy internationally. It had been there on his cell when he got off his flight that morning

Wanderer One buddy setting up 3pm in Meshchansky. More locally

Wanderer One was the team's code name for Hazel Ingliss.

The Nines didn't believe in long messages. Incomplete arrangements were commonplace. Hugely annoying but an essential part of the job, security being paramount and all that. They could often leave you a bit high and dry though whilst trying to piece things together.

Like now, for instance.

'Well, she seems to know something about what might have happened.'

'How do you know?'

'We get to hear things.'

'Why would a golf pro be involved in this?'

'That's not what I said, is it?'

So it's her father, and maybe his friends, who've heard something, Paul thought to himself.

He needed to position this properly now

'My rather obvious question is why do you need me?' he said, realising that his 3pm trip to Meshchansky was likely to be accompanied, albeit not in quite the way he'd imagined, 'when everything we're talking about here involves Russia. Russian people, Russian places, Russian power and Russian intrigue. If all this has happened in Russia, why can't you sort it all out internally?'

It was a good question.

He wasn't expecting the answer though.

'It hasn't.'

'It hasn't what?'

'It hasn't all happened in Russia'

Paul knew the fine art of staying silent.

'I know two of The Nines are here in Moscow, Mr. Lambert' she continued. ' But Harry Shepperton and Colonel Wyatt have opted to go somewhere else, haven't they?'

She held his stare.

'Maybe they just needed some fresh mountain air to help them think clearer.'

Chapter 27 – The replacement currency

Launching a new currency is a tricky process. There is much to consider, not the least of which is the impact and effect on the existing currency, the one it will replace. The timing has to be perfect and not allow for any overlap.

Ideally the old currency will be withdrawn at a particular time, which will be laid down by the Government on behalf of the issuing Authority, let's say, for example, midnight on the first of June. At that exact moment it ceases to be legal tender and all and any physical manifestations of it are finally withdrawn in the culmination of a process which will have happened over a period of time starting several months earlier.

Central banks will continue to honour the old money indefinitely and will exchange it for the new currency, which will have become the new legal tender for that particularly defined territory – usually a country – at one second past midnight on the second of June.

Difficult though it is to execute properly, that part of the whole operation is, nonetheless, quite easy to understand due to its rather mechanical nature as a sequential process. Much harder to calculate and implement is the perennially controversial decision on the rate of exchange which has to be used in order to convert the old to the new.

Over the years legions of honest citizens have seen their savings decimated and wiped out by the imposition of poorly thought through monetary policy. One day you have ten thousand of the old ones, next day you have one thousand of the new ones, which is ok if the purchasing power changes proportionately as well. But if there is parity – i.e. the old and the new are deemed to have the same or similar value, then you stand to lose ninety per cent of your money.

Unsurprisingly revolutions and civic unrest quite often accompany these changes which, by their very nature, tend to affect everybody in the country or territory in question.

These matters are further complicated when political change is prevalent in the background, as was the case with the establishment of the Euro across Europe in the

mid Nineties. This was no simple internal change, requiring, as it did, the withdrawal of several major and long established national currencies. The German Deutschmark, the French Franc, the Dutch Guilder, the Spanish Peseta, the Italian Lire, the Austrian Schilling, the Greek Drachma and several more, all vanished to be replaced by The Euro, as a long term plan to create a federal Europe slowly gathered political momentum in the background.

Making the seismic decision about the exact value of one Euro in relation to the twenty or so national currencies that were being withdrawn fell to the ECB, the European Central Bank.

It was this august body that Andrei and Georgi spent most of February 2022 researching.

They now had enough tech knowledge from their experimentation model, Crypto One, to set up Crypto Two, a second derivative cyber currency, and the one they planned to use for *Ischeznoveniye*. But they now needed to understand the procedural aspects of introducing new currencies, starting with the basics. This was a logical step despite seeming counter-intuitive. Why the need to know about setting up new currencies when their plan was to disrupt all of the old ones at the same time?

Simple answer. If you plan to knock a house down, it's a whole lot easier if you understand something about its foundations and supports first.

'It's not much like a normal bank, is it?' Andrei commented, as they ploughed through all the available ECB data.

'No, I don't think we have a branch in Moscow.' Georgi laughed. ' And if we did, I don't think it would have an ATM. It doesn't look like the sort of place that's designed to give money out to normal people.'

'No, it's a politicians bank, a place where they can fuck about with people's lives at arm's length, at least as far as I can see.'

'More think tank than bank bank then. Lots of ideas, policies, strategies and inflation guidance principles. God, no wonder the current system is teetering on the edge, if that's all they're focused on.'

'Looks like they've got a small army of people working there. There's thousands of them.'

'What are they all doing? Does it say?'

Georgi watched as his friend continued to scan page after digital page of rambling information.

'It seems half work on central banking…' he said, tracing his finger across his laptop.

'Wow. Big surprise for a central bank. Who'd have guessed!'

'……and the remainder oversee supervisory mechanisms.'

'What's that supposed to mean?'

'Well, as a minimum, it means there's definitely not much normal banking going on. I think it's just code for *'we are the regulator'*.

'So don't mess with us. Just do as we say and follow our rules'

'Exactly. Certainly looks that way. There's a request here from an EC citizen under their Freedom of Information act asking about employee demographics. Not a particularly sensitive area, one wouldn't have thought. They took three months to tell him to fuck off.'

'Hmm. Not looking too sweet, are they? Be nice to put one over on them in addition to all the other stuff.'

'Well, I don't think we'll need a separate plan to do that. They'll just get caught up in it as we go along.'

'How do you mean?'

'Well, reading between the lines, all this guff is really saying is that they are a control function. Implementation and compliance. That's what they do. So if things derail, they'll be in the pot straight away, whether it's anything to do with them or not.'

'Great. So what else do we need to know?'

'They've been faffing about with a digital Euro for years. That proves how political they are as an organization. All talk, no action. I mean why isn't something like that one of their top priorities?'

'Maybe because they're still so worried about keeping the regular Euro afloat. Hardly out of the woods yet, is it?'

'I thought it had survived its last scare.'

'It did.'

'You mean there might be more?'

'Bound to be. Most of the major EC countries would much prefer to control their own financial affairs. All nation states would if they could. Some can't because they are inherent basket cases. Others get mugged into joining a big rich club in the hope that their membership will help save their economies from either drowning in too

much debt or just from sheer incompetence.'

'Is that how it works in practice?'

'It's how it works in theory. In practice it doesn't work at all because, guess what, the whole point of a rich club is to look after the rich members. The poor members are only there to salve their consciences.'

'But they bail them out, don't they? Isn't that what they call it? A bank bail out.'

'Where, if you examine them carefully, the bail out is nothing more than a short term loan that leads to even greater debt, sometimes even doubling it, as happened with Greece in '08.'

'Sorry Andi, I was barely five. What happened.'

'The country lost control of its finances in pursuit of a set of conditions drafted as a basis for their membership of the latest rich club.'

'Namely, the E.C?'

'Correct.'

'And they got screwed?'

'Correct'

'And let me guess, those conditions were set by the good old ECB?'

'Correct. Three in a row. You win today's star prize.' Andrei clapped his hands.

'And they lent Greece the money, as well?'

'Not directly, no. A private Wall Street bank did that.'

'To balance the country's books so it could meet the club's entry conditions?'

'Correct again. Four right out of five. Well done Georgi. We'll make an economics professor out of you yet.'

'So those individual countries inside the Euro all share a currency, even though their wealth and poverty levels are totally different?'

'And that's the reason why the theory doesn't work in practice. Well, at least one of them anyway. The interest rates are all set centrally meaning that the basic cost of money, the costs of lending, are the same for each club member, for each country. Which causes innumerable problems and lots of financial pain for the countries that are in trouble. And guess what. They're not the rich ones.'

'And the countries who didn't join the money club? What about them?'

'Notably the UK, Denmark and Sweden. They have some of the most vibrant economies anywhere, so independence doesn't seem to be doing them any harm.'

Georgi slumped back on the sofa and stretched out, hands crossed behind his

head as he absorbed this quick trot through some of the more recent highlights of life in the EC.

'Well, I'm glad we're not in,' he declared eventually.' Sounds well dodgy. I think I can understand why the English did that Brexit thing and left. Good on them.'

Andrei nodded.

'And that's another good thing about the size of Russia too. We're not likely to get bludgeoned into joining like all those smaller European countries did. Not that Russia is in Europe anyway, whatever the organisers of that Eurovision song contest charade seem to think.'

'Are Switzerland in it?' Georgi asked, rather randomly.

'The song contest? Yes, I think so?'

'No, not the bloody song contest. The rich club. The EC?'

'No, I don't think they are.'

'Well, isn't that a bit odd. One of the richest countries in Europe, the people who look after everybody else's money, and they're not in the club. Didn't they get invited then, assuming that's how it works?'

At an earlier stage in their planning for *Ischeznoveniye* the boys had attempted to roughly plot the location of the world's money, thinking that there might need to be a geographic basis to their heist. They quickly concluded that computerized and digital distribution didn't work like that. There were no obvious epi-centres of storage; the world's money was actually spread out pretty evenly everywhere, as was general access to it.

The exercise had not been completely without value though, highlighting as it had, one particular and rather interesting anomaly.

For such a sophisticated piece of analysis they had resisted the temptation of multiple spreadsheets and just used crayons on a big wall chart which showed a world map broken down by national borders. They chose a variety of indicators to support levels of wealth and money by country including *assets under management* which showed where money was being looked after by a host nation or, more specifically, by an investment vehicle in a third party country. This method not only showed where the money actually was but also who was holding it and looking after it on behalf of other people.

It had been one of those all-nighter tasks and they both remembered the growing sense of shock and surprise as the hours rolled by and a massive green splodge had

started to obliterate the middle of their chart.

On a world map laid out end to end with the West coast of the USA on the extreme left and China on the extreme right, Europe will always be in the middle. And right in the heart of Europe one particular country was no longer visible as an ever-increasing large number of green ticks, each representing one billion American dollars, covered it in a thick layer of colour.

'Now, don't tell me. They're not in the Euro either.'

'Actually they're not.'

'So this relatively small country at the heart of Europe is home to a hugely disproportionate amount of the world's wealth but chooses not to be a wealth club member nor a user of the club's own currency."

'Correct. They still use their own Swiss Francs. Have done since seventeen ninety something in one form or another. It's considered a safe haven currency.'

'A what?'

'One that's more trusted than most. In times of trouble, people tend to convert their money into things which are considered to have better survival chances than others.'

'How do you determine which is one of those and which isn't?'

'That's a bit complex. Lots of factors feed in. Historic performance is usually the starting point, which is then combined with some more recent economic data about the country in question. In the case of the Swiss, this is a country that never goes to war so they don't have an economy that's saddled with the astronomical debts caused by the kind of reckless military spending which seems to afflict most other countries. All that kind of stuff helps make its core currency very attractive.'

'Have they not got an army then?'

'They have a compulsory military service which all young male citizens are obliged to participate in for about nine months. After they leave and return to civilian life they're allowed to keep their weapons. So in reality they are probably better prepared for a fight than many other countries, at least in terms of raw manpower. They essentially have a citizen army of well-equipped soldiers who spend most of their lives working on farms, running restaurants, teaching in schools and just generally going about their normal everyday business. It's almost the perfect model of how to actually have a defence force without incurring all the costs normally associated with it, without all that procurement spending crap that's slowly crippling

other countries.'

'Wow. They're not daft, the Swiss, are they?'

'No, they're really not. Plus it's a lovely country full of lakes, rivers, mountains and Alpine pastures. On the face of it the kind of place that one might reasonably expect to get constantly attacked by outsiders. And yet they never are. You have to wonder why!'

'Because of the green blob?'

'Got to be.'

'So if we can crack them, then we're in.'

Andrei smiled at his friend.

They often came to significant conclusions at the same time.

'Great minds think alike.' he agreed.

Although in reality they often don't, it does always helps as part of forming a plan if people readily agree on a course of action.

And so the Fort Knox of Europe, sitting at the mountainous heart of the entire continent, became the key target entry point for *Ischeznoveniye.*

'I still prefer Millstatt though' Georgi muttered.

'Austria is really so beautiful.'

Chapter 28 – Hank's new buddy

To say that Hank Wyatt was comfortable around money would have been either an understatement or an exaggeration, difficult to know which. As someone who had once possessed a small fortune – several small fortunes in fact – he had known what it was to have money. However, these had only been fleeting relationships as a result of how it had come to him through the roulette wheel and his previous dyscalculia, another of those imperfectly understood brain conditions which had manifested itself in him in a very strange way.

For Hank's sensory compensation for number blindness was an uncanny ability to interpret and read colours in a way that defied logic and analysis. Something which he had tried to explain over and over to his CIA interviewers back in the day. He kept right on telling them that he didn't have a system but they recruited him anyway, determined to believe that he had something, just not sure what.

Well they'd been right on that score, he had plenty about him, starting with a huge streak of charity towards his fellow man which prompted him to give away all of the casino windfalls.

He wasn't particularly proud or self-satisfied in doing so because, to him, it was just so obviously *the right thing to do*. That most momentous of phrases which marks out a real man, something completely lost on so many people these days in their hurried and squalid pursuits of ambition, fame, glory, power or materialism.

So Hank was also a man who knew what it was to no longer have money. Not to have lost it, which is something different entirely, but to have given it away because he felt no need for it.

Or, to be more accurate, because he felt that others needed it more than he did.

He wasn't poor, he had all the basics, the shelter, the food, the sleep, the security, the human relationships, the ability to continually study, to learn and grow as a person. He hadn't heard of Maslow's hierarchy of needs but he could have been the model for it. And he saw so many around him who lacked so many of those things.

Life could be so unfair

So the man walking along the travellator at Cointrin that Wednesday lunchtime en route to the Fairmont Grand was no stranger to money, nor the people who looked

after it, loved it, slept with it, and lied about it. He knew all about that crowd and what made them tick.

Harry Shepperton knew all this of course, knew it only too well. Hank had nearly become a Nine, was shortlisted but didn't get as far as those now legendary interviews where The Six who were to become The Nines were put through their paces by the gruffly amiable Blinky Duff and his dour Scot pal Archie Webster. He'd read the file one last time before sending it back to Langley with his personal thanks and enclosing a note -

'Can't really imagine a future where we're not going to need him, one way or another. Keep him close.
Best from London
Ten'

And now that time had come. The man who could read colours could also read bankers.

And he could visualize Blockchain algorithm movements in his mind.

And he was in town.

Time to call Professor Rivera again and make sure they had their stories straight. Jake had beaten him in by about two hours and was just arriving back at The President Wilson.

'Alright for you guys on the official payroll,' he quipped when Jake mentioned his hotel by name. ' That's one beautiful establishment. I think I'm in an Air BNB.'

'You're in here tomorrow.'

'What?'

'We essentially swap over tonight, well in the morning actually. I check out. You check in.'

'Well, err, okay.'

Hank struggled not to sound surprised.

Jake chuckled.

'And I head over to your Air BNB. So make sure you pay your mini bar bill before you check out.'

'I don't understand.'

'Officially. It's a security thing. Keeping us apart so as not to arouse suspicions anywhere.'

'And unofficially?'

'Harry Shepperton is the fairest minded guy on the planet. It's just his way of doing things.'

Hank smiled inside.

Nice.

Really not necessary.

But nice.

'So how was it with the Banker's? Did they welcome you with open arms?'

'I don't think I'd phrase it quite like that, no' Jake told him.' To be fair they've got an army of people working on it and they've barely been together forty eight hours so the fact that they managed to cobble that statement together earlier this morning is at least something.'

'Have you got a decent contact?'

'She's a local banker, well from Zurich, not here. But she's obviously been told to manage me rather than let me in.'

'So they're being a bit coy.'

'I'd say a mix of careful and suspicious. They know there's a general feeling that this can't have happened without their involvement so I think their priority right now is to manage that perception rather than solve the problem.'

'Lots of chickens coming home to roost then!'

'Yes, exactly. The old trust issues are still there and they've got their reputations on the line.'

'Well, if they're being driven by that then they've got the wrong motivation.' Hank asserted. ' We're going to have to change that. By the way, who are we again?'

'We're FSCSC.

'Aren't they the compensation unit?'

'No, that's the FSCS. The Financial Services Compensation Scheme.'

'And the difference is...?'

'We're Fraud Squad Cyber Security Compliance. They really exist, we don't. Not that anybody's likely to check in the eye of this particular storm. But if they get distracted and worried by the thought of compensation, then so much the better. They need to start focusing on the realities of this and getting it fixed and stop worrying about themselves and their image.'

'Absolutely right. Big opportunity for the world banking community to come up smelling of roses for once.'

'And that's part of our task when we go back later. I told them I had a colleague flying in which allowed me to just sniff about a bit and then leave. We're due back in together at five.'

Hank checked his watch. Two hours. No wait, one. Lost an hour on the way over.

'Ok, I was planning on going straight there anyway so why don't I do that. I'll grab a coffee and wait for you.'

The ride in from the airport barely took twenty minutes. Geneva is a bit sprawly like a lot of main cities but it's not a huge place. Until you get close to the lake its actually rather nondescript and a bit concrety, the more beautiful parts being higher up in the hills behind the main town. Like so many other sea, river and lakeside spots all over the world, the place is instantly transformed as soon as one gets close to the water.

The Quai de Mont Blanc runs most of the way along the front of the lake and is home to several grand hotels. The Fairmont has one of the more commanding positions with its direct views out over the lake towards Le Jet d'eau fountain, the city's most famous landmark which shoots water over four hundred feet up into the air in a plume of shimmering droplets. It is an almost obligatory location for any kind of press conference where it has been deemed necessary to indirectly inform viewing audiences about the location.

So this was the chosen venue for le Force d'Intervention des Bancaires, the unfortunately named FIB, who had virtually commandeered the whole hotel for its hastily planned investigation into *Ischeznoveniye*.

An English acronym would have worked much better under the circumstances but international suggestions ranging from the slightly cheeky GITS – the Global Investigation Team Specialists – through to the even worse Cyber Unit National Team Squads, were all politely declined. This was the French part of Switzerland and the French can be touchy and quite insistent sometimes when it comes to the use and deployment of their beautiful language.

So the Bank Task Force got off to a shaky start with the world's assembled media. Even before they'd started their main work, they'd been forced onto the back foot almost straight away with their opening statement at that morning's press conference

"We are FIB and we swear to tell the whole truth and nothing but the truth. Our motto is FIB won't FIB." they announced to a slightly surprised press pack.

Gee, did they choose that stupid name just so they could say that, they all wondered. And why do they sound like they're in court already?

Bankers. Huh. What can you do?

Colonel Hank Wyatt (Ret'd) of the US Air Force was not a guy who generally had trouble getting in anywhere. Upon his early retirement he had negotiated the right to maintain certain access credentials, which meant he had no difficulty walking into most military facilities. And years before that, when he'd left the Bureau, he also negotiated the right to keep an honorary FBI pass, something which could get him into most places in the States, no questions asked.

But this was a Swiss hotel, and, at the moment a rather heavily fortified one. The global mood was still one of shock but there was a creeping yet palpable awareness that those charged with the resolution of this problem were on borrowed time. There were no angry baying mobs yet, no cries for blood, but how long would it be?

As a consequence the authorities were not taking any chances and sensible, if not somewhat severe precautionary measures were being taken to protect the investigation teams.

Parked up on the promenade just to the right of the main entrance was a Leopard 2 battle tank, and over to the left a LeClerc borrowed from the French Army in a show of local support. Not that anyone was going to storm the hotel demanding answers – not just yet anyway – but a show of force can always be a useful deterrent

As his taxi pulled up, Hank reached into his inside jacket pocket and took out a small soft case, flat and just over two inches square. He slipped the tricoleur ribbon out and clipped it to his breast pocket. He had figured correctly that the local authorities would probably deploy some of the soldiers from the tank regiments onto door duty, men in camo always being more effective for that than men in suits.

He checked the uniforms as he got out of his cab and drifted slightly left. The afternoon was quiet now but the young French soldier was nonetheless alert and watchful. As Hank walked towards him the sun did him a favour as it glinted on the Medaille d'honneur he had been awarded a few years previously for saving the lives of two French citizens.

Members of the military tend to like and respect things like that and they will generally recognize the awards and their significances, those particular ones usually being presented personally by the President of France for acts of selfless bravery and courage.

You don't get the Medaille d'honneur for just turning up.

The young tank commander snapped to attention and saluted, eyes now straight ahead.

'Bonjour Monsieur.'

'Bonjour Capitain. Merci beaucoup.'

'Mille mercis a vous pour votre service, Monsieur'

Hank didn't speak much French.

Didn't need to.

He was in without declaring himself.

The tank commander stood at ease.

Mission accomplished.

Five minutes later he had his coffee and started mingling with the journalists on the terrace facing Lac Leman.

It was a real throng with journalists from all over the world wandering in and out of the afternoon sunshine. Most of them seemed to be biding their time and awaiting the next announcement from the official team who had promised another update but not until the next day.

Under the circumstances that just seemed like an eternity.

As is always the case when people from the same profession get together, it looked as if a lot of them already knew each other, and, judging by the amount of hugging and general kissy kissy that was going on, a lot of them seemed to be very close friends as well.

Hank was trying to figure out the best way to break into one of these groups when he spotted Ivan Terrtroothski from Izvestia on his own at the far end of the balcony about to light up a large cigar. He recognized the largish bear of a man from the recording he'd watched on the plane.

'You really think they'll keep us waiting till tomorrow?'

He extended his hand in the customary fashion.

'Hank Wyatt.'

Ivan blew a large puff of pungent smoke out towards the lake and introduced himself.

'You East coast, not West, right?'

'You've got a good ear, Ivan.'

'I play cello when I'm not running round like idiot. Music good for the soul as

well as the ear.'

'Well, I cant disagree with that' Hank told him.' I notice they didn't really respond to your question properly at the end of the press conference.'

'No. And I approached them after for comment. And you know what I got?'

'No idea. They fobbed you off maybe?'

'Their comment was *no comment*. What do you say to this?'

'I think it's odd, to say the least. Like you touched a nerve or something.'

'I think this too. Same thing.'

'Did you have a good reason for asking that particular question?'

Ivan blew another cloud of smoke out towards the fountain and eyed Hank suspiciously.

'You not reporter are you, Mr. Wyatt. Who you work for?

Ivan knew immediately that a fellow journo would not have been asking him to betray his sources like that.

'I'm with one of the Government agencies, Ivan.'

'CIA?'

'Not any more, no'

Ivan screwed his eyes up a bit, pondering his next question. Thirty years in the business had given him good instincts. He could smell his next story.

But Hank was way ahead of him.

'I'll tell you but I can't feature directly in any of your reports. You can use the material but it will have to be non-attributable.'

Ivan's lengthy experience was telling him that he might suddenly have a potential new angle on a story which had really gone quite cold for the past few hours.

'Ok. I consider it. No payments.'

'Understood.'

'And you only tell me, not other reporters.'

'It's a deal.'

'You working for DGSE then, right?'

Hank looked puzzled.

'When not playing cello, I study military history. My second hobby, you can say.'

Hank looked even more puzzled.

'Including all awards and commendations. So I know what this is.'

He tapped Hank on the chest.

'You must be very brave man, Mr. Wyatt. You saved somebody's life one day and put yourself into danger.'

Hank took the medal off.

'Just used it to get in actually. French soldiers on the door, they love all that stuff.'

'You mean DGSE gave you medal to literally open doors, so to speak?'

'No, Ivan. A former President of the Republique gave it to me personally although I told him in my dreadful French that I hadn't done anything that most normal people wouldn't do.'

Ivan was beginning to like the first paragraph of his new story.

'What did he say?'

'He said most people weren't normal like me, which was very gracious of him.'

'May I see, please?'

'Of course.'

He handed his bravery award to the Russian who studied the small bronze medal intently.

'I never hold one before. Only see pictures. It's a beautiful thing, thank you. Can you tell me the story?'

'One day maybe, Ivan, but not today.'

'But how come an American is working for French intelligence. Is it connected with that?'

'I'm not DGSE. The guys I work with use numbers with their letters.'

Ivan's second paragraph was now starting to write itself.

An ex CIA operative with a French Medaille d'honneur who was working for MI6.

Shouldn't have too much trouble getting a decent headline out of that.

'You part of some Brit task force then? Come investigating the disappearance, something like that?'

'Something like that, Ivan, yes'

'You here alone?'

'No'

'How many are you?'

'Two here, two in Moscow.'

Ivan stopped puffing and stared hard at his new acquaintance.

'Two in Moscow?'

'Two, yes'

'Can you tell me what you know?'

'Some, not all.'

'Well, obviously, I suppose. Why have you targeted me, Mr. Wyatt?'

'It's Colonel Wyatt, actually.'

Hank pulled one of his new business cards out of his top pocket. Just got the things printed so might as well use them, he thought. And an experienced Russian journalist could always come in handy.

Ivan looked at the card.

'You ex Air Force and ex CIA colonel? What happened? They both kick you out?'

Hank Wyatt chuckled. He had to admit he'd had a very interesting life but now was not the time to expound on that either.

'No Ivan, I've always been a good boy. Got a medal to prove it, remember.'

And so began a friendship that would last a lifetime as the two men bonded slowly leaning on a terrace balcony overlooking a Swiss lake. Such relationships almost always being based on a kind of sharing, usually of experiences, stories, and matters concerning family, friends and life journeys.

Hank had always found it easy to open up and talk to people, being naturally garrulous by nature as Paul Lambert had found out when they'd first met back in Boston a few year earlier on their Wuhan mission.

Ivan was much more cautious, a product of his Russian background where one had to think twice about what was being said by who and about whom, but his vast knowledge would inevitably find an outlet in any conversation.

Hank opened him up with a simple question. *"What got you into journalism Ivan?"* and then spent the next fifteen minutes listening to tales of growing up in Siberia and a struggle through college and the local education system that had led him to Moscow and his present job.

'And why the interest in military history, Ivan. Can you tell me that story?'

'One day maybe Colonel, but not today. We have more pressing business to attend to ' he nodded in the direction of the large open bi-fold doors where he had the better view of what was happening inside the main salon just over Hank's shoulder

and where there seemed to be a sudden flurry of activity.

A youngish looking blonde woman in a smart lemon trouser suit had mounted the small podium and was tapping the microphone.

'Ladies and Gentlemen. Mesdames et Messieurs, if I could have your attention for a moment please.'

Hank and Ivan joined the others as the crowd on the balcony started to move inside.

'My name is Sylvie Danton and I am the new spokesperson for the FIB. I just want to bring you all up to speed on where we are at the moment.'

She paused for a few moments allowing the crowd to break off from a hundred small conversations and tune in.

'Thank you. This is just a short statement. I will not be answering any questions afterwards. They will be dealt with by my colleagues tomorrow morning in their main update.'

To his credit, Ivan had learnt that directness helped a lot in his line of work.

Short sharp questions always seemed to work best.

'Why not?'

The young blonde scanned her audience seeking her interrogator.

'Because there is only limited new information.'

Short sharp statements also worked well if delivered with enough bite.

'It's always a spokesperson's job to answer questions.'

'And they will be answered in the morning, I can assure you.'

Persistence also helped a lot.

'What are we supposed to tell the good people of the world tonight then? Just go to bed and stop worrying about your money.'

'I think you can reassure them that we are all doing everything we can to help to fix the problem.'

'So you think you can fix it then?'

This was turning into an object lesson in how not to be fobbed off.

'All problems can ultimately be fixed, is that not so?'

She was getting dragged into a dialogue now, the exact thing her training – and her boss – had warned her against.

'*Ultimately* sounds like code for *a long time.* So is that the message you want us to give out tonight. That this could drag on for ages?'

And now she was being asked pointed questions.

It was an uncomfortable place to be but, to her credit, Sylvie's unruffled nature was holding up well so far.

'I cannot say at this stage. It would be very remiss of me to speculate on that. This is a very complex investigation.'

'What have you done since 9am this morning? That would be a real update. It's been over six hours. The world is watching and waiting.' asked Hannah Freiheit from Bild, as Ivan's colleagues started to follow his lead and pile in.

This was not a good sign. They were starting to turn on her a bit now before she'd even gotten started.

Hardly surprising though, when you keep a large group of people hanging around all day.

Even if there is a nice view from the terrace.

'I can tell you that we are, and have been, concentrating on unraveling the technology.'

Ah, ok, well now she'd actually told them something.

'Are you referring to your own internal systems' Jacqueline Trouvére from Le Monde wanted to know, just as suspicious as she had been in the morning about the banks' own role in what had happened.

'Yes, but not exclusively.'

'And have you found any of the money yet,' asked Bruce from the Sydney Morning Herald. ' Anything at all would be a start.'

'I am afraid not, Mr. Buggameeblue. Not at this stage, no.'

'Are you not concerned that your prevarications will lead to panic and unrest across the world?' asked Rob Watchinit.' There have been more kidnappings this afternoon.'

'We are working as fast as we can to make sure that doesn't happen. I can assure you we have the concerns of the victims uppermost in our minds.'

Victims! Was she inadvertently telling them something else now?

'So it definitely wasn't an accident then' asked Lucy Diggs from the BBC. 'You're ruling out any kind of technical glitch?

'I cannot rule anything either in or out at this stage, I'm afraid. It's still far too early for that.'

'How long do you expect your investigation to last then? asked Charlie from The

Straits Times. 'People have a right to know that much, at least.'

'I agree. They do. But it's another question I can't answer right now. Maybe in the morning.'

As suddenly as they'd started the questions suddenly stopped and a hush fell on the room.

Sylvie Danton had weathered the storm.

Or so she thought.

She paused briefly to compose herself before reading out the short statement which she had originally come to deliver, and then, feeling a tad over-confident, made her one single slip up as she turned to leave the podium.

'Merci beaucoup, ladies and gentlemen. I will see you in all in the morning.'

She looked out at the crowd.

'Any last questions?' said the lady who had said she wasn't going to answer any.

Ivan pounced quickly.

'Any news about those nutters in Moscow?'

Chapter 29 – Monique

Monique Sagné was an industrious kind of girl, always busy, busy, busy with something or other.

She had no fixed routine apart from her morning yoga, which she did religiously around 7am every day, straight after getting up. No tea, no coffee, no toast, nothing. That was the received wisdom, always do the routine on an empty stomach so that all of the physiological benefits of the twists, turns and stretches are undisturbed by any digestive tract or bowel activity. That way the detox effects are maximized.

As a result of those forty-minute sessions and the natural dietary discipline which had been with her since she was a little girl, Monique had a beautiful slenderness that made her the envy of other women and the involuntary target of hundreds of admiring glances from legions of men down the years.

Her lovely toned curves were further enhanced by her love for her garden where she would spend two or three hours most days when the Alpine weather permitted. It was a place that reflected her character, hugely individual and unlike any other, dotted around, as it was with what appeared to be a random mixture of plants and flowers from all corners of the world. If they were happy to grow in her garden then the lovely Monique was more than happy to host them, to tend them and to derive happiness from them.

Like Guillaume she knew a lot of people but only a relatively small number were blessed enough to be able to count her as a close friend. That smallish group would often be invited to their lovely home high in the hills above Geneva with its tranquil setting and distant lake views where they would spend hours around the heavy marble dining table laughing and joking the hours away.

On these occasions Monique not only managed to prepare and cook wonderful meals but would also somehow strive to integrate her kitchen duties with an ability to sit and participate. Her food was as wonderful as her garden, just as varied, always fresh and full of new surprises, and she would always throw herself one hundred percent into her hosting duties and enjoy laughing the night away.

She was more than a one in a million.

Willi was the luckiest guy on the planet and he knew it.

Among her many other talents, Monique had also once worked in the same industry as her husband and had become one of only a very small number of bank officials to attain the elevated rank of B.O.B before the age of thirty. At that point she made the right life decision, chose family over money and swapped the daily rigours of being a senior Bevollmaechtiger for the equally challenging but much more delightful and fulfilling joys of motherhood.

She still maintained regular contact with some of her old friends from those days so, in addition to her husband, she had several other alternative sources who kept her constantly informed of the latest updates and developments in her old profession. As a result her phone had been much busier than usual over the previous twenty four hours as she did what everybody else in the world was doing and grappled with the effects and implications of *Ischeznoveniye*.

So it had been with much interest that she had learnt about the imminent arrival of her lunch guest for the day. Although discussions about clients are supposed to be treated confidentially by Doctors, Lawyers and Bankers, pillow talk exists in all walks of life so Monique knew quite a lot about her husband's English friend, Harry Shepperton. And yet, at the same time, she knew nothing, apart from the fact that he worked for the British Government and was very coy about saying too much about exactly what he actually did.

As Leo was winding the Mercedes way up into the hills she'd had that quick recap with Willi, just to make sure she had her facts straight before their guest arrived. Nothing new to report, it seemed, at least from her husband's perspective. She would have to use her own redoubtable talents to find out more.

The natural charm and feisty intellect of the lovely Monique Sagné who could melt hearts at a hundred paces pitted against the wits of some sort of top professional agent. Willi had already decided in advance that this would be one lunch where he would probably be keeping very quiet.

'Bonjour Arri' she embraced him on both cheeks in the proper Continental manner ' How lovely to see you again.'

Harry grinned back at her, correctly assuming with his own infallible instincts that this would be the point in his relationship with his own personal private banker where he would need to open up a bit more, partly because the occasion demanded it if he were to use Guillaume's knowledge of the banking industry to help him with his enquiries, partly because he sensed that his teasing with Monique should probably

stop now. She had, in her own sweet way, been trying to pin him down for the past couple of years. Now he probably needed both as allies.

It was time.

'Bonjour Monique, the pleasure's all mine.'

He extended the loveliest bouquet that the Concierge at the Crowne Plaza had been able to get his hands on at short notice. The purples and yellows and oranges complimented the colours on the newly installed splashback in her kitchen perfectly. The flowers were a lovely touch, always appreciated by a hostess, but the fact that he'd thought about the colours, well, that was a bit unusual for a man, to say the least.

She was genuinely touched and told him so.

'It's the absolute least I can do' he told her. Willi looks after me so well professionally and you look after me so well as a guest. You always have, Monique. I am truly privileged to know you both.'

She was already arranging the flowers into a beautiful shape in one of the many vases she kept tucked away in her utility room. She ran some fresh water into it and pulled gently at the petals and blossoms until she had the nice full shape she was happy with.

She came back beaming, with a big smile on her face and poured out some Marsanne.

They toasted.

Santé.

'Arri, I hope you don't mind if I ask you something before we sit down to eat.'

'Of course not.'

'Are you involved in trying to solve this, err, what shall I call it? Cette disparition.'

'The disappearance. Well that's as good a name as any for it'

'Oui, yes. The disappearance.'

'Yes, I am. That's why I'm here in Switzerland, actually.'

He took a long draft of the honey flavoured white wine.

'In fact, that's why I'm here in your house'

Monique looked at him quizzically.

'It's not here, 'Arri.' She told him, a bit sternly. 'We don't 'ave it. We 'ave nothing to do with it.'

Harry backpedalled quickly.

'No Monique, of course not. I'm so sorry. That came out all wrong. What I meant was Willi agreed to see me at very short notice today to figure out if he could help and then you, as always, were kind enough to invite me to lunch and so, here I am.'

Monique knew what she was doing. She had him slightly on the back foot now.

Only slightly.

So she pushed on.

'Help you how ' Arri? You're not a banker are you?'

'No Monique, no I'm not. I work for the UK Government.'

So far so good.

'Oh, is this a British matter then? I thought it was everywhere.'

'It is.'

'And 'ave you told Willi exactly what you do so that he knows if he can help you?'

And there it was.

Checkmate.

Swiss style.

'Not before today I haven't, no.'

And he looked at them.

And they looked back at him, expectantly.

Monique walked away from the old marble table that had been the scene of so much late night revelry down the years. The fondue base for her raclette was bubbling away nicely.

'But I suppose now would be a good time' he confessed.

And so he told them.

About The Nines and a few other things. About the Wuhan Mystery, as his team had christened their Covid -19 investigations. About the White House heist and Johnny Marriott, that patent guy. Plus his latest suspicions about La Disparition, as Monique had called it.

About The Disappearance.

A raclette is a patient dish. It will wait for you if you feel the need to chat for a while before eating. So it turned out to be an inspired choice by Monique for lunch that day as Harry Shepperton explained what had happened already, what he thought was happening now, and then his suspicions about what might happen next.

Finally Monique brought over the fresh bread from the oven and the cold meats

from the fridge and they started to tuck in.

She was feeling a whole lot better, her womanly instincts confirmed about her husband's English friend and business acquaintance.

Willi was also feeling a strange sense of relief. He hadn't quite known what to expect but now it was out in the open his mood also lifted considerably and he focused in on the details as his guest continued.

'And, much as I love Switzerland and especially seeing you two, I did need to validate my thinking Willi, you know, with someone who properly understands the mechanisms of banking.'

'Mais oui, d'accord, mon ami. Yes, of course I understand. And I can see why you would choose to come to me as well.'

'Good. What do you think then?'

'I think you are in the right place but talking to the wrong person.'

Harry's blank expression didn't say much but deep down he was suddenly disheartened, faced with the sudden prospect of, well, of what, having to undertake another journey to another part of Switzerland. Something he hardly had time for given the ticking clock and the rapid pace at which events were starting to unfold.

'I don't follow. Who is the right person?'

Willi grinned at his lovely wife as she sipped her coffee.

Not just beauty, plenty of brains too.

'C'est moi 'Arri' she said softly. ' It's me.'

Harry looked surprised because Harry was surprised, something that didn't happen too often.

'I don't understand.'

'Back in the day and before I left to have our Marcus I did all the computer stuff at the bank. That was how we described it in those days. There was no I.T department and the Internet was in its infancy. There was no broadband and you had to go through dial-up to get online.'

Harry nodded.

He remembered those days.

Long time ago.

'I used to get in at 6:30, do the alarms and then check all the systems. It was kind of extra on top of my actual job but I enjoyed it and I seemed to have an aptitude for it, so my manager sort of put me in charge of everything that needed to be done in

those areas.'

'And you became the expert?'

'Well, only in the sense that I knew more than the others who were working in the branch. In the land of the blind, the one eyed man is king. You know this saying?'

Harry did.

'And it all developed from there. When the Siemens guys came to do the software upgrades I watched and learned. Pretty soon I was helping out at our other local branch around the corner in Herrengasse as well. Whenever they had problems they would call me. Word got around.'

'And you became the tech expert.'

'Well not overnight, no, but gradually I learned more and more. The bank started sending me to Zurich and Berne on courses, even Vienna a couple of times. I enjoyed them immensely and I learnt how to code.'

'But I thought Willi told me you were BOB before you left. Doesn't that mean signing stuff off, authority levels, and being heavily involved in all the daily grind, the routine banking stuff.'

'Exactly. I did all that as well. That was still my day job.'

'As well as fixing the systems when they crashed.'

'Yes. And installing the upgrades.'

Harry realized that he'd probably found the insider that he'd been looking for, the one he could really trust. The lovely housewife who spent most afternoons pottering around her flower filled garden had been involved in building bank networks almost from the beginning.

'And you took your interests into retirement, so to speak?'

'I never really stopped. I had a short break from being a salaried officer to comply with the leaving-service rules then, after a while, they hired me back as a sort of independent contractor. Essentially it was supposed to be about security and the new protocols, but in reality I was consulting on the integration of IP and ATM networks into the banking infrastructure backbone'

Harry looked over at Willi.

'Don't remember you ever mentioning this,' he ventured.

'I don't remember you ever mentioning that you were a spy, Harry.' Willi countered with a grin.'

'Now bring your coffee upstairs and I'll show you something.' Monique offered,

and she led the way up some winding polished pine stairs to the first floor of their chalet style house, built in the picturesque Austrian / Swiss tradition. Lots of wood, both inside and outside, and a large wraparound loggia balcony, deep enough to sit six or eight comfortably around what appeared to be a second dining table.

'We like to eat out here when it's warm enough,' Willi explained, 'you can't beat alfresco dining in the fresh air, especially when you have a decent view.'

He nodded his head towards the distant alpine peaks.

'The White Mountain,' he confirmed.' Much better known by its French name of Mont Blanc, of course. At just under sixteen thousand feet, she's the highest in Europe.

'Thought that distinction belonged to Mount Elbrus.' Harry queried.

'Only if you believe that Russia is in Europe, and most Europeans don't think it is. Elbrus is way over off the far Eastern coast of the Black sea, it's further east than Moscow and most of Iraq. How is that Europe?'

Harry conceded the point. Hard to argue with that.

Monique brought some cake and biscuits and set some plates out on the table. Next to them she unrolled some old blueprints.

'Pretty old school.' Harry commented.' Not very digital.'

'They're mid and late nineties mostly,' she concurred,' some a bit earlier.'

She continued unravelling and splayed the drawings out across most of the table, anchoring them with some bottles of Old Boxer to keep the schematics flat and legible and safe from the occasional waft of breeze that would drift in as it blew softly along the valley.

'I imagine this is the kind of stuff the FIB team are reviewing right now back down there,' she commented, indicating the small urban sprawl that was Geneva, way below at the bottom of the hillside, ' albeit they'll have a much more modern version on their screens and tablets.'

'What exactly am I looking at here?' Harry sought clarification.

'These are some of the first telecoms' engineer's plans that were devised to map out the systems integration necessary to start computerising the banking network's backbone.'

'OK. I've seen this stuff before but remind me. Integrating what with what.'

'The two different systems that you need to do the job. A data network to carry all the coded messaging required to protect the systems and keep them safe from

unwanted surveillance, piracy and theft. And a comms network to link up all the different nodes, hubs and customer locations, basically those input and output terminals where people withdraw and deposit their money.'

'But isn't that all one and the same network?'

'It is now, at least in terms of the operational day-to-day. How it's run and how its managed.'

'But it wasn't always like that?'

'No, even today, where it's essentially seamless, any systems engineer looking at the overall infrastructure can see the joins pretty easily. It's run as one but built as two.'

'OK, understood.'

Willi waved a bottle at him.

Harry resisted the beer, still a bit early.

And he was going to have questions.

'But essentially one large interconnected global network rather than several smaller ones?'

'Yes, correct.'

The coffee was good and strong anyway, proper European stuff. Needed to concentrate now.

'And the implications of that on the present situation are what then?'

'That its main strength is also its main weakness.'

'How do you mean?'

'The end-to-end design is great for customers of course. You can get your money out pretty much anywhere in the world.'

'But?'

'But it also means that if the bad guys manage to break in anywhere they are not confined or restricted to their access point. Essentially if the location of forced entry is in Australia, you can do damage in Japan, entry in Frankfurt, you can do damage in California, and so on. There are essentially no firewalls to hinder or stop the geographic spread of any malware that is strong enough to create bad infections. In fact the latest ones positively thrive on resistance. You can think of them as flesh eating bacteria, cannibalising their hosts aimlessly as they go. At a certain point, if left unchecked, they possess the inherent power to self-destruct, essentially to destroy any network that they've invaded.'

'That sounds like a suicide mission.' Harry noted.' Why would they do that?'

'Well, they're not thinking, are they.' Monique said rhetorically. 'They're not human. They don't have a logic, not a human one anyway. These are essentially nothing more than electronic impulses, hugely randomized and only given shape and purpose by the existence of a technical instruction or set of instructions. They are data bits and bytes. Nothing more.'

'Ah, the rise of the machines.' Harry observed. ' The rise and rise, to be more accurate. And I do recognize that there's almost no end to it. But the programmes themselves still have to be written don't they, and the codes and algorithms developed. And I thought that the fail-safes, the roadblocks, the cut outs and the safety valves were all being created in parallel. I can hardly believe that they weren't. Not to do that is sheer madness. It's just asking for trouble.'

He looked at Monique and Willi rather askance.

'So there is the opportunity for immediate contamination anywhere inside that network even if the intrusion happens somewhere else half way round the world? 'he asked, seeking more clarification and validation of this rather surprising piece of information.

'There are localised firebreaks, of course. They're an inherent part of the designs and are upgraded constantly. You can think of them like the regular security patches issued by Apple and Microsoft to constantly protect their operating systems. They get downloaded automatically and will almost always fix any new problems and shore up the breaches. That's the good news, of course. The bad news is that they have to keep on issuing them. They have become a constant feature of digital life.'

'So all systems, even the best ones, will always have their vulnerabilities. Is that what you're saying?'

'That it's inevitable, a fact of life, at least for the moment.'

'And what? Somehow that's how all this happened?'

'No, no 'Arri. But that is vital background. You must understand that first.'

'Ok.'

'An' now you have to consider these overlaps.'

She pulled a couple of the larger drawings towards the middle of the table.

'If you look here,' she indicated a specific point ' you can see some gateway markings.'

She traced her finger to the relevant area.

'What are they exactly?'

'They are like interconnections. If you want to link two different types of network together then this is where it will 'appen'

'Well ok, I understand that but what's the relevance? I don't quite see.'

'You have to maybe think about it like a train.'

'Like a train! How?'

'Have you ever seen a train...?'

She was searching for the right word in English.

'Qu'est que c'est decoupler en Anglais, Willi?

'Uncouple.'

'Have you ever seen a train uncouple 'Arry?'

'Yes. Of course.'

'So there is a place where they usually do this, mainly in the middle between the carriages.'

'Yes, that's right. They do that a lot with the long distance trains.'

'And what happens?'

'Part of the train stays behind in one place, usually in the station and ...'

Harry paused as he thought back to the rowers going round Barnes bridge.

'Bloody hell.' he exclaimed suddenly

'And the rest of it ' Arry?'

'The rest of it carries on as normal. But the train is now smaller. Much smaller.'

'And the people who want to use the train?' Monique continued to guide him gently forward. Always better if people reached their own conclusions rather than having them imposed.

'The people who want to use the train will have to…...'

He paused to think.

'Well the ones that wish to make the journey to the new destination will have stayed on board. They will already be travelling somewhere else.'

'D'accord. Yes, of course. And the others…?

'Will still be where they were before.'

'And, if my guess is right. And please remember it is only a guess, for I cannot know for sure, the first group of passengers are like your thieves. They have done the uncoupling and are now somewhere else, while the people who are still waiting at the station are the other group. In other words, they are us. The people who cannot see

where the uncoupled part of the train has gone because it has moved.'

Harry nodded slowly.

So, somebody else had had a David Copperfield moment as well. Only this time it was somebody who understood how bank networks functioned.

'OK, so taking your example further, where does that lead us to next?' Harry wanted to know.

However unlikely explanations sounded, he would always give them the benefit of the doubt until they either crashed and burned or turned out to be feasible.

'To a portal.'

'What portal?'

'You know what one is of course?' Monique was checking.' A portal?'

'Like an overlap area, a kind of doorway from one place to another.'

Monique nodded in agreement.

'Oui, c'est ca. Yes, of course, that's right.'

She smiled at him, like a schoolteacher who had managed to coax the right answer out of an uncertain pupil.

'And do they have them on the Internet, for example? ' she led him again.

'Of course. People talk about them all the time in that particular context.' he confirmed.

'As an area to pass through?'

'Yes. On the way to somewhere else."

'And what will 'appen if you decouple the train half way through. Half way across?'

Now that was a hard question.

Hard and a bit weird.

Harry tried to think of an example of this so he could get his head round what Monique was suggesting.

'So would that be the same as clicking a hyperlink and getting no response?'

Monique was seemingly impressed with this answer. She clapped her hands together, palm against palm, and waggled them together towards Harry in a kind of praying motion.

'Yes, exactly. You have given an instruction but there is no response. You have basically said " *I'm finished reading this story and I would now like to read that story over there please."* Click and hey presto. Only this time. Rien. Nothing. Ne rien.

Nothing at all. Nothing happens.'

Harry was still thinking.

Yes, of course, that happens. Happens all the time. But what was the significance of it and how did it apply to La Disparition. To The Disappearance?

'Now I will complete my train analogy.' Monique said with a certain tone of finality.

'Did you ever see a film called *The taking of Pelham 123?*'

Harry froze.

Not only had he seen it, the brilliant original with Walter Matthau and the later version as well. It was one of his all time favourite movies. He knew the story backwards.

He glared at his hostess and her husband.

'It didn't really disappear at all, did it?' he muttered out loud.

It was half question, half statement.

'They've just moved it somewhere else. Like the uncoupled train. There are now two bits, two pieces. One in one place, one somewhere else'

'Oui 'Arry. I think so. As I said before, I cannot be sure but I know it could have been done like that.'

'Using a portal instead of a tunnel'

'Or maybe both.'

They all paused for a moment.

Willi had managed to do something that he hadn't really expected to be able to pull off that afternoon.

He'd stayed out of it.

Now it was his turn to make a contribution.

He stood up and fetched a bottle opener from the covered side pocket of their Traeger barbeque parked over on the corner of the balcony, still covered up against the crisp spring weather.

He cracked open three bottles of Old Boxer and poured out three glasses.

'It's always five o'clock somewhere,' he announced in the old time-honoured tradition, as he raised his glass.

'And if that doesn't deserve a drink, then I don't know what does.'

He kissed his wife gently on her forehead and nuzzled a few soft words into her ear.

The three of them sat back in silence, alone with their thoughts, and studied the beautiful distant alpine mountaintops, glinting away in the crisp late afternoon sunshine.

The view was idyllic and the silence was golden, broken only by a brief exclamation in English.

'Bloody hell.'

Chapter 30 – The Energy King.

Liam's original plan had been to meet up somewhere with Paul at some stage in the afternoon. They'd kept things fluid to allow for the kinds of eventualities that pop up in their line of work. In this instance, the surprising, albeit not totally unexpected fact, that Paul's potential ally was turning out to be FSB and that Liam's own trail in pursuit of the communiqué, the only really serious lead they had, had gone rather cold.

Liam had wanted to check out his colleague's 3pm, the one which Jake had alerted him to, albeit briefly, so he didn't know the full details. However, his short video dialogue earlier had at least informed him that Paul was already making headway with his own contacts so he made the decision to leave him alone for now and concentrate on his own faltering lead. If he got any help from local surveillance courtesy of Valeria it would be a bonus. For now, he was on his own for a few hours.

He called Jojo in Chelsea and told her about his wild goose chase.

'So dat particular trail's gone a bit cold for now.' he told her.' 'n I just called Paul but he's busied himself out with the locals for now.'

'Did you catch the FIB press conference?'

'I heard 'dey was just stallin' till tomorrow.'

'That's about right. The Q and A was interesting though, especially the Russian journalist guy at the end.'

'I didn't actually see it Jo, I was still in the air. What did he have to say, then?'

'Well, it wasn't too specific but there's obviously some information from within Russia that we could probably use to our advantage.'

'And what would datt be denn?'

'From what he said it sounds like they've got wind of something about some strange behaviour locally. The journalist was from Izvestia who are pretty respectable as Russian media outlets go, so I'd imagine his sources would have been reliable.'

'How can we get to him?'

'Well, Hank and Jake are both in Geneva to see what else they can get from the FIB unit. You could try them.'

Jake was enjoying a coffee out by the pool area of the President Wilson when

Liam caught up with him.

'Just on my way over to the Fairmont now, actually.' he explained by way of an update. 'It wouldn't surprise me if Hank hasn't found Ivan and tapped him up so either give me half an hour and I'll call you back or try him direct.'

'Ok, ta. Will do. Anytin' else?'

'Did you hear about Wanderer One's tennis and golf connection?'

'No,'oi didn't, no. Go on."

'She's pals with Mags Mollinsky, you may have heard of her, the up and coming golf pro?'

'Yeah, black baseball cap and blonde pigtail, oi know who ya mean.'

'And Mags likes travelling, in what little spare time she has, likes to get away from the circuit. So it turns out that she, in turn, knows Yelena Alliskiya, who is one of her regular holiday buddies.'

'Sorry, dat's somebody I've never heard of.'

'Well, she's that rarest of all things at the moment, a Russian golfing sensation. Or at least an emerging one. Big sport over there right now, apparently. I mean, who knew?'

'Well, certainly not me, dat's for sure.' Liam confirmed.' So Yelena fits into this how?'

'She doesn't. Well, not personally, anyway. But her dad might because he's very wealthy and very well connected. Right at the top apparently, if you catch my drift. The very top.'

Liam whistled.

'And he was Paul's intended three o' clock.'

'You mean that's not happening now?'

'Not unless you do it Liam.'

'Why ,what's happened to Paul. I barely spoke to him an hour ago.'

'Well, you'll recall Harry nominated me as liaison when we hit ops mode last night, so all emergency messages come straight into me.'

Liam stopped walking.

This wasn't good news.

'Which code?'

'Blue three.'

Liam breathed a sigh of relief.

Trouble, but not big trouble.

The Nines had their own colour coded internal message system, largely based on the extent to which they were either delayed, compromised, needed something urgently or were in personal danger.

Broadly speaking red was bad, yellow was an annoyance or a distraction, but one which could be managed without external intervention, and blue was a temporary hiccup, usually solvable without any kind of reinforcements. Green was reserved for progress, the only one of the colours that was good news. They didn't get too many green messages.

The numbers from one to five were an indication of severity. So red five, the code none of them ever wanted to see or hear, meant imminent danger to life, need immediate assistance / evacuation. Help, drop everything , I'm in real trouble.

Blue three, based on what they knew about Paul's current situation, almost certainly meant he'd just got stuck and bogged down with something.

The Nines were all infinitely adaptable.

Liam didn't hesitate to pick up. They were all trained to cover each other in the widest range of circumstances.

'I'll need something though,' he told Jake.' If I'm meeting with one of the most powerful men in Russia, what's my back story?'

'Paul was thinking of posing as an emissary from the FIB, either seeking information or bringing some. You know, intended for the top.'

'Pretty high stakes then. Don't know if I've got sufficient blagging skills to turn myself into a credible banker. What happens if the conversation gets all finance tech ? I might struggle with that.'

'Then don't let it happen. Avoid it.' Jake instructed.' I don't think you'll be getting a grilling. He'll just want to know what the fuck just happened. You know, like everybody else really.'

'Ok, no probs. What else?'

'Get yourself over to Meshchansky district, it's about an hours walking from where you are right now. '

Liam's location was clearly marked on the GPS app on Jake's phone. They both knew each other's exact location.

'Just head North and keep going. Soon as I find Hank in the Fairmont I'll ping you.'

'Ok, that's the Izvestia angle covered. But what about the Oligarch?'

'His name's Viktor Alliskiya, He's generally known as The Energy King. Made all his money from monopolizing the country's natural resources, the gas, the coal, the minerals, and so on.'

Jake paused for a second while Liam took all that in.

'You wouldn't happen to know anything much about any of that stuff, would you now, Mr. Geologist, Sir?'

Ten seconds later Liam rang off, turned around, walked back past the apartment where Andrei's body still lay stretched out on the sofa in the top floor apartment, crossed back over the open park at Staraya Square and strode briskly along Lubyanskiy Prospekt.

The rather ominous Lubyanka building, infamous for its repressive prison, glared at him from a distance. He wondered what secrets it held today as the current headquarters of the FSB, the modern day KGB.

Did they know what he knew?

Or did he know more?

Was Viktor Alliskiya just a rich oligarch?

Or did he have another job?

Was Russia complicit in any of this?

Or just another victim?

The dance of the spies was about to begin.

In an unintended reversal of roles Paul was now waiting for the Staraya park surveillance video to come through on Raspo's smartphone. It turned out that Valeria outranked him as the youngest Major ever appointed by the FSB and, after a couple of hurried calls of her own, declared that she needed to keep her own phone free awaiting further instructions.

The clip didn't take long to arrive and the three of them looked at it together. Paul quickly spotted the distinctive female shape of a tall curvy young woman crossing the park in a Southerly direction.

'Almost hundred percent that's her.' he announced.' But where's the food.'

The figure in question wasn't carrying anything but she did have a small sports backpack.

'Well, she can't be going far if it's in there, can she? Nothing worse than cold

burgers and soggy chips.'

'Davat' bednym' suggested Raspo.

Paul looked up from the phone blankly.

'You have read the communiqué I presume, Mr. Lambert?'

'I have.' Paul confirmed. 'Of course.'

'They have a Robin Hood agenda, do they not, these people, whoever they are?'

'It seems they might do, yeah, although we don't really know if that's just some kind of smoke screen or not. What does that mean, what you just said. I'm really sorry, I don't speak any Russian.'

Aaagh.

Britguilt.

Again

'It means, *give to the poor.*' RR explained with a sudden and unexpected smile.

'There is a trend among today's youth to do that differently. Being the young, they like to find their own ways of doing things so, if they see a homeless person or a down and out, as I believe you also call them, they won't give them money because they suspect, quite rightly, that they will probably spend it on Vodka. So they give them food instead. The arrival of so many relatively cheap take-aways in our country over the past few years has just accelerated the trend.'

Paul thought back and remembered a few homeless guys lying on the pavement somewhere when he'd been walking around earlier.

But not many.

'They tend to get moved on by the cops, especially in the major city centres. Don't want to frighten off the tourists you know, we like their dollars too much. But the kids always seem to find them, even if they're just sat on a park bench.'

He rewound the video.

'Look. There,'

And sure enough, right at the beginning of the clip, their target had quite deliberately placed a brown paper bag next to a shabbily dressed man with torn shoes who was rubbing his face as if he'd just woken up.

'What, and this is something your kids do a lot?'

'The ones who have a bit of money do, yes. And there are more and more of them.'

Raspo looked at Paul, slightly angrily.

'You see, despite your Western media portrayal Mr. Lambert, we are no longer an impoverished country. Nor one without morals. So yes, it's a growing trend, and a rather fashionable one. Personally, I hope it catches on.'

Hmm, Paul thought, modern Russia continues to surprise.

'Well, that explains that, I suppose. What about her bike though?'

'Possibly a rental and she just dropped it off at the nearest rack.'

'There'll be a record of payment then, assuming we can find and identify it.'

'Not necessarily. The schemes are still quite new here and to encourage take-up the organisers are still having lots of free promotional days. They lose quite a few of the bikes of course, but they're all heavily branded so they figure the overall exposure is worth it as people see them more and more around the city.'

Paul thought quickly.

'Ok then, lets see where she's going.'

The cameras were not completely ubiquitous and the clips only covered certain areas of the City. They picked her up again on CCTV as she left the park on the west side, just across from the Kitay Gorod metro station where another of Moscow's three lane boulevards bustled along.

Georgi had left the apartment a few minutes earlier. They saw him meet her. The couple spoke together in a rather agitated fashion for a few minutes before she grabbed his arm and seemed to hug him before they disappeared back into the park and down the steps into the Metro.

'Have you got face recognition installed yet by any chance?' Paul enquired.

Valeria had now come off the phone and joined them.

'Only in selected locations as part of the broader rollout' she confirmed. 'That isn't one of them,'

'So even if we follow their Metro journey it won't help us identify them.'

'Correct. But we should probably find out where they were going anyway. It might provide another clue and, let's face it, we still haven't got many.'

A few seconds conversation on the phone and Raspo received a new video file.

Georgi and Ans could clearly be seen walking along the long underground station corridors before turning off towards a platform entrance.

'Where does that go? Paul enquired

'That's the purple line, the seven, north west direction.'

'Heading where?'

'Out into the suburbs eventually, but it passes through Meshchansky and some of the other wealthiest areas first.'

On the day after *Ischeznoveniye,* Viktor Alliskiya left the Kremlin using one of the less known entrances of which there are several. It is, in any case, not a building with a traditional front door and many of its guests tend to arrive and depart quietly and unseen.

Viktor was not bothered about being in the limelight. It came with the territory as a Russian billionaire and his picture was often attached to a whole variety of stories in the local and world media, some of them true, some made up, all interesting and good copy – which was all that mattered to the editors and proprietors of the newspapers and other digital outlets.

Sometimes people do actually look like their stereotypes. Gangsters with stripey suits and fedoras. Rock stars with long hair and blonde starlets on their arms. Controversial scientists with unkempt beards and open toed sandals.

But what is an Oligarch supposed to look like?

Probably older and fatter than the average with a defensive manner and a shady personality.

But Viktor Alliskiya was none of these things.

Still in his thirties he looked more like a pro tennis player. Tall, slim, athletic and sun tanned, he gave interviews freely and was skilled enough to bat away the usual tricky questions about raping the state economy, being involved in corruption, and instigating bribery.

As such he was a marmite figure, the darling of many but a devil to others. In his very Russian way, Viktor quite liked the conflict between these two opposing views and played on it and up to it whenever he could.

The fact that he was instantly recognizable didn't bother him either. A pair of shades and a warm beanie and he could immediately be as anonymous as the next guy so, for the most part, he lived an almost normal kind of life.

His meeting with the officials had been impromptu. Known as a man with a huge network of contacts, he had effectively been summonsed to give his take on matters.

It was one thing to have one's views considered but yet another to be invited to contribute to the resolution of the problem.

He had seen it coming of course, so it hadn't been too much of a surprise.

'How can such a thing happen, Viktor?'

'I really cannot say. It is almost beyond belief.'

'Do you have any contacts who could help, maybe in finance or banking?'

'I can ask around, certainly. I will be pleased to help.'

'It will be appreciated. By everybody. You understand that of course.'

'Yes, yes, of course. I am in great pain myself as a result of this attack, as you can probably imagine.'

'Your first task should be to ensure that Russia herself is not incriminated.'

'Ok, understood.'

'By which we mean two things. Firstly, it didn't happen here, secondly there were none of our citizens involved.'

'Yes, of course. I can see why.'

Viktor was not blind to the unfolding politics of such a dramatic situation. Whichever country had unwittingly hosted the perpetrators of this global crime could become an international pariah overnight for allowing it to happen, even if, as was almost certainly the case, there was nothing much they could have done differently to stop it.

'I will see what I can find out.' he said robustly. ' Do you have any early leads at all that might be of assistance?'

'We know that Izvestia have heard something. They are sitting on their sources but we, in turn, are sitting on them, so we should have something soon.'

'Ok, well that's good. I know people there as well so I can ask around.'

'And we can expect some Government personnel to start arriving from the West. We don't have exact details yet but they always suspect Russia when things like this happen so it's a pretty safe bet they will do what they always do.'

'And send some agents?'

'That's what we expect, yes.'

'Won't your own guys want to deal with that in their own way?

'They will, of course, but they always appreciate extra assistance. Who doesn't?'

'Will I have to travel away from Moscow?'

'Don't know, at this stage. Unlikely, I would have thought, but not impossible.'

A few more details and eventualities covered off and they were finished.

As Viktor rose to leave he had one last question.

It was rather hard to see the connection with what they had been discussing for

the past hour yet it was something that mattered greatly to Viktor Alliskiya, to the Energy King.

'And the Tbilisi pipeline contract renewal?' he pondered.

'Shouldn't be a problem.'

Matters of global cyber-sabotage aside, business was, after all, still business.

Chapter 31 – The trick

As March dawned across the planet Andrei and Georgi's self-imposed deadline was suddenly upon them. All the preparations had been completed and they had reviewed, double-checked and then checked everything again. Where such meticulous thoroughness is involved, one could be forgiven for thinking that nothing much could go wrong. However anybody with any experience of the military will quickly attest to the opposite.

Whether it be the army, the navy, or the air force, the level of advance thinking that goes into almost any activity is quite excruciating in its detail. There are lots of meetings between lots of people who talk about lots of things and the outputs from those meetings then get disseminated and cascaded down to teams of other people who then talk about most of the same things – albeit sometimes including a few new ones – so that everybody is *" on the same page "* when it comes to the execution of the plan or the implementation of the strategy, or whatever.

The whole point of these activities is to improve the chances of success and to reduce the chances of failure and, to that end , they are, without doubt, worthy endeavours.

But what they will never do – never can do – is guarantee an outcome.

The world tends not to want to work that way, preferring instead, to create unseen risks and spontaneous uncertainties. Why this happens is anybody's guess, and there have been no shortage of possible causes expounded down the years by all sorts of philosophical, scientific and religious theorists, some well-intentioned, some ill-informed, some genuine, many charlatans.

The reality is simple. Things have a habit of not always working out according to the plan, no matter how well rehearsed that may be.

There are increments involved in these never ending mishaps ranging from the slight miss all the way through to the globally ubiquitous military *FUBAR*, the term applied by those unfortunate enough to get caught up in a mission that is *fucked up beyond all recognition.*

To their great credit the two teenage boys were mature enough to know this as well and were sufficiently pragmatic to try to include some mitigation into their last

minute plans.

'So on the day, we need to leave early' Andrei started.' Even though the hit will look like it happened in Geneva, there's no way of telling how quickly things might unravel.'

'That's true Andi, but connecting any clues back to here, back to the flat cannot possibly happen that quickly, surely?'

'I agree, but we don't really know, do we. There's a first time for everything and this will be the first time that anybody has attempted to launch a Crypto that's directly linked to all of the existing global currencies at the same time. The whole exercise should take place from start to finish in the digital domain of which our bedrooms definitely do not form part.'

'OK. First things first. What do we use for data erase?'

'Well, you're the python guy. Can you tweak the USBKill Linux programme?'

'Already done'

'And Ninja OS for flash drive rapid recycle.'

'Also done.'

In most cases where authorities seek to track and close down anything which they deem to be rogue software applications, they will require password bypass, something which immediately creates a dependency on the accused for cooperation who, in turn, may be able to successfully claim violation of their rights, given that the creation of such passwords are generally classified as mental creation procedures – a bit similar in concept and in law to intellectual property – and, as such, are very often protected by those very laws.

The way they will often get round this is by attempting to seize any offending computing equipment while it is still switched on and active. Easier said than done but a tactic used successfully by the US feds in closing down the now legendary dark web Silk Road operation in 2014.

In turn, in one of the many bizarre twists and turns in this particular game of cyber cat and mouse, a kind of auto destruct instruction can now be deployed by the owners of any suspect software, instantly destroying all evidence as soon as any unauthorized device – in other words anything belonging to somebody else – is introduced into the machine to either read, copy or download its contents. All and any evidence on a suspected machine is therefore instantly destroyed and prosecution – at least in a 'clean' legal system – becomes impossible.

'I've tested it over and over,' Georgi continued,' which was pretty scary because I could have fucked up weeks of development work if I'd got it wrong. But anyway, it's done now and I'm happy with the programme.'

'And we can remote access them?'

'Of course. All of them have got RAT's deployed. As long as we have Wifi, we can connect from anywhere.'

Remote Access Trojans – as the name very graphically suggests – are secret "back door" entry points inside software systems which support unauthorised and virtually invisible access and monitoring by those who install them.

'How do we do that and hide our IP address?'

'Go through multiple TOR servers and churn the IP's, the underlying MAC addresses will kick in then for security reasons. That's plenty of obscurity.'

He looked at his friend across another scene of scattered coffee cups and discarded McDonalds bags. They might have been computer geniuses but they were still nineteen-year old boys.

Tidying things up was way down their priorities list.

As i-day drew closer, they were still managing to stay on the right side of cool. But only just.

i for *ischeznoveniye*. The day their lives would change forever.

The Onion Ring servers were a randomly distributed set of international nodes. Mostly individually owned and mostly non-corporate they were, and are, collectively known as TOR and support broad access to the dark web where privacy rules.

Well, almost.

'In the short term, at least. Although nothing's perfect Andi. We shouldn't forget that.'

'Yeh, course. Agreed. So that's our escape plan covered, at least in terms of the tech. What about physically?'

'What do you mean?'

'I mean we obviously can't stay here, can we.'

'No, I know. Been thinking about that quite a lot.'

'Or together either, probably.'

'No, been thinking about that too. That's gonna' be almost as weird as what we're actually planning.'

'Do you think it might turn out to be necessary to leave? To leave the country, I

mean?'

The two friends looked at each other.

Another less than pleasant moment in the overall adventure.

'Might be for the best, I suppose, yeah. Just in case. Although I don't think we'll ever be able to outrun this, will we. It'll be too big.'

'Wanted, Dead or Alive' Andrei laughed. 'Just about everywhere. The ultimate wanted poster with our mug shots on them.'

'Well, let's hope it never gets that far,' Georgi responded.' Cos if they ever find out who we actually are, either one of us, then we really are as good as dead. Poster or no poster.'

'What about Ans. Have you told her yet?'

'I can't can I? We're sworn to secrecy, remember.'

'Well, how's that gonna' work then? She just turns up here one day and we're both gone. Just at exactly the same time that the story breaks and you and me both go missing. At the same time.'

'Well, I must confess, that's been on my mind a lot too. Not quite sure what to do about that?'

'She knows us Andi, knows us inside out. She'll know it was us. You know what she's like. She'll just know.'

'Yeh, I know you're right but I'm not sure the best way to do it. I've thought about that quite a lot too but I haven't figured it out yet.'

He puffed his cheeks out and exhaled.

'I do like her a lot, Georgi. Do you think I should marry her?'

Georgi's face had a kind of strange blank expression for a moment.

'Well it's one idea, I suppose.'

JoJo and Caitlin had been wrestling with the mechanics of Cryptocoin most of Wednesday.

'All right for some, jetting off round Europe in the line of duty,' Jo quipped.

'Russia's not in Europe, Jo,' her colleague reminded her.' Plus having no more than half the team abroad on Ops is the unwritten rule, remember. Just in case anything blows up back here at home. Plus Harry's in Switzerland as well, so with Jake, Paul and Liam all away as well now, that really makes four out of seven if you include the boss. That's more than half.'

'Ok, I know, I was just kidding. And I managed to fluke a nice trip to Ireland when that White House project was going on, so I'm not complaining. Goodness, seems ages ago now, that one.'

'That's because it was Jo. Four years to be exact. And we're all still talking to each other. Quite an achievement.'

'And it's actually five people if you count Hank,' Cait suggested as a disconnected afterthought, 'although he's not really a Nine, he kind of is in a way.'

'Yeah, I can't help thinking he's going to be key to this somehow, what with all his knowledge about the finance sector.'

'Well that is why he's in Geneva, Jo. Somehow that seems to have started self-selecting as the epi-centre for Jumbo. I wonder why.'

'Well, lets get back to the hacking theories then and review our assumptions to date then we might find out.'

Another take out package from one of Chelsea's finer Deli's was quickly swept off the kitchen table as they cleared the decks for the afternoon.

'If you wanted to create a mirror, how would you go about it? That's where we got up to before we stopped for lunch, wasn't it? '

'Exactly.'

'So do you think it's going to be based on spoofing.'

'Good chance, yup.'

'Only instead of a masquerade or a copy, it just creates a reflection.'

'Do we think that's really possible?'

'Well, lets think it through. There are really only two options here. Either it happened exactly as everybody is being led to believe and everything has really disappeared.'

'Which still seems unlikely/borderline impossible.' Jojo commented. 'Even though that really is what it looks like.'

'Or that didn't happen.'

'In which case it's some sort of trick. An illusion.'

'Which has taken place in the digital domain. Essentially in Cyberspace.'

'So, let's start with that. The borderline impossible option. How would you do it?'

'What about creating a set of dummy accounts.'

'A set? There's millions of them. Hundreds of millions.'

'Sure, but computer technologies deal in hundreds of millions all day and every day, don't they. Billions in fact, if you're talking about Quantum algorithms, like the ones that increasingly make all the trading decisions for the major investment houses. Billions of computations in milliseconds in fact, each one culminating in a decision, a buy or sell signal to the dealers. Every market uses them nowadays. FOREX, equities, currencies, all the derivatives. In fact they're so well established, they're almost old hat.'

'How would our perpetrators get hold of the basic data required for that?'

'How about the dark web?'

'No way, some of it maybe, not all of it. We're talking about the world's bank accounts. I mean how many will there be?'

'Well that at least should be in the first FIB output. Lets see?'

Cait scanned her laptop

'Here. One point six billion as of last year. That's individuals. Private citizens. And let's say another twenty percent on top for business and Company accounts. That gets us up one point nine billion.'

'So nearly two billion sets of very well encrypted data. Not held centrally anywhere, but distributed. Sourcing that in the way you would need to in order to create replica accounts is just impossible.'

'Well, it's not Jo, is it? Because it looks like somebody might have actually managed to do it. And if we're sticking with this theory, then that's got to be our working assumption.'

Caitlin Yang was not a girl to be defeated easily, neither by work nor play. She had developed a series of conditioned reflex responses to most of the situations in life that a tall curvy athletic woman in her prime of life would be likely to face. These ranged from managing male advances, unwanted or otherwise, through to the types of vigorous debates with the boss which are experienced by senior professionals everywhere these days, whatever their line of work.

She still thought back often to the day her life had changed forever at her Nines' interview in London and how Colonel Blinky Duff and his interviewing sidekick old Archie Webster had spotted something in her that allowed them to forgive her temporary blubbering, pass her and offer her her dream job.

The Nines had an especiallly transparent recruitment policy where the interviewing board made their full notes available afterwards to all candidates. It was

a smart psychological move, designed to create trust and insight. All six had benefited from it.

Caitlin had hers framed.

The words in the summary were emblazoned across her heart.

Capable of selfless bravery of the highest order.

They could have failed her for her temporary emotional lapse. But the two seasoned old pros hadn't seen it that way. Once they understood that she had once saved somebody's life, her tears had made sense.

But such an inspirational girl. Other than that, she breezed through.

From the moment she'd first been privy to the innermost thoughts of her bosses she had pledged her full allegiance to the team. Who would ever want to work for anybody else when it was clear that one was held in such genuine high esteem?

She may have been specifically recruited for her internet and software skills but Caitlin Yang was a naturally bright spark, a wild Californian free spirit from 'Frisco, matured partially by her time on the East coast at Harvard but still more than capable of moments of wild abandon, as many of the men who passed through her young life had found out, very fortunately for some, much less so for others.

Her natural courage and sense of adventure combined with a restless curiosity made her a formidable ally.

Cait was not a girl who gave up on much.

She was now in deep thought, a kind of Zen like state that Jojo had seen her in before.

She recognized it straight away for what it was.

Time to shut up.

Cait was trance thinking.

Jojo was not from America.

She was English.

She went to the kitchen and put the kettle on.

Chapter 32 – Meshchansky

Like all great cities, Moscow has its good places and its less good. The rich have to live somewhere and, as a general rule, tend to cluster together. Whether this is because they feel safer like that and it's some kind of primeval survival instinct is debatable. Just as likely is the notion that the nicer parts of any large town are usually separate from the other areas and so it just becomes a simple matter of geography.

Rather intriguingly, exactly the same can be said about the poor.

Another odd characteristic is to do with the mixed nature of inner city regions, which often reflect those disparities in microcosm. And so it can be that the difference between desirable and unappealing can often come down to just a few streets.

Being a born and bred Muscovite, Viktor Alliskiya knew perfectly well the differences between the various Oblasts, the smaller administrative areas which made up the city. He owned several houses across Russia, and several more around the world, his considerable individual wealth being barely impacted by those numerous purchases, large and extensive properties though they were.

Such things become possible only with extreme riches, and, as they say, behind every great fortune lies a great crime.

In Viktor's case, as with so many others, life had dealt him a hand that included some auspicious timing and he just happened to be in the right place at the right time when the old Soviet Union was breaking up.

Such social upheavals are the end for many but also the beginning for a select few who are cute enough to spot the opportunities and have no qualms about taking advantage of them. Life, according to those people, is all about winners and losers, and they have no doubt whatsoever about which of those groups they belong to.

As his Maybach glided its way back from his early morning meeting he was also, like Caitlin in London, in deep thought about Ischeznoveniye.

But there was a significant difference.

He wasn't trying to figure it out, or understand how it had happened, or even why it had happened.

He was purely focused on the who.

Because that was the primary concern of his benefactor.

So that was not just his main concern. It was his only concern.

For Viktor was a pragmatic man. Although the Disappearance had temporarily parted him from his billions, he had no doubt that this would only be a temporary matter, a minor blip on his smooth and gilded passage through life.

The rich are always best placed to ride out life's storms so he was as calm and untroubled as any man with twenty houses and apartments – all fully stocked with provisions, amusements and stimulants of varying descriptions – can ever be.

His comfortable lifestyle was so extensive that it would take seismic events of a completely different kind to disrupt it. And by looking after those who looked after him he was intent on making sure that never happened.

"Whatever happens Viktor, somebody somewhere always knows". That was what his father had told him all those years ago.

It almost seemed ridiculous when you said it out loud, just so obvious. And yet the world was full of endless mysteries that had remained unsolved for eons of time. Why? Because people had stopped asking questions too early in their investigations, in numerous cases before they had even gotten anywhere close to that most significant person, the one who knew.

Convincing that person to then talk was another matter altogether but there were ways and means to do that.

That would be stage two.

Stage one was where he was now. Find the person or persons responsible and hope that they weren't Russian. If they were, they were in even more trouble than they knew.

As his comfortable roomy saloon cruised the thirty minutes back to the home he called triple M – My Meshchansky Mansion – Viktor was busy making calls. All of them brief, barely two minutes, not chatty, very succinct and very business like. All of them identical.

All of them like orders to soldiers.

Do this and do it now.

The numerous recipients all understood. These were *drop everything* messages. Whatever else you happen to be doing, stop it now and do this. They understood intuitively, without any further explanation, that Viktor too had probably received some similar orders.

So they also made their own calls and gradually a small spiders web started to

appear, spinning itself first across Moscow and then beyond, south towards the breakaway republics, north towards the former capital of St Petersburg, east out towards the frozen wastes of central Asia and Siberia, home to many of the country's prison camps and a likely destination for the audacious perpetrators of this astonishing crime. After they had been interrogated, of course, and finally explained how they had pulled it off.

But, Viktor reminded himself, that was stage two.

First things first.

By the time he reached MMM he had made about twenty calls and each and every one of his contacts would have done the same thing. It was an object lesson in activating a network and by early afternoon the word was out right across Russia.

That evening the official he had visited in the morning contacted him again and he was alerted to the imminent arrival of various representatives of foreign Governments searching for clues.

"Their agents will be sent to other countries as well, of course, but it is inevitable that some will come here. They always like to suspect Russia of collusion and involvement, even if we are an innocent party, so we must manage them as best we can while they sniff around here like dogs."

Viktor got the message and awaited further instructions.

He wondered who would be first to make contact and how they would do it. That was always an interesting part of the game.

Probably be the Brits or the Yanks taking the lead, he thought.

And he was right, although the method of contact, as was so often the case, surprised and caught him off guard.

'Papa, I might need to go to Austria for my next tournament. Do you want to come?' Yelena asked him that same evening.' It's supposed to be a really beautiful country.'

'Yes, my sweet. I have heard such things too. When will it be?'

'In the spring. Mags is in a tournament there at the same time. You remember Mags, she's on the pro – circuit.'

'Yes, of course, the English girl, bit older.'

'Well, she's in her thirties I suppose, yes. But she's so well connected, papa. She's like a female version of you, well, if you see what I mean.'

Viktor laughed, the proud father with the beautiful daughter.

'And her manager is coming to Moscow tomorrow. I think she said once that he's one of those mega agents, the ones who seem to know how to fix most things in sport. Mags says he can probably get me in, even though I'm a bit borderline with my current rankings, you know, being out with the injury for the past couple of months hasn't helped too much. She texted me earlier saying she could hook us up.'

Viktor's ears pricked up.

'Coming tomorrow? To Russia? With everything that's going on!'

'Well the world hasn't completely stopped yet, has it? Life goes on doesn't it until, well, until it doesn't, I suppose.'

'What's his name?'

'Lambert. Paul Lambert.'

Viktor made a quick call.

Not for him, hours of aimless Googling. He could get that done by other people, better and younger, skilled in knowing more precisely what to look for.

'Well, do you want to invite him here to the house. Maybe some hospitality is in order if he's going to help you get in.'

Viktor checked his diary quickly, only a couple of meetings mixed in with the never-ending phone calls, all scheduled for around lunchtime.

'If he's free in the afternoon, I could be here and say hello as well. Sometime around three, maybe? '

Yelena unwound her long tanned legs from the scatter cushions on the velvet sofa, walked over to her father and kissed him softly on the forehead, nearly always a sign of love and a very difficult thing to do unless you have a strong affection for somebody.

She was a modest girl who was eternally grateful for his support, whatever it was he did for a living.

Those news reports were always so confusing, some said his business talents kept the lights on and ensured that peoples' homes were warm through the long dark frozen Russian winters, others suggested he was some kind of gangster.

To Yelena, he was her lovely Papa, always was, always would be.

Many others, however, saw him very differently.

'Thank you Papa, that's a nice idea. I'll ping Mags and see if she can set it up.'

Back in London, the Nines' support team had been busy creating some false social media profiles to support Paul's cover story. A string of news articles slotted in

nicely just behind them. To the casual observer he looked the part, an up and coming super sports agent with a roster of talent.

However, the people who called Viktor back half an hour later were not casual observers, they were the black ops digital media team from St Petersburg, the guys who ran bot farms for a living and were masters in their own rite of scamming the world's media.

'It's a decent cover,' they told him, ' quite skillfully done, but its still a cover. We haven't been able to confirm his real identity, which, in itself, is telling us something. He's been professionally washed, whoever he is.'

That told Viktor most of what he needed to know.

He immediately had mixed feelings. Good on the one hand, because one of the first of the expected foreign agents was hopefully going to walk into his house the following afternoon and that should be of considerable assistance in helping him pursue the task he'd been given earlier that morning.

But it was worrying on the other hand because he realized straight away that he himself had been targeted.

That was a bit puzzling. Why would they do that?

But mostly his feeling was of anger because the golf tournament story had dragged his beautiful Yelena into his work, something that he always tried to avoid at all costs.

The guy on the phone from St Petersburg understood straight away what he needed to do next and made a couple of calls of his own. Within a couple of hours a young blonde major from the FSB had her assignment for the following day and was using her department's own resources to try to evaluate the suspicious Brit that she had been charged with intercepting.

Another couple of phone calls uncovered where he was going to stay and Valeria was booked in for the morning shift, the regular girl at The Metropole suddenly finding that she had some holiday entitlement she didn't know about which was about to expire unless she took it quickly.

Nobody ever argues with an unexpected day off work.

'What is the tournament called?'

'The Austro Power open. It's in a place called Millstatt. Look, its right in the middle of the country. The course looks so beautiful.'

Viktor looked at his daughter's laptop.

'Isn't that a slightly strange name. Are the sponsors a sports drink or something? Red Bull are Austrian aren't they? Is it one of their new brands, maybe?'

Yelena tapped away for a few minutes.

'Doesn't look like it, no. I think they're a green fuel company of some kind. Loads of stuff about climate change and sustainable renewables, providing for the future needs of the planet. Bit impenetrable, really '

She handed it over to him.

'Here, you read it. You might be able to make sense of it. Looks like your kind of thing.'

And he did.

And it was.

But, due to a rather unexpected twist of fate caused by events in Raspo's bar the following day, it was Liam Dempsey not Paul Lambert who arrived at the gates of MMM. While Jake had been point man in London he had spotted a potential advantage in making a change and had initiated a switch.

The large wrought iron gates would have been intimidating were they not so artistically crafted. Liam admired them for a few moments before stepping forward to announce himself.

The intercom beat him to it.

'Mr. Lambert.'

'O'im afraid not, sir, no. He's currently indisposed. I'm Liam Dempsey, his assistant.'

'Mr. Alliskiya only sees people who are on the list,' the disembodied voice told him.

'Oi, understand sir, but Mr. Lambert thought that I might be more suitable for this particular meeting.'

Viktor's head of security muted the volume and looked across the bank of screens to where Viktor was watching proceedings from his study.

'What do you think, boss?'

'Is he armed?'

An infrared beam scanned Liam for ten seconds.

'Doesn't look like it, no. Not unless it's something unusual.'

'Ask him.' Viktor suggested.

'Are you armed, Mr. Dempsey?'

'No, not at all. Why would oi be armed when I've come here to talk about a golf tournament?'

'Because Mr. Alliskiya is a very important man and some people would like to kill him.'

Well there's some unusually refreshing truth, Liam thought to himself. *Ten out of ten for honesty, at least.*

'Well, o'im not one a'dem,' Liam assured him.' We don't kill people in my line of work,' he added forcefully, swapping a truth of his own with Viktor's unseen security man.

The Nines were an unarmed unit, expected to use brainpower instead of firepower to achieve their objectives. They didn't announce that of course, it worked better in the dark

The security guy was suspicious by nature, had to be in his line of work.

'Why you more suitable?'

'Because we share a common interest?'

'And what might that be.'

'The four fundamental states.'

'Mr. Alliskiya does not get involved in politics. '

The security guy had heard enough.

'Goodbye, please give our best wishes to Mr. Lambert. We hope he is not indisposed too long.'

He flicked his mic switch off and was just about to shut off the camera feed as well when Viktor spoke across to him.

'Ask him which ones.'

He switched the mic back on.

'Which ones?'

'We can start with solids, liquids and plasma although I will fully understand if the fourth one turns out to be more interesting.'

The security guy looked at Viktor on the screen.

He had a quizzical expression on his face.

'Ask him what Brownian motion is.' he instructed.

Liam smiled inside when he heard the question.

He was in.

'It's the mathematical model used for describing the random movement of particles in fluids.'

'Does it have a practical application?' came the response.

'It measures drag coefficients caused by the frictional forces that are generated by molecules under pressure.'

'Why is that important?'

Liam was a bit surprised. Were they going to keep him out here all day with their vetting questions?

But then he guessed that three would probably be enough and he guessed right.

'It's measurement theory for the essential laws of fluid dynamics, how they move from A to B. Pretty useful if you're building a complicated flow system, maybe something like a pressurised pipeline, for example.'

Viktor nodded to his man in the control room and the gates swung open.

'Welcome to Meshchansky, Mr. Dempsey. Please walk up the driveway and I will meet you.'

It would be fair to say that most people finding themselves in this type of situation would feel apprehensive.

Liam didn't fit into that category. The Paddy in him always took over and his natural enjoyment at meeting all sorts of new people would always be there to help him navigate the trickiest of situations.

At three on the dot Viktor walked into his sumptuous lounge and the two men met and shook hands. It was a warm enough greeting, but underneath the civil exterior there were a lot of calculations going on.

On both sides.

Yelena joined them a few minutes later but her father obviously had his own reasons for meeting this tall athletic looking man with the laughing eyes and the trendy stubble.

Liam Dempsey definitely looked more sports star than secret agent.

'Pop upstairs Bubla and bring the paperwork down please' he asked her softly in his best loving father voice.' I had some draft contracts prepared last night for our meeting. Mr. Dempsey can tell me how he likes Russia so far while you're gone.'

Yelena wisped out of the room.

'Now Mr. Dempsey. Please let us not waste each other's time. I only have three things I wish to discuss with you. The golf, The Disappearance and, as you happened

to bring it up, the fourth state.'

'Da gas, ya mean? Yeah, oi like dat one most of all, yeah. Dat's definitely me personal favourite.'

Viktor glared at him, looking decidedly unamused.

'I take it you have a rudimentary training in geology Mr. Dempsey, something which is always admirable. It is a proper subject to learn, unlike media studies or sociology or those kinds of modern nonsenses. But you have used it to gain audience with me. Why?'

'Well, we didn't really, did we? We used da golf tournament.'

Viktor glared again, it was a bit stormier this time, and he was about to launch into a full-on attack based on dragging his innocent daughter into something unnecessarily when Liam disarmed him.

'Which is all legit, by the way.'

'What is?'

'The tournament.'

'I know it is. I looked it up.'

'No, I mean Yelena's entry. She's in'

He produced a letter from his jacket pocket.

It was on the headed paper of the Golfverein Milstaetter See, based in Carinthia, the Southernmost of Austria's beautiful provinces, and it confirmed the entry of Ms. Yelena Alliskiya into the May 2022 international all-comers tournament sponsored by Austro Power.

Viktor read it, very slowly, as he did all documents. A lot of the ones he read contained more traps than the average golf course so he had learnt to be careful with them.

They could also mean the difference between small, medium, large and very large sums of money so they were always worth spending time over.

And because this one concerned a matter near to his heart – his daughter – he read it twice.

Then, with more than a hint of surprise in his voice, he handed it back to Liam.

'Well, if it's a forgery, it's a very good one' he admitted,' how did you….?'

'It's not, sir. It's not a forgery. She's in. And on merit too, if I may say so. I watched her last round at Troon, before her injury. If you can battle through the weather on any course that directly faces the Irish sea then you have my full respect, I

can tell you that.'

'Technically it's the Firth of Clyde, Mr. Dempsey. Scotland not Ireland'

'Well, whatever you want to call it, it's where the Irish Sea and the Atlantic meet. That's a pretty lively environment. Guaranteed wet and blowy nearly every day. Only top golfers need apply.'

Viktor thought for a moment.

'And did she?'

'Did she what, sir?'

'Did she apply?'

'I don't really see how she could have gotten in otherwise, do you?'

Liam smiled his Paddy charm offensive smile.

Viktor got the message.

Liam's ultimate boss – whoever it was – was more than a bit like his own, somebody with an extremely long reach. He knew enough about his daughter's profession to know that entry lists were normally closed months, sometimes years in advance. No need to ask too much more about that at this stage. With all of his suspicions now fully confirmed, he diverted slightly.

'Are you a geologist by trade, Mr. Dempsey? Or is it just a hobby?'

'Well, it's not my day job, if that's what you're asking. But I still like to dabble a bit.'

'Ah, yes. your day job. Perhaps we could come back to that in a minute. But with the four states I thought your answers sounded a little too fluent for a dabbler.' Viktor prompted him a bit.

'And you've obviously heard about my problems in Georgia.'

'Can't quite remember the detail. I hear so much. You know how it is.' Liam agreed.

Viktor wasn't so easily dissuaded.

'Any suggestions?'

'I wouldn't be so presumptuous as to tell you your business, sir.'

'But if I were asking?'

Liam had spent most of his flight from London to Moscow catching up on the latest edition of *'The Global Geologist'*, his favourite monthly for keeping abreast of all the latest issues and stories from that fascinating world.

Among them were several articles on the setbacks being suffered by the owners

of the planned gas distribution network between Russia and Western Europe. They had also received much coverage in the mainstream press although there it was mostly geo-political, not scientific. His niche magazine had covered the story differently and, reading between the lines, Liam knew exactly what the issues were.

'I think maybe the external equilibrium forces are out of kilter' he started.' In the absence of a natural balance, when an energy transfer ceases you may incur temperature differentials. That instability can cause a lot of weird effects which, I'm guessin', keep leading to your operational managers having to constantly shut down various parts of the system for fear of leakage and, heaven forbid, explosions. If you have to keep doing that a few times every day then it'll take you forever before your lovely Georgian gas arrives in Munich.'

He fixed the Russian with his friendly Paddy stare.

'So oi'd maybe be starting to look at something like that if oi was you.'

Viktor considered this unexpected piece of advice from the most unexpected of sources for the briefest of moments.

'If that's what it is, do you know how to fix it?' he asked.

'I could hazard a guess.' Liam told him. ' But your technical energy consultants are probably better placed. They're actually there, aren't they. On the ground, as it were?'

'Yes, but you're actually here.'

Liam was smiling inside for the second time in about half an hour.

Got him.

He was in again.

Chapter 33 – Daylight robbery

Anastasia was going through her spring wardrobe. As the seasons changed, so she would track the climate and temperature variations with her clothes. Moscow in winter was a deep freeze, all mink coats, heavy jumpers, trapper hats and ushankas.

Like all young girls she got a big thrill out of fashion. The colours, the styles, the elegance, the dressing up, the fanatasies, the always – on chance to be someone else, or, at least, to pretend to be someone else. Oh, the sheer escapism of it all. She just loved it.

The thing with fashion though was the constant movement. The trends meant lots of change. And that meant keeping up. And that meant more shopping. Which was not a problem in and of itself. She loved the whole experience of being out and about. Moscow had changed so much and could now rival pretty much anywhere in the world for choice, not just in clothes, but in everything that you needed for a good wholesome day out with a light lunch in the middle and then some vibrant nightlife at the end of the day.

And such was her life.

Unencumbered by the drudgery of a day job, she would flit from shop to restaurant to boutique to coffee shop to department store to bar to club like the colorful and lovely butterfly that she was. It was her good fortune to be in that most desired of all positions for a woman, for she had a man to look after her, or rather a teenager, although, in the case of Andrei, who had packed so much into his very short life, it almost felt like a sugar daddy.

But he was good to her, as befitted a childhood sweetheart type of relationship. For the most part the sweet tenderness of fourteen or fifteen rarely survives more than a few years as it gets overtaken by curiosity and adventure. Many in number are the young teens who then spend years in a kind of sexual and loving wilderness having decided that the grass might be greener on the other side.

Because, most of the time, it isn't.

But Ans and Andrei had survived those turbulences, the temptations of the fruit of another, squeezed into illicit embraces, of some harmless slap and tickle, had not been for them. They were cool as cats, now as then, and, as she went around with her

own girlfriends, she became aware, as lots of women do through the gossip, that their lives, by comparison with others, were really pretty good.

This dawning realization, one could reasonably expect, would normally be sufficient to allow for a smooth passage into a marriage or something similar as those teen years slide silently into something else.

But life tends not to do smooth passages. Even kings and queens are not spared rough rides. It is in our nature, in life's nature it seems, to be subjected to turbulence, sometimes unexpected and driven by external forces, then other times caused by our own actions, self-inflicted, like the wounds of the cilice.

This is where heartache comes from. It's not a medically proven condition, nor one that a doctor can do much about, even if it were possible to behold the ailment and diagnose it. One of the most painful afflictions known to man seems to remain permanently beyond the reach of the medical profession, not because they are unaware of it but because it is just so mysterious.

The pain it can cause is genuinely physical.

The mental distress it can cause distracts like the worst toothache.

The confusion and soul searching are both inevitable symptoms.

There are no tablets.

Whisky just makes it worse but that doesn't stop people reaching for it.

There is no operation because, short of removing the patients heart – a rather drastic measure – the condition is incurable.

There is only one effective treatment and that is the passing of time, which, in most cases, will enable the pain to go away.

Obviously, and regrettably for all concerned, that is never quick.

Much of this distress can be attributed to the power of love, the strongest of all the emotions, and the one which binds us more intricately with our fellow humans than any other. It is those feelings which play such a huge part in the pleasures of being together as well as the anguish of being apart.

There had never really been anyone else serious in Anastasia's young life apart from her long-standing boyfriend. With the single yet remarkably important exception of his own – their own – long-standing friend.

Georgi.

These things should never happen of course, but they do. There should always be plenty of fish in the sea but, for whatever reason, for some people it just doesn't work

out like that.

Maybe it's a kind of fatal attraction, where two people become so infatuated with each other that the third party is inevitably doomed, even if they happened to have been there first. It might be sexual, it might be romantic, it might be intellectual, it might be shared interests, it might even be, as is often the case, something indefinable, a kind of magnetic tug that attracts in an inexplicable, primeval kind of way.

If, therefore, one had asked Anastasia why, all of a sudden, after so many years she had, almost overnight, started to fancy Georgi, she would have been hard pressed to come up with a reason.

Or the reason.

Or any reason.

But then all of a sudden one day, there it was.

He had, of course, always made it pretty clear that he liked her, in one of those teasy kinds of ways that would leave one feeling a bit unsure. The signals could be misinterpreted so easily. Was he just being friendly, so often such a tricky proposition between boy and girl, or was he just being nice to her because she was his best friend's girl?

She hadn't really analysed it or agonised over it or even thought about it very much but then, one day, there it was.

She suddenly fancied him.

And from that moment on things had progressed very quickly to the point where, within days, they became lovers.

It was consensual, not forced by either party, so despite the resulting conflicting emotions, which they both felt, it had, at its start, a naturalness about it as well. This acted like a salve on both their consciences for a short period although neither knew if or when it might wear off.

As if all that were not turbulent enough, there was also the rather non-trivial matter of when it all happened.

They say that good timing is the secret to many things in this world.

The converse is probably equally true where bad timing can often make situations much, much worse.

This was the exact situation that Andrei, Georgi and Anastasia now found themselves in as the calendar flipped over into March and their deadline for

Ischeznoveniye was suddenly upon them.

The two boys had now reached the appropriate level of confidence with Blockchain technology that they considered necessary to allow them to pull off their extravagant heist.

Their experiences with CryptoOne a few years earlier had also, without them even knowing it at the time, provided them with both the knowledge and the platform for the design and implementation of CryptoTwo, their intended vehicle for The Disappearance.

They had settled on the fifteenth as the perfect date to trigger the chaos.

It was the Ides of March in the old Roman calendar. Traditionally the day on which all outstanding debts were expected to be honoured and settled. The symbolism of this ancient custom had appealed to them and they frequently wondered if the authorities would figure out the association between that and the theme of the communiqué.

Had they studied the clues a bit harder and combined them with the Sig cypher evidence they might have reached the boys much earlier.

But they didn't.

And by the time they did, it would be too late.

In the week leading up to the launch there was a flurry of last minute activity, all of it behind the scenes. As the world drew nearer to the day of global financial chaos, nobody was aware of it apart from two young Russian teenagers in a swish apartment off Staraya park.

And their extremely hormonal girlfriend.

They started off by penetrating the soft underbelly of the ECB, that European Central Bank, and obtaining not only a huge number of account details but also bridge access to large groups of parent and daughter institutions around the world, those who were either affiliated with or controlled by various of the Banks' practices. This exercise, which they had planned meticulously, yielded much directly but it was the indirect harvest of data which surprised and delighted them most.

Due to a series of Beta trials which the ECB had been conducting with other policymaking and regulatory bodies all over the world, their internal systems, once breached, provided entrance points into a large number of similar institutions. There was a mass domino effect as, one by one, large numbers of individual firewalls were compromised and a high capacity mainframe in the Nevada desert started to become a

repository for more and more client information.

It was being stolen in Russia, but, in keeping with the distributed nature of global fintech systems, Andrei and Georgi's growing horde of data was being transferred out of the country as a never-ending stream of data packets and onto an anonymous cloud server nearly six thousand miles away.

As stage one unwound and started to deliver, the boys began phase two.

Their secondary target was the other home to most of the world's money. If it's not being held in the banks, a large majority of which are privately owned, then its probably being held, much less privately, by world governments in their individual exchequers.

These are the deposits that create state assets and their value forms much of the backbone for the finance systems that support Government policies and the associated spending.

Without them, all of their plans, initiatives and actions will grind to a halt. So although stealing from individuals is bad enough, stealing from Governments has always been regarded as the ultimate threat to the stability of our way of life. It's a hanging offence, not just metaphorically, but also in reality. Those that choose to go down that path and undermine the modern world by messing with the very fabric of the system that supports it should be prepared to face the direst of consequences.

And those very issues had been at the heart of most of those late night discussions that the boys had been having for the previous few months. They had waded through all those issues in considerable depth and had made their choices fully aware of the consequences.

Now they were burning their bridges.

There was no going back.

Government exchequers might sound like they're very different to banks.

They're not.

They operate in very similar ways in the key areas of holding, storing, looking after and handing out money. The key major difference is their clientele.

Or, to be more accurate, their client.

For individual Exchequer banks only serve one master, have only one customer.

The Government of the country in which they are set up.

So, in the UK, for example, the Exchequer bank is The Bank of England, an

institution which is replicated, almost exactly – at least in terms of theory and systems – all over the world by the state banks of all individual countries.

These are the individual Fort Knox's of National Governments and, in keeping with that world famous institution in Kentucky, they also hold, either directly or indirectly, much of the other wealth owned by the individual exchequers – the gold and the bullion.

These are the hard assets which are allowed to fluctuate in value in line with global market movement but which underpin the base security of national economies. As such, selling them off to shore up poorly managed balance sheets is a strategy that should never be undertaken by responsible politicians although, with the number of those people in permanently short supply, it still happens and is seldom anything but extremely damaging in the short term.

As an example of this idiocy the UK Labour chancellor Gordon Brown adopted one such approach in 1999 and sold over 400 tonnes of the UK's total holding of 715 tonnes of gold, representing well over half of the country's reserves. The market value at the time, coming off the tail end of an extended bull run, had dropped to a low of $275 per oz. Ever since then the value has been consistently between $1200 and $2000 per ounce, even hitting an all time high of $2036 per ounce in July 2020 as the shock of Covid prompted a global retreat into the world's safest value store.

Brown's timing was so appalling that in retrospect it almost looks like a deliberate attempt to undermine and destroy the whole country and its economy. Various soft estimates, both before and since, have calculated the loss and damage to the UK economy to be in the order of £7-8 Billion.

That's bad enough but a more brutal assessment based on a more astute market timing tells a completely different story.

Brown's total raise of $7.5 billion dollars would have been totally eclipsed by a sale price of $261 billion dollars if the UK Government of mid 2020 had followed his lead and sold the equivalent amount when the market hit one of its newer peaks. They didn't, of course, only being bothered at the time with printing money to pay for Covid-related economy lockdowns, a strategy almost as bad as Brown's in terms of future destruction of the value of the currency and the creation of a complete range of inflation related disasters for the normal hard working citizens of the UK.

His unnecessary and desperate decision in reality left the British exchequer about $255 billion dollars short and remains one of the more extreme examples of financial

ineptitude imposed upon democratic electorates anywhere in the world in recent years. Anybody else perpetrating such a crime would be locked up as a very minimum.

Brown became Prime Minister.

'No wonder they had no money left,' Andrei said one evening, as the boys read about this extraordinary tale from modern day England for the first time. 'One of the other blokes in charge of the finances even left a note saying so.'

Georgi looked across at his friend.

'Admitted stealing it you mean?' he queried.

'Well, he might as well of done. *Dear Chief Secretary. I'm afraid there is no money left.* That's what he wrote. Some bloke called Liam Byrne. Can you believe that? And these were the kind of people that the electorate had entrusted to look after things.'

'Is that just a Brit thing then, do you think?'

'I doubt it. They're probably everywhere. To make matters worse, they don't ever seem to get sacked, they just get promoted. The more damage they do, the greater the opportunities that seem to come their way. Brown even got another position as advisor to the World Economic forum a few years later. How mad is that?'

'About as mad as making that warmonger Blair a peace envoy. Didn't those two work together for a while? Whatever did the poor people of the UK do to deserve those two cunts?'

It was the steady accumulation of so many of these and other similar stories from all over the world that made the boys increasingly feel a whole lot better about what they were planning to do.

The more they read, the more they realised that the biggest thieves were not people like them, but the people in charge, the people who were running things, taking ever stranger decisions allegedly on behalf of the honest citizens who voted for them.

Most of them qualified by their perversions and not very much else.

The more they read, the more Andrei and Georgi hardened their resolve and any feelings of guilt which they may have had right at the beginning of their adventure steadily dissolved and evaporated.

If they were going to be responsible for knocking over a corrupt system and

getting something better built in its place then so be it. The only trouble with that idea was the rather worrying reality that it was the people who were corrupt and not the systems.

By the 8th of March, one week ahead of i-day, they had used their combined twelve years of accumulated black hat experiences to breach the defences of most of the bastions of national and international wealth.

Country by country they had infiltrated the systems one by one, continually learning as they went along, increasingly surprised to find so many similarities in the methods that were being adopted to protect those sources of national wealth.

The physical assets would remain untouched of course and would eventually form the basis for whatever recovery the authorities managed to put together. But the electronic links were fully compromised and set onto rafts of timers, synchronized to click into action all together at a pre-determined time when the Ischeznoveniye operation was initiated on the fifteenth.

Until then they would do nothing further for fear of tripping any one of the several highly sensitive security systems charged with the twenty-four hour protection of those depository facilities. The slightest suspicion that there had been a breach could have been disastrous, resulting, as it almost certainly would, in an immediate lockdown of everything pertaining to the location, both in it and around it. Their task was hard enough without making it any more difficult than it needed to be.

They already had the personal account data. Now they needed to focus on business and company accounts around the world. Some basic homework was needed to calculate the effort and the likely time required.

How many banks were there? That would be a good place to start.

'This is going to take ages,' Georgi declared one morning, as they started out on their latest fact finding mission. 'There's about sixty just in Austria alone and that's a pretty small country.'

Andrei laughed, fully aware of his friend's plan to relocate to the heart of Europe with a few million and the associated ongoing personal requirement of finding a nice friendly local bank to put it in.

'So just the EC alone on that basis could easily be about two thousand.'

'Hmm, not so sure it works like that though,' Andrei told him, continuing to flick through the pages on his screen, 'France is seven or eight time bigger than Austria by head of population but only has half as many banks. Bit weird that, but it's suggesting

to me that there may not be any one formula that we can use to compute that accurately.'

'Well, for argument's sake, lets just call it two thousand per continent. There may be more than that in the States and Asia, because of the sheer level of economic activity, and maybe less in South America and Africa, probably even fewer in Australasia. But let's guess at around ten or eleven thousand all together, or about five thousand each if we split them up.'

'That's kind of what I was getting at Andi,' Georgi told him. 'Unless we can find some way to automate things then that's Mission Impossible right there. At one bank per day that's about fourteen years work each, assuming we go straight through with no days off. Not exactly what I had in mind.'

The importance of doing your homework had just become apparent. There was a massive logistical problem with this part of their scheme and a potentially gaping hole in the middle of their plans.

However, the two boys were nothing if not resourceful and by the evening of the same day they had developed a way to address the fact that, without an all-embracing solution to this rather unexpected potential setback, their plan would become impossible.

'We'll pick three or four at random to trial it first,' Andrei had said, after they had agreed on a method for tricking the individual banks' firewalls into believing they were being re-set. 'If it works for them, there's no reason why we can't do an automated rollout. With a new set of security protocols in place which we can control remotely, all we'll need to implement is another synchronisation exercise so that all the actions are triggered at the same time on the fifteenth. No advance warning again. Everything happens at once. Like we agreed, that's our only chance of success. They mustn't know we're coming, otherwise all of the defence barriers will go up.'

Georgi nodded.

That was, indeed, the only way.

But he'd spotted an anomaly

'I agree.' he said.' But we're going to have to do those three or four trial sites separately, aren't we? Because what if one of their alarms gets set off?'

'Well, that's a chance we're just going to have to take. I admit its risky but even if the worst happens, there's no way of them knowing for sure that it's part of a concerted attack. They're hardly likely to compare notes, are they?'

'Why not? I would have thought that's exactly the kind of thing they're likely to do.'

'Well, let's just spread the tests out geographically, that's about as much as we can do. I can see the Italians talking to the Swiss, for example, or the Americans talking to each other. The people involved will likely all know each other socially. But will the Portuguese talk to the Japanese in the same way? Or the Chileans talk to the Norwegians?'

It wasn't perfect. It was a plan with a flaw. But it was all they could come up with.

So they picked their four trial sites and on a frozen Moscow evening they sent their malware off on its secret mission to the four corners of the earth.

Objective: Penetrate the bank accounts of approximately two hundred thousand individual businesses situated in a few carefully selected countries and gain operational control of them by securing and transmitting the basic account details back to base.

Unseen.

And undetected.

The first part difficult but, with their skills and experience, perfectly feasible.

The second part much harder, especially since the hit was designed to get inside the four source code repositories of those organisations.

But they had little choice.

'The real weakness with this, of course, is that we won't actually know if they've spotted anything unless they publicise the breach. We're gambling a bit that they won't really want to do that. It's hardly good for business is it?'

And, indeed, the recent history of acknowledgements of such leaks supported that assumption.

Terrified of the impact of litigation most companies will lawyer up pretty quickly and do everything possible to reduce the financial damage that comes with admitting a security breach and the ensuing and inevitable modern day compensation claims. This legitimate tactic is generally referred to as mitigation, a nice soft respectable sounding name for hoovering up a pile of shit.

Although it is seldom deliberate, the carelessness associated with these losses of personal and private data cannot be underestimated.

The Adobe hack in 2013 happened to one of America's largest corporations, a

company who are in the business of designing and selling fancy audio – visual content creation tools into the global digital marketplace. That's a very big market and Adobe are a very big fish in it. As a manufacturer of software products one could be forgiven for expecting only the highest of security standards from a Company that professes to be a leading player in that sector. Their own laxity and overall attitude towards such matters might best be summed up by a rather reluctant initial announcement that 3 million records had been affected, a number which was later updated to 38 million, and then finally reported to have actually been, in reality, about 150 million.

The full level of compensation payments made out of court are never disclosed fully but somehow in this case the Company seems to have got away with payouts in the order of around two million dollars, half of which went to the lawyers. That can only be said to be a rather paltry sum for a Company with total assets in the region of USD 21 billion.

In a subsequent 10-Q filing to the US Securities and Exchange Commission – the organization who police financial matters relating to American companies – Adobe admitted the breach but not only said they did not believe that such attacks had a materially adverse impact on their business, but added that their own efforts to fight cybercrime might not be successful, but could well incur potential liabilities and cost the company a lot of money.

So much for customer care.

Perhaps even worse is the behaviour of Equifax, another massive US Company whose actual core business consists of collecting and aggregating that very consumer data for credit monitoring and assessment purposes. They claim to work with the individual records of around 800 million consumers so, again, one could reasonably expect a robust level of protection to be afforded the highly valuable and sensitive personal information which all those people entrust them with every year.

But in September 2017 they announced a hacking breach of their own which also affected about 150 million users.

One hundred and fifty million!

That's the size of the total populations of two very large countries.

Incredibly the hackers had been burrowing away deep inside the company's internal systems for nearly 3 months, allegedly undetected. Between discovery in July and announcement in September senior management within the Company sold their

company stock using insider knowledge about these events before the price plunged.

Ultimately the courts awarded $650 million in settlement to consumers, a sum subsequently downgraded by a judge in Atlanta to $77 million which represented the insulting sum of a measly $6 payout to each claimant in the ensuing class action lawsuit that the fiasco had created.

Latest official records show the company to have assets of about USD 8 Billion.

Its chairman is a lawyer.

Many US States have data breach notification laws obliging companies to come clean when such events occur. Their requirements vary and the ensuing legal landscape is a patchwork quilt of inconsistency. Victims may never even find out that their own data – which can range from passwords to credit card details and PIN's – has been exposed until they find out the hard way.

Other countries around the world also like to play games with the private data of individual citizens,

In Europe, the EC, the unelected federalist governing body that likes to tell individually elected national Governments what to do, decided to do its own tidy up exercise. Finally launched as GDPR – the General Data Protection Regulation – it unfortunately became law in 2018 and proceeded to immediately tie everybody up in knots, apart, of course, from the lawyers who had both drafted it and were now getting paid millions for interpreting the act's nonsense and policing its content.

In order to comply with GDPR rules, each and every individual internet user now has to agree to a set of obscure and usually invisible terms and conditions with almost every click before being allowed to go through the GDPR wall of fog and access what they are looking for.

It is a truly monstrous thing, which could only have been contrived to create mischief. It does nothing to support, promote or allow the individual user to transact his or her own data, that set of highly personal assets which should never belong to anybody else apart from the individual owner under any circumstances, unless they have actually agreed to sell them.

As the boys first began navigating these stories they were further strengthened in their resolve, yet again, to carry on with their daring yet outlandish plan.

'How long again?' Andrei had asked, when Georgi read out the Equifax story.

'How long what?'

'Were the hackers in there before anybody spotted them?'

Georgi scoured the story again.

'134 days, it says here.'

Andrei threw his head back and laughed, a raucous, almost violent laugh.

'How fucking long?'

'It says 134 days. That's what it says' he repeated, starting to giggle a bit himself.

'What kind of dumb fucks did they have working security at that company? Does it even still exist?"

Georgi read out Equifax's latest asset valuations from the SEC filing.

'And on top of that they had an operating revenue figure of about 4 billion dollars last year.'

Andrei started laughing again, holding his sides and leaning forward in his chair.

Georgi couldn't help himself and within seconds the two boys were writhing on the floor, helpless in the face of truth being stranger than fiction

'Was it us?' he asked finally.

'What do you mean?'

'Were they Russians, the crew who did it?'

Georgi was still reading.

'No, apparently not. Chinese. As was the company CIO, who got banged up for it as well as for conspiracy of some sort. He was the one who flogged his shares. At least, he was the one they caught.'

Andrei finally stopped laughing and Georgi also began to quieten down.

Then, just as quickly, he started off again.

'Now what is it?' Andrei asked.

'They said,' Georgi started to explain, but then had to stop and compose himself.

'Yeh, they said what?'

'They said that the poor people shouldn't take the money but would be better of accepting free credit monitoring services from Equifax instead.'

Andrei looked at his friend aghast.

Then they both started laughing again.

'I don't suppose it says how much the lawyers got?

Georgi tracked his finger over the article again.

He looked up.

He could barely speak now.

'Eighty ...' he began

Andrei waited expectantly.

'Eighty what. No, don't tell me. Eighty free credit reports.'

'No, not quite. They got….'

And he doubled up laughing again

'Eighty eight million.'

Andrei wiped his eyes.

'Eighty eight million fucking dollars!'

Of course it wasn't really funny.

It was ridiculous, right down to the judge's ruling.

But it made the boys feel better and better about themselves.

And that's always a good thing.

Plus 134 days undetected.

That was also surely a good thing.

'How long will we need?'

'Couple of hours most to get in. Couple more twatting about, set up the spoofing, get out. I'm guessing ten, twelve hours, tops, not more than a day, anyway.'

'So about 133 days less than the Chinese had inside Equifax.'

'Yeah. If even that's the truth.'

Several days later their soft strikes in Argentina, The Philippines, Iceland and Kenya retrieved the first sets of data relating to business accounts held by some of the smaller banks in those jurisdictions. They re-formatted all the files so that they were compatible with everything else which had already been retrieved so far. The burgeoning database in the Arizona desert was starting to get quite chunky.

Several weeks later it was way, way bigger, a growing monster that had a mirror collection of the individual details of millions of bank accounts of customers from both retail and savings as well as investment banks all over the world.

They had the account numbers, the sort codes, the account holder names, the branch identifier codes, the BIC's and the IBAN's, the addresses of the customers, both physical and e-mail, the addresses of the banks including the individual branches as well as the various H.Q's, and a whole host of associated passwords and PIN codes which, for their intended purposes, were actually superfluous to requirements.

In short they had enough to empty the worlds' banks of all the money which they held on behalf of all those customers.

Georgi would have had enough to buy all of Millstatt, a hundred times over had he wanted.

But that was not the plan.

Raping the innocent had never been their intention.

No.

That was not their game.

Others do that.

Despite what a lot of American lawyers think, it is possible to have enough.

And be happy with it.

There is actually such a thing as just enough.

And more than enough.

Chapter 34 – Le trou noir

As Hazel Ingliss drove back along the river after her tennis club lunch her phone had pinged non-stop. She had the UK Cabinet and the P.M. breathing down her neck, both clamouring for updates. In Switzerland Jake made it back over to the Fairmont just before 4pm local time just as she called Hank for the first of her afternoon updates on the situation.

The world had stopped briefly for most people earlier that morning when FIB issued their first briefing. It was an event that rivaled the World Cup final for sheer audience size. Billions tuned in and watched. Streets were empty, bars and coffee houses were full. Not quite the same atmosphere of sheer excitement as the sport though, in fact quite the opposite as people sat in subdued silence, spending the cash they had in their wallets, not quite knowing where their next top up would come from.

Most were hoping for Government intervention of some sort. Wasn't that what they were there for? To act as a safety net, the lender of last resort when the world imploded.

Which it just had.

Seasoned observers of how official bodies deal with such matters were not surprised by the bland holding statement and reassurances from Geneva, but huge numbers of ordinary people were.

They had expected action. Immediate action to fend off what that morning's papers had been unanimous in calling a global disaster of unmitigated proportions.

And what did they get?

Not even a high-ranking Government spokesman but, instead, some sharp suited functionary from the world of banking.

Of course it was, and remained, a bank problem in terms of explaining what had actually happened, so, in that regard, the choice of spokesperson was understandable.

But, interesting though that was, it was not really the uppermost thought in most people's minds that day.

Everybody wanted answers.

Not just the who, the question that Viktor Alliskiya was increasingly focused on in Moscow, but all the rest of it as well.

The how, the why, the where and the when.

All of it.

But they didn't need or want everything right now. As the good people of the world sat around gloomily watching this momentous broadcast they just wanted to know three things.

Where is my money?

When will I get it back?

How do I get by in the meantime?

And Geneva man, as the smooth talking representative from the FIB had become know, had not told them any of that. Which had an immediate effect on the attitude of the general public whose suspicions were becoming increasingly aroused.

Why isn't he telling us?

What's he hiding?

How come he doesn't know, when they've been looking at the clues for nearly a whole day and a half now?

What are they up to? What the hell is going on?

Then there was the vacuum.

Between about 9:30 London time and 4 in the afternoon Geneva time, nothing much appeared to happen.

Or at least that was the perception of ordinary people who were just continually treated on their global TV screens to hours of street view shots of the Hotel Fairmont, a beautiful jet spout out on the lake, and a non-stop procession of so called experts who all delivered various judgments on what they thought had happened, mostly preposterous, none of them even close to the actual truth, which was unsurprising because their own individual wacky theories never even got anywhere close to what the two boys had pulled off.

Finally somebody pointed out to the FIB team that the world was now listening to a deafening silence and it was at this point that Sylvie Danton had been pushed forward by her boss to make a holding statement.

At the end of it another three things were starting to become clear.

The banks were looking clueless.

The media were getting exasperated.

Something was definitely going on in Moscow.

To the assembled politicians in the UK cabinet – and their counterparts around

the world – there was a fourth concern.

The people were starting to get edgy and agitated.

And that was a concern because civic unrest was their area.

Hazel explained this to Harry first, disturbing his reverie as he continued to gaze out from Willi's lofty terrace across at Mont Blanc, still absorbing and computing Monique's highly plausible assessment of the situation.

'I'm just about to call 9-4' she told him, referring to Jake.

The Nines all had numeric code names which harked back to the order in which they'd been interviewed at GCHQ four years earlier.

Jojo had been first in that morning so she was 9-1. And so on.

'But I wanted you to be aware of the politics first.'

'Hardly surprising ' Harry replied.' Probably the biggest crisis any of us have ever known and the people in charge still look like they're faffing about on the afternoon of the second day.'

'Agreed. Let's hope him and 9-9 have made some progress.'

The Nines had three honorary members, who helped out in varying capacities as their complex missions unfolded.

Billy Poppitt was 9-7. Brigadier Zhang T'ang of the CSB, from their Wuhan mission, was 9-8, and Colonel Hank Wyatt (Ret'd) of the US Air Force was 9-9. Hazel also had a 9-10 in mind from the team's very first mission at The White House but that was the last thing on her mind right now.

Johnny Marriott was a maybe for the future.

'What did you find out over there from your own personal banker, Harry. Anything of interest?'

'Possibly, I'm still working something through. I'll know by this evening.'

'Ok, well, soon as, please. I'm starting to get roasted here.'

Hank picked up second ring and waved Jake over as he saw him pass the LeClerc and the Leopard 2 on his way in.

The two tanks, fearsome in full battle mode, had made quite a stir. Just as Sylvie's speech concluded, they had chosen that precise moment to swap positions outside the main hotel entrance. The sight of two fully armed beasts-of-war trundling around the Quai Mont Blanc on the banks of Lake Leman in the heart of genteel Geneva had briefly set hearts a flutter all over the world as the TV crews attempted to alleviate hours of boredom by filming this changing of the guard manouevre in great

detail.

People saw revolution in the air.

In reality, it was just a piece of theatre designed to keep a lot of sleepy people and two tank crews awake.

Hank was bringing Wanderer One up to speed as Jake joined him. He put the call on loudspeak.

'Any luck with that Izvestia bloke?' Hazel wanted to know.

'I'm working him.' Hank confirmed. ' Nice guy, bit intense like they can be, but my bet is that he knows more than FIB do and he's just leaning on them to flesh out his own story. We'll probably be on the vodkas in an hour or so, hopefully I'll get more then.'

'What are we making of FIB so far. Friend or foe?' she continued.

'I was with them earlier on for a bit' Jake confirmed.' A strange bunch, mix of managers, tecchies and PR people, one of whom has been assigned to me.'

He fished a business card out of his pocket.

'Sylvie Danton. Haven't met her yet. She was busy.'

'Oh, you just missed her,' Hank told him. 'She did the afternoon update. That's her over there. Look,' he continued, pointing across the salon.' Blonde bun, big glasses, small earrings, the tall girl.'

'Talking to the bloke with the cigar, you mean?'

'So she is. Good old Ivan. That's my 5pm vodka date.'

Jake had suddenly screwed his eyes up, turned his head very slightly and was biting his lip.

'What's up, Buddy?' Hank asked.

'Does Ivan speak French?'

'No idea. Why?'

'Well, they're not speaking English.'

'How the hell can you tell that from fifty paces.'

'I can lip read. And that's definitely not English.'

'Show me.' Hazel instructed.

Hank swung his phone round and held it steady.

'Just a tick.' Hazel said,' bear with me.'

She pressed a button on her handset, captured the image on her screen, pressed another button while the database from her office fired up, and then ran the jpeg file

through it.

'She's a Russian national, Government affiliation unknown but she works for the ECB. Bit suspicious maybe but hardly a criminal offence, not yet anyway. You'd kind of expect the FIB team to have some Central Bank representation on it. What time you meeting her, Jake?'

'How' bout now,' the Texan cowboy from Laredo answered and he abruptly headed off into the throng.

Hank watched him go, juggling a few thoughts in his mind about the one item that had caused the most worldwide interest in both press conferences.

Those nutters in Moscow.

In a room full of English and French speaking people why was Sylvie Danton talking to Ivan Tertroothski in Russian?

Maybe just because she was Russian and they shared a mother tongue. That was certainly a possibility. Or maybe it was something else, something she didn't want anybody else to hear or overhear.

"If all this has happened in Russia, why do you need me to sort it out?" was the rather sharp question that Paul Lambert had asked Major Valeria in Raspo's bar over in Moscow just a few hours earlier.

Her rather oblique answer had pointed at Switzerland.

Nutters in Moscow, indeed.

What the hell was going on?

Texans and Paddies wouldn't appear, on the face of things, to have too much in common.

Wrong.

The menfolk of those two places are gifted with an over abundance of natural charm and courtesy when it comes to dealing with the ladies.

Jake's southern drawl was a powerful weapon when he chose to use it.

'Evenin' maam,'

He kissed the back of her hand as Sylvie extended it.

More than a bit unusual in that particular context.

'Least it will be soon. Jake Rivera, at your service.'

'Oh' Sylvie exclaimed, breaking off from her chat with Ivan. 'I'm sorry, I was not expecting you to be American.'

'Well, maam, ain't nothin' too much 'ah can do about that, seein' as how's 'ah

was born there.' he replied, laying on the full Laredo sound effects.

She studied him for a moment, something in her female intuition ringing an alarm bell, or maybe it was just something somewhere else in her female system that was ringing.

Tall, polite, rugged looking Texans have a certain effect on women, with hat or without.

'Ah was told you gonna' be mah contact in this extravaganza. 'Ah mean, how lucky can 'ah guy get?'

Although flirting was slowly being reduced to criminal status by the global woke brigade, to Jake it was just common courtesy to pay a lovely woman a complement.

Him and several million other men actually, un PC though that now was.

Sylvie remained calm and professional again, just as she had been earlier under pressure from the media pack.

'Well Bonjour Monsieur Rivera, you are very welcome. I'm so sorry I missed you earlier. There's a lot going on right now, as you can see.'

She waved her arm across the salon, highlighting the packed room and the size of the crowd, as if it were something Jake might have failed to notice on his own.

'Your office said you would like to have some inside track on our investigations.'

'Yes, maam. We figured we could probably help more if we were a bit closer to the action, to your deliberations, so to speak.'

'Yes, mais oui, d'accord. Yes of course. I just had the same request from Mr Tertroothski here,' she said, turning to Ivan who had been hovering.

'Do you two know each other?'

They didn't, so they said so.

She did the honours.

'I meet Hank already out on balcony.' Ivan told Jake ' We go to bar at five. Will you come?'

'Of course, definitely. As soon as I complete my debrief with Madamoiselle Danton, I'll be right there. Shall we go?' and Jake took charge of the situation by leading Sylvie away from the heaving crowd in the middle of the room and out towards one of the lifts.

'Allons y.'

He didn't know exactly where he was going but figured correctly that the FIB team hub would be on one of the other floors. Plus the centre of that particular scrum

in the large ballroom area was not looking like the best place to unearth any secrets.

'You were talking Russian just now. May I ask why?' Jake's professional warmth switched suddenly to professional cool as he asked her his first question.

Sylvie was a cool customer too, easy to do when telling the truth.

'Because we're both Russian, Professor. You really shouldn't be so suspicious. We're all on the same side in this, you know.'

'Yes, of course. So what have you found out and how can we help.' Jake noted her acknowledgement of his professional credentials. Somebody had been doing their homework. And she'd just addressed him as plain Monsieur just a moment earlier when Ivan had been there.

Interesting!

'Well, what I have to tell you must remain confidential, of course. We will announce it tomorrow morning formally at the next press conference but until then it must remain out of the press. Do you accept this condition.'

Jake had just agreed to meet a journalist for a drink in about half an hour, one who's exact relationship with the cool, calm and collected lady from FIB was not entirely clear.

Hmm!

Tricky.

'I will need to share with my boss and I will pass on your request. But you probably know that his immediate superior reports in to the Prime Minister of Great Britain who will take his own view.'

That was about as diplomatic as he could make it.

Sylvie obviously took that as a yes.

Either that or she was just going to tell him anyway.

They wandered down a long corridor and went into another, much smaller conference room. It must have had about forty or fifty people in it, all staring at banks of screens. It reminded Jake of a trading floor.

'Where's the others?' he computed quickly.

'Next door. They didn't have anything big enough and it was essential that we were all together in the same building. So we had to split. Half in here looking at the States and Europe, half next door looking at Asia Pac, Oz and everywhere else.'

'And what exactly are you looking at?'

'You will recall the four key questions that my colleague mentioned at this

morning's briefing?'

'How. Where. Why. Who. Yes, I remember. How's that all going'

'We have something on the first two, but nothing on the last two.'

'I'm all ears.'

'There was a massive hack. It seems to have spread out from four different locations after initial attacks in Buenos Aires. Manila. Reykjavik and Nairobi. Using some kind of backdoor technique, which we're still investigating, they then seem to have broken out into one of the more mainstream centres of global banking and used that as a springboard into the rest of the world.'

Jake reflected for a second.

'Can you say where? London or New York I suppose.'

'Bit closer to home.'

'What Frankfurt?'

Sylvie smiled, raised her delicate eyebrows to the heavens and shrugged her shoulders.

'Bit closer.'

'Fuck. So that's why we're all here.'

He bit his lip.

'Your colleague also said that these were probably the best hackers in the world. What else do we know about them?'

'Well, we're still building up the whole picture but it looks like they are also highly trained finance specialists. Up to speed on the latest of everything.'

Jake's southern charm was still there with Sylvie but it was wearing off quickly with his feelings about her work colleagues in general.

'You mean there were definitely bankers involved? That's really not good.'

'I didn't actually say that, did I?'

'Meaning?'

'Do you know much about crypto currencies?'

'Not personally, if I'm honest. But I know a man who does.'

'When can you talk to him next?'

Well, in about half an hour actually, he thought to himself, quickly remembering that Hank was supposed to be flying under the radar, his secondment to the Nines being wholly unofficial and only sanctioned by Harry based on his intuition.

Which nearly always turned out to be right!

'My team are available 24/7. How should I brief him?'

'We think the Disappearance might be linked to the launch of a new Crypto.'

'Ok. How?'

'We only know some of the how, I'm afraid, not all of it.'

'Ok.'

'Our suspicion is that all of the various currency denominations of the affected accounts were converted into something that would have effectively taken them out of the system, albeit on a temporary basis, while they were being transferred into something else.'

'Ok. And that would be what exactly?'

'When you talk to your friend ask him or her about the Blockchain, especially the part that allows and supports multiple transactions in and out, irrespective of whichever established currency is being used.'

'You mean they accept all of them?'

'They have to in order to work properly, to fulfill the brief.'

'What brief?'

'A large part of the original concept, if we use BitCoin as an example, and we should because they were there first, was to disintermediate. It's a strange word, a dirty word in fact in my community, because it attempts to cut banks out of the transactional mechanisms.'

Jake was following but sometimes its best to pretend not to.

'Sorry, you're losing me.'

'Our traditional role down the years has been to act as middlemen. People wish to exchange money with each other for a whole host of reasons. If you happen to be standing next to the person you wish to transact with, then the process couldn't be easier. You put your hand in your pocket and give him ten Euros, a hundred pounds, a thousand dollars or whatever. They give you whatever it is that you are buying and they are selling. And that's it. Job done.'

'Yes, of course. That's why people like cash. Simple and straightforward.'

'But we don't. And we're not alone because Governments don't like it much either. And increasingly so.'

'Understood. That type of transaction can't earn the bank any kind of cut and, from a Government perspective, its invisible and, presumably, therefore pretty much untaxable.'

'Oui, c'est ca, Professor. Exactement. That's it exactly.'

'So, what, they see Cryptos as some kind of magic solution to that?'

'No, no, it is the opposite. They are scared of them. And so are we. Cryptos are eating our lunch, as you Americans like to say.'

'Because of the disintermediation thing, you mean?'

'Partly, yes. As long as the banks can continue to function in the way they have been doing for hundreds of years, they are essentially a major part of the tax collection system. They are all-seeing because they know where everybody's money is, they know who's got what and where they are keeping it.'

'Indispensable knowledge when you want to tax somebody. Or a company. Yes, I can see that quite clearly.'

'Well, Bitcoin doesn't really involve the banks. The nature of those transactions bypasses us completely.'

'How can it do that?'

'Because it is a stand–alone system. The only grip we ever had on it was the fact that you had to convert any BTC you owned back into *"real money"* in order to be able to spend it on anything. No point in owning a thousand BTC if you cannot do anything with them."

'BTC is BitCoins?'

'Yes, that's right. But then at some point in their evolution over the past few years they started to become acceptable as payment media in their own right. Admittedly, mainly for larger transactions. You wouldn't want to try buying a pint of milk with BTC, for example. But once that happened, we started to lose control. And so did the Governments. Or, to be more accurate, they could see what was going to happen, the writing on the wall, so to speak.'

'Ok. So what is their plan to counteract that and how does it fit with Jumbo?'

Sylvie jerked her head back and gave him a strange look.

'Interesting. I assume that's your project name for all this. Ours is a little more descriptive.'

Jake waited.

'We call it Le Trou Noir.'

Jake waited again.

Most Americans don't speak any French.

Sylvie explained.

'It means Black Hole.'

Just over half an hour later he recounted all this to Hank and Ivan in the Floor Two lounge bar. The panoramic South East facing view out across the lake was a soothing contrast to the fevered mood inside the hotel where the assembled multitude had just been promised an evening update.

The sun splayed a thin river of gold sunshine across the water and out as far as the fountain in an attempt to calm everybody down by providing an early evening glimpse of nature's astonishing beauty.

'Did she let on what they've found, then?'

'No more than what I've told you already.'

Hank had vouched for Ivan, trusting his own instincts and some pretty serious training as a senior CIA officer in one of his previous lifetimes. Jake was slightly less sure but decided that having such sudden and unexpected access to some inside track from Russia might outweigh any disadvantages so he played along.

Ivan could sense the slight mistrust.

Russians were used to it.

'I know her from before she work for bank' he offered. 'She bright as button. Have good understanding of how everything works.'

He frowned at the barman who was politely pointing to the *Pas de fumer* sign on the wall.

No smoking allowed inside.

Having a cigar with his vodka was one of life's pleasures for Ivan.

He complied reluctantly and put his Arturo Fuente Dominican back into his Humidor case.

'What did she do before, then? ' Hank asked his new buddy.

'Something in Government. She not tell me exactly. I learn long time ago when to stop asking.'

'Do you think she's retained her links?'

'You mean is she a spy like you Hank? Like you and your nice friend, the Professor, here?'

Jake winced a bit.

People had really been doing their homework on him.

Ivan laughed and knocked back a shot of his drink.

'Not everybody in the word is spy, you know. You guys should get out more.'

'Still, an interesting choice for spokesperson or PR lady or whatever we're calling them these days.' Jake observed.

'Maybe she just good at her job,' Ivan concluded drily. ' What else she say?'

'She told me a bit about CBDC's. Basically the way that the Governments of the world are planning to fight back against the Cryptos.'

'The Central Bank Digital Currencies.' Ivan was checking.

'Yep, that's them. Dead right. Pretty scary it sounded too. Programmable money, all controlled centrally. The reverse of disintermediation by the sound of it. The way the Authorities plan to wrest control back. And once they do, they will have more power than ever.'

'In what sense it programmable?' Ivan asked, waving his glass at the waiter for some top ups.

'Well the key question is always going to be who is in control. If the issuing authority is in charge, like the State for example, they will design a set of checks and balances into the availability of the money.'

'How that work then? In practice, I mean, not theory.' Ivan was a clear-headed journalist, even when he was on the vodkas. He needed to understand this for his readers.

'Let's look at the Chinese example because they are rolling these out faster than almost everyone else.'

Ivan nodded. ' Yes, I hear this already.'

'And the basis for it is a kind of points driven society where people are rewarded for whatever it is the State considers to be model citizen behaviour.'

'Rewarded? How rewarded?'

'Can be anything. Access to better interest rates on savings, cheaper deals on loans, first choice on new car models, maybe even choice of housing or the types of jobs people are offered.'

'And the difference between those CBDC's and the Cryptos?'

'Cryptos like Bitcoin are structured differently. For a start they are not owned or created by the State.'

'So most of the old traditional players are out of the loop.'

'Exactly. And even more so since BTC has become an acceptable method for payments with no bank involvement. There is a kind of critical mass to these things.

Nobody wants to be the first person to join a club. Conversely, if the club has a limited membership of, say, one thousand, then by the time it gets to around six or seven hundred members, there is likely to be something of a stampede to join because people equally don't like losing out.'

'And at what point in this cycle you are describing does that momentum actually start to pick up?'

'Well, that's probably the best question I've heard in a long time.' Hank decided to contribute, sensing that Jake's insights from his brief chat with Sylvie were only going to take him so far.

'With BTC its probably taken a little short of a decade, not so long really when you think about the generally slow pace of most revolutions.'

Ivan's ears pricked up.

Being a journalist he was a words guy.

And he liked that word.

Revolutions.

That was a word which could sell a story.

A word that could get him on the front page.

'You really think this will revolutionise money?' he asked, taking a noticeably smaller slug of his drink. He needed to follow this.

'No doubt about it. The more I read about it, the better I realised it was. It's not virtually incorruptible. It actually is incorruptible.'

'I like to believe this,' Ivan commented,' but I cannot. Humans will always cheat their way through these things.'

'But this is different,' Hank reassured him.

'And why, may I ask?'

'Because it's a totally automated computer-based system. Once set up and established, there is no human intervention.'

'I don't understand. It is not possible. It cannot be.'

'Well I'm sure I don't have to remind you Ivan that, until two days ago, it would have been considered impossible for all the world's money to disappear. And yet here we are…' and he waved his arm at the people in the bar and on the terraces outside and down below on the streets,' all of us, gathered here together from all over the world, trying to make sense of just that.'

'Ok, but I still struggling with idea in practice. How I get one then, one of these

BitCoin? And how I spend it? Because if the banks don't accept them as money, then my options must be very limited.'

Hank waved the waiter over again to get some bar snacks.

As the daylight outside began to fade and the city lights on the other side of the lake started to twinkle, he felt his BlockChain moment coming on.

Chapter 35 – Crosstown traffic

Midnight on the Ides of March, a time that manages to sound ominous and a bit sinister in a Shakespearean kind of way.

The boys were well rested.

There had been no booze for a while, plenty of sleep, lots of quarter-pounders, and no disturbances or distractions.

They couldn't shut Ans out of course, didn't want to, she was part of the gang, always with them, always around them, brightening up their days and their lives with her light headed view of the world.

She never asked too much and sometimes that can be just as much of a virtue as the hard-hitting questions posed by the likes of award-winning seasoned investigative journalists such as Diggs, Watchinit, Buggameeblue and Oyeh-Wright.

That didn't mean she wasn't curious, or even a bit nosey, she was a girl after all, but she did have an innate sense of her own good fortune, a sense of how lucky she was with the two bright, funny and sparky computer geeks who inhabited her life but who were, for the most part, off in cyberspace while she was off at the shops or out clubbing, off in dance space.

Andrei and Georgi didn't mind her doing that, it seemed to make her happy.

And Ans didn't mind them paying more attention to their multiple screens than they did to her; it seemed to make them happy.

A lot of people could have learned a lot from their attitude to each other.

But in the couple of weeks leading up to i-day she couldn't help noticing a change of some sort come over them, as if there was something in the air.

Her female intuition told her it was probably connected with that message they'd asked her to deliver. That had been a funny day and they never really explained what it was, never really said that much about it.

She was always asking if she could help. It was kind of automatic; they always seemed so busy, barely having time to look up from the numerous screens and digital devices that littered the flat.

And it went with her seemingly sweet nature. Not just lovely to look at, but sweet by nature too. Everybody said so. So it must be true.

Well, most of the time!

So when the regular mid-afternoon trot across the park to McDonalds turned out to involve a detour that day, she was slightly puzzled, although also quite a bit excited because it gave her the chance to try out her new prize toy, the moped which the boys had clubbed together and bought her for her sixteenth.

The sheer thrill of the independence that comes with having one's own transport at that age can never be understated. It is a true and beautiful sense of pure freedom and the simple delight of just travelling somewhere else under her own power washed over her like a mild aphrodisiac, making her feel a bit giddy, just at the very thought of it.

It would be her first opportunity to cross town on her own so, as she began concentrating on trying to memorise most of the journey, she didn't really think too much about the content of the envelope she was being asked to deliver, nor the fact that the boys had never asked her to do anything remotely like that before.

So off she went that wet afternoon, wrapped up tight from head to toe against the inhospitable January weather, found the address in between the Arbat and Presnensky districts after a shaky twenty minute ride, located the external mail drop next to the front door of the rather swanky looking building, delivered her jiffy bag envelope, chugged back over to Ulitsa Maroseyka to pick up the boys' lunch, ran out of petrol just as she passed the Bolshoi, dumped her bike to collect later, was obliged to walk the rest of the way, met Piotr from one of her dance classes who'd lost his wallet, gave him half of the food and finally made it back about six o clock to two very hungry teenagers who laughed at first at her exploits but then hugged her and hugged her again.

Their lovely Anastasia.

What would they ever do without her!

But it was only really now, several weeks later, as she started to agonise over this current situation, that she thought back to that day and the sheer weirdness of it.

She began to worry, only slowly at first, but then it started to build in her

Was there something wrong?

Had they broken the law maybe?

She knew enough about them to know that they had spent large parts of their formative years with some pretty unsavoury characters.

Had their pasts come back to haunt them?

It started to prey on her mind, the more she thought about it, the more it actually seemed as if something different was happening.

They always had several of their "projects" on the go at any one time and had always seemed adept at juggling the work and the deadlines without too much fuss.

But this was a bit more frantic somehow, like something bigger, or maybe more important.

She pondered her options and, as girls will do sometimes, tackled the subject from a rather obscure angle.

'How far should my moped go?'

'What, before you put petrol in, you mean?'

'Yes, I'm always nervous now since I ran out that day in the rain.'

'Well we got you one with a 50cc engine' Andrei told her ' So I think the sales guy said about a hundred miles or so on a full tank. You just need to pay attention to the gauge and you'll be fine.'

'I couldn't see it that day, it was so wet.'

'Well, just learn to always look at it before you drive off.'

'I do, but I just got so nervous after doing four miles on strange roads. It was bad enough going there but then I couldn't find the right turning coming back. Now that I think about it, what the hell was that all about anyway? Halfway across town with a bloody envelope. Are you getting into the spying business?'

Andrei laughed.

'No, not at all. Don't think we'd be any good at that.'

'What was in the envelope then? You haven't turned me into a drugs mule, have you. Taking advantage of my nice nature.'

'It was just something to do with our latest plan.'

Anastasia's ears pricked up.

Their work was always "projects."

Projects not plans.

Maybe it was nothing but at least it gave her something to hang her next question on.

Like the Swiss, Ans wasn't daft.

Again, she came at it sideways

'Did it work then?

'What do you mean?'

'The message. The one I got soaked delivering before having to walk three miles home. Well, back here to the apartment anyway I mean, although it's hardly like home anymore, since I barely seem to have any time with you these days. Either of you.'

Andrei pulled up sharp.

His girl was upset and he'd not noticed.

Of course, he and Georgi had been flat out on launching CryptoTwo for days now and Ans had become part of the furniture.

'I'm sorry I….'

'Well, did it?'

'Did it what?'

'The message. Did it bloody work. Aren't you listening to me?"

Upset and more than a bit angry it seemed.

Better try to answer the question.

But how? Without giving the game away, the one thing that he and Georgi had sworn not to do. Because that would involve her. She would become implicated and she was way too lovely for that.

Way too innocent. Lovely Ans.

Was it time to tell her, to tell her straight.

But then the whole plan-of-escape conversation that he'd had with Georgi just a few nights previously started to replay itself in his head.

'I, err.., I think it maybe did work, although not in the way that I was expecting' he said, making up his mind suddenly about something that had actually been on his mind for years, although he had only been dimly aware of it.

'It wasn't meant to do that, you see, it was meant to do something else, something else entirely, not something like this, not connected with us like this, with me and you like this, no, it was meant to…..'

'Andi, what the fuck are you gabbling on about ' she was cross now, eyes blazing away.

Why was he fobbing her off?

He was going to leave her, that was it. Like all boys, he was really a bit of a bastard. And now he'd found someone else. After all these years. And all she'd done to be nice to him, to look after him as best she could while he lived on planet Zog or somewhere with his stupid friend, that other nutter, as Piotr had called them, and she

suddenly realized that she hadn't seen him either since that day when she'd given him half the food, and he was a good friend, a nice friend, somebody she could go out clubbing with and have a good time, not like these two fucking...., yes, nutters. Fucking nutters. Piotr was right. That was the right word for them.

She suddenly collapsed into an involuntary bout of uncontrollable sobbing, her lovely young body wracked with the emotional pain of rejection. Her bosom heaved and the tears ran down her cheeks in streams as she yelled at him.

'You fucking bastard. Fuck you.'

She wiped her eyes.

It didn't help. The tears ran and ran.

'Fuck you, fuck you both, the two of you. Why are you smiling like that? Can't you see I'm upset, you fucking nutter?'

'Ans' he said suddenly, in a rather strange voice, assertive, gentle, unaffected by her outburst.

'What is it?'

'I love you. I never loved anybody or anything more in my life.'

'What are you doing? Where are you going? '

Andrei was suddenly down on one knee in front of her, grinning like a Cheshire cat.

'My beautiful Angel.' he said softly.

She glared at him, although she sensed it wasn't quite the right time for a death stare.

'I love you so much. Will you marry me?'

Chapter 36 – Corroboration

'So that would definitely work then, would it?' JoJo asked, after a short period of contemplation.

They'd been up most of the night wrestling with the intractable problem of how the Disappearance might have happened.

'It's the only way that makes any sense,' Caitlin replied, 'if you factor in all of the available evidence, although I'm using that word very lightly at the moment in this particular context.'

'There's certainly nothing in the available bank outputs from this morning that contradicts it, so that's a plus. But then they didn't really give us a lot, did they?'

'No, they didn't. Typical banks. Them first, everybody else second. We can only hope they're a bit more open about it tonight. She didn't give a time though, did she, Sylvie whatshername?'

'Sylvie Danton. No but Jake just spoke to her and his text said probably about 8 their time, so that's 7 here. So in a couple of hours.'

'Ok, so do we wait, or do we call Harry?'

A few seconds later Harry's mobile lit up on Willi Sagné's balcony, high up in the hills above Geneva.

It was just beginning to get dark. A few miles down below him the town was starting to twinkle in the early evening light as Jake completed his group text message update and headed off to the lifts to find Hank and Ivan in the Floor Two lounge bar in the Fairmont.

He looked at the caller ID on the screen.

9-1 Everett.

'Hi Jo, how's it going?'

'We may have cracked it Harry, or at least Cait has.'

Harry suspected the theoretical explanation put forward by Monique earlier was probably correct. Her assessment had tallied pretty accurately with the complete sequence of events, as he understood them to have happened.

But he was not a man given to guesswork. He knew Hazel Ingliss was taking a personal interest in the case, as indeed was everybody, all the way up to the PM. He

needed to be sure before he briefed her.

Plus he trusted his team implicitly and would always listen to their view.

'Ok, shoot. I'm all ears.'

As he listened Cait laid out the various steps involved in launching a crypto. A few years earlier each and every new one of them was a major news story. But by the spring of 2022 there were so many of them that even the seasoned traders were spoilt for choice.

Ethereum.

LiteCoin.

Ripple.

XTZ

Doge

Eos

Neo.

Dash.

Cardano.

Stellar.

Tron.

It was a longish list, and one that continued to get longer with each passing month as more and more wealth piled into the digital variants and global interest in them grew.

What he heard was broadly consistent with Monique's interpretation.

So much for the how.

'Why'd they do it Cait? If they're putting it all back, what was the motivation?'

'Well that part is still guesswork. And remember, they could put some of it back, but not all. Even keeping the tiniest percentage would make them mega-rich, whoever they are. And we still don't have an answer on that yet either.'

'Agreed. But you must have some thoughts on the rationale. The Robin Hood note thing, what were we calling it?'

'The communiqué?'

'Exactly, yes. What about that.'

Just then Monique appeared with some blankets and a carafe of freshly made Glühwein, the perfect way to keep an early evening Alpine chill at bay.

Harry smiled at his gracious hostess, stuck his thumb up by way of thanks and

tapped his mobile.

Monique nodded her understanding and withdrew discretely.

'He's doing proper spying stuff now.' she whispered to Willi when she got back downstairs. 'Exciting isn't it?'

Harry drew the warm fluffy material up his chest and settled back to listen.

'Ok' Cait started 'so for what it's worth and from what I'm seeing and from what I understand of it all so far, I think I'm gonna' buy the social agenda thing. At least for now, pending whatever else we hear from FIB later on.'

'And your thinking?'

'I think the perpetrators are very young, highly idealistic, technically proficient bordering on brilliant and must have already had years of ops behind them despite their tender years. That's a very potent and dangerous combination of factors.'

'I didn't know you were a profiler as well Cait, in addition to your numerous other skills.'

'Well, it's just deduction isn't it.'

'I don't know, is it?' Harry was testing her a bit now, probing her logic, pushing, thoughts of his impending conversations with Hazel, possibly even later on with the PM as well, now colouring most of his thoughts.

'Plus they're already probably long gone.'

'Ok, well that's a fair bit of deduction, so lets have it.'

'Older people would be unlikely to leave the note, it's just too risky. Why leave clues at all, it's unnecessary. So our culprits are either risk takers or just careless. The sheer ingenuity of coming up with the spoofing combined with the launch of CryptoTwo indicates a very high intelligence level, which doesn't mean they're perfect of course, we're all human and can make mistakes, but clumsiness, with these two anyway, just seems so unlikely.'

'Two?'

'Way too much work for just one person. Plus the pure psychology of it would suggest the need to continually bounce ideas back and forth, to and fro. You can't do that alone'

'More likely a team then?' Harry pushed again. How far had she thought this through?

The fact that JoJo chose to come back in and answer told Harry something else very valuable. The Nines were working well together and continuing to gel as a unit.

Even in the midst of a crisis that was pleasing. He made a mental note.

'Unlikely,' she said, her soft Hertfordshire accent in stark contrast to Caitlin's West coast lilt, 'we thought about that in a risk context too. Two's company, three's a crowd and all that. The fewer people who know, the better. In any large gang, by which I mean four, five or more, history tells us that somebody will inevitably become unhappy, didn't get enough of the cake, wasn't cuddled enough by the others, stole somebody's girl, or whatever. With two, that hardly ever happens. It's much harder work, but, if you've got time on your side, eminently doable. And, let's face it, nobody was timing these guys. They didn't have a deadline, not an external one anyway.'

'And years of ops?'

'Just not possible that this was anybody's first rodeo,' Cait came back on.' Way too complex. There's a level of sophistication about this that almost guarantees it was done by people with previous vast experience. But you'll struggle to find all the ops track record, the hacking knowledge, the coding skills, the spoofing tricks and the sheer audacity in anybody over thirty.'

'Why not?'

'Because of the other characteristics and the sheer balls of it.'

'I can think of plenty of people over thirty with balls the size of melons' Harry suggested, rather too graphically. 'So we may have to disagree on that one for now. What's with the idealism though? I have to say that note never sat easy with me. I always thought it was probably a red herring although I really couldn't ever figure out why, just couldn't put my finger on it.'

'There's no doubt that there's a distinct distraction component in there, so you got that bit right' Jojo told him. 'The theme suggests maturity though, an appreciation of human nature, an understanding that people have a tendency to repeat their own mistakes. That doesn't really sound much like teenagers, does it? But we think they probably are. And they used the communiqué wording to try and disguise the fact, as camouflage if you like.'

'Teenagers. Really.'

Harry was surprised.

That didn't happen often.

'It's the latest spoofing stuff. You wont find it in any of the regular chat rooms, even the dark ones.'

'Spoofing?' Harry enquired, testing them a bit once again. 'Remind me.'

'Generic term for falsifying data. There's a number of ways of doing it, each new iteration usually more devious than the last. It's a continuing downward spiral, especially from our perspective.'

'And that works with the banks customer data?'

'It shouldn't but it can. In practice their systems should always spot an attack using their own packet inspection firewalls, which are kind of like Hi Definition X-rays which should be able to see through superficial material and spot underlying trouble.'

'I would dearly like to think my bank's security was way ahead of the bad guys,' Harry offered, quite reasonably. 'Are you saying it's not?'

'We're saying it's an ongoing tussle. The banks are generally a step ahead. Obviously. They have to be. But these things run in cycles and every so often there will be a small window of opportunity when the reverse is true, the bandits get ahead of the game, and there is significant vulnerability. It won't last too long, but it will be there'

'Which is what happened on Monday night?'

'Exactly. They would have spent ages setting things up on the quiet. Nobody could have been aware of anything until such time as they attempted entry.'

'And then the banks internal alarms systems would have all gone off at once?'

'They should have done, yes.'

'Then why haven't FIB told us that?'

'Good question. They'll have their reasons, no doubt. Will probably claim it's a small part of a bigger investigation or something like that. Maybe we'll hear more this evening.'

'So the breach is triggered by fabricated data?'

'No, not quite. It's more likely the actual act of fabricating the data.'

'Don't understand.'

'There's a lot of mis-direction involved in these scams. For example, caller ID's on mobile phones can now use a bad number to show a good number. Let's say your phone is telling you that your bank is calling because their telephone number comes up on your screen. But they're not. The caller ID has been forged by a gateway device inserted illegally in the network and you're suddenly talking to a thief.'

'I think something similar happened with my e-mail a while back,' Harry

recalled. 'One of the people in my contact list made a rather odd request so I rang him up to ask some questions and discovered it wasn't even him who'd sent the message.'

'Exactly. That's spoofing, the phone call version and the e-mail version.'

'And this particular version? The Jumbo version that seems to have made all the world's money disappear overnight. What the hell version is that then?'

'Well, first off you have to understand that not all of it's illegal. Although making something appear to be something which it is not sounds very dodgy, there are plenty of instances where it's perfectly legit. Like with VPN's for instance. I take it you know what they are?'

'I do, yes. Virtual Private Networks. Where you get assigned a temporary IP address located somewhere else so if I'm in London, for example, it looks like my computer activity is being generated elsewhere.'

'Exactly. So it's entirely possible that it's going to be a bit of a fine line proving that these guys did anything wrong.'

Harry was surprised again.

Twice in about five minutes.

Now that really didn't happen very often.

'You telling me it's possible to steal all of the money in the world and not be guilty of a crime.'

'We're not lawyers Harry, are we?' Caitlin reminded him. 'We're just pointing out that there may be a jurisdictional element to all of this which makes it a cyberspace crime. Hence it didn't really happen in any one single location, but rather in several. That could make prosecution difficult.'

'Ok, point taken, although it had to have started somewhere didn't it, the action or actions that triggered this? But we're getting ahead of ourselves. Can we get back to the spoofing and how they did it, or how you two think they did it.'

Harry was now getting close to the corroboration he needed.

This was starting to sound very close to Monique's explanation from two hours earlier, the one that he'd been thinking about ever since, was still mulling over, the one that had seemed ridiculous at first but now seemed a lot less so, especially as it was now beginning to sound as if Caitlin and JoJo were headed in the same direction.

'There's another kind of spoofing which is a bit less well known' Jojo started, 'although the hacking community are pretty au fait with it. It involves mirror imaging, the actual fabrication of alternative data sets designed to mask and masquerade.'

'Ok, interesting. Go on.'

Harry was now having a déja vu, seeing Monique's old network blueprints from the early nineties splayed out across the table again.

'It's a technique that the blacks play about with a lot, but usually it's just out of a kind of mischievous curiosity.'

'The blacks?'

'The black hats. Malign hackers.'

'Ah, ok. What about them again?'

'Well, it's always been generally accepted that they would never really be able to do much in anger with those types of tricks because of the capacity and scale issues.'

'Explain.'

'Because you'd pretty much need a server farm in the Nevada desert or somewhere like that to host all of the replicated files. There would just be too much of it for normal data storage locations, just way too much data. Fortunately those mega sites are still owned and managed by the good guys so we can generally see everything that's happening in those domains. For the most part they're all pretty much totally transparent.'

'Ok, so if you're assumptions are correct and that's how it was done, then it poses two rather obvious questions as I see it.' Harry steered things along.

'Firstly, where are those mirror files being held? And secondly, has the money been detached from them or is it all still there? Or at least some of it?'

'Yup, agreed. That's what we thought.' came the response from Chelsea. 'In terms of sheer feasibility, it's probably one for Hank now. He's probably best placed to comment on the practicalities. Unless you happen to know any other banking infrastructure experts of course. Outside of the FIB team that is. Somehow it would be nice to get an alternate view of things without having to be too dependant on them.'

They concluded the call and disconnected.

Just then Monique appeared again at the top of the stairs with another top up carafe of the lovely home-made Glühwein, some warm sausages and a basket of bread.

'Ow is it going 'Arry?' she enquired, placing the tray down on the table next to him. 'Av your team found the money yet? I hope I was able to help.'

He grinned up at his lovely hostess

'More than you can possible know actually.'

He raised a glass in her direction.

'More than you can ever possibly know.'

He took a long swig of his invigorating Swiss winter – warmer.

'Santé.'

Chapter 37 – Cat. Mouse. Fish.

Viktor's phone was red hot most of the time but he was not a man given to idle chat. His calls were strictly functional and strictly business with only the absolute minimum of pleasantries and courtesies to keep things civil. But his contacts all understood that. He was a very busy guy, and well connected too, right to the top it was rumoured, so not a guy to mess with.

Even during meetings he would constantly be pawing at his mobile, flip it over, scan a message, then tune back in to whatever real conversation he happened to be having.

His phone was never off, even at night. He had his personal staff on a twenty-four hour rota and those on midnight phone duty were under explicit instructions to wake him if certain people or their representatives got in touch.

For his part, Liam was also used to the inhospitable nature of cellphone intrusion, it just being a facet of everyday life. It was very common, but what was unusual was the sheer frequency of the buzzes, pings and bleeps that emanated from Viktor's phone, all denoting different people and/or different regions.

'Dat's a whole lot of friends ya's got there Mr.A', he commented somewhat laconically. 'Or are ya just busier dann usual today?'

Under most circumstances Viktor Alliskiya would have moved his surprise guest on by now but, in truth, he was enjoying himself rather too much to do that.

The agent that he had been warned about was turning out to be a hugely knowledgeable source of information about rock formations and mineral deposits, not most people's cup of tea, but subjects very close to the heart of The Energy King, mainly because he spent millions on research each year as his teams beavered away across the vast expanse of the Russian mainland in search of new oil, coal or shale deposits. Any additional advantage he could gain over his competitors in any of those areas could save him some of those millions and Liam sounded like a man who knew what he was talking about.

'I'm always busy Mr. Dempsey, it's how I like things.'

'Well, me too but moi phone don't go off every foive seconds.'

'Ah, yes, well, I like to keep updated on things you see, a man in my position

needs to be on the ball all the time.'

'You can put a stop-loss on your positions, ya know, denn you don't have to be worrying about your investments all the time.'

'I am aware of the available strategies in those areas, Mr. Dempsey. Do I look like a man who just started making money yesterday?'

'Unless you happen to be investing in Cryptos, that is. They tend to have different rules.'

'And you're an expert on them as well are you, as well as matters pertaining to geology?'

'Not really, no, I wouldn't put it like that. In fact I only got interested in 'dem last month. Started reading about one that was being launched here in Russia. Or at least it seemed that way. Some of the ownership rules surrounding them can be pretty arcane so wasn't entirely sure.'

Viktor shifted back in his comfy high-backed red leather chair and continued to size up his prey. He had already decided that it might be a good idea to try and deliver an English agent to the officials he had been talking to the previous day. That appealed to him, would be novel and quite interesting, something he'd never done before. One more string to his bow, as it were, with the people who mattered.

In the meantime Liam was continuing to be more than stimulating as a conversation partner.

First the tennis, which he had to confess, had been a pretty good angle, almost one hundred percent certain to get through to him using Yelena.

Then the whole gas stability equation, which he had drawn out rough on a notepad and which neatly addressed one of his current headaches down in Georgia.

And now, by the sound of it, he was about to start talking about CryptoTwo, something which did indeed form part of Viktor's extensive and diverse international portfolio of stocks, shares and other tradable assets. He'd heard something somewhere on his long and winding grapevine and had got in early, the tried and tested way of making huge profits from insider knowledge, illegal though that was now supposed to be.

So, yet again, the young man before him had his attention.

Which, of course, Liam knew.

"Got him", he smiled to himself as he noticed Viktor mentally engage with his third gambit. *"Again."*

'And what did you make of it?'

'Well, not too much at the time actually. I'm a pretty busy guy Mr. Alliskiya, as I'm sure you will have been told.'

'Yes, of course. As an international sports agent you must be running around like a mad thing.' Viktor gave him a knowing grin.

'So I just give all my spare cash to a professional money manager. She's authorized to make all those decisions for me then I don't have to worry about stock picks or asset classes or any of that stuff. I find it a bit tedious as well as a bit confusing to be honest, so I generally leave it alone.'

Viktor nodded in quiet agreement.

'And then there's the daily temptation to keep looking at how things are going. Are you up or down? If you're down, do you sell before you lose too much? If you're up do you sell and make a profit, or wait longer in the hope you'll make some more. You could easily be looking at making those decisions every half hour. I ask you, what kind of life is that?'

'Every minute for some.'

Liam had hooked his fish but continued to play along, reeling him in slowly.

A game of cat and mouse with a fish in the middle.

Two fish actually, only one of whom would eventually swim free.

'Sorry?' Liam put on his puzzled Paddy face.

'For the professionals I mean, the guys on the trading floors and at the dealing desks. Their days are spent looking at screens every minute, just constantly tracking the prices and movements of hundreds of those things. That really must be quite debilitating, I agree with you.'

'But the pay's good, so I hear, so dey'll be happy enough come Friday and when the Christmas bonus arrives.' Liam continued. 'But aren't their lives being made easier with these fancy algorithms, the ones that use predictive computing power to tell you which horse to back.'

Viktor gave him a strange look.

'Sorry, that's the Irishman in me comin' out. I meant which investments to pile into.'

Viktor was canny enough to realize that something was going on now, just not quite sure what.

It was Liam's third bullseye in a row, for he was now touching on a subject for

which Viktor had what could only be described as a fascination.

He thought quickly on his feet, as befitted a man of his worldly experience, and immediately saw a way to maybe kill two birds with one stone.

'Well, that's one of my pet subjects actually,' he offered. ' I have an idea. If you know as much about that as you do about golf and pipelines, might I suggest that you stay for dinner this evening and I'll get one of the guest rooms fixed up so that you don't have to worry about traipsing back across town to your hotel in the dark. In return, perhaps you could share your playbook with me and we could have a chat about how those algorithms could start to work with the Cryptos.'

'With CryptoTwo, you mean.' Liam asserted, suddenly a bit more forcefully. 'That's the only one I know about.'

'Ok, lets start with that then.'

Viktor picked up his cordless house phone and spoke to somebody, somewhere else in MMM.

'Make up the west wing please Krystina. Male guest.'

"*Got him.*' he thought to himself, quietly smiling.

As he put the house phone down, his mobile pinged yet again on the table next to it.

He flipped the screen over.

Finally, one of the messages he'd been waiting for.

Piotr from The Bolshoi knows who the nutters are.

Liam read it upside down.

" Hmm. Got them too."

Chapter 38 – The escape route

Hank had finished off his telephone call with Hazel earlier whilst watching Jake head across the crowded salon towards Sylvie Danton.

'So I think you should just mooch around a bit with the media crowd' Hazel was concluding her briefing with the Bostonian, the second of her two ops guys on the ground in Switzerland just as the first one was introducing himself to his FIB liaison.

' See what you can sniff out.'

'Ok, that's what I thought too. Good to be a bit unstructured sometimes and just hang loose for a while. What's happening in Moscow? Any news?'

'They're my next call,' Hazel told him. 'Last I heard Liam was trying to find out what the local authorities really know about all this and whether they're mixed up in it in any way.'

Hank thought back to his phone call with Jake while he was snacking on his pizza at Monica's in the Logan departure lounge.

'Thought Paul was doing that? Something happen?'

'Jake switched them. Him and Liam. Decided that the situation called for some blarney involving geology and gas stability with the local contact. I don't know the detail but he was on point for several hours last night so he would have had the necessary overview to make that call. Jake doesn't do things without a good reason. You can ask him later.'

'Ok, will do. Where's Paul?'

'He's pursuing pigtail girl; you remember the one from that communiqué thing. We're trying to work backwards from the drop off to find out who she is and where she went next. Getting hold of the CCTV is proving a bit sticky though, not that I'm too surprised by that, it is Russia, after all.'

'Are we still believing the Robin Hood angle then?' Hank asked, partly surprised to hear that it was still being taken seriously, but then again, as he knew Hazel would say, they didn't really have very much else to go on.

'Well, maybe' she concluded sensibly. ' A lead is a lead after all. Let's see where it takes us.'

'Be a bit bizarre if this turned out to be some kind of global charity stunt by one

of those anti-capitalist groups.'

'Well they're all bonkers enough to do that aren't they, but they do also tend to be exceptionally well motivated so I'm keeping an open mind. I'll have the PM and his team on at me again this evening so if anything new turns up, whatever it is, please let me know straight away. And tell Jake the same. Reports are starting to come in now of a few street riots and civic leader kidnappings in France, Spain and Italy. Various different protest groups seems to be claiming responsibility and we think it's their way of pointing the finger of suspicion at officialdom. It's probably the first signs of things starting to turn nasty so anything we can say to calm all that down will be very welcome.'

'Ok, will do' Hank concurred. 'Catch you later on.'

Hazel had barely rung off at her end when her screen flashed.

Lambert 9-3.

'Hello Paul, beat me to it by half a second. You on a train?'

The GPS based geo-locator app on her mobile had popped up a map with a moving blue dot in it.

'No, I'm hitching a ride across town actually.'

'Who with?'

'My two new best friends Major Valeria and Raspo the pretend barman.'

His companions in the muscular semi-military looking SUV ignored him.

'Well, since an hour or so ago anyway.'

Hazel took this news in her stride. She was experienced enough to know that it was more than a joke to think that any foreign agent could wander into Moscow undetected.

'Where you going?'

'There's a district called Meshchansky that's suddenly become of interest. It's a bit north of the centre, not too far out, so quicker by car than the metro.'

Hazel minimized Paul's location on her cell screen and tapped a couple of buttons on her phone's keypad. A second blue dot appeared close to the first one, just off to the right and up a bit. She enlarged it.

'That's where Liam's gone.'

'Why, what's happened?'

'He picked up your three o clock after checking in with Jake earlier.'

'Well, that's a bit weird. Our two headed out that way too before we lost them.

'Your two? Who do you mean?'

Paul told her about the old FSB video surveillance and brought her up to speed on his days work thus far.

'So checking into The Metropole this morning turned out to be an interesting experience. They knew I was coming, it seems.'

'Ok,' Hazel was following.' So getting back to your two. Who are they?'

'We don't know yet.'

'Are you sure it's the same girl?'

'Not one hundred percent, no. They haven't got the face recognition software rolled out everywhere yet.'

'And he just met her on the street. '

'Yes, just by the park. But it looked arranged. Then they took off together.'

Hazel panned out of the screen map of Meshchansky on her phone so that she could see a larger picture of the whole Moscow metropolitan area.'

'You lost them in the Metro system somewhere, you said?

'Yes. Correct.'

'What line were they on?'

'The seven. It goes right through Meschansky. We ran the Kuznetsky-Most station surveillance tape over and over in case they got out there, but we couldn't see them. Maybe they did a quick change of clothes or something because the video's been checked and checked but to no avail. '

'Maybe that's because they're not there,' Hazel suggested. 'Maybe they never even got off.'

She was now looking in detail at the map image on her screen.

'Try checking the airport.'

Paul looked quizzically at Valeria but it was actually Raspo, who was busy driving, who made the connection first, as the two Russians listened in to Paul's conversation on loudspeak.

'She's right. The seven goes out as far as the old Planernoye yard,' he said excitedly. 'That's the end of the line. It's a fair bit out from the City centre but from there it's only a short taxi hop over to Sheremetyevo.'

'And if you wanted to buy an airline ticket anonymously, you wouldn't want to use your bank card, would you?' suggested Hazel.' And most travel agencies won't take payment in cash anyway these days because of the money laundering

regulations.'

'But the Airlines will.' added Paul. ' And the airport video will be way better. We might even be able to track their purchase if we can time stamp it.'

Suddenly they were all on the same page.

If it was the right girl, this could be the breakthrough they needed. She, or the boy, might be involved, might even be the actual perpetrators.

'When was all this again? 'asked Valeria.

'Last week.' Paul replied.' So they could be long gone out of the country by now.'

'Let's not get ahead of ourselves too much,' the calm voice of Hazel Ingliss reminded them.' It's still a long shot. One thing at a time.'

'Ok, we're on our way.'

'Good luck, keep me posted, please.'

Hazel rang off.

'I am not your best friend.' Raspo said to Paul suddenly and rather sternly. ' Why you say this? You English are very strange.'

'It was a joke.'

'Yes, and I have heard many of your English jokes. This is also why I say you are very strange.'

Paul glared at him, only to suddenly notice Raspo's face in the rear view mirror grinning back at him.

'Just kidding,' he smiled.' Russian joke.'

The considerable authority of a major in the FSB was on display very quickly as Valeria introduced herself to the first security patrol at Sheremetyevo. The armed soldiers eyed her with professional suspicion until she tapped a couple of codes into her mobile.

Five seconds later the two guards got messages of their own which obviously provided them with all the clearance and reassurances they needed. They saluted and within minutes their own senior officer appeared and all four of them headed across the concourse to a set of escalators and then up to an elevated control room with a panoramic view of the taxiways and the apron.

They joined a fifth man sitting in front of a bank of cameras showing images from all across the airport. It was a bustling scene, no different to the way Logan had looked over in Boston when Hank had passed through it the previous morning.

It was still the calm before the storm.

'What date and what time?'

'Tuesday of last week, about four in the afternoon.'

'Travelling to where?'

'Not sure?'

'You won't know the airline then, I suppose?' the CCTV guy queried.

'Sorry, we don't, no.'

'Better sit down then, we'll have to trawl through several possible locations to see if we can find them. When you say about four, can you be any more specific. It'll help narrow it down a bit.'

Paul, Valeria and Raspo did some quick computations based on the last sightings of Georgi and Ans on the metro.

'Probably left the station about four actually, now we come to think about it, so allow fifteen minutes on top for the taxi ride across from the Planaernoye terminus to here, so maybe a bit later, about four fifteen.'

'They arrived by taxi? You sure?'

'Almost certainly, yeah.'

The CCTV guy wheeled his chair down to the last set of monitors, which showed the throng of arriving and departing passengers outside the main terminus building.

Two of them showed the taxi ranks.

'Well, at least we got a focused area to check now.' he said, tapping the screens.

'Now what do they look like?'

Paul described the couple based on the video which had arrived on Valeria's phone earlier.

While they started to concentrate on the images of hundreds of travellers scurrying to and fro, the senior security officer was busy explaining the airport layout.

It seemed that the ticket sales desks were not associated with the individual airline check-in counters, but were all set off over to one side, tucked away in a corner.

'It keeps the pedestrian walkway areas free' he explained. 'Most people already have their ticket when they arrive. They buy it in advance before they come here. Those desks are only there as a convenience for the very small number of customers who either forget their ticket or leave it all to the last minute. There's not many of them but there's always a few.'

'Got to be easier than the cab rank then,' suggested Paul, getting up from his seat and walking back to the middle of the bank of screens.' Which camera am I looking for?'

'Twenty two' said the CCTV guy, 'wait while I fast forward the playback to four fifteen.'

While Raspo stuck with the taxis, Paul started to watch a few rather bored looking women who were busy chatting together behind a long counter.

'And they sell on behalf of all the airlines ' he asked.

'They do, that's right.'

'Ok, well let's see then. '

He stretched out on the swivel chair and waited.

It was Raspo who saved the day when the clock ticked round to five and the others were about to give up and go home.

'They wouldn't necessarily have come straight here though, would they?' he suggested, 'might easily have wandered off first to get some food or a coffee or something.'

So they stayed an extra hour and sure enough it was just before six that two familiar looking figures came into view and approached the ticket desk.

Valeria noted the exact time and logged it before instructing the local security official to use his pass clearances to access the central server. From that moment on the identification process was relatively straightforward since the ticket sales desk, as they had been informed, was very quiet.

Ans and Georgi had needed to produce travel ID and passports for their plane tickets to Vienna, scheduled for departure just over a week later.

A couple of internal systems kicked in providing names, addresses and some basic profiling of the two teenagers.

'Goodness, they look so young don't they,' Paul wondered out loud.' Do you think we could have the wrong people? Maybe we're not reading all these clues properly.'

'No, its definitely her,' Valeria told him. 'She's the girl from the communiqué video alright. And the fact that she's shaping to leave the country with her boyfriend just at the exact time when all this happens makes me even more suspicious. We'll know more when we search their flat.'

She said something in Russian to Raspo.

Paul looked at her expectantly.

'I just asked him to check if we've got an extradition treaty with Austria.'

Chapter 39 – Dinner in The West Wing

In the world of spies all sorts of things get swapped and exchanged but the most commonly traded commodity is information. This is the most basic of all forms of espionage. One country has something that another country does not. Their leaders cannot bear this affront to their misplaced egos so they embark on a series of wild adventures to redress the balance and correct the dastardly perceived wrongs.

This may just sound like cold war stuff.

The iron curtain.

The evil Empire.

East v West.

Checkpoint Charlie.

The politics of the big wall down the middle, a notion thought up by blockheads based purely on short-term expediency, and a strategy which can never be sustainable.

But it is way more pervasive than that.

The stuff of secrets is as old as the hills, something whispered by advisors to kings in ancient times and consultants to businesses today.

Knowledge is power, so they say, and he who knows things is oft well advised to either keep them to himself or only speak with judicious selectivity.

The rewards for applying these laws consistently range from great power and wealth when done properly to interrogation and death when not.

So spying and espionage are not for the faint hearted and should only be undertaken by those of a certain character. Training on the job does not come as standard for the purveyors of these crafts. Rather it is imperative to know exactly what you are doing on day one, even before you leave base.

The slightest miscalculation can be deadly.

Having said that it would be easy to conclude that the strange breed of people who choose to do these things for a living must all be ice – cold killers.

Nothing could be further from the truth.

The modern day agent needs a host of positive attributes, most of them social. The ability to shoot straight and mix up poisons furtively and slip them into someone else's drink is way down the list.

After all these years, 007 still has a lot to answer for.

A cool head is more essential, preferably alongside the ability to read situations and people, an intuitive nature that tells you when to be flexible, and the sheer character and strength of mind to be loyal and courageous.

Contrary to popular opinion taking orders blindly is now several places further down the instructions list which is, these days, more commonly topped off by the ability to think independently and make good and quick decisions based on the specifics of individual situations.

Old Blinky Duff and Archie Webster knew all this when they interviewed for The Nines a few years earlier. Their mentor and boss Sir Walter Tweedie had set up the sessions and insisted on something new for the candidates.

'Give them all a left field question,' he'd advised, 'each with three feasible default options as answers. The type of people we're looking for will always come up with one of their own which will invariably be a better choice than the ones we've provided. That is going to be, primarily, how the final six get selected. Quick reactions and independence of thought '

So Jojo Everett got the plane crash, Mark Wright got the sports star, Paul Lambert got the astronaut, Jake Rivera got town planning, and Caitlin Yang got the swimmer.

Liam Dempsey had been the sixth one through the door that day.

The sixth of six.

The final candidate.

It was a day he'd never forgotten.

"Well that's about it from us," old Blinky had said after an hour or so.

Liam had been feeling pretty good at that stage, he was confident all had gone well.

"But before we let you go, there's just one final question. There's no right or wrong answer. We're just interested in seeing how you think through problems."

Liam was suddenly apprehensive.

One final tripwire.

Deep breath.

"Ok. Is dis my specialist subject question then? Loike on Mastermind?"

"Well, not really Liam, no. They're completely random actually, so not really designed around you in any way at all. In fact they're even multiple choice and come

complete with a set of possible answers. All you have to do is tell us which one you prefer."

More apprehension.

He knew he'd done well so far on geology, geopolitics and tech futures.

Now they were throwing him a curve ball.

"Ok. Fire away.'

"So I want you to imagine that you're away on a business trip and you're trapped in a large house which is owned by your host. You feel threatened by certain aspects of his behaviour although you're not quite sure why. Which of these three options do you choose to address your predicament?

Number one – confront the situation upfront by being assertive and making your excuses to leave.

Number two – stick around to try and sniff out exactly what it is that's going on.

Number three – contact base, make them aware of where you are and ask for reinforcements.

Now, three years later, as he sat in the MMM in the Meshchansky oblast in central Moscow, Liam replayed the final part of that interview in his head.

"Well, they're all possibilities." he'd started.

Blinky and Archie exchanged glances.

Bit worrying.

"But they all have considerable weaknesses too. Number one suggests I might be backing out of the mission at a crucial stage. Never a good idea to bail unless you absolutely have to."

Blinky and Archie looked at each other again but they were smiling slightly this time.

That was better. He'd caught the drift of the question.

"Number two sounds a bit too passive, like hang in there and see what happens. Not exactly a dynamic response to the situation, is it."

The two interviewers made some brief notes on the pads in front of them.

"Whereas number three sounds like the option of last resort, something to keep up your sleeve in case all else fails. Feeling threatened – which is what you said – is probably a regular part of this particular day job, so if I called for back up every time I got a bit nervous I don't think I'd be doing the job properly."

Blinky and Archie waited, pens poised.

"So are you telling me you haven't got a preferred answer then, Liam? " Blinky had asked him finally.

"Ah, no, sorry. You asked me which one of those three I'd choose. My answer is, obviously, none of them."

Liam flashed his warm paddy smile across the desk.

"But if you're now asking me for my own solution, which you didn't, but I tink now maybe you are...."

The two seasoned interviewers waited patiently.

"Then it would depend on some specifics. Am I alone in the house?"

"No."

"Are the other inhabitants neutral?"

"No"

'Am I armed?"

Blinky and Archie exchanged another meaningful glance.

The Nines, as an operational unit, were all going to be unarmed.

"No."

"Am I looking for something?"

"Yes."

"Or somebody?"

"Yes."

'Do I know their exact identity?"

"No."

"Does my host know?"

"No."

"Are we looking for the same person? Or persons?"

"Yes."

"Does my host think I know who they are, or who he or she is?"

"Maybe."

"Is my host armed?"

"Probably. His security detail will be anyway."

"Am I actually locked in?"

"No."

Liam had digested the data for a few seconds.

"Then it sounds like I might be at the half way point of some kind of mission –

assuming that's what the "business trip" actually was. The situation is tense because the next thing that's going to happen will probably determine the final outcome. So there's probably a kind of game of chess going on, both sides bluffing a bit, being cagey, not wanting to reveal their hand too much. My best short term option is to persuade my host and captor that I know much more then he or she does. In turn I would expect him to probably humour and indulge me rather than kidnap or kill me. So my preferred option would be to try to engineer a social situation to jolly that along."

"A social situation like …"

"Like I'd try and get him to invite me to dinner."

Chapter 40 – A digital gold rush

The thing with the Blockchain is that it is pure technology.

It has a genesis like quality. In the beginning there was the blockchain.

And so on.

As such it follows a lot of rules, some of which are programmable and individual, others of which are not. But, partly because of its very nature, there was another biblical characteristic which pertained to it equally well.

It went forth and multiplied. After a while there was a second one, then a third. And so on.

Within a decade or so, a whole raft of Blockchain based digital currency network variants had emerged. Such was the speculative frenzy that greeted these new financial instruments that their values on the global markets went into overdrive.

Even in the labyrinthine world of options and derivatives many of the investment plays were wildly esoteric. They needed some specialist knowledge in order to deliver returns. The pitfalls and traps for the leveraged unwary were many and varied and, although fortunes were made, many, many more were lost.

It had been exactly these thoughts that had prompted the intuitive part of Harry Shepperton's nature to get in touch with his old colleague Colonel Hank Wyatt in Boston a couple of days earlier.

It was a feeling he had – you could call it his gut – that Jumbo was going to need a very detailed knowledge of all sorts of financial futures if The Nines were to unravel its mysteries.

Hank hadn't known it all, but he knew plenty. The rest he quickly worked out as he studied the recent history of the world's new money system, for that is what the Blockchain technology is and is destined to be.

The scramble had started about five years after Nakamoto and BTC. The visionaries could see it and some of them started work almost straight away, the new pioneers, few in number but unfettered in ambition.

But the remainder – and they were far and away the vast majority – were reactionary.

The opponents of change.

The deniers of progress.

The Luddites.

They were all out in force, partly because the status quo suited them – and that is a position that should never be underestimated – but mostly because they simply did not understand.

The new era of computerization only really started to take hold in any significant way in the eighties, driven largely by the global might of American business and the sheer power of the Yankee dollar.

Soon the first terminal devices started to appear in the shops and in people's homes and suddenly, almost imperceptibly, the revolution was under way.

Then the generational thing happened, where there is no need for acceptance of the new – because it has always been there – and no need for rejection of the old – because it is increasingly not there at all.

And so it was that about thirty years into what is now called *The Digital Age*, the first credible signs of a wholesale upheaval in the world's monetary systems could be seen. Given that they are more than the lifeblood of the world's economies in so many ways, a hugely dramatic reaction could have been expected.

Instead, it was quite muted.

Now, just two days after that phone call, Hank was imparting this very quick history lesson of the early Noughties to Jake and Ivan in a Swiss hotel bar.

Like a lot of people, they knew some of it already.

Like a lot of the same people, they were actually amazed how much of it they didn't know.

Hank was doing his best to keep it simple. His own understanding in many ways reflected the exact workings of the new technologies, his savant intelligence capable of its own spontaneous programming functionality.

As the tech shifted and moved constantly forward, so his own understanding and comprehension constantly realigned around it.

To say that his small audience was captivated and enthralled would have been an understatement.

By six o'clock they had grasped most of the basics, their questions were becoming sharper and, without them realizing it, much more relevant to the puzzle they were all trying to solve.

'So it's a rival system then, is it?' Ivan asked, seeking clarification.

'In the sense that it can stand alone in its own rite and function independently, I suppose it is,' Hank agreed.

'Won't that cause a lot of problems though?' Jake enquired. 'Like trying to run a country with two legal systems. They'll constantly clash.'

'It would do, but that's not really the case. They can work separately, but they don't have to. In fact transferring across to and from Cryptos is almost what you might call an inherent design feature.'

Jake and Ivan looked puzzled.

'In that particular regard, just try to think of them as another bank. All of those are highly independent, yet they can – and do – all trade with each other quite easily. It's just that we don't refer to it like that.'

'Trading with each other?'

'Yes, it just sounds strange when you say it like that because it's more commonly known as moving money around, or as transferring funds from A to B. Nothing mysterious about it at all, we all do it all the time. It's a very basic functionality, actually the bedrock of how the whole system works.'

'So if I have a Crypto account, it's just like another denomination of currency, like having an account in Euros instead of pounds?'

'No, not quite. Those are both examples of traditional established currencies. Old world. Analogue, if you will. Anything that runs on Blockchain will be different, predominantly because they are electronic only in nature. They are designed to be non-physical assets. Easiest way to think about it is, you can buy one but you can't hold one.'

Jake and Ivan still looked puzzled.

'But I can trade one?'

'Yes, you can, very much so. Their values change from day to day, just like equities or commodities. The movements are a constant source of speculation, especially right now at the beginning of the new era. It's a bit of a Wild West time. A kind of twenty first century Klondike.'

'And then I can convert my profits into dollars? Or Swiss Francs, or whatever?'

'Or your losses. Yes, you can. And people do exactly that, they move in and out of BTC, or whichever one they happen to choose, all the time, either winning or losing as they go.'

'But you just said it's not really another currency?'

'Correct.'

'So how does the trading work?'

'The same way it does for anything, actually. Trading principles are just buy and sell. Sell boat, buy car. Sell flat, buy house. Sell your labour, buy some freedom. Nothing much really changes there, probably never will.'

Ivan had been nodding along, taking it all in.

He had been thinking about things back home ever since his editor had called him earlier, just before he went into his huddle with Sylvie Danton.

Word was starting to get out regarding two teenage ultra hackers, the same two that Viktor Alliskiya was now slowly but surely beginning to run down.

'How you start one then?' he asked in his rather brusque but amiable manner.

'What? A crypto?' Hank was checking.

'Yes, Crypto, like we had CryptoOne in Russia not long ago. Who does that and how they do it?'

This time it was Jake and Hank's turn to exchange glances.

Now that was a good question.

And in the context of Jumbo, a really good question.

Chapter 41 – The Ides of March

The Ides of March had broken softly, one of those mildly warmer days in Moscow when the chill is less, the sunshine is more and the world feels lighter and fresher, awoken from its dozy hibernation slumbers by the eternal movements of sweet mother nature. A few drizzly on-off downpours in the morning, brighter and lighter predicted for the afternoon.

The boys were alone in the apartment. Ans was coming over later. They'd told her it was going to be a busy kind of day, busier than usual.

That usually meant lots of head down, lots of keyboard tapping, lots of furrowed brows, interspersed with the occasional swearing.

A day when things would go wrong, would be going wrong a lot, most of the time in fact, a day when they were trying to do something new, a day of unchartered territory, a day of being true adventurers, genuine pioneers in this brave new digital world which she didn't really understand, although she loved the life it gave her.

Or rather, she had loved that life until very recently. She had loved it very, very much, with that depth of longing and passion that is almost the exclusive preserve of sixteen year old girls who can possess an intensity of feeling that is both natural and unnatural, natural as a strong love, but then unnatural in its extremity.

For the truth of the matter was that poor, beautiful, sweet, innocent Anastasia had managed to get herself swept up into a whirlwind of emotions about the two young boys who filled up her days, filled up her nights, filled up her dreams.

For all the years she had known them, everything had been fine. And that had already been quite a few years. But to a sixteen year old, two or three years is a complete lifetime. Somebody who is twenty-one is old, twenty-five is almost another generation, everybody over thirty ancient.

So, in her head, Ans had known Andrei and Georgi forever. There had, of course, been a time when she hadn't known them at all, a time way back in the distant past, in the dark ages when she had been about ten or eleven, but that just seemed so long, long ago that it barely seemed to have been her.

They had been a permanent fixture, Andrei her lover, the boy who'd taught her the joys and delights of sexual exploration and adventure, and Georgi, his lovely

friend, the other handsome nutcase in her life.

The two boys had a bit of a reputation and a profile to go with it. They always dressed so smartly, always had plenty of cash to splash in the nightclubs, at least once they were old enough to get in, always had the latest sports cars, at least once they turned eighteen and were old enough to drive.

That's the kind of thing that's guaranteed to attract attention, whatever country one lives in.

And so it was with Andrei and Georgi.

People started to talk and gossip.

What did they do for a living?

Where did they get their money from?

And it doesn't take long, never takes long, for the truth to emerge.

They didn't have regular jobs but they worked in IT, worked with computers, fixed them maybe, or quite possibly they could be website designers, or alternatively they might be creating new apps for a living, or maybe they wrote those blog things about coding, did teaching perhaps, because everybody knew that computing was huge as an industry and the demand to learn was massive and growing every day, so maybe it was just that, freelance teachers could earn a lot and work all the hours they wanted at fifty or sixty bucks an hour – US dollars still being the preferred method of payment -so that would mount up pretty quickly.

But as the gossip raged, those closer to the boys would speak of their associates, the crowd they ran with, those older guys, people who definitely did not have any kind of regular jobs but certainly had close working relationships with those other organisations, the ones that liked to work in the shadows.

And, at that point, one stopped asking questions.

But it is, of course, perfectly possible to stop talking and keep listening.

So now that people had their curiosity aroused, the two boys became even more of a talking point than ever before and, as people started to put two and two together and add the clues up, it became apparent that Andrei and Georgi were part of the hacking sub-culture, that worldwide community of computer experts who were, for the most part, guns for hire.

Now that world definitely paid more than sixty an hour.

Way more.

Way, way more.

And then word started to get out about the nature of some of the tasks that they had been asked to undertake on behalf of their unseen sponsors, their patrons in the background, those who were pulling the strings in the darkness.

Outlandish and extreme by any measure, these tasks were a mix of international politics and gangland crime.

Aerial drone border mapping.

Denial of Service DOS attacks on foreign institutions.

Messing with the balances in salinity plants.

Switching the lights off.

Creation of ransomware.

Random acts of civic disruption.

And many, many more.

"They must be really good at what they do" people speculated, *"because that stuff is just so dangerous. They could easily get themselves killed doing it. They must be nutters."*

And yet they hadn't been killed.

Or arrested.

Or deported.

So they carried on doing it.

And the more they did, and the more they got away with, the greater their reputation became, they became admired because of the undoubted skill sets which they had to possess to be able to do such things.

"But so high risk. They must both be nutters"

So gradually, the label stuck, as labels tend to do, and after a while, in the small local circles within which they moved, that is how they became known.

Ans loved all this of course, hardly seeing any downside to it at all, just the glamour and notoriety that came with the success which, although it was happening in a counter culture, still had the vibe of rock star fame.

And yet now, as they began to mature, they had started to reduce what they saw as their dependency on the old world, the place where they had done all their training, had honed their skills, had learnt their trade.

The time, it seemed to them, had come to try and go it alone.

And so *Ischeznoveniye* was born, the scheme that would allow them to deploy all of their accumulated skills into one dash for freedom and leave those remnants of the

past that connected them to the Moscow underworld behind forever.

Ans, who kind of did and yet kind of didn't really know exactly what they did or exactly what was going on, was always going to be part of this turbulence although, as is so often the case with the innocent of heart, it was going to be a much more tumultuous ride than she could have ever expected.

By eleven that morning she'd already been to the local artisanal bakery and picked up some doorstep sandwiches and a mix of coffees and cold drinks before riding the rest of the short distance over to the apartment.

She was in a happy mood as she wisped her way into the building, juggling her warm scones and buns as she pinged the lift buttons for the top floor and then again as she groped in the depths of her handbag for the front door key.

'Hi guys, grubs up.'

Two sets of bleary eyes greeted her.

'Wow, you both look like shit. Didn't you get any sleep?'

Truth was, something else had intruded into the morning, something rather unexpected

A green-eyed monster.

The two friends, who had hardly ever had a cross word in all their years of friendship, had had a bit of a spat.

Well, that's how it had started out anyway.

It wasn't even the main event, the launch of CryptoTwo scheduled for 3am that coming morning, which was turning their world upside down.

No, it was the fact that all of a sudden two men found out that they loved the same woman, and that, at around 9am that very morning, had suddenly conspired to turn their worlds upside down.

Ischeznoveniye was on autopilot.

The escape plan was not.

The spat had rather quickly escalated.

'Well, you didn't tell me that, did you?'

'Well, we have been a bit busy, haven't we!'

'Yes, but getting married Andrei! I mean, come on, you're only nineteen years old.'

'What's that got to do with it?'

'No, I just mean, couldn't you have waited, you know, waited till all this is over.

I mean, it's the biggest thing we've ever done and right in the middle of it, you decide to go and get married.'

'I'm not.'

'You're not what?'

'Not getting married in the middle of it.'

'No, well maybe not, but you told me right in the bloody middle of it. Same thing.'

'No it's not, it's not at all. How is that the same thing?'

'You know I'm fond of Ans, too. And now I find out you're going to marry her.'

'I'm sorry. That doesn't make any sense at all.'

And so Andrei's surprise announcement, intended only as an introduction to a chat about their final escape plan, was suddenly threatening to overshadow and disrupt the main event.

'I had a plan too, you know.'

'Well, I would have hoped you did. What was it?'

'You're not really interested, are you!'

'God you're just being impossible now.'

'Me? Impossible! You're always the bloody difficult one. Always have been.'

'Will you please shut up. Just stop it. We're squabbling like children on what is arguably the most important day of our lives. Please calm down Gigi, I didn't know you'd prepared anything. How could I when you didn't say anything. Now, what is it?"

'I bought us some tickets.'

Andrei was clearly taken aback by this revelation.

'Tickets for what? Tickets for the bloody circus?' he laughed.

'No Andi. Tickets to Austria. Plane tickets. For all of us. Ans and I went out to Sherry and bought them last week.'

'You went to the airport? When? What day?'

'Last week. Monday or Tuesday I think, can't remember.'

'Tickets to Austria. Why?'

'Because I didn't think we'd be safe to stay here anymore. You remember Andi, we spoke about it' Georgi said, a bit exasperated now.

'I remember you spoke about Austria, of course. But we were just chatting. You never told me about any plans. How did you know that I didn't have any plans of my

own?'

'Because I figured that if you had, then Ans would have known about them because she would have been part of them.'

'Not necessarily!'

'What do you mean?'

'I might have booked her a surprise honeymoon trip.'

This notion obviously did not sit very well with Georgi either.

He looked at his friend in a slightly horrified manner, the way you can only look if someone is threatening to steal your girl.

Shocked.

Surprised.

Mortified, even.

And yet she wasn't his girl.

Not really. Not yet, anyway.

This was getting confusing.

'And have you?'

'Have I what?'

'Booked her a honeymoon trip. Christ, can you even get married anyway? She's only sixteen.'

'I may need judicial consent but I can probably buy that. It's only a piece of paper. A marriage license they call it. I mean, what the fuck! Whose business is it anyway really, who marries who? If two people love each other, isn't that enough?'

Georgi suddenly looked downcast, inconsolable.

'What's the matter now. You've gone all pale. Are you feeling sick?'

'She never said.' Georgi mumbled dejectedly.' All the way out to the bloody airport and she never said anything at all. Took us all afternoon. Bloody hours on the Metro, there and back. She never said a word.'

'Well, why would she, especially if you bought a ticket for all of us. She probably just thought it was a perfectly natural thing to do. Book a nice little trip together after a few months of hard slog and get away somewhere. You know how she is Gigi, she's scatty as fuck. This is Ans we're talking about, remember. Not asking questions is totally consistent. I mean, that is just so absolutely so her, isn't it? Now come on, I don't see why you're getting so upset about it.'

'It's not the trip.'

Now it was Andrei's turn to look puzzled.

'But you just said....'

'It's the marriage thing.'

'What about it?'

Georgi was slowly backing himself into a corner, almost without realizing it.

And then it all came out.

So a couple of hours later poor Anastasia, without either realising it or expecting it, had just chirruped her way into a firestorm.

There was one of those gloomy silences in the room where normally there was just a lot of banter, cheery bustle and subdued excitement.

Atmospheres like that don't need to be experienced for too long before one deduces that something is a bit off. Females seem to be especially sensitive to them, detecting black moods like barometric pressure drops ahead of a thunderstorm.

Irrespective of her age, there is not too much guaranteed to infuriate a woman more than being in the middle of an emotional storm without being able to understand what has caused it.

The two boys glared at her.

Pretty disturbing to say the least, especially when you don't know why.

She placed her basket of warm goodies down on the table.

'Well if something doesn't work with your silly bloody algorithms don't blame me.' she offered valiantly, knowing intuitively that this wasn't work related, yet totally unsure what else it could be.

She thrashed around quickly in her lovely mind for something, anything.

'I got here quick as I could,' she continued, glancing up at the large kitchen clock, fully aware of how dark a young man's mood could become if his stomach has been rumbling for too long,' It's not my fault this town is one large traffic jam. Do you know how close I come to death trying to keep my bike upright while I'm hanging on to your stupid sandwiches.'

They glared a bit less.

'Plus its raining cats and dogs out there and I'm bloody soaked. Look, at me ' and she peeled off her leather jacket and her helmet, swishing and shaking her lovely long hair as if to prove the point.

'And I spent all yesterday afternoon at the hairdressers and all this morning trying something new with my make up and do you know why?'

Her bosom heaved a bit now.

'I'll tell you why. Because I know today is such a big day for you both and I wanted to make it extra special for you. That's why. Because I thought I'd try and do my best to make sure it was a day to remember. Because that's what you said wasn't it. That's what you both said. The fifteenth will be a day to remember. You told me, didn't you, both of you. So I wanted to look my absolute best. Even though you wouldn't tell me what was special about it, would you. It was just another of your bloody secrets, wasn't it.' she quivered.

Oh, no.

Both boys could see it coming now.

They'd seen it before.

And when that happened, it was game over.

Ans was going to cry.

'And good old Ans, doesn't need to know, does she! Because she's just a stupid girl. Go and deliver this letter Ans. Did I ask why? No, I fucking didn't.'

'Ans ' Andrei started ' please don't....'

'Pop over and get some burgers Ans, no lettuce on mine today but I'll have two of them Barbecue sauce dips please, don't forget now and, oh yeah, can you get a warm apple pie with ice cream and I'll have a hot chocolate today instead of a coffee and good old Ans will always go and …'

'Ans, we didn't mean..' Georgi tried to intervene.

Can you stop an avalanche, once it's started?

No. You cannot.

'…get them, even if it's midnight and freezing fucking cold outside and, oh yeah, sorry, I'd forgotten we live in the middle of fucking Moscow and guess what, well surprise, surprise IT'S ALWAYS FUCKING COLD AT MIDNIGHT HERE' she screamed at the top of her voice, she was blubbing a bit now.

'Ans, darling..' Andrei stood up, under the misapprehension that he could do something about the runaway train.

He couldn't.

'Don't you fucking darling me, you shifty bastard. Do you know what I did last week? I spent another afternoon of my life doing something for you, something else that was supposed to be a nice surprise. I even paid for it.'

Andrei looked across at Georgi.

The atmosphere in the flat was definitely not improving.

'You let her pay?' he said, questioningly. ' You let her pay, even though it was your idea to go there. You tight bastard.'

All of a sudden Ans picked up her helmet and launched it with all her might at Georgi.

'You told him?' she screeched, unbelievingly. ' You fucking told him. It was supposed to be a secret. S E C R E T ' she spelled it out, letter by letter for him, for emphasis, just in case he'd forgotten what the word looked like or sounded like.

Or meant.

'We agreed that, didn't we? That it would be a secret. Or did I dream that bit?'

Georgi sort of half ducked, half covered his head and hunched up a bit. The flying helmet crashed full on into an open laptop, broke the screen and sent it flying off the coffee table at a weird angle, taking some glasses, a few cups and a plate with it on its way to the great laptop cemetery in the sky.

Not satisfied that she hadn't damaged her target properly, Ans rounded the table and grabbed Georgi's collar.

She was weeping now.

Uncontrollably.

'You promised me. You fucking promised me.'

'He kind of got it out of me, Ans. I didn't mean to tell him.' Georgi said, rather unconvincingly, as she scrunched up the top of his Tee shirt.

'What do you mean "*he got it out of me*?" How? What did he do? Invite the whole of the Spanish fucking inquisition to our flat to force you to tell him a secret,' she sobbed. 'And not just any secret, was it. It was our secret. And you promised me you wouldn't tell.'

She was furious now, shaking.

She suddenly stopped gripping his collar, let go of him and stood back a bit.

'Did you tell him our other secret as well? You know, while you were at it. While the Spanish inquisition were here, ripping your fingernails out. Did you tell him that as well?'

Georgi looked horrified.

'No, Ans, please don't.'

'What other secret?' Andrei thought he'd spotted a break in the clouds, that the storm was about to pass.

He was wrong.

He hadn't.

It wasn't.

'Did you tell him that you fucked me, you shitbag? Did you tell him that as well? Our other little secret.'

'I only told him about the tickets because you're getting bloody married.' Giorgi responded, miserably ' I didn't know that, did I?' he continued accusingly. 'You never told me, did you? So I suppose that was your little secret, was it? And there was I, thinking we were all going to go away together and enjoy ourselves for a while after all this.'

He waved his arm around, indicating the mess that had become their flat.

'After all this was over. After *ischeznoveniye.*'

Suddenly it went quiet.

Andrei had a look of horror and disbelief on his face.

Georgi started to weep softly.

But Ans had suddenly stopped in full flight.

She wiped her eyes and cheeks with the sleeves of her jumper.

'Disappearance!' she exclaimed. 'What disappearance? What are you talking about now? '

She had a look of blazing fury on her lovely young face.

"What else don't I know? Tell me, you fucking nutters.'

And then slowly, from somewhere, crawling out from under the terrible wreckage of the past fifteen minutes, came the truth.

All of it.

As the dust started to settle, it taught them all something, as the truth always does.

Ans learned about *" the plan".*

Georgi learned about heartbreak.

Andrei learned about betrayal.

The room was very quiet for what seemed like a very long time.

'Coffee'll be cold by now.' Ans said finally, in a very subdued quiet voice.' I'd better pop out 'n get some refills.'

She didn't bang the door on her way out. She shut it softly and very deliberately with a movement that had a certain finality to it, like it was something she might

never ever do again.

The two boys stared at each other.

Neither of them felt much like doing anything.

Fortunately they didn't have to.

In true twenty first century style, everything that needed to happen later on that evening had already been pre-programmed.

A Russian dye would soon be cast out onto the world causing a massive and irreversible seismic shock wave, the first ripples of which were currently being felt in a swanky top floor apartment just opposite Staraya square, albeit for quite different reasons.

"*i minus fifteen. i minus fifteen*" said a robotic disembodied voice from the shattered laptop over in the corner, sounding rather like a naughty parrot.

"*i minus fifteen.*"

Chapter 42 – Departure

'And so they're probably in great danger right now.' Harry was reporting in to Wanderer One on his latest deliberations. The chilling of the early Swiss evening had driven him back inside Willi and Monique's snug chalet, where the sparkling glow of a roaring fire threw flickering patterns across the ceiling.

His two hosts had once again absented themselves for a few minutes to provide him with some privacy for his call.

'Well, I'm hardly surprised to hear that, considering what they've done.'

'Yes, of course. But there's a much bigger risk here.'

'Which is….?'

'That others find out how they pulled this off. At which point we're likely to very quickly have a whole new series of copycat hits on our hands. The banks will be saying in their statement later tonight that they can restore credibility and I think, by and large, most people will want to go along with that. But, if it happens again, ……'

'Their reputations are completely shot.'

'Exactly. So it's become critical that we get to them before anybody else does.'

'And you're totally convinced that it was these two that did it.'

'Well, Liam is, and that's good enough for me.'

'Did he ever get as far as the father of that golfer girl, Yelena….'

'Yelena Alliskiya. Yes, he did. He's become a main source, actually.'

Hazel smiled inside.

Good old Mags Mollinsky. Her tennis buddy had actually played a small part in helped to solving a Nine's case. Now that would really be a good lunchtime story down the club at some stage in the future, although Hazel already knew she would have to be very circumspect in how she told it.

'Is he credible?'

'Extremely. And connected at the highest levels. Liam said he span a spider's web out across Russia within the space of about two hours just by calling people up. And then, lo and behold, one of the silken threads got snagged and we had our guys. Or, to be more specific, Viktor Alliskiya had them. Or, to be even more accurate, he at least knew who they were. And that's exactly the danger.'

'You mean they're likely to disappear.'

'Exactly. And without trace. But not before spilling the beans about everything. Which is why I'm concerned about a repeat performance.'

'Carried out by people with greater resources than those boys had?'

'Yup, that's my point. From what Jake has been able to learn from the FIB guys, this present situation is likely to be recoverable. The damage resulting from it, however, will doubtless last a lot longer, although that's another matter entirely.'

'So what is their current status?'

'Undetermined. We know who they are but not where they are. Paul's trip to the airport unearthed some video of Pigtail girl. You remember her?'

'The one who delivered the Robin Hood communiqué?'

'Yes, exactly. She bought three plane tickets out of the country about a week ago so we were quickly able to identify the individuals concerned. Turns out that Paul spent the first half of today trying to get himself a local girlfriend to bolster his cover only to discover that his preferred squeeze turns out to be a major in the FSB. So I told him to team up and offer them any assistance they wanted in the hope that some collaboration might work in our favour.'

Hazel went a bit quiet.

'That's hardly standard practice, Harry.' she felt obliged to remind him. 'How much did he have to reveal about The Nines?'

'I wouldn't worry about that too much.' he responded. "Paul knows how to look after himself. If he had to say anything at all, I'm sure he would have worked it to his advantage. Plus it's not really too smart pretending that the locals don't know what's going on. Especially in Russia.'

Not for the first time Hazel Ingliss found herself slightly conflicted with her professional managerial priorities. The working ethos of Harry's team, of her team, was based on very large amounts of trust.

DDD they called it.

Decide.

Delegate.

Deliver.

It required much discipline to work effectively and, seasoned operators though they all were, Hazel and all of her other top-level colleagues sometimes had to just take a deep breath and let it go.

So Hazel took a deep breath.

And let it go.

'When were the tickets for?'

'Today. We must have just missed them. While Paul and his two FSB accomplices were trawling through last week's video out at Sheremetyevo, the people they were actually looking for must have been busy checking in downstairs, not so very far away in the same building.'

'Did you check the airline manifest?'

'Yes, of course. They made the flight. Well, two of them did anyway.'

'So two are presently en route out of the country, presumably to somewhere half way across the world where we have little jurisdiction and probably no extradition arrangements. Let me guess, they've gone to China? Or Bahrain maybe, if they wanted some sunshine?'

'Well extradition might be tricky because before you can even start to establish a real case, you have to determine two things. Number one – exactly what crime has been committed? Number two – where was it carried out? I would say, at the moment, we'd probably be struggling with both of those.'

That's all true. Plus there is the rather non-trivial matter of Jumbo being a highly international matter, as all Nines' cases are of course. So there's likely to be a long list of countries queuing up to get hold of these three.'

'Well, before we get too far ahead of ourselves I should mention that the girl – Anastasia – doesn't really look like she's part of this. She is, far as we can tell anyway, an innocent party, just the girlfriend.'

'Ok, and what then, she's decided to stay behind. Or got left behind?

'No, no, not at all. She's definitely on the plane.'

'Where's the third one then?'

'Andrei Umnyblodoski. He's currently under observation.'

Hazel was surprised.

'You mean you think there's a mastermind in all this, somebody even higher up that he might lead us to?'

'No, no. He's not going to be leading anybody anywhere for a while.'

'And why's that?'

'Because he's in the hospital.'

The long reach of Viktor Alliskiya's network was not just confined to the interior of Russia's vast borders. The world isn't like that anymore.

He needed to be confident in his ability to track down people or items whoever they were and wherever they were. They could be in the middle of Moscow or in the middle of the Sahara, it made no difference to him. He had a reputation to worry about as the go-to guy for finding people and for finding things. It meant a lot to him, helped hugely with his business affairs, so it was something he liked to nurture at every opportunity.

Nonetheless it still came as a considerable surprise to find out that the two prime suspects for *ischeznoveniye* were not only his fellow countrymen – that was bad enough – but also that they had been literally operating right under the noses of the authorities, deep in the heart of the capital, less than a one mile walk from The Kremlin.

'Are you sure, Piotr?' he asked.

Despite his undoubted toughness Viktor had a soft spot for the ballet, so he had been immediately concerned for the wellbeing of the sensitive young Bolshoi star when his rougher contacts had first told him their source.

'Because I need to be sure. To be very sure. Do you understand me?'

'Yes, yes, of course. I am only repeating what I told the other guy on the phone earlier.'

'Ok, well now just tell me.'

'There's this girl who hangs out around the park.'

'Staraya?'

'Yes, and in Zaryadye as well, the larger one right next to it. She likes to dance so we do light training exercises there together, whenever it's warm enough.'

'And how exactly does she fit into my requirements today?'

'Because she goes there to get away from her two boyfriends, something I always found a bit strange to be honest, but anyway, that's how she always described them. *"My two guys"*, she always called them. *"My two lovely nutters."*

Viktor's ears pricked up.

That phrase was starting to get about a bit.

'Hmm, well a bit curious admittedly, but maybe it was just a term of affection.'

'Yes, partly I think it was, but she did also say that they did genuinely drive her mad with all their computing stuff. Dawn till dusk, it seemed, they were always at it.

And supposedly red hot as well, by all accounts. But then that day when my desktop packed up and I needed some help they were always just way too busy with their own work.'

'And what was it they were working on, exactly?'

'Well, that's what I kept asking, but she would never say. Either couldn't or wouldn't, I was never sure which.'

'Do you know their names?'

'The two boys? No. She might have mentioned them but I never took it in. Sorry.'

Viktor was less than pleased and was just about to say so when Piotr continued.

'But the girl I knew of course. Anastasia Yurilenko. Everybody called her Ans for short. She was lovely, just the cutest thing, she was so bendy. All sweetness and light.'

Viktor's ears pricked up again.

'Just a second,' he said, muting his cellphone and looking over at the wall screen that linked the West Wing of MMM to his security and control team in the main house.

The two men on duty that evening had been listening in, as instructed, and quickly ran down the list of possibly relevant activity that had been reported to them since the morning.

The name was ringing a bell. Within a few seconds they found it.

'She came up on an FSB airport ticket check, just flew out of Sherry a couple of hours ago.'

'Did she have two boys with her' Viktor asked.

'Negative. Two travellers only. One female. One male, Georgi Podlyavitch. Aged 19.'

'Where are they flying to?'

'Vienna. SU2352. Gets in 7 our time.'

'Text Stefan in Bratislava for me. Tell him to get over to Schwechat asap.'

He clicked his volume back up.

'Ok, Piotr, we're just checking that now. But please tell me again, apart from the possible hacking connection, what else made you think these youngsters might have been the ones we were looking for?'

'Well,' Piotr continued hesitantly,' it was something else she said the last time I

saw her.'

'Ok. And when was that?'

'At lunchtime. In the park.'

'You met for some training?'

'No, we were meeting because she said she wanted to give me something.'

'And what was it?'

'I don't know.'

'Sorry. What do you mean? *"I don't know."* '

'I never found out because she didn't turn up.'

Viktor was puzzled but pleased at the same time, which was a rather confusing feeling, although this odd occurrence sounded, on the face of it, like exactly the kind of thing someone would do if they were running away. If they were disappearing. And that, for very understandable reasons, seemed to be exactly what was going on.

'I tried to ring her but her phone was off,' Piotr continued, trying to be as helpful as possible as he remembered the advice of his friends when they heard he was going to be speaking with the fabled Energy King that same afternoon. 'I didn't really know what to do for a while so I just carried on with my headstands and waited.'

Viktor knew how to be patient. He took a deep breath.

There would be more, he thought to himself.

He was right.

'About ten minutes later Dimitri came along with some lunch. '

'Dimitri? Who's he?'

'The Assistant manager from McDonalds on Ulitsa Maroseyka, just across the park. It was from Ans. She knows I never have much money so she would treat me now and then. Which was a bit strange, because she never really worked herself, not far as I know anyway, but she always seemed to have loads of money. I guessed from the boys.'

'And that's what she'd wanted to give you?'

'No, I don't think it was, no. I never really found out what that was.'

Viktor took another deep breath and waited again.

'But he did know that I was friends with Ans and it was actually him who gave me *a* message. Or maybe it was *the* message. I really don't know which.'

'And what did he say then, this Dimitri?'

'He said Ans was having to go away, and that people would come looking for

her. That was the thing that connected in my head when I heard about your search.'

Viktor was relaxing a bit now. Still a lot of work to do but it seemed almost certain, with each passing minute, that he was on the right trail.

'And that she was right because they're here already.'

'Sorry. What?'

'That was the last thing Dimitri said to me before he went back to work.'

Viktor was puzzled again.

'Sorry. I didn't understand that last bit.'

'And then he pointed out this guy who just happened to be walking past and said *" and he's one of them." '*

'Did he explain what he meant? Or what he thought Anastasia had meant?'

'Only that the guy had been nosing around in the restaurant earlier trying to find out who Ans was. Nobody told him of course, although everybody knows her. Apart from being totally unmissable, she's just so lovely. Nobody wanted her getting into any kind of trouble, especially with foreigners.'

'Foreigners?'

'Yeah, Dimitri said the guy only spoke English, but with a funny accent.'

'You say you saw him Piotr? You saw this guy."

'Yeah. Dimi actually waved to him when he walked past because he'd been talking to him just an hour or so earlier in the shop.'

'What did he look like?'

Piotr described Liam.

Viktor switched over to screen four, the guest quarters in the west Wing.

Yup, no doubt about it. He suddenly realized that he was going to have even more to discuss with his impromptu dinner guest than he had first realised.

However, it was not going to be anything like the conversation he planned.

Chapter 43 – The FIB

The assembled might of the world's media were gathering yet again in the largest salon the Fairmont could offer. It was more than a full house. The morning session had been busy enough but the number of journalists had swelled considerably since then, filling up hotels all along the lake as far as Montreux, a hundred kilometres away on the opposite Eastern shore of the lake.

There was no single other story attracting such global interest. How could there be when everybody on the planet was affected? And so even the smallest provincial media outlets had decided it was essential to have representation.

As a result the inevitable happened and the evening session was hopelessly over-subscribed. It was scheduled for 7pm but, even an hour before, the room was already full to bursting. A row of desks was placed along the back so that as many cameramen as possible could get some decent shots of the protagonists as the world waited expectantly for the FIB team to take the stage.

Two tank commanders, one from the French Armée de Terre, one from the local Armée Suisse, both in full battle dress, had moved inside the main doors to add some much needed colour and variety to the proceedings.

Positioned, as they were, just along from the temporary TV gantry, their striking presence again managed to spook the world for several minutes until the commentators confirmed that no hostilities had broken out, Switzerland was still at peace - as she always is - and that the military were merely on guard duty.

The good people of the world, as expected, were getting ever more jittery.

As per the morning briefing, most of the planet was tuning in. There wasn't much else to do. Until such time as the Disappearance was solved, nobody could really think straight about anything else anyway.

Ivan, Hank and Jake had dragged themselves away from the comfy delights of the hotel bar in good time and were now at the front of the gathering throng.

'Did you hear back yet?' Jake asked him.

Ivan nodded.

He had made the strategic decision that the chance of two new friendships with the CIA and what appeared to be the SIS were worth sacrificing something for. His cellphone had been red hot with updates from his editor about activity in the area

around Meshchansky and Staraya Park.

'They've got them,' he confirmed, 'or, to be completely accurate, I should say they will have soon. Once identified its pretty much game over. Only a matter of time now.'

'Can you say who they were?' Hank enquired lightly, as if discussing the football results.

'Couple of kids from the hacking community. Pretty well known locally by all accounts. Surprised it took this long to find them actually.'

'And the money?' Jake asked.

'Don't know enough to comment yet', he answered, a bit obliquely.

The two Americans were beginning to wonder about Ivan's seemingly impeccable sources but were both experienced enough to know when to stop asking. So they did, leaving his last words hanging strangely in the air.

'Well, let's hope Sylvie can tell us then' said Hank, as the so far unflappable Russian from the ECB climbed the four steps up onto the small podium and gazed out at the world's press. 'Here we go.'

'Bonsoir Mesdames et Messieurs, Good evening Ladies and Gentlemen', she began, the French language taking precedence for the French speaking spokesperson in the French third of Switzerland, irrespective of the fact that 95% of the audience didn't speak a word of French. That small courtesy observed, she carried on in perfect accentless English.

'I would like to thank you all on behalf of the international FIB team for your patience and good humour since this morning. It has been a long trying day for all concerned and I am pleased to be bringing it to a close now with our latest findings.

My colleague who addressed you this morning promised an update by tomorrow morning. However it is my hope that this bulletin, the third one today, will provide many of those answers tonight so that we can all start to better understand what has really happened.

Firstly please let me reiterate that this was not and is not a bank run. Much of today has been about crunching data and I can tell you all now, with absolute certainty, that this was a robbery, pure and simple.'

A wave of soft noise washed across the room, a kind of shared murmur of agreement. Everybody already knew that, of course, but good to have it confirmed, nonetheless.

'Neither was it a technical glitch or some kind of catastrophic accounting oversight. Our systems were compromised by a very smart organization. And no, I do not know their name, but that is something we will find out.'

Hank and Jake glanced at Ivan who was biting his top lip with his lower teeth and shaking his head. It did not look as if this latest explanation was fitting very well with whatever he had heard on his own personal Moscow Hotline.

'Secondly, I am afraid to say that despite our best efforts the precise location of the money remains unknown at this stage although we are continuing to work on several leads which we expect will be productive very shortly.'

'Thirdly, I am pleased to report that our colleagues from the Official Liaison Department at the Government's International Taskforce will be able to announce a temporary initiative shortly to provide short term relief to all those affected, that is to say everybody.'

And then, without a shred of irony, ' A spokesman from that OLD GIT unit will reveal the details of this initiative later on here in Geneva at midnight tonight.'

She beamed out at her audience, seemingly very pleased with herself now, possibly because she had managed to get so far uninterrupted compared to her earlier appearance in the afternoon.

The calm before the storm.

It wouldn't last.

'And finally' she continued ' I would just like to say…'

But Ivan interrupted her.

Clearly he'd heard enough.

And so he said so.

And with a lot of passion

Although exactly what he said was lost on most people in the room because it was a tirade of Russian.

He was clearly angry about something.

Extremely angry.

Furious and highly agitated, he continued to lay into her as the astonished onlookers, both in the room and around the world, watched Sylvie get slaughtered for the second time that day.

'Must try some of that vodka before we leave town.' Hank commented.' What on earth do they put in that stuff?'

'Don't think it's that buddy,' Jake replied.' I don't hardly know any Russian but I do know what Izhets means.'

Eighteen hundred miles away Liam, like everybody else around the world, was watching in amazement.

'What's he saying?' he asked his host, as Viktor's butler glided along to his end of the long heavy oak table with some more Russian red.

The two men had agreed to dine earlier than usual at 7pm Moscow time so that they could break off at 8 to watch the press conference taking place an hour earlier in Geneva.

Viktor's hospitality had been splendid and specifically designed to disarm his target, who had continued to intrigue, entertain and, if he was being honest, to educate him on some rather mundane matters concerned with soil sub-strata properties and infra-red aerial scanning techniques, both subjects which he seemed to possess an inordinate amount of knowledge about for one so young.

It was a joust and, to the untrained eye, it looked like a pretty even battle.

Viktor, the Energy King, hugely wealthy and skilled in business, was not talking too much, was concentrating hard, was watching his prey, was stalking and waiting, waiting to pounce on that lie, that lie that still wrankled.

Sports agent, indeed.

Such impudence.

And yet, as his guest had proven to his satisfaction, Yelena was now a confirmed all-comers invitee for a major golf tournament in Europe.

It was all a bit puzzling.

And Viktor was now making the uncharacteristic mistake of underestimating his opponent in this psychological game of chess.

He was being led.

And he didn't know it.

His short term plan to deliver a valuable asset to the sponsors of his pipeline project seemed to be going well enough, the conversation headed in the right general direction, as Liam explained several different ways how the adoption of A.I. could make both his basic explorations as well as his delivery mechanisms much more efficient.

'You'll need to have the technology approved at both ends though' he told

Viktor,' and get some transit rights granted and approved as well. It's a bit like international airspace, if you pass through it, you need to abide by the local regulations. Obviously, in your case it's different because you're underground, but the licensing regime will still be jurisdictional. So country by country.'

'You are a man of many talents Mr. Dempsey. I wouldn't have thought such a detailed knowledge of geological matters would be a requirement in your line of work.'

'I find it helps to know a little about a lot,' Liam assured him cryptically,' rather than the other way round.'

He gave Viktor one of his best Paddy grins.

'So I know people who can help with that, you know, just in case you ever get stuck.'

'Do I look like a man who gets stuck much, Mr. Dempsey?'

But just around then, as it was coming up to eight, the butler had pressed a couple of buttons on a remote control unit and a sidewall turned into a 85" OLED screen, quickly diverting their attention back to matters in Geneva.

'He said she's a lying bitch,' Viktor translated, in answer to his guest's question, 'and that she should be ashamed of herself for betraying the people.'

'The people?' Liam was surprised. ' That seems a rather odd phrase to be using in that context.'

'She's not Swiss. She's Russian.' Viktor offered, as an attempted explanation. 'We are a comradely folk, Mr. Dempsey, something quite hard to explain to outsiders and, I regret to say, even harder for them to understand.'

On the TV screen Ivan was continuing his rant. The cameramen had him in full focus now and the world's eyes were upon him.

Liam was suddenly pleased to see the slightly surprised face of Jake Rivera in the crowd, right alongside Ivan in fact.

He started to wonder.

Then, next to him on the other side, was another familiar looking face.

'Colonel Hank' he muttered, half under his breath, and thinking quickly on his feet.' To deal with the FIB. Of course, the perfect guy.'

'Care to share?' asked Viktor, from the other end of the lengthy table. ' You seen something unusual?'

'I get to see a lot of unusual things in my line of work,' Liam answered teasingly.

'Although this particular performance, if it is what I think it is, is going to take some beating.'

'Mr. Dempsey,' his host sought to remind him,' it is supposed to be us Russians who speak in riddles.'

Viktor took a large draft of his Massandra.

'Might one reasonably enquire what the fuck you are talking about.'

'I'm guessing he's now saying they've hidden it,' Liam told him. 'Although my Russian is virtually non-existent, I do, as I just told you, like to know a little about a lot. And I do happen to know what the word skrytyy means in your language.'

Over in The Fairmont, Ivan continued to blaze away.

It was turning into quite the show.

Jake and Hank continued to look slightly taken aback although Liam knew that all members of The Nines had terrific acting skills for deployment as and when necessary.

Sylvie, enduring her second onslaught of the day, was continuing to keep her cool under the relentless force of Ivan's comments, which, although they were totally incomprehensible to most of the onlookers in the room, were clearly very strong accusations of some sort.

Although it had seemed like forever, it was only really seconds, rather than minutes, before the translators working for the TV broadcasters caught up.

Liam didn't need them.

He suddenly had his own guide, sitting at the far end if the table.

As well as watching the screen, Viktor had also become busy with his cellphone again, prompted by several more pings in the space of a couple of minutes. His calm, unflappable exterior seemed to be changing as he read successive messages and a look of consternation came over his face.

'It seems as if we might have a problem.' he said abruptly, looking down the table at his guest, 'although I gather from what you said just now……' , and then he paused briefly to digest a few more sentences of inflamed rhetoric from Ivan, ' that oddly enough you are slightly ahead of me in this charade and you already know that.'

Liam had a wry smile on his face.

But it wasn't quite one of his happy Paddy grins.

Chapter 44 – Millstatt

A lot happened on the Ides of March 2022.

At 4 in the morning in London Harry Shepperton had gone to his bank and found that he had no money.

In Moscow, the *ischeznoveniye* software had kicked in and transferred all liquid funds in all the world's bank accounts into electronic deposits for CryptoTwo.

A couple of the peta-byte servers in the Nevada desert awoke and hiccupped briefly to digest this massive temporary spike in traffic activity before dozing off again.

Gradually over the next few hours, everybody else in the world found themselves in the same position as Harry.

The Nines' third full-on Op had been launched under the code name Jumbo as the UK Government deployed its crack Rapid Response Team to investigate.

By the following day they were in full swing.

In Moscow Andrei Umnyblodoski and his best friend Georgi Podlyavitch had quarreled again violently over their girl.

Nines team member 9-6 Liam Dempsey had wandered right past their penthouse apartment at lunchtime just as Georgi struck the almost fatal blow.

Nines team member 9-3 Paul Lambert had finally identified Anastasia Yurilenko as "pigtail girl" who had delivered the Robin Hood communiqué.

Commander Harry Shepperton finally caught up with his old banker friend Willi Sagné in Geneva, he whose lovely wife Monique turned out to be full of surprises.

Nines team member 9-4 Professor Jake Rivera identified some high level activity close to The Kremlin and dispatched 9-6 to Meshchansky to investigate.

In Chelsea 9-1 JoJo Everett and 9-5 Caitlin Yang figured out how Andrei and Georgi had managed to compromise Sakamoto's brilliant blockchain architecture.

At the Fairmont, Ivan Tertroothski was standing tall for journalistic integrity everywhere by turning down the Bank's bribe and calling them out.

At MMM Viktor Alliskiya realised that, even as The Energy King and one of Russia's richest men, he could still be duped by treacherous bankers.

Wanderer One reported to the British Prime Minister who immediately launched

an inquiry into the banks' role in what became known as The Disappearance.

Over a protracted period of time dribs and drabs of the money slowly resurfaced as the FIB continued their seemingly endless ongoing investigation.

The global price of BTC dropped to a yearly low of 99000 USD before heading off once more into the stratosphere while all the Central Banks tried yet again to capsize it.

Down by the beautiful lake in Millstatt, Anastasia parked her new scooter and walked the short distance into town.

She had learnt from the "useful phrases" section of her guidebook that *Immo*, short for *Immobilien*, was the local Austrian word for estate agent, or realtor, and she was off to do one of her favourite things.

Ans was going shopping.

It had been a few months since her eventful departure from her motherland but she was gradually settling down into her new life. The cleanliness and sheer beauty of Carinthia captivated her and she was having no trouble making new friends, the arrival of young Russians with money in Europe no longer being any kind of real surprise, there were just so many of them.

None had anything like Anastasia's small fortune though, the one that she had inherited from her husband who had died so tragically attempting a night swim, despite a plethora of notices from the authorities warning of the dangers of such activities in the Country's many natural lakes.

The brevity of the marriage and the amount of money in his bank account had prompted a short investigation by the local coroner's office who ultimately found no signs of any foul play. Their report was sufficient for a local notary to deem her claim legitimate. Although he did have some suspicions of his own when she told him some of the details of her husband's short life, they were not sufficient to hold up her inheritance.

The nice British lady with the fedora who'd met them off the plane at the airport in Vienna had been so helpful in getting everything sorted out and had explained a few things to her, some of which she hadn't known, most of which she had. She had made England sound very alluring as well.

Her Andrei, the only true love of her life, was recovering well from his fractured skull and was due to leave hospital in Moscow in a few weeks.

His involvement in the global scam which had come to be best known by it's Russian name *Ischeznoveniye* – The Disappearance – was now a matter of public record. Under normal circumstances he would have been in big trouble and probably gone to prison for life.

However his legal team, claiming some as yet unpublished special insights from the British authorities, were mounting something which had been christened by the media as " The Robin Hood Defence", and were hopeful of not just getting him off, but also of obtaining considerable compensation for their client who had, so they claimed, merely been seeking an equable redistribution of wealth on behalf of the world's dispossessed.

The case was complex, taking as its central theme an issue which has troubled society forever, namely getting the balance right between rich and poor. It was probably not something particularly well suited to a legal case, but then nobody else has ever managed to solve that problem properly so why not let those guys have a go?

His lawyer had insisted on the case being heard in Switzerland in an attempt to satisfy most of the jurisdictional conflicts surrounding it. Paul Lambert was optimistic, as he always was, not just about his chances of winning the case, but also about debriefing the young hacker back in London, once he'd recovered his health fully.

'Use the medical angle,' Harry had told him, as he finished off the last of Monique's sweet and nutmeggy glühwein.' Swiss Doctors are the best, so get him transferred here first and then on to Guy's in London for the convalescence. I'll sort out some UK papers for him once he's there.'

'We'll need to take him Viktor, you do realize that, don't you.' Liam had told his genial host quite forcefully as they finished off dinner that night.' Because every other eventuality will look as if it implicates Russia, as if he were working for some people here. And I don't think you'll want that, will you? You and your friends?'

'But you know that's not true.'

'And I suspect the media will know it as well. But that won't stop them from printing it, will it, or from pointing the finger? That's just what they do. Nothing much I can do about that, I'm afraid.' He shrugged and deployed one of his bigger Paddy grins.

The Energy King contemplated this little white lie for a moment.

'Ok, then we will help you as long as it is made clear he was acting alone. I will expect you to keep your word on that. Now, what do you need?'

'Tell Stefan he'll be met at the airport in Vienna. And we'll take it from there.'

Anastasia looked once again at her beloved's last text as she took off her protective helmet and shook her lovely hair free in the late spring breeze.

PROBABLY BE A YEAR AT LEAST

PLEASE DON'T LEAVE ME

I WILL LOVE YOU FOREVER

ANDI

A flat would do to start with, although she did love the look of those large Austrian chalet style houses in the beautiful local *baustil*.

Who doesn't?

Her daydreaming was interrupted by someone calling out to her.

'You can't leave it there. It says *residents only* and you haven't got a badge. Look'

The smart looking Chinaman was just getting into his green sports car a few bays further along.

He pointed up at a sign.

"Nur anrainer"

'Oh, sorry, I didn't know what it meant,' she admitted, absorbing the scene in front of her, the way only a woman can.

Good looking guy.

Older.

Fit and tanned.

Sporty.

Obviously wealthy judging by the mint Lambo.

65M it said on the plate.

What the hell number was that?

'No problem' he waved back.' You in the tournament?'

'No. What tournament.'

The Chinaman pointed at another sign, much larger, next to the first one.

'Not very observant, are you?' he laughed.

Ans looked up again.

Welcome to the Millstatt Allcomers International Golf tournament proudly sponsored by Austro Power.

'Oh,no. I don't play golf.'

'You should. You've got the shape for it. Give it a try.'

The Brigadier pressed a button and clambered in, his gull wing doors closing behind him..

'You're right Johnny,' he said, turning to his companion in the passenger seat.

'Austrian women are really incredibly beautiful.'

'I already know that.' the Englishman agreed. 'Although I don't think she's one of them.'

An even more stylish car pulled up next to the Lambo in the end bay.

Austria is full of Mercs, not too many Maybachs though.

Another funny number plate, this one with a small Russian flag in the corner.

The driver checked the steep driveway and the sign to make sure he was in the right place before purring the limo smoothly up towards the clubhouse.

The mint green Lambo followed behind with a throaty roar, creating a small shower of gravel and small stones as it growled its way up in the wake of Viktor's luxury saloon.

Anastasia couldn't wait to be seventeen.

Life was just so exciting.

******

About the author

Johnny Johnson is an English writer of contemporary fiction. He is the creator of The Nines, a special unit in the British Secret Services who are tasked with solving the problems that other agencies cannot fix. The team members have all been specially selected for their high IQ's and their ability to think their way – rather than shoot their way – out of trouble.

"We don't do dead bodies in Hotels," the team's leader, Commander Harry Shepperton, likes to remind people. "Hell, people have to sleep in those places."

Other books by the author in The Nines series

How To Steal The White House

The Wuhan Mystery

Arrival

john@thezapcorporation.com

Printed by Amazon Italia Logistica S.r.l.
Torrazza Piemonte (TO), Italy